INTERNATIONAL ACCLAIM FOR

Why Not?

"A romp of a read!"

—*Mango*

"A giggle from beginning to end."

—*U* magazine

"Highly entertaining."

—*Books* magazine

And praise for *What If?*,
Shari Low's sassy romantic comedy
that introduced Carly Cooper
from *Why Not?*

"More fun than a girls' night out!"

—*OK!* magazine

"One of the funniest books I've ever read."

—Marisa Mackle

"Excellent. . . . Chuckle-inducing. . . . A cross between *Sex and the City* and Billy Connolly."

—*Caledonia* magazine

"Fun!"

—*The Bookseller*

WHY NOT?

Shari Low

doWn
tOwn
press

New York   London   Toronto   Sydney

DOWNTOWN PRESS, published by Pocket Books
1230 Avenue of the Americas
New York, NY 10020

This book is a work of fiction. Names, characters, places and
incidents are products of the author's imagination or are used
fictitiously. Any resemblance to actual events or locales or
persons, living or dead, is entirely coincidental. Except for
Sir Richard Branson, who is real, very much alive, and appears
with his kind permission.

First published in Great Britain in 2002 by Judy Piatkus Publishers, Ltd.
Published by arrangement with Judy Piatkus Publishers, Ltd.

Library of Congress Cataloging-in-Publication Data

Low, Shari.
    Why not? / Shari Low.—1st Downtown Press trade pbk. ed.
      p. cm.
    ISBN 0-7434-8312-X (pbk.)
      I. Title.

PR6112.O835W47 2004
823'.92—dc22

                                                        2004050245

First Downtown Press trade paperback edition November 2004

10 9 8 7 6 5 4 3 2 1

DOWNTOWN PRESS and colophon are
trademarks of Simon & Schuster, Inc.

Manufactured in the United States of America

For information regarding special discounts for bulk purchases,
please contact Simon & Schuster Special Sales at 1-800-456-6798
or business@simonandschuster.com

This book is dedicated to Isobel Cook,
who has survived more "head on the table" moments
in the last few years than most people
experience in a life . . .
F*** *all going for us, but we're still chipper!*

And to the memory of John Thaw—
Carly's favourite hero and mine.

Acknowledgements

The acknowledgement section in my first novel *What If?* carried a health warning. It was so nauseatingly emotional that the NHS almost buckled under the demand for stomach-settlers. I'll try to do better this time but keep a bucket on stand-by just in case.

To my mates, who are always there in times of good, bad and alcohol—huge thanks & love to Wendy Morton, Isobel Cook, Pamela McBurnie, AnnMarie O'Connor, Phil Oakden, Linda Lowery, Janice McCallum, Clare Barwick, AnnMarie Low and Emma Vijayaratnam.

To my family, the Murphys, (especially to Betty, an amazing lady without whose babysitting service this book would never have been written) and to the Hills.

To the lovely Val Lawson, whose help has been indispensable.

To my phenomenal agent, Mary Pachnos. Everyone has their cross to bear in life and I have a terrible feeling I'm yours, yet you *still* return my calls. We'll get to the Caribbean one day!

To all at Piatkus, both in the office and the reps out on the road, thanks for being such a pleasure to work with.

To the wonderful management and staff of the spectacular

Old Course Hotel in St. Andrews for providing me with the most luxurious weekend of research ever . . . Sometimes I just love my job. And to the Virgin icon, Sir Richard Branson, for allowing me to take his name in vain.

Boundless appreciation to the poor unfortunates who have to live with me as a deadline approaches; Gemma, a fantastically cool step-daughter and big sister, my beautiful babe Callan, who makes every day more special and comical than the one before and the impending new arrival who has reminded me how much heartburn sucks. To my gorgeous, smart and ever-patient husband, John Low. If all men were like you then I'd have nothing to write about. More than words, more every day, always . . .

And finally, to all those who bought *What If?*, and the journalists and reviewers who said such nice things about it . . . thank you.

Now that wasn't so bad, was it . . . ?

Why Not?

PROLOGUE

Why Not Serve My Kidneys With a Good Lambrusco?

June 2001

I can't decide what to wear. Should I go for fat, black, baggy jumper or fat, blue, baggy jumper? At least the bottom half is easy: a pair of jeans that look like two tents sewn together and topped with more elastic than a support bandage.

I used to be attractive. Not Jennifer Aniston—drop down on my knees and thank God for my genes—gorgeous, but pleasant, passable and after a good scrub up, attractive. I guess I still am—if you're one of those guys with a fat fetish.

So I've decided that God is definitely a man. If She were a woman this whole pregnancy thing would be far more efficient. We'd be able to unzip our bump and put it in the oven while we were washing windows or doing a trolley dash round Sainsbury's.

I've just realised that I sound more domesticated than Nigella Lawson on cleaning day. I think I need a long lie-down in a dark room. My tenth one of the day. That's the other thing. Whoever says pregnancy makes you glow is lying. Or mistaking the shine of perspiration, as you try to manoeuvre more flesh than a fully grown seal from place to place. And don't even start me on piles. Whose idea of a sick joke is that? I know, I'm ranting. I'm allowed. I'm nine months and three days pregnant. I therefore qualify for emotional extremes, including self-pity.

I weigh up the options: get dressed and go meet the girls, or close the blinds and get horizontal. It's an easy choice really, because if I'm so much as five minutes late there will be a stampede of high heels rushing to my door with hot towels, a kettle and bicycle pump to blow up the birthing pool.

Black baggy jumper wins and in ten minutes I'm out of the door and safely ensconced in a cab. It's the one highspot of being pregnant—the panic-stricken look on every cab driver's face as you use a crane and Vaseline to prise yourself into their back seat. That's followed by a fierce look of concentration as they speed to your destination quicker than a space shuttle, meticulously avoiding speed bumps and cobbled streets. Don't they realise that careering round London streets at ninety miles an hour causes enough terror to induce labour?

On second thoughts, driver, put your foot down—let's get this bump on its way into the big, bad world. Poor bugger. It doesn't know what it's coming into. Or maybe it does and that's why it's refusing to come out. I've got a mental picture of it with one foot on either side of my cervix, suction pads in its hands, shouting, "Don't make me jump."

As I enter Paco's I spot the girls at our usual corner table. It's the worst one in the restaurant—right outside the kitchen doors and camouflaged by several plastic pot plants. Paco has made us sit here ever since we had a party for fifty which two hundred turned up at and caused so much accidental destruction that he was forced to refurbish. We still come every week figuring that our contribution to his turnover will go a little way to paying off his decorating bills. I'm sure they do illegal things to our food before they serve it to us.

The girls see me coming and start singing the *Jaws* theme in their Scottish accents. It's amazing that we've all lived in London for years, yet we still sound like Lulu. Except when we sing, unfortunately.

It's getting louder as I get to the table. The other diners are wide-mouthed and there's a stampede of waiters to the kitchen to request the night off. I sit in the chair with reinforced steel legs.

Kate, Carol and Sarah eye me anxiously. I can tell they're trying to deduce my emotional state. Is it tears and tantrums, or earth mother karma calm?

"Hi, sweetie, how're you doing?" Kate asks with obvious trepidation. That's usually my cue to break down into uncontrollable sobs, or rub my belly gently and smile serenely. I shrug my shoulders, point at my ever-expanding mass and reach for a garlic breadstick. "Not a contraction, not a drop of broken waters and it's still doing the salsa."

They groan. So do I. Why didn't they warn me about pregnancy? This lot have seven children between them. Seven! And Carol has twins, for God's sake. It's bad enough carrying one, but two would definitely tip me over the edge—I'd have been giving myself an internal with a sink plunger to get them out long ago.

"Any word from him yet?" Sarah ventures. Now "him" is not a reference to my gynaecologist. Nor does it refer to God, my boss or Butch, my long-lost poodle. "Him" is Mike Chapman, father of bump and the man I joined in matrimonial bliss barely a year ago. Don't ask: do you want to see me cry?

I shake my head. To be honest, it's probably a good thing. If he walked in here right now I'd end up in jail for assault with a deadly ciabatta. I can feel the tears welling up. Don't cry. Don't cry. I try to replace sorrow with anger. Bastard, bastard, bastard. It's working. I take a deep breath and I'm back in control.

The girls look relieved. I've put them through so much stress in the last few months that it's a miracle they haven't developed stutters and nervous tics.

Kate rubs my hands, concern oozing from every pore. She was born maternal and spends her whole life worrying about our welfare. Although lately she's had enough dramas of her own to keep her occupied. You see we all have very defined roles in this little group. Kate: soft, motherly. Sarah: sensible, reasoned. Carol: tactless, glib. Carly: hopeless, hilarious. We've been friends since primary school, since the biggest decision in our day was what to spend our dinner money on. Even then, Kate would fuss and make sure we ate a balanced lunch.

Kate was a hairdresser until she married Bruce Smith, a highly successful architect, and had three children, Zoë, Cameron and Tallulah (we're sure that the after-effects of an over-enthusiastic epidural were responsible for the name of her last born). Thereafter, she decided to devote her life to creating a haven of family bliss in her Richmond semi. Fortunately, we girls constitute family members too, so she does everything from serial nagging (in a nice way) about our cholesterol levels, to buying our condoms. She must have been on holiday nine months and three days ago.

Lately, though, Kate's been a bit distracted. In fact, the onset of the distraction can be traced back to when Keith Miller (alias Builder Bob), construction entrepreneur, bought the other half of her semi. She's been weirder than Tantric sex ever since.

Carol, on the other hand, is our in-house beauty consultant and provider of salacious gossip. She's a "just a wee bit too old to still be called super" model: auburn tendrils that hang to her twenty-four-inch waist, eyes like chestnuts and a figure that mannequins would kill for. She's in more demand than ever as she now comes complete with the most beautiful twins that were ever put on this earth. This is obviously down to hereditary blessings. Her husband Cal also struts the catwalks and he makes Brad Pitt look average. It would be easy to be jealous of her (OK, sometimes in my extreme emotional state I do have the odd encounter with the green-eyed monster). But Carol is so lacking in pretension, has more hang-ups than the fashion floor at Harvey Nicks, and is so hilariously shallow that you can't help but adore her.

Sarah has taken on what was previously my role: sensible, focused and utterly devoid of madness. She teaches primary children and honestly enjoys it. Personally, I'd be threatening the little buggers with violence, but Sarah is more compassionate than Claire Rayner. What's more, since being rescued from a life of impoverished singlehood by her lovely husband Nick, she radiates happiness from every moisturised pore. Now that makes me insanely jealous. I know, I'm a terrible person.

Nick was actually an ex-boyfriend of Carly (sister of Cal, are you confused yet?), who just for a change is obviously late. Yes, I'm being sarcastic. Carly has never been on time for anything in her outrageous life. She is our entertainment co-ordinator and social convenor. Mostly, the entertainment is just listening to the weekly events in her perpetual soap opera. Only Carly would have a mid-life crisis at thirty-one and go off round the world seeking out her ex-boyfriends (Nick being one of them) to re-evaluate their husband potential. She single-handedly proved that you should always take chances in life because her insane man-mission was successful—enter one Mark Barwick, lawyer and Carly's childhood sweetheart who has the wisdom of Solomon and the patience of a school bus driver. I'm sure he's aged ten years since he married her.

There's a sudden commotion at our table. I look to check if my waters have broken, but no, it's just the girls shuffling round to make room for Carly as she launches herself through the door and sprints to our corner in her usual manic manner. She's a sight to behold: five feet eight inches of sexy curves, white T-shirt, ripped jeans, hair that resembles a blonde toilet brush and carrying a motorcycle helmet.

"News, news, news," she yells. "First, Kate, any developments on the Builder Bob front that you wish to share yet?" That's the thing about Carly; she breaks the ice quicker than the *Titanic*.

We laugh as Kate simultaneously shushes her and shakes her head sheepishly.

"Ok, Carol, did my brother get the Calvin Klein contract and did you get the Mothercare one?"

"Yes to both," Carol smiles. I bet her bank manager will too.

We raise our glasses and do a Mexican wave—two pints of celebration margaritas (non-alcoholic for me of course) coming up.

"Sarah, does Nick have the opening date for the restaurant yet?" Nick is opening his second London restaurant specialising in traditional Scottish food. His first one has been full every night since Sean Connery was spotted there with Pierce Brosnan and Roger Moore on some kind of weird Bond reunion night.

"One month from today—get your sequins and Jimmy Choos ready, girls."

Carly turns to me. "And what about you, fatty, ready to drop the sprog yet?"

I splurt my drink as the whole table collapses in laughter. The world would be a duller place without Carly Cooper (she refuses to change her name to Barwick, because she says it keeps Mark on his toes and reminds him that she's an independent woman of the new century. The truth is she just couldn't be bothered changing her name on her forty-seven different credit cards).

I clutch my ever-expanding sides. My arms would need to be made of Silly Putty to go all the way round my stomach now. Ouch! A sharp pain just shot through my abdomen. I bend over double, but it's not easing. Oh, holy cow, don't let me give birth in Paco's, he'll have a stroke.

The girls suddenly stop laughing and dive to my side. Kate has her arms round my shoulders.

"Deep breath, take a deep breath," she's urging.

"I. CAN'T. FUCKING. BREATHE," I stammer.

Carol orders Paco, "Call a cab!" He's gone a whiter shade than snow.

"I. Don't. Think. There's. Time," I whisper between pains.

"Did anyone bring their car?" Carly looks desperately at the girls. They all shake their heads.

"Oh, fuck, Jess," she tells me, "there's nothing else for it. We'll have to go on my moped."

Never in all my nights lying awake and imagining the arrival of my first-born child, did I envisage being rushed to hospital on the back of a bright pink moped called Martha. The pain ceases long enough for me to get outside and strapped on. Thank God the hospital is only five minutes away, although it takes us ten because I yell to stop halfway when another pain comes. My waters finally gush while doing thirty miles an hour down a main road.

"It's OK," Carly shouts. "It'll give the guy behind us something to wash his windscreen with. And don't worry, Jess, I've seen *Scrubs*. I know what to do if we don't get to the hospital in time."

If I wasn't crying, I'd collapse in hysteria. This is the most ridiculous thing that's ever happened to me. I try to breathe a sigh of relief as we screech to the reception of the maternity hospital.

"Baby coming, baby coming, clear a path," Carly shouts to the receptionist. The stunned woman's training kicks in and in five minutes I'm on a bed in the labour ward, being examined by the most George Clooney-like doctor I've ever seen. Oh, the indignity. I finally meet a gorgeous, successful, single (no wedding band) man and I'm sweating like an Eskimo in a sauna and screaming like a banshee. Fuck it. I hate men anyway. The doors open and Kate, Sarah and Carol rush in.

Aaaaaaa! Oh, my God, nobody warned me it would be this painful. I feel like the midwives are doing a Hannibal Lecter and whipping out my kidneys for a bite of lunch. Served with a good Lambrusco, of course. Well, Chianti is a bit upmarket for us. And it doesn't have any bubbles. I think I'm delirious.

Aaaaaaah! This isn't a baby I'm having; it's a rhino. A rhino with a large horn, which is tearing through my internals like an Exocet. How do other women do this more than once? I swear I'm never having sex again. I'm officially celibate. Not that I have much choice in this at the moment, since I don't have the rhino's father lovingly holding my hand and whispering endearments. Bastard.

I open my eyes a millimetre just to check he hasn't sneaked

in on his belly like the reptile that he is. But no, it's females only. I'm giving birth to my first child surrounded by four women. I suddenly feel like one of the Nolans.

Kate's holding my hand, saying, "Push, push, push," like a removal man trying to get a piano down a flight of stairs. Sarah is holding an ankle, with a look of sheer terror on her face. She can obviously see the rhino's horn. Carol is putting on her make-up in the corner. I don't know if that's for the after-birth photos or because George Clooney is due back any minute. And Carly, well, she passed out about ten minutes ago and is lying face down in a pile of coats.

Aaaaaah! I can't do this for much longer. Get this baby out *now.* What's it doing in there, having a picnic? I would cry, but it would get in the way of my glass-shattering screams. This isn't the way it should be. I should be in a state of euphoria, staring into the bastard's eyes and planning the christening. How could he do this to me? I swear as soon as I can stand I'm going to hunt him down, tie him up and remove his testicles without anaesthetic. Slowly.

Oh, God, another pain! This baby has body armour on and it's fighting its way out. I thought this labour lark was supposed to last for hours? I've had facials that have lasted longer than this.

The doctor is back now. He's looking very serious and telling me to push. Then stop. Then push. Make up your fucking mind. I squeeze my eyes so tightly shut that I'll need a crowbar to open them. That's if I survive this. I swear I'm dying. This is what death feels like.

"Push, come on now, one more push," Dr. Delicious urges.

I want to punch him. I know he's never done anything bad to me. He's never promised to love me then betrayed me quicker than a double agent. He hasn't promised to spend the rest of his life with me then baled out at the first sign of parole. But I don't care. He's male, therefore I hate him. I hate all of them.

Suddenly, I feel a slipping sensation down below.

Kate bursts into uncontrollable sobs. Sarah's hand flies to her mouth. Carol puts down her mascara. Carly sits up, sees what's happening and collapses back into the coats.

"The head's out," Doctor says. "One more push, come on, one more."

My mind is racing. I want to have an out-of-body experience. Amputate from the neck down please. Now! And get this bloody man away from me! Don't you realise I hate the male species?

Another slipping feeling. Then suddenly, there's an indignant wail. I stop breathing and look down at the doc as he lifts what looks like a green blancmange and puts it on my chest.

"Congratulations, Mrs. Chapman. You have a son."

Book One

CHAPTER 1

Why not
start at the beginning . . .

1996–1999

Much as I hate to admit it, I was the ultimate cliché. Like many kiss and tell headlines before me (and no doubt many to come), I was the House of Commons researcher who was shagging her married boss. I know; I was heading for disaster quicker than a dinghy in a hurricane.

Three years before, on the day of my interview with the Right Honourable (HA!) Basil Asquith, MP, I dressed meticulously: navy blue Jaeger suit, crisp white shirt, leather Gucci briefcase (a present from my parents for graduating top of my class at Aberdeen University). I was feeling confident; I had a degree in Politics and a first in common sense. Plus I felt sure that my previous years of experience as an administrator at Party Headquarters would do no harm to my prospects. Indeed, I was the Conservatives' idea of a veritable ethnic minority: Scottish, female and left-handed.

As I was shown into his office, I strode forward purposefully and shook his hand. His photos didn't do him justice—he oozed presence and charm like royalty on a state visit to the Commonwealth.

In preparation for the role, I'd researched him thoroughly, studying not only his high-profile career, but also the countless *Hello!* and *House & Garden* articles he'd featured in with his wife Miranda. She was the archetypal Conservative wife: tall, blonde, early fifties with an aloof posture and a rich heritage. She baked for the village fair, raised money for countless charities and dressed in blue for daily lunches with other party wives. Carly called them FANNIES (Far too Affluent, Needing No Income, and Extremely Smug).

Basil was a different story. Looking back, I can see now that his whole persona was the result of years spent in public life; a presence manufactured to win votes and endear him to all lesser mortals. The well-groomed grey hair, the custom-tailored Savile Row suit, the warm-as-toast smile and the firm handshake. Think George Hamilton without the sunbed then add a sharp political mind and an expense account.

The interview flowed smoothly. I competently lied about my political orientation (as a working-class girl from Glasgow, I couldn't even spell Conservative until I was eighteen) as I had done for so many years before in my previous role as an administrator in party HQ. Well, politics is full of people claiming to "believe passionately" in things they don't give a toss about. When in Rome . . . or Parliament.

I'd done my statistical homework too. We discussed in depth the current manifesto and reviewed his constituency's demographics, history and issues. By the time his assistant interrupted us with a reminder of his next appointment, I was feeling confident and visualising how my name would look on official notepaper.

The offer letter came through a few weeks later and before you could say, "Hope the security check doesn't uncover my brother's police caution for shoplifting," I was Jess Latham, House of Commons researcher.

My job was to make sure that the Right Honourable One was well versed on every political situation that arose. When there was a new bill in the house, I provided Basil with the background, origin and aims of the legislation. When he was to speak in public, I researched the audience, and compiled a thorough analysis of all the topics that would be discussed. On every political situation, from the environment to the Welfare State, I kept Basil up to date with all national and international developments and viewpoints. It wasn't so much a full-time job as an overtime job. My work was my life and I had never been happier. I was focused, I was in control and I was in Armani; everything was just the way I liked it.

We hit the campaign trail almost immediately. It was less than a year until the 1997 general election and although the chances of the party securing leadership were up there with William Hague lifting a Mini Metro with one hand, Basil was relatively confident of retaining his position as MP for Oxford.

The hours we slogged were horrendous. My girlfriends forgot what I looked like as I cancelled every night out for three months due to working sixteen-hour days to secure the country's (or at least the county's) political salvation.

Occasionally, Miranda would sweep in to whisk Basil away for a joint interview or photo shoot. She always looked so utterly composed and in control, but I knew it was a fragile veneer that covered a fragmented reality. I knew that theirs was a marriage of convenience, one completely devoid of intimacy, which was endured for political conformity and public approval. I knew that Miranda barely tolerated her husband for the sake of her windswept lifestyle and, in turn, he made all the right comments and appearances on the family values bandwagon. In truth, their relationship was no more than that of acquaintances of many years who occasionally supported each other for mutual gain. In fact, the last time they'd had sex was around the time of their second son's conception. He was twenty-nine.

And how did I know all this? Because Basil and I had fallen into the habit of having a nightcap after our long, hectic days and he would frequently bemoan the sorry state of his personal life. Now, this is where I shake my head like a mountaineer with frostbite in disbelief at my gullibility.

The night after the election, our team had a celebratory dinner in a private dining room in a prestigious London club, courtesy of Basil's obscenely wealthy and extremely well-connected father-in-law.

We deliberately chose this venue because although we were elated at having won our battle, the big boys had lost the war and the whole party was officially in mourning. I dressed all in black, not out of solidarity with my colleagues, but because too much hectic snacking had resulted in the slight expansion of my size twelve hips and I was doing a damage limitation exercise (as opposed to the aerobic exercise that would have been far more effective).

As I sat on Basil's right-hand side, he leaned over and whispered that I looked stunning. I smiled, but as I met his eyes I suddenly realised that it wasn't just one of those throwaway compliments that bosses uttered in an attempt to boost employee morale. No, I'd seen that look before—every time Basil wanted something badly, be it a new ministerial Jag or a jolly to Europe at the taxpayer's expense, he got that look. It was one of the Conservative commandments: thou shall covet whatever thou chooses and attain it at any cost. I checked behind me to see if Michelle Pfeiffer had just walked into the room, but no, it was definitely me he was staring at. Oh bugger.

My brain automatically went into analysis mode. These were uncharted waters. My own personal Bermuda Triangle. Basil was my boss, a respected MP, a pillar of society. This scenario wasn't in the three hundred and thirty page career-plan that I'd written on leaving university. But then, in my militant youth I had envisaged working for left-wing female activists, not a right-wing, upper-class, smoother than ice Tory MP. And a hugely attractive one at that. A sharp intake of breath accompanied that last thought. It was the first time that I'd actually admitted to myself that I found Basil attractive. How could I not? He was fiercely intellectual, blindingly brilliant, fascinating company and to cap it all, pretty easy on the eye (I've always fancied George Hamilton). With horror, I realised that I was contemplating breaking another of the Conservative commandments (and the exception to the rule of the last one): thou shalt not, under fear of death, covet thy FANNIES' husbands.

For once, my steely control threatened to slip. I struggled to come up with one definitive, resounding argument as to why I should not entertain intimacy with the man who was now tickling my kneecap under the table. I blame it on hormones. For years my libido had been firmly repressed and it had suddenly decided to rebel. The only defence I can muster is a physical one: I was more sexually frustrated than a poodle in a cattery, due to a distinct lack of time or interest in any activity that was outwith my career. I was ripe for the plucking. Or should that word begin with "F"?

I needed a second opinion. I excused myself and rushed to the nearest phone. I contemplated calling Kate, but I knew she would talk me out of whatever it was that I was possibly, maybe, potentially, thinking about planning. Carly was a better bet, but she was working in Shanghai. Or was it Hong Kong? It didn't matter anyway because I only had a pound in change and that wouldn't get me past Europe.

I called Carol. Carol and I had always had a very close but fiery relationship. She is direct, blunt and unfailingly honest and when that is matched against my similar nature and frequent disregard for tact, it often causes sparks to fly. We're a bit like Geri Halliwell and Mel B when they were in the Spice Girls, only taller and with more clothes. However, when it came to meaningless sex with older men she was the expert, as she was subsidising her modelling career with countless dates with rich fiftysomethings who showered her with more gifts and holidays than you could a win in a whole year on *The Price Is Right*.

"Carol, it's me and I'm in a phone box so I have to make it quick. I'm out with Basil, he touched my knee, told me I look stunning, my hormones are surging and I'm seriously considering molesting him. Help."

There was a pause. "You're not Jess Latham," she blurted. "Jess Latham couldn't *spell* 'indecisive.' You're an imposter. What have you done with the real Jess?"

I suppose I deserved that. For years I had sanctimoniously tutted at my friends' antics as they careered from one relationship to the next, disparaging their lack of focus as they allowed their emotions to overrule logical actions. Now I was either the pot or the kettle.

"Carol, I'm serious. Forget it, I shouldn't have called." It was the reality check that I needed. Time for a fast cab home.

There was a laugh on the other end of the line. "OK, OK, I'm sorry, Jess. Now, when was the last time you had sex?"

"With or without another human being present?"

Another giggle. "With."

"Do you want it in years or will decades do?"

Another laugh, then, "And he's definitely not married in the devastated wife and children, potential broken home kind of way?"

"Definitely. It's strictly an in-name-only, can't even remember the wife's dog's name, kind of set-up."

"Then I think you should . . ." Bugger, the line went dead. You get nothing for a pound. But I hazarded a guess that she would say, "Dive in, feet first." (Carol has a *major* problem with metaphors.)

I returned to the table and as calmly as possible, hoping the noise of the others chattering was covering the chugging sound of my sex drive going supersonic, I sat back down. This was insane. I would *not* be so stupid as to get personally involved with my employer—I had worked too hard and been too successful to resort to that. I was a competent professional. I used my brains in life, not my body. I was an intelligent, driven, female of the nineties and I would not be distracted by something as trivial as sexual lust.

Unfortunately, those thoughts ran round my brain, but didn't quite make it as far as my hand, which had just grabbed Basil's fingers under the table and returned them to my knee. Well, why not? I was attracted to him. I was in control. I was assertive . . . I was toast.

By the time dessert was served, his hand had wandered into my private manifesto and was doing a thorough review. All I could think was thank God I'd worn stockings, because there's nothing worse than fingers trapped in a gusset for quelling the fires of passion. I've never eaten pudding so quickly in my life— a Dyson couldn't have polished off that tiramisu any quicker.

After coffee, Basil whispered, "My place, twenty minutes." It was now or never. One cab directly home would remove this nightmare dilemma. I should fix my face into my most professional expression and say that I was far too tired to do any more work tonight. But no, I nodded and smiled. In all honesty I was relieved he made the offer, as nothing, but nothing, could have dissuaded me from diving under his duvet that night and this would save me from having to break his window and make an illegal entry.

As he left in his chauffeured limo, I hailed a cab and gave the address of Basil's Mayfair flat. Was it my imagination or did the driver look at me with a knowing sneer? No tip there then. En route, I contemplated the sense of the imminent encounter. It was official, I decided, there was none. But somehow, I couldn't form the words that would have the driver doing a handbrake turn and whisking me back to the safety of my own home. What was worse, as the journey went on, I was actually starting to justify my actions in my head. Why shouldn't I be entitled to a relationship? After all, most of the adult population of the country embarked on one at some point in their lives. Why should ambition preclude intimacy? Couldn't I have both? Why not?

I thought back to my previous plethora of relationships with members of the opposite sex. OK, so it wasn't exactly a plethora. Oh, all right then, so discounting the odd snog behind the youth club wheelie bins and later the occasional drunken one night stand, there had only ever been one and a half relationships in my whole life. But you have to understand I had other priorities. That coupled with the fact that I had, let's just say, *unusual* taste in men, made sex a lower priority in my life than de-fleaing my cat. And I didn't even own a cat.

It had been this way since puberty dawned. I was almost outcast from the school common room after completing a questionnaire in *Jackie*.

Which man would you most like to date? General consensus from my schoolmates: Simon Le Bon or Tony Hadley. My answer: Jeremy Paxman. Swoon!

Which man would you least like to date? General consensus from schoolmates: Morrissey from The Smiths, Limahl from Kajagoogoo. My answer: Simon Le Bon or Tony Hadley.

What would be the perfect date? Schoolmates: a night on a deserted island with either of the two mentioned above. Me: dinner at the House of Commons, followed by seats in the audience of *Question Time*.

When I was twelve, I was convinced that I was adopted. I was not the Glaswegian daughter of a postman and a school dinner lady. I was the secret love child of Henry Kissinger and an exotic, fiercely intelligent Scottish beauty, who had been forced to abandon me so that she could continue her campaign for world peace and the end to Third World debt.

It wasn't until my first year of university that I had my first actual relationship, when I met my Jeremy. Only his name was Miles Frombay and he was a professor of Political Studies. I didn't care that he was twenty years older than me. I didn't care that he was two stone overweight and his fashion sense consisted of leather patches on the arms of his tweed jackets. I didn't even care that our trysts extended to sandwiches in his office, followed by a spot of romance on his battered sofa. All of this was conveniently overlooked due to the fact that he was the most intelligent man I'd ever met. We could debate all night on the merits of the American Star Wars strategy. He could quote every Prime Minister this century on their plans for social reform. He'd even had dinner once with my biological father, Henry Kissinger. Miles Frombay was a god. For a while.

Our relationship lasted the four years that I was at uni but on my day of graduation, the last one we'd spend together, I didn't shed a tear. I would miss Miles, I thought regretfully for about a nanosecond; he'd been a great companion and we'd had some fantastic times on that sofa. But nostalgia was swiftly replaced with excitement. The adrenalin took over and my brain was bubbling with plans for the future. I was going to embark on my new life in London. Granted, it was not as I'd planned, to work at the heart of the Labour revolution, but to take up the only post that I'd managed to secure: administration assistant at the Conservative Party's Headquarters. It had almost given my father (adoptive father that is, not Henry) a heart attack—his golden child off to join the *other side*. But I had to go. London was my Mecca, the centre of the political world and this role was a step in the right direction. I would work my way up the ladder. I would change things from inside the system. I was more of an idealist than Che Guevara. Oh, and Miles who?

I voraciously absorbed every element of my new surroundings. The players and every event in the political world fascinated me. It was an all-consuming lifestyle and my personal life took such a back seat that it was almost in the trunk.

My social life consisted solely of monthly nights out with Carol, Carly and Kate, where I would listen with huge amusement to the latest episodes in their neverending quests to find, recognise, seduce, attract, or hold on to "Mr. Right." It was beyond my comprehension. Only two things were important in my life: my work and my mates. If my "Mr. Right" had camped on my doorstep, I'd probably just have stepped over him as I came home after another sixteen-hour day, then given him directions to the nearest homeless shelter. I suppose in the back of my mind, there was always the image that one day I'd settle down, marry a Jeremy Paxman and breed, but that could wait. No, men definitely were not my priority. Friends were. Success was. Oh, and not forgetting . . . Meaningless sex was another thing altogether. I may have been a touch on the clinical side, but I was still human. Thus my other relationship, which even with generous scoring would still only rate a half. Enter Colin Fuller, personal trainer, party animal, lovely bloke, great in bed. We'd met when I answered an advert for a flatshare in Chiswick. Colin answered the door wearing nothing but shorts and a smile. I said a silent prayer that he lived here and wasn't just repairing the plumbing or visiting his sick eighty-year-old aunt. Someone in the heavens must have been listening. It was the start of a beautiful relationship. For five years we shared the flat, shared the beer in the fridge, shared the remote control for the telly, and initially, shared the same bed. No strings, no demands, no expectations. Not only did our relationship satisfy my libido, but it also burned off 550 calories an hour.

Alas, it was a sad day when we realised that an intimate relationship could threaten to destroy a beautiful flatshare. You see, Colin was as ambitious in life as I was. Like me, he was born into a working-class background (he took elocution lessons to lose his broad Dudley accent). He never hid the fact that he was intent on marrying well and forging his way into the lifestyle that he wished to become accustomed to (since he had the body of a young Sylvester Stallone, he was never short on offers from wealthy wives who were being neglected by their busy husbands). Monogamy lasted for the first year or so, until two things became perfectly clear: a) due to the long hours we both worked, we saw our window cleaner more often than we saw each other, and b) I didn't have enough money to be his Mrs. Right and since he thought politics was about as interesting as fly-fishing, he wasn't my Mr. Right either.

On one rare Saturday night together, over a crate of Budweiser and a botulism curry from the local take-away, we amicably decided that we would continue to share the flat, but in all other respects go our separate ways.

There were, however, a few exclusions to this deal. We would continue to accompany each other to all weddings, christenings and funerals if no other partner was available. We also wouldn't rule out the occasional night of passion if neither of us was involved with anyone else and we had an urge for physical activity.

We shook on the deal, and then had a quickie to seal it. It was one of the very few encounters we would share over the next few years. Colin swept from one affair to another, accumulating expensive gifts and high-profile contacts as he went, until the day that he won his proverbial lottery—a slightly overweight, but ridiculously wealthy American heiress called Tamsin. She was having a sabbatical in London and fell madly in love with him at first abdominal crunch. Before you could say hup, two, three, four, they were lunging down the aisle and Colin was swept off to her penthouse in Houston, Texas. I was delighted for him. After all, the fluid in my contact lens case was deeper than our emotional relationship. We had always been very open about the fact that we were mates first, occasional bed-sharers second.

The day before Colin's wedding I had lunch with Kate. Before we'd even sat down, she was giving me her very best sympathetic expression.

"Are you OK, babe? Do you want to stay with us for a few days?" she asked, concern in every syllable. I was missing something. Had someone died? Was I supposed to be distraught about something?

"Why?" I replied, confused.

"Well, I just thought that with Colin getting married, you might be feeling a bit, well, lonely. You could stay with us for a while until it's all blown over."

I was astounded. It had honestly never occurred to me that I should be upset. Sure, it was sad that a friend would be leaving the country, but it wasn't like I was losing the love of my life. We hadn't shared anything more than a toothbrush since he'd met Tamsin almost a year before. And anyway, I had an interview for a research position with Basil Asquith a few weeks later and that was the focus of all my thoughts at the moment.

I gave Kate a hug. "Thanks, sweetie, but I'll cope, honestly."

She gave me an admiring look, as if she was proud of my bravery. I smiled back. There was no point in trying to explain my feelings, or lack of them, to Kate. She had been happily married to her first love, Bruce, for years and would sooner run naked down Bond Street than indulge in a spot of casual sex.

It was probably just as well I hadn't called her tonight, I mused as the taxi drew to a halt outside Basil's impressive Georgian townhouse, she'd have been at the restaurant armed with a chastity belt and padlock before I'd Dysoned my pudding.

Basil answered the door before I'd even taken my finger off the bell. His face had a look of unadulterated lust and excitement that would have shocked and disgusted old ladies at coffee mornings all over Oxford. I lost my coat at the door, my dress in the hall, my underwear as I entered the bedroom and my shoes, well, they stayed on—turns out he had a thing about stilettos.

Now, I'd love to say that it was an orgasmic experience: that my earth moved, there was a crashing drum-roll and the angels sang. But in truth it was, well, average. Passable. Satisfactory. In a no orgasm, couldn't find my clitoris if you won it in a raffle, kind of way. But hey, it was sex and I was desperate. And short of paying for it, this was my only opportunity to be hot and sweaty with a member of the opposite sex. I made a mental note to get out more.

CHAPTER 2

Why not
say it with 'cuffs?

I intended it to be a one-night affair. I really did. After all, having sex with your boss could be a career-limiting move and I was very focused on having a long-term political career. But it was just so difficult when my whole life revolved around my job. Soon giving Basil his daily briefings took on a whole new meaning. We quickly fell into a pattern of work, work, work, sex, work, work. This was punctuated only by Basil's return to the family home every weekend, for the sake of appearances. Yes, it sounds lame now, even to me.

I reasoned that I had the best of both worlds. I had a relationship with a man to whom I was seriously attracted, a more than healthy level of carnal activity, great conversations with one of the country's finest political minds *and* I still got to spend the weekends with the girls, invariably giving them a blow by blow (job) account of my week's activities. We were always careful to be highly discreet. After all, the party seemed to be careering from one sex scandal to another and the tabloids were like locusts when it came to MPs. Basil had made a wise choice though. He understood my ambitions and he knew that I would never let anything jeopardise them, so I was as skilful as a big game hunter when it came to covering our tracks.

As for my complaint about sex being a tad on the boring side, it would be fair, indeed an understatement, to say Basil produced an unexpected revelation in that department. One night, about six months after we'd consummated our working relationship, I sneaked into his flat in the middle of the night, using the back door key he had issued to me (this ruled out the possibility of a maverick paparazzo snapping a photo of him opening the door to me in his jim-jams).

As we undressed, we clinically discussed the day's workload. Passion? I've felt more passionate about control top tights.

We slipped under the duvet and I readied myself for our usual sexual encounter. It was easy—just lie back, eyes tight closed, think about Liam Neeson. I hope Liam isn't psychic because I'd hate him to know how many times we've had virtual sex.

Basil leaned to kiss me (Liam whispered rude suggestions in my ear). Basil's hand then strayed down to my breast (Liam disappeared under the duvet and began to lick every crevice). Basil climbed on top (Liam pulled me on top of him, all the while talking to me in that delicious Irish lilt). Basil came, fell off and started to snore (Liam still had hours to go, although there was now the faint sound of a battery-operated device). I screamed in ecstasy, so loudly that Basil woke up with a start.

"Are you OK, my darling?"

"I'm fine, Basil. Just a touch of cramp in my foot."

"Darling . . ."

"Yes?"

"Have you ever thought about, well, spicing up our sex life a little?"

Thought about it? Mmmm, only for hours.

"What did you have in mind?" I asked. Surely he wasn't contemplating deviating from the missionary position? I didn't know if I could take the shock.

He reached over to the bedside cabinet and pulled out . . . handcuffs. I couldn't contain my astonishment. Knowing Basil, he was about to launch into a full-scale debate about police in the nineties and these were his props. But no.

"Why don't you use these, my little haggis? Make Uncle Basil a happy bunny."

I'd seen *Blue Peter*. I could make bunnies out of felt, a Fairy Liquid bottle and sticky-back plastic, but not out of four metal hoops and two chains.

I suddenly realised what he meant. Oh shite. I bet Liam never used handcuffs. I reprimanded myself. What was it that Carly always said? Try anything once to see if you like it, then try it again when you're sober just to double-check. I pondered for another nanosecond, then my general attitude to life kicked in. Why not give it a go? The worst that could happen was that he'd lose the keys and we'd have to get the bolt cutters out.

I took them from him, snapped one set on to each wrist, securing them to the rosewood posts on either side of the antique bed. I don't think that's what the Georgian carpenter had in mind when he designed it.

"Now what?" I asked, not really wanting to know the answer.

He struggled to speak, his face flushed with excitement and his breaths coming rapidly. "I want" (pant, pant) "you to" (pant, pant) "tickle me."

Don't let me laugh. Please, God, don't let me laugh. Was he serious? This brought a whole new meaning to police brutality. If the Oxford pensioners could see him now, their pacemakers would explode.

I tentatively reached over and tickled his stomach. Then under his arms. He was moaning like a Brazilian porn star and sweating like Bill Clinton when he heard the word "Lewinsky."

I moved down to his feet and suddenly it was all too much for him—he almost wrenched the bed posts from their joists as he screamed out then collapsed into the pillow. Mmmmmm. I clenched my teeth together so tightly that I removed a filling. Don't laugh, don't laugh, I repeated silently.

"Oh my darling," he whispered, "That just blew my mind." That was the thing about Basil, he occasionally liked to use teenage vernacular because he thought it made him sound hip. It did. In the sixties.

In ten seconds he was fast asleep again. What should I do now? I summoned up Liam but he wasn't interested in a second bout. And anyway, I was about as horny as a hooker after a night shift. On my left shoulder, a wee devil was whispering, "Just leave and let the cleaner find him in the morning. Or call the *News of the World* and let the paparazzi attack. This image would put a photographer's kids through college."

But the angel on the other shoulder was showing mercy. She must have had a sense of humour. She persuaded me to release him, grab my clothes and make a swift exit.

In hindsight, I really should have called it a day at that very moment, but to an extent, I was cornered. If I ended the relationship, then not only would I return to a life of boring celibacy, but I had no doubt that it would make my professional life very uncomfortable as we worked side by side every day. No, best to just carry on regardless. Well, why not?

The next morning, I waited in Basil's office as usual with his coffee and his day's schedule. I couldn't contain myself. I was desperate to see if he would hang his head and sheepishly claim a mental aberration for his behaviour. Or would he be too embarrassed to face me and go straight to his first meeting? But no. At eight thirty sharp he strode purposefully in to the office in his normal manner.

"Good morning, Jess. Are we organised for the day?" He asked this every morning in life. One day I vowed to reply, "No, I couldn't be arsed, so sod all is prepared." But not that morning. I just nodded.

"Great." He smiled. "Then let's get started, shall we."

I was dumbfounded. He was acting as if nothing untoward had happened at all. Surely any minute now he would look at me through mortified eyes and whisper an explanation. He hung up his jacket and sat behind his imposing mahogany desk. He clutched his hands together and leaned forward. My eyes were on stalks.

"First of all, Basil, a small recommendation about your dress code today."

He looked perplexed.

"I think it would be advisable to keep your jacket on."

"Why? Are we expecting heating problems?"

"No sir," I replied, "It's just that you seem to have developed strange marks on your wrists. Must be some kind of allergy, I presume. Maybe your housekeeper is using a new soap pow-der." I could have won an Olympic medal in laughter suppres-sion.

"Yes, well, good advice, dear, good advice," he murmured as he pulled his sleeves down, covering the welts. "Right, what's first on the agenda?"

He was priceless. Not a flicker of embarrassment, shame or, well, anything. Now I knew it: he was a true politician.

I couldn't wait to tell the girls. This would have them chok-ing on their chocolate pud for hours.

I can remember the exact moment that I started to want more than just being an old guy's mistress. It was eleven thirty p.m., New Year's Eve 1998, and I was standing in Kate's kitchen sur-rounded by enough food and drink to save a starving nation and keep them celebrating for a year.

I was dressed from top to toe in grey (it was the new black that season) Prada, courtesy of a premenstrual shopping spree the day before. Well, I had nothing else to spend my money on, I reasoned. It wasn't as if I was saving to get married, or for a romantic two weeks in Mauritius with the love of my life.

I had been at Kate's house since the day before, figuring that it was better than staring at the four walls in the flat in which, since Colin's departure years before, I lived alone. I had arrived at ten o'clock on the morning of the thirtieth, armed with a pile of books that I'd been trying to find the time to read for ages, a bottle of plonk and a box of chocolate eclairs. It would be a relaxing chill-out end to the year. Wrong. By twelve o'clock I was losing the will to live. The house was like a non-stop episode of *Sesame Street* and I was Big Bird. I sang songs with Zoë and Cameron, helped them tidy their rooms, and fed them their lunch while Kate readied the house for the following night's celebrations. By two o'clock, I was contemplating forging a note from my mother saying that I had to go home early. But by nine o'clock that night, when an exhausted Zoë fell asleep snuggled beside me on the sofa, a startling realisation dawned—I hadn't enjoyed myself so much in one day for years. In between the bribery, blackmail and coercion (not much different from politics really) deployed to get the kids to do what they were supposed to, I was actually, shock horror, *laughing*.

This was disturbing. I'd always put kids in the same category of desirability as colonic irrigations and enemas. Had I been kidding myself all this time? My head started to throb. This was major. I'd never devoted more than three seconds to contemplating the future of my personal life and suddenly I was awash with doubts and questions.

In bed that evening I stared at the ceiling (it was hard not to, as I was in Zoë's top bunk and the Artex was ten inches from the end of my nose). Maybe, I pondered, it was time for a slight shift in strategy. Now that I'd hit my thirties running, perhaps I should widen the scope of my aspirations. After all, couldn't women have everything now? Couldn't I have a political career *and* a family? Margaret Thatcher managed it (bad example . . . think Mark and desert—not a good role model). And anyway, it's not as if I aspired to be Prime Minister; my aims were more targeted at a whip (political, not leather) position. I'd set myself a ten-year timescale to achieve that, by which time I realised my ovaries would require serious coaxing to perform. I needed to give it serious thought, I decided, as my eyes closed. I'd think about it tomorrow.

I woke with a start at the sound of Cameron riding a pretend motorbike (Bruce's golf bag on wheels) up and down the hallway outside at seven o'clock the following morning. So much for chilling out. Kids? What *had* I been thinking about the night before? I didn't want kids. A budgie was too much of a responsibility. And as for a husband, why bother? Wasn't I getting most of the perks of marriage already (regular sex, intimate dinners, stimulating company) without any of the drawbacks (laundry, grocery shopping, in-laws)? I shook off the remnants of last night's melancholy—it must have been a dodgy bottle of wine, I decided. Kids? Book me in for the colonic irrigation. I was a career girl; I didn't *do* domesticity. I didn't *want* a husband. I didn't *want* children. End of story. Finished . . .

Until later that evening. The party was in full swing, after a mighty procession of couples had crossed the front door and I was in the kitchen contemplating starting a petition to have all celebrations banned on the premise that they were too depressing for words. I was preparing the wording of the motion in my head when Carly came in.

She was a sight to behold in leather trousers that must have been painted on and a white off-the-shoulder gypsy top revealing boobs that no bags of potentially harmful jelly had been required to enhance.

"Why are you in here on your own? Carol is dancing on the living room table with one of Kate's silk rhododendrons between her teeth. She needs rescuing."

"Sorry, Coop, I don't think I'm ready to start celebrating the New Year yet."

"Oh God, Kleenex alert," she exclaimed as she pulled up a chair. "Just close your eyes, pretend I'm a Samaritan on the other end of the phone and spill the beans. Take your time—it's a freephone number."

That's the thing about Carly. She could make world famine and the threat of nuclear warfare seem amusing.

"Don't overreact, Coop, I'm hardly an emotional wreck, just irritated, I suppose. It's just that I'm bloody sick of always being on my own. Birthdays, Christmas, New Year. And don't even start me on Mother's Day. I've got less chance than a Franciscan nun of ever getting a card for that. Look at me, Carly—I'm thirty years old and if I carry on like this I'll be fifty and still tickling Basil with a feather duster."

"I thought the distinguished MP for sado-masochists suited your career, career, career lifestyle? You always said a normal bloke would be too much hassle. Not to mention too boring, if he didn't know the difference between a mandate and a manifesto. By the way, what is the difference?"

I ignored the last bit. "I know," I agreed, exercising a female's right to change her mind about anything at any time. "But what's the point of putting time and energy into something if you're not going to get anything out of it? I'm achieving nothing. Why am I wasting my time on a fruitless affair when there's a wee part of me that wants marriage, babies, the whole shooting match."

Carly laughed. "The only thing that needs shooting around here is Basil for being a perv."

I gave her the most evil stare I could muster. "I thought Samaritans were just supposed to listen and not answer back?"

"Sorry, caller, please carry on."

"It's just, well, where am I going with this? I want to be spending New Year in New York, dancing the night away at a government ball in the Plaza, not eating chipolatas on a stick and singing "The Carpenters' Greatest Hits" in a semi in Richmond. No offence to present company."

"None taken."

"How do you deal with it, Carly? You've been an official noman's land since you came home from Hong Kong and that was years ago."

"Don't exaggerate. It was two years, two hundred and ninety-six days, eleven hours and fourteen minutes ago. And anyway, it's not as bad for me because I've accepted that I am to relationships what Mike Tyson is to female rights. I couldn't be a bigger disaster. Have you talked to Basil about this?"

"No. I don't want to do the clingy mistress thing; I'd hate myself. And anyway, it's so predictable."

"Would you want him to leave his wife and move in with you, lock, stock and handcuffs?"

I didn't say anything for a moment; partly because I was thinking, but also because I was chewing on a chipolata that was harder than a brick. Carly must have cooked them. "I guess I would," I finally admitted. "I know he's got some strange habits . . ."

Carly snorted. "That's like saying Pavarotti's a trifle plump."

I ignored her. "But I've never met anyone more intelligent, or interesting. And I love who he is. I love how he makes a difference and the way he deals with people. I suppose I love, em, him."

Carly groaned. "Jess, have I taught you nothing? Always go with a guy for his body, his money or his sense of humour. That way, when the love has gone you'll still have something to keep you amused."

"Can I remind you that you're single, pissed off and sitting in a kitchen with me on New Year's Eve?"

"Good point. Well, you have to tell him how you feel. If you want a future as the next Mrs. Asquith then it would be an idea to let him in on your plans."

I thought about it for a while longer. She was right. I did want more. Maybe I did even want to marry him. I wanted to end all the sneaking around, the late-night commando crawls into his flat and the furtive fumbling under tables. I wanted to work alongside my husband, not under my boyfriend (he was still sticking to the missionary position when he wasn't locked up in 'cuffs).

It was no big deal for a politician to divorce these days. Even royalty did it. And after all, his marriage was in name only. It's not as if Miranda would be devastated. As long as she was financially secure I didn't think she'd be too perturbed. In fact, she'd probably welcome not having to keep up the pretence of being a devoted spouse any longer. She might even find another man, one who could have an honest relationship with her. Yes, I decided with gin-soaked logic, I'd be doing her a favour.

It was settled. As we counted down the seconds to midnight, I made my New Year's resolution. By this time next year, I'd be Mrs. Jess Asquith. Now I just needed Basil to agree.

He couldn't have been more stunned if I told him that I'd voted Labour in the last election.

I thought I'd planned my moment perfectly. It was a freezing January night and as I let myself in to his flat I made some last-minute adjustments to my attire. I opened my coat and surveyed myself in the hall mirror: bronzed skin, courtesy of Clinique tan in a bottle, white lace bra, matching G-string, and white hold-ups. The finishing touch was stilettos that were so high I required a Sherpa and oxygen.

I dropped my coat and went upstairs. As I leaned against the door frame, Basil's eyes lit up like a neon Santa in those over-decorated gardens at Christmas.

He reached over to his drawer and pulled out handcuffs. Without even speaking, I snapped them on his wrists (he'd need to wear long gloves for a week after this session) and climbed on top of him. As I stood on his chest, my heels made puncture marks that would have made open heart surgery a painless exercise. But he didn't complain. Not even a murmur of rebuke.

I lowered myself down and got to work. It was a short shift. In ten minutes he was purring like a pussy cat and swearing undying devotion. I dived in with both stilettos.

"Basil, sweetie, I've been thinking. You know all this sneaking around is really no good for your stress levels. So I think I may have a better option."

"You mean you want to move in here as my housekeeper? But Mrs. Mollins would be devastated if I let her go, she's been with the family for years." I could see his mind whirring. "I suppose it would make sense, though."

I was apoplectic. His fucking housekeeper! I took a deep breath. Confrontation was not the way to win with Basil; I'd watched him in enough fraught negotiations to know that. Can I just say here that I know you're shaking your head and wondering what possessed me to want a relationship with what was at worst an arrogant, chauvinistic prick and at best an old-fashioned, kinky twat. I often wonder this myself. But the truth, although I'm highly ashamed to admit it, was that I was delusional. I was so blinded by his brilliance, so entranced with his mind, that I completely overlooked his idiosyncrasies.

I was so caught up in my vision of us forging a public life

together that I omitted to notice that in private we had nothing in common except work. I think it was the old "bird in the hand" theory. Noddy would have been smarter than me.

"No, darling, I was thinking more along the lines of making our relationship a little more formal. In the marriage sense."

He looked at me aghast. He couldn't even speak. I wasn't sure if I should run for my life or call an ambulance for his imminent heart attack.

I rushed to the drawing room as quickly as I could in those shoes without endangering my life and returned to the bedroom with a brandy. The consummate professional, he had recovered his composure.

"Darling, we need to discuss this," he said calmly, as if he were about to tell me the week's shopping list. "I thought you understood that this could always only be between the two of us. That's what makes it so special, you see. I thought that was what you wanted too."

"But I want more now, Basil. I'm thirty years old and I want a proper relationship. Maybe even children." I still wasn't sure that I did actually want children, but it was worth throwing in to see the renewed expression of panic that washed over him. He lowered his head for a few moments. I resisted the urge to fidget. I felt like I was ten years old again and the headmaster was about to mete out my punishment for throwing toilet paper bombs at the loo walls.

When he looked up, I could see the genuine sadness and regret. Detention for a year and a million lines.

"Then I'm sorry, my darling, this has got to end. It would be career suicide for me and that must always come first. I have to say that I care deeply for you." He paused. "Love you? Yes, I think I can certainly say that I do. But please understand that I could never give you more than we have already. I suppose I've been selfish. I never considered that you would want a more permanent arrangement. I'm so sorry."

I couldn't reply. Suddenly, I just wanted to be anywhere but there. I frantically looked around for my clothes, then realised I hadn't been wearing any. I stood up, turned and as gracefully as I could manage, walked out of the room. It's hard to make a dramatic exit when you're wearing a G-string and your bum is wobbling.

The next day I did what was for me unthinkable—I called in sick for the first time in my life and spent the day working on my CV. After the débâcle the night before, it was time for a change. I contemplated applying for postings in Borneo, Mongolia or Ecuador, anything to get me as far away from London as possible.

I was on my twelfth cup of tea and twenty-seventh Cadbury's chocolate finger when my stubborn streak kicked in. Why should I damage my career just because of Basil Asquith? Why should I leave my job, my friends, Prada, just because I'd fallen into the age-old scenario of getting hot and sweaty with a married man? Sod it! I was stronger than that. I hadn't worked my arse off to end up shuffling paper in a country that most people couldn't spell!

I called Carol for encouragement, advice and general telephone hugs. She answered her mobile after ten rings.

"Carol, it's Jess. Where are you?"

"Don't ask. But since you already have, I'm on a beach in Shetland, in a Chanel bikini filming a Scottish Tourist Board campaign."

"But it's January! It must be minus ten degrees up there."

"I know. One of my nipples just sank a passing ferry." I brought her up to date. Right up to what was now the twenty-eighth chocolate finger.

"And how do you feel now?" she asked. "Do you still want him?"

"Do you want the truth or the politically correct answer?"

"Truth."

"I think it's a definite possibility," I conceded.

"Well, there's only one thing for it then, babe. You're going to have to make him see how much he needs you."

"How do I do that?" I wailed. I was no good at these male/female mind games. Luckily, I was speaking to the master. Or mistress.

Carol laughed. "That's easy, babe. Just ignore him."

I took Carol's advice. For the next four weeks I was the person-ification of courtesy and efficiency. I carried out my duties meticulously, but at six o'clock every night I packed up my briefcase and headed for home. No more overtime. No more nightcaps. And definitely no more late-night rendezvous.

Occasionally I would catch Basil looking at me with a searching expression. By the end of the second week I felt that I was making progress, because searching turned to pleading. In the third week, he invited me to his home on the premise that we had "to talk." I was resolute.

"I'm sorry, Mr. Asquith, I couldn't possibly. After all, this is purely a *professional* relationship."

He stared murderously at me. That was the thing about Basil: he was used to getting his own way and to people dancing to his tune. Well, not this babe. I was wearing a Walkman.

In the fourth week, he cracked. I was sitting at home in my

particularly attractive teddy bear towelling dressing gown (a Christmas present from Carly) and pink thermal socks (Kate), when the doorbell rang. I grabbed my Avon catalogue—it was collection night. When I opened the door, I almost keeled over with shock. It was him. I didn't even know that he had my address. In all my years as his garnish, he had never once set foot across my doorstep.

"You're not the Avon lady." It was out of my mouth before I realised what I was saying. Blame catatonic shock.

He looked puzzled. Bless him, he thought Avon was a river in Somerset. Why would I be having a visitor from there?

This was all going horribly wrong. I salvaged the situation by opening the door wider and beckoning him inside. I wished I'd tidied up. I may be the personification of efficiency in most areas of my life, but I am to housework what Imelda Marcos is to budget control.

He stood in the living room and for the first time in all the years that I'd known him, he actually looked nervous. Here was a man who had entertained some of the most important people on the planet, who spent his life dealing with potential mine-fields, and he was standing in my front room looking decidedly disconcerted.

He pulled me to him, holding both my hands.

"Jess, I'm sorry. I can't stand it any more. I miss you more than you could ever imagine. I suppose I never realised how much I'd come to need you."

I needed Carol. Was it OK to drop the Frosty the Snowman approach now? Better not.

"And?"

He surreptitiously shifted from foot to foot.

"And you're right. A permanent arrangement would be far

more sensible. I, em, well, I've been thinking things through and I've decided to leave Miranda."

Frosty was melting and making a puddle on my shag pile.

"You will?" I asked with just a touch of scepticism "When?"

The cynic in me wanted deadlines, all promises counter-signed in triplicate and witnessed by a Justice of the Peace.

"After the local elections. I've been so silly, my darling. But I promise I'll make it up to you. Can you forgive me?" That was the other thing about Basil. When he wasn't trying to sound hip, he slipped into the vocabulary of a bad soap opera.

I thought about it. The local elections, which would select new councillors for the area, were three months away. Although they didn't affect Basil directly, I could understand him not wanting to court any adverse publicity before those—the big-wigs in the party would never forgive him. I could wait that long. After all, I'd waited years already. I conveniently over-looked the fact that I'd only decided I wanted to marry him a few weeks before—I was in martyr-mode.

I nodded my head and put my arms around him. A feeling of victory mixed with optimism washed over me. My future flashed before me. Jess Asquith. Thank God I suited blue.

I squeezed him tightly and as I did I heard the jangling of metal coming from his jacket pocket. He'd come prepared. Oh bugger, where were my stilettos?

The days seemed to drag by. Outwardly, we acted as if nothing had changed. I was Superbabe, the all-action political researcher, during working hours, and Superwhip the sad-action dominatrix, after hours.

Occasionally, doubts would creep into my mind (usually while I was creeping through the shrubbery that led to Basil's rear entrance), but then Basil would throw in a "next year when we're married," or "when you're living here," comment and I'd slip back into quiet confidence that I wasn't being taken for a bigger ride than the Lone Ranger on a canter with Tonto.

The local elections were held on the first Thursday in May. The whole team had thrown its weight behind the Conservative candidates, knowing that Basil's job would be a lot easier if his constituency had a Conservative majority on the council. The day before was a frantic rush of phone calls, meetings and publicity. By eight o'clock our team looked like we'd run a marathon then been dragged a hundred yards behind a speeding bus. And we felt even worse. Exhaustion was seeping through every pore of my over-exfoliated body, but my mind was whirring like an overwound clock. Only twenty-four more hours of being a mistress. This time tomorrow I'd be out of the closet.

I helped Basil dress for a formal dinner with the party chiefs and as I kissed him goodbye, I actually felt something like pride that this man was going to be my husband. At least I thought it was pride. In hindsight it was probably just hunger.

"Good luck tonight, darling," I whispered. Not that he needed it. We'd already heard through the Commons grapevine (which was more reliable than an official government announcement) that as long as the elections in his constituency went in their favour, he was going to be offered "something big" in the Shadow Cabinet.

"Thank you, my sweet."

"I'll see you later. I'll come by around midnight."

Was it my imagination, or did one of the country's leading pillars suddenly look more shifty than a shoplifter in Wal-Mart?

"Let's not meet tonight," he replied. "Tomorrow is going to be a big day. Let's conserve our energy."

What were we, the National Grid?

But it made sense. The last thing we needed to be doing only hours before a life-changing event was playing "tickle my toes with a feather."

I went home and tried to sleep, but I was hearing more voices than a schizophrenic on a conference call.

I watched the hands on my bedside clock tick round.

Ten o'clock. He would tell Miranda tomorrow and we'd start our life together without secrecy or subterfuge. My darling.

Ten thirty. He would tell Miranda but she'd refuse to release him on the grounds that she was evil and twisted. My poor darling.

Eleven o'clock. He would postpone telling Miranda until his Shadow Cabinet position was secured. My manipulative darling.

Eleven thirty. He would chicken out of telling her altogether and I'd go down in history as the longest-running mistress since Camilla Parker Bowles. Bastard.

I couldn't stand it any longer. I pulled the pillow over my head and was on the verge of suffocation when the phone rang. I knew he'd call. He could obviously telepathically sense my apprehension and blind panic.

I picked up the receiver. "Hello."

"This is the Samaritans ring-back service."

I chuckled. "Hey, Carly. What's up?"

"I just wanted to wish you good luck for tomorrow and to say that I'm available, for a nominal fee, to stand guard outside your door in a ski mask and bulletproof vest just in case the Conservative Wives' Club form a posse and come to hunt you down."

"Thanks, but I don't think you'll need to. I'm sure he's going to change his mind, Carly. He won't go through with it, I just know it."

"Don't be ridiculous. Why would he stay with a miserable, boring old cow who spends her whole life talking about flower arranging and de-fleaing her dog, when he could have you?"

"Carly, you've never even met her—how do you know that's what she's like?"

"I don't. I'm just making this up as I go along to try to cheer you up."

It wasn't working.

"Look, seriously, Jess, it'll be fine. He will tell her, I'm sure of it."

I wished that I had her confidence. How come I was having serious doubts?

"Why don't you call him?" she added.

"Because it'll make me look totally insecure, needy and neurotic."

"And the problem with that is what? Those are the strengths that I list in interview questionnaires. Stop trying to act so bloody invincible all the time, Jess. You're only human. He'll understand."

She's right, I thought as I hung up. If I was going to spend the rest of my life with this man, then I should be able to let him see that I had the odd moment of weakness; just one or two in a lifetime. Surely he'd love me; failings and all.

I lifted the phone to call him, but then changed my mind. If I was having a once in a decade moment of weakness, then I wanted to get full value for it. I'd much rather be with him, I decided. That way, he could put his big arms around me and run his fingers through my hair as he told me how silly I was.

I dressed in ten minutes and called a cab. As it sped through London, my confidence slowly returned. It would all be OK. Basil would break the news over a civilised meal tomorrow evening and Miranda would agree that it was for the best and ride off into the sunset on the back of her Irish setter.

I let myself in through the back door. The house was silent and in darkness as I tiptoed up the stairs. He must be asleep. Conversation could wait until morning, I decided. Tonight I'd just climb under the duvet, nuzzle up close to him and fall asleep with a big smile on my face.

I opened the bedroom door and immediately squinted as my eyes adjusted to the light. I wished they hadn't. My whole body froze as I surveyed the scene before me.

Lying on the bed, with each limb tied to a post, wearing only a gag and a look of total horror as he saw me, was my future husband.

And standing above him was a blonde escapee from an Ann Summers party. All I could see was the back of a scarlet basque, two firm buttocks, black stockings, and shoes with heels that looked like knitting needles.

My heart thundered. I blinked furiously in disbelief, which was no mean feat as my eyes had popped out so far that they were resting on my cheekbones. A hooker! One bloody night! One night without me and he'd enlisted the services of some tramp! I couldn't breathe. I would have put my head between my knees but I was paralysed from the hair down.

The blonde registered Basil's sudden seizure and following the direction of his eyes, slowly turned towards me. As she twisted her body, one breast popped out of the basque, but she didn't even notice. Her two eyes and one nipple were soon focused intently on me.

My hand flew to my mouth, paralysis forgotten. This wasn't a hooker. Although I think I wished it was. Standing above my beloved, feather duster in hand, in all her semi-naked glory, was . . . his wife.

CHAPTER 3

Why not bet on the horse that's scratching its bollocks?

June 1999

The Press Office had a photograph of me on their wall, which, four weeks after I had caused them to work more overtime than reindeers in December, they were still using for darts practice. I still maintained that I was the victim in the whole débâcle. After all, how could I be blamed for losing my temper when catching my betrothed in a compromising position? Even if it was with his wife.

And how could I possibly have restrained myself from picking up the nearest object (which just happened to be an antique Victorian lamp) and launching it at said betrothed? At which point, like the miserable coward that he was, he broke free from his restraints, whipped around me and bolted down the stairs. I blame my next action on exhaustion, stress and the outrageous shock that consumed me when I realised that Miranda had less cellulite than me. I grabbed Miranda's duster and went after him, closely followed by said lady, still with one protruding nipple.

Basil was fear personified, which is the only excuse I can muster for his suicidal actions. Instead of locking himself in a downstairs room and calling the police, he grabbed the first thing that came to hand, unfortunately his ministerial red case, and launched himself out of the front door. By the time he reached his top step, he realised the insanity of this manoeuvre and hastily retreated. Sadly, this was too late to avoid having his picture snapped by a lurking photographer from the sleaziest tabloid in the land, who was on a stakeout, prompted by a faint rumour of Basil's extra-curricular activity.

So there it was: the potentially devastating picture of the MP for Oxford on the front step of his house in the middle of the night, stark naked with only government property covering his privates. You couldn't have made it up. It was a newspaper editor's wet dream and a politician's worst nightmare.

Fortunately, both Basil and the Press Office had friends in high places and outstanding debts owed by the owner of the newspaper group. Not to mention a bill that was about to go to vote, which proposed to curtail the activities of the press.

I'd never be so bold as to claim that bribery, blackmail and coercion were a factor, but suffice it to say that the vote was postponed and the photographs never saw the light of the high street news stand. And I was now on the Press Office's most wanted list.

At least some good came out of it though—it certainly brought our affair to Miranda's attention. Although I'm sure it wasn't how Basil had intended to break the news (if he ever *had* intended to). In fact, her calmness stunned me almost as much as catching her acting out a scene from "Miranda Does Mayfair."

When Basil darted back into the hallway (at this point he

was unaware that he had been snapped) the sight of him was so ludicrous that somehow the wind gusted from my axe-murderer's sails and I collapsed in a fit of giggles. The tears of mirth washed off my make-up and I reached for a shelf to support me as I doubled in hysteria. When I recovered my faculties, the three of us looked at each other, not quite knowing where to start. Well, it wasn't exactly a situation you could have rehearsed.

Basil looked from woman to woman and, for once in his polished life, was totally speechless. Miranda recovered the power of her vocal cords first and in a hesitant and embarrassed voice announced, "Well, I think we could all do with a cup of tea." Only in Britain . . . There could be a ten-minute warning for the end of the world and while you and I were clutching our loved ones in despair or looting shops (that would just be me in Gucci), the upper classes would use it to have a nice cup of Earl Grey.

I stared, gob-smacked, as she turned and headed in the direction of the kitchen, tucking her anatomy back into her basque as she walked.

She returned with a tray laden with teapot, cups, milk, sugar and a plate of Cherry Bakewells (usually my favourite, but they were just too breast-like for the current situation). She turned to Basil, who by this time had donned a robe for the sake of modesty and removed the gag for the sake of speech.

"Well, dear, I think you'd better explain to me why your researcher is here in the middle of the night and showing violent tendencies." Cool as a packet of frozen peas.

Basil stuttered and stammered, incapable of even a basic sentence. I interjected. There was nothing else for it but to come clean and I was determined to have my say before Basil could think of a ludicrous excuse to extricate himself from this situation.

"I'm so sorry, Miranda. You see Basil and I have been, well, seeing each other for quite a while now."

I ducked to avoid potential flying objects, but only her eyebrows rose. "Really?" I was sure I saw a hint of a malicious smile on her face and the daggers shooting from her eyes could have speared Basil to the wall.

The can was open and there were worms all over the floor.

My notion of sisterhood pushed me to reveal all. I reasoned that the situation was so bad that lying would be pointless and the least Miranda deserved (other than my head and Basil's balls on a plate) was the truth.

Basil visibly shrank as I told Miranda the whole story, including the not-insignificant little fact that Basil planned to divorce her and marry me. You have to understand, I didn't do it in a spiteful manner. More in the manner of a serial killer who's been caught with twenty-six bodies under the floorboards and realises that confession is the only option that might save him from a death sentence.

Miranda listened carefully to every word. I finished my soliloquy with another apology. "I am so sorry, Miranda. If I'd known that you were still a couple in every sense of the word then I'd never have allowed this to happen."

Well, I wouldn't! I admit that it was immoral doing the naked hokey-cokey with a married man, but I'd never have pursued it had he not sworn to me that their marriage had been in name only for the past twenty years.

There was a pause that felt like hours, while Miranda absorbed the sorry tale. I looked for signs of tears, hysteria, disgust, any kind of emotional response, but there was none. She just sipped her tea and contemplated her response. I admired her composure. If it were me in her sex-shop shoes, I'd have my husband in a head lock by now. If this was the kind of composure that a public school upbringing instilled, then I was signing any future children up for Harrow first thing the next morning. If I lived that long.

And Basil? He was still visibly shrinking. He was losing a height competition with a garden gnome by the time Miranda spoke.

"Well, my dear," (there was the merest hint of sarcasm) "here's what we're going to do. You can have my husband—God knows, I've tired of him after all these years. But it'll be when *I* say. For the moment, we'll carry on as before. I expect utter discretion from you until *I* decide the time is right for divorce. No one, and I mean *no one,* hears about this until I say so."

I was stunned. She then unleashed her controlled fury on Basil.

"You know you really are pathetic. I've ignored your long line of little dalliances over the years . . ."

Whoa!! What long line? I cursed myself for not realising that I wasn't the first. I kicked his ankle—my school hadn't taught deportment, we went for revenge and pain. ". . . but I think that it's time to leave you to it. I'll divorce you when I'm ready, but until then, you can see how the world feels without my connections or my daddy's cash." She paused, as an expression of relish overtook her delicate features. "You know, you really are welcome to each other."

With that, she stood up and calmly left the room. I turned to Basil the Gnome. His face was ashen.

"So, what do we do now?" I asked, not sure what the next move in this emotional chess-game was.

He slowly turned to look at me, as if he was in some weird meditative trance. Eventually, for the first time since the arrival of the Cherry Bakewells, he spoke. "Well, I think you've just been granted your wish."

The only problem was, I didn't know if I still wanted it.

That evening, I should have been in the constituency, showing solidarity for our party as we awaited the results of the local election, but I knew that Miranda, never one to shirk her duties, would be there. I decided that she had seen quite enough of me (although not as much as I'd seen of her) that morning.

And I needed some time to think. What did I want out of life now? Dumping Basil, politics and my career ambitions and digging out those applications for far-flung postings seemed like a good idea again.

Shite, what a mess. Did I still want Basil? Did he still want me? Or was he at that very moment lavishing his wife with gifts from Perverts R Us, pleading insanity and begging for another chance? I was more confused than a rabbit on a motorway and totally disgusted with myself for allowing my focused, sane life to turn into the second half of a Jerry Springer show.

I was just about to settle down with a bottle of Bailey's and *Dirty Dancing* when I realised that the girls would be at Paco's for Thursday night dinner. Thank you, God. I was dressed, taxied and sitting at the table with Carly, Carol and Kate within half an hour.

I recounted the whole story, stopping only for huge slurps of frozen margarita.

Carly's chin was in her tortillas as she listened. "Good grief, this is worse than the time I got caught in bed with my ex the week before I was supposed to get married." It's a long story. Carly was the first half of the Jerry Springer show.

"So what are you going to do now?" Kate asked, her brow knitted with worry and concern.

I thought for a moment. There was nothing else for it.

"Drink more margaritas," I replied.

The boys in blue won the election as expected and the next day it was announced that Basil had been awarded the position of Shadow Minister for the Environment. Are handcuffs bio-degradable? The next few weeks were mayhem as we relocated our office and Basil ran the publicity gauntlet, delivering more sound bites than Tony Blair on speed. He and Miranda knocked up a record number of magazine covers, and in every one Miranda sported a cool, composed, patrician expression. She could have won a Bafta for "Best Wronged Wife in a Photoshoot."

I saw Basil in a different light now. No longer did I look up to him in childlike reverence, hanging on his every word like a devoted groupie. But somehow, I couldn't quite bring myself to break off the relationship. I changed my mind twenty times a day. One minute I was sure that continuing to see him was the right thing to do. After all, I'd backed my horse and the fact that it was now limping round the track and stopping every five minutes to scratch its bollocks, didn't mean I wasn't still hoping it would make it to the finishing line.

Then, common sense would take over and I'd resolve to dump him, move on, refocus on work and get my mates to promise to shoot me if I so much as breathed near another man. I was so irritated with myself for switching the focus of my thoughts from my professional life to my personal life. It was as if the floodgates had opened and my brain was drowning in emotional twaddle. Worst of all, it seemed like I'd passed the point of no return. Now I knew how the girls had felt for all those years—I couldn't concentrate on a single thing. Words like *vulnerable, sensitive* and *emotionally fulfilling* were now creeping into my head and replacing all other words of more than five letters. It was devastating.

I refused to discuss it with Basil. No way on earth. If he realised that his Miss Cool was turning into a serving of mushy peas he'd be banging down Miranda's door and begging for forgiveness. No, I was cool, I was calm, I was articulate and I was composed. And I was still his regular night-time partner.

Over the next few weeks I used every ounce of resolve and discipline I possessed to get those floodgates closed again. They were almost there. They were closed, the chain was around them, the padlock was on one link, then another, then . . .

Another night at Paco's threw me into a major relapse.

There were three announcements from the girls. Normally, all revelations and developments were dealt with by the old Jess in a detached and almost amused manner, because they were invariably about love, romance or feelings and therefore totally alien to me. This night was different. In my new "in touch with my emotions" state, I was affected by every one of them. And not in a good way.

Carol was first. She announced that Clive, her current OSCAR (Over-Sexed, Careered and Rich), with whom she traded affection for an American Express card and a charge account at Harvey Nicks, wanted to take her on holiday for a fortnight.

Now, to mere mortals, this may seem like not so much of a problem, more a bonus, but not for Carol. Long ago, Carol had decided that until she met "Mr. Right" she would look on men as being merely a means to a lifestyle. It was almost clinical. They wanted the trophy girlfriend. She wanted jewellery, the cars, the expensive hotels and restaurants. In short bursts, the deal worked perfectly. However, the prospect of being with a man she didn't even particularly like for twenty-four hours a day, seven days a week was daunting. She was getting colder feet than a polar bear.

The situation with Basil flashed into my mind. Was that what I was doing with him? Was I attracted to him just because he was a successful, important, powerful guy, with a distinguished career and no shortage of funds with which to send our future offspring to Eton? Would I still want him if he was an impoverished plumber, whose dinner conversation revolved around ballcocks and u-bends?

The answers made my stomach turn. Yes and no. In that order. What had happened to me? I'd become shallower than Carly and Carol put together, and they could drown in a puddle.

That was it! Basil had to go, I decided. Tomorrow morning I was going to resign and cut all the madness out of my life without the aid of an anaesthetic. I was going to return to the sane, independent, focused female I had been before I had allowed myself to fall in love with a serial adulterer. Basil was history, gone, finito.

We put Carol's situation to a vote and decided that she should go with Clive. My new, moralistic self was going to vote against it until I noticed that she already had her Ambre Solaire in her handbag. Who was I to spoil her chance of a suntan?

It was Kate's turn next to deliver her news. With huge hesitation and even huger tears, she announced that she was pregnant again.

There was a stunned silence. I don't know if I was more shocked at her news or at the fact that she was crying. I'd never seen Kate upset like this. She had always been our group's Doris Day, going through life singing "Que Sera, Sera" and taking everything in her stride. What a nightmare; you finally think your days of nappies and vomit are long over and then you become the one percent exclusion to the contraceptive pill's ninety-nine percent reliability record.

And yet . . . I had a sudden realisation that I wished it was me. Since I had finally decided to be honest with myself, I had to admit that the thumping noise I was hearing wasn't Paco's dodgy plumbing, it was the definite beat of my body clock going into blind panic.

I thought it through. I was now thirty, and since I'd just decided to chuck Basil, my exposure to sperm would be severely diminished. I tried to deploy logic. It could take me years to find a potential mate and with the hours that I worked, any chance I had to find Mr. Fertilise Me Now would be reduced even further.

My mind went into overdrive. What if, after years of searching, I finally found him only to discover that my fertility level had plummeted like a jet with engine failure? My stomach turned. What if that was what happened? What if, by saying goodbye to the dishonourable MP, I was resigning myself to a life more barren than the Gobi? Oh, my God, there were so many what if's. Someone could write a book about them.

Maybe I should have a rethink. Basil was looking like not too bad a choice after all. Or at least his sperm was.

Carly suddenly leaned over and took my hand. Sometimes her psychic sadness detector is scary.

"What's up, Jess?" she asked gently. "You OK?"

"Sure. I was just thinking that in my present situation, the chances of me having children are up there with winning the Lottery and shagging Mel Gibson." I shrugged my shoulders and made a mental note to rethink the whole "chucking" thing. I took my mind off the dilemma by shining the over-table light in Carly's face. "Anyway, Cooper, it's your turn. Spill the story."

She paused, then reached into her backpack and pulled out two letters and her purse. Oh fab, she was obviously selling raffle tickets for Save the Petunia or some other equally obscure cause. But I was way off the mark.

"This," she said, placing the first letter down on the table, "is my letter of resignation. Goodbye bog rolls." No big deal, I thought. She always hated her job as a sales manager for a toilet roll manufacturer.

She placed down the next letter, excitement oozing out of every pore. "And this is a note to my landlord, terminating the lease on my flat."

Where was she going to live? Astonishment was starting to creep over me. Had she bought one of those canal boats she saw on some holiday programme last week? Was she going to spend a year walking from John O'Groats to Land's End in aid of Save the Petunia? Absurd. Carly. Same meaning.

"And these are my credit cards, which are going to take me around the world to find every poor bugger who has ever had the misfortune to exchange bodily fluids with me."

"Whaaaaaaat?" Kate was the first to regain her voice. "Have you been taking drugs? What are you talking about?"

Turns out that Carly had given up on finding an eligible bachelor waiting outside her door with a rose in his mouth. She'd been single now for years, ever since her return from working abroad. At the time she had sworn off men for life—four engagements and two near misses had proved to her that she was to relationships what Scooby Doo was to crime detection. Now she'd decided to travel the world on an insane mission to track down these guys and take them for another test drive. It could only end in disaster. But she refuted all our objections. She was going and there was no changing her mind. I had a dreadful thought. If Carly, who was gorgeous, funny, smart (well, most of the time) and a good person, couldn't find an eligible man under forty with no criminal record and a decent personality, then what chance did I have? She'd been looking for years and the nearest she got to a hot date was accidentally feeling up a waiter in Paco's when he served her tortillas.

There was no hope for me. I was doomed to a life of take-away dinners for one and *Coronation Street*. Nope, it just wouldn't do. Basil was looking better by the minute. At least he was almost single, articulate and I was pretty sure that I loved him. He didn't set my knickers alight (although no doubt it would transpire that he had a fetish for that too) but we could make a good life together. That was it. The relationship was back on. Why not marry Basil Asquith? It just might be the best move I'd ever made.

CHAPTER 4

Why not
binge on green stuff and grout?

July 1999

As I got ready for Carly's "going away on a mission that can only end in disaster" party, I viewed my reflection in the mirror. It was a special night, and not only because one of my best friends was embarking on the journey of a lifetime. I would miss Carly. She was the one female guaranteed to be a comfort in a crisis because no matter what disasters fell upon us, she had been there, done it and laughed about it. Her first port of call was going to be in Scotland because one of her ex's had last been seen in St. Andrews. I really hoped it would work out for her. Otherwise we'd be bailing her out of the bankruptcy courts.

The other big news that evening was that I'd won the battle to force Basil to accompany me. This was a first. Persuading him to come with me had been up there with forcing Elton John to act butch, but I was determined that I wasn't going to yet another party on my own. People would start to think I had the personality of an armchair if I turned up at yet another function with only my Jimmy Choos for company. I couldn't understand his reticence. It wasn't like I wanted to snog him in full public view—I just wanted him to share in one night out with my friends.

He resisted every plea, bribe and attempt at blackmail, until I finally resorted to sex deprivation. That old chestnut. It worked every time.

The phone rang as I was locking the door. Bugger. If it was Basil calling to cancel then I was going to leave him in handcuffs for a fortnight. I snatched the receiver.

"Jess, it's Carol. Just wanted to check you hadn't been stood up by the political perv."

"I don't know yet—I'm meeting him there. He didn't want to be seen entering with me. Is Clive picking you up?"

"Nope, I decided that a change is as good as a sleep so I'm bringing George—he's replaced Clive as the OSCAR of the month. I met him in the duty-free section of the airport. He's a big-shot publisher in the newspaper world. Plus, he's rich, gorgeous and still has his own teeth, so I swapped him for Clive. Saves packing Fixadent every time we go away for the weekend."

Was there a single man in London between the ages of fifty and sixty that Carol hadn't been out with? Only the ones who thought stocks were what you used to make soup. Like I could talk. At least hers didn't put a blanket over their heads when they were out together.

As usual I was the first of the girls to arrive. I made a mental note to buy them all new watches for Christmas.

My eyes were trained on the door like heat-seeking missiles and the sigh of relief that I exhaled when I saw Basil's car draw up knocked over two napkins and a candle-in-a-bottle.

As he entered, he scanned the room looking like an under-

cover cop on surveillance and it took much cajoling and a
pitcher of margaritas before he started to relax. We took advantage of the crowds and Paco's enthusiasm for naff plastic plants
and settled in a semi-concealed corner table.

Kate arrived with Bruce, her three months' pregnant stomach still flat as Holland, closely followed by an over-excited
Carly, her arms gesticulating greetings to all around her.

I introduced everyone and was highly proud that the girls
managed to greet Basil without so much as a knowing smirk.
There we were, two girlfriends down and one to go, and not an
innuendo had passed their lips. Maybe tonight was going to be
fine. My shoulders loosened up as much as my Wonderbra
would allow.

"There's Carol!" Carly exclaimed. I grabbed Basil's hand and
dragged him out of his seat. May as well get the final introduc-
tion over with. I hugged Carol.

"How's it going?" she whispered in my ear.

"So far so good. No dramas or disasters."

"See! I told you it would be OK." We disentangled ourselves. "Let me introduce you to George." She turned to the
gent behind her. I could see what had attracted her to him.
George was tall, mid-fifties, and looked like he'd just stepped
out of an advert for "Armani for the Mature Man." In fact, I
was sure I recognised him.

"George, this is Jess."

I stepped forward to shake his hand, allowing Basil to move
forward too.

"And this is her boyfriend, Ba—"

"Bastard!!" George yelled.

Carol and I stared in horror. What was wrong with this guy?
Had he suddenly developed Tourette's Syndrome?

But it was worse than that. Before I could say, "Pleased to meet you and have you seen a doctor about your disability," George had pushed past me and had a horrified and shell-shocked Basil by the neck, propelling him towards the door.

My margaritaed brain couldn't keep up. My eyes focused on where my other half had been standing but he wasn't there. I looked at Carol. I couldn't understand why her face was a mask of serenity, but then I remembered that she'd overloaded on the Botox this month. She was as stunned as me but she just couldn't show it.

I grabbed her hand and raced after Basil and Rocky. We got outside just in time to see George blast Basil with a right hook that propelled him back ten feet and over the bonnet of a Ford Fiesta. I dived to Basil's side and tried to pull him to a vertical position, but it was impossible without the aid of a forklift.

As I struggled, I heard George tell Carol that he was leaving. She obviously made no move to join him and with an indignant "Fine then!" he jumped into his chauffeur-driven limo and roared off like Batman on a crisis call. By this time, the entire population of the pub was hanging out of windows engrossed in the drama. Mortifying didn't even begin to describe it.

Basil pushed me aside and staggered to his waiting car. I suppose if you're going to have a street brawl, the classiest way to end it is by both parties strutting off into twenty-foot vehicles with smoked windows. Limos at dawn . . .

I walked back in to Paco's in a daze.

"What the hell was all that about?" asked a confused, but still calm-looking, Carol. Somewhere among all the chaos, it had all become clear.

"How was I supposed to know that 'George' was George Milford? You never mentioned his surname," I blurted.

"What's the problem with that?" Carol replied, puzzled.

If it were a scene from a movie, I'd have paused for dramatic effect. "George is the publisher of the *Sunday News*, isn't he?"

Carol nodded.

"He's also Miranda's brother," I whispered. Even the waiters groaned. This just couldn't get any worse.

I should have collected my things and gone home. It's a scary thought that if I'd just beaten a hastier retreat than Zsa Zsa Gabor in the presence of Marigolds, my whole life would have been different. But in my drunken haze, I figured that where better to lick my metaphorical wounds than with the girls and surrounded by food and alcohol.

Carol and I headed for the bar. "Give us doubles of whatever is closest to hand." This was no time to be selective, I thought as I downed a large glass of crème de menthe. "Thanks for providing the cabaret, girls. It saved me having an impromptu karaoke competition." It was Carly.

"I'm so sorry, Carly," I groaned. "I hope this hasn't spoiled the night."

"Don't be mental, Jess; remember we're from Glasgow—a party isn't a success without a striptease and a punch-up. So who's volunteering to get their kit off? I'll pay for it out of our entertainment budget."

"Another crème de menthe and I'll do it for free," replied Carol, downing another glass of the green stuff.

After another few drinks, Carol was getting profound.

"That's it, Jess. I've decided. No more older men."

"What's brought this on?" I slurred.

"Well, look at us. I've stuck to older guys because they're mature and sensible."

"Not to mention filthy rich, generous and grateful," I added.

"OK, that as well. But so much for sense. You've ended up with the Invisible Man" (I thought that was unfair—Basil *had* actually turned up tonight) "and I'm dating Rambo. So I've decided, the next man I get down and dirty with is going to be under forty. What they don't have in experience, they can make up for with energy."

She was obviously visualising it, because she was smiling from ear to ear. I don't know if it was being reminded of the débâcle or the mental image of Carol shagging that did it, but I suddenly felt my stomach turn upside down. I bolted for the loos and felt a huge relief when I pressed my head against the cold tiles of the toilet walls.

My temperature was beginning to return to something near normal when I heard a voice behind me.

"You don't mind if I just carry on, do you?"

I turned around so quickly I gave myself whiplash and a fresh bout of nausea.

"I do mind as a matter of fact. This is a private moment. Get the hell out of here before I call the manager." At least that's what I meant to say. In my drunken haze it came out as, "Piss off to your own toilets, you perv."

"Actually, this is the gents. It's you who's taken the wrong turn in the corridor."

Oh bugger. I thought Paco's new porcelain wall ornaments were a bit unusual. I shrugged my shoulders and returned to the wall. Unless he was an off-duty cop who could arrest me for indecent wall-hugging, I decided to ignore him. Behind me, I heard the distinct sound of water hitting a hard surface then a zip being pulled up. Classy guy. But then, I couldn't talk—I was getting intimate with grout.

"Sorry to interrupt your meditation, or whatever you're doing, but can I ask you something?"

I turned again, slowly this time, to stare at him. Had I not been in such an indisposed state, I'd have automatically checked my hair, pouted my lips and pulled in my stomach. But even I realised it was a bit late to try to impress. This man was gorgeous. He was over six feet tall, with short black hair interspersed with the occasional fleck of grey à la Richard Gere in his prime before he went all religious and political. His eyes were blue and framed with lashes that could have tickled Basil's toes from a distance of several inches. I guessed that he was mid-thirties and I could see the outline of a well-toned bod under his black T-shirt and black jeans. For the first time since that fateful night that I seduced Basil, I got a hormone surge. It must have been the crème de menthe.

I brought my mind back to the present. He wanted to ask me something. Please don't let him ask me for a date because if he fancied a deranged women in a drunken stupor in a gents' toilet, then he must be twisted. And I already had a twisted man, thank you.

"What's the question?" I asked fearfully.

"It was you who was with Basil Asquith earlier, wasn't it?"

Was this a trick question? And why did he want to know anyway?

I articulated to the best of my ability. "Why?"

I asked, but I didn't really want to hear the answer. Since Basil's family members were coming out of the woodwork tonight, this was probably his long-lost son.

He washed his hands (good-looking *and* hygienic) then pulled a business card from his pocket. Through blurred vision, I read it. "Mike Chapman. Journalist. The *Daily Echo/Sunday Echo.*"

My groan echoed off the toilet walls. The *Daily Echo* and its sister paper, the *Sunday Echo,* were the most scurrilous tabloids in publication. They weren't quite "I Gave Birth To An Alien," but it was close.

"Don't take this personally, Mr. Chapman, but there's more chance of me standing up and peeing in that wall thing than there is of me talking to you."

He laughed. What a gorgeous grin! His teeth were perfect and his eyes crinkled at the sides. He was definitely related to demi-god Gere.

"OK, well, keep the card. And if you change your mind . . ." With that he turned and left.

I stumbled back into the restaurant and cornered Carly. "Coop, why are there people from the *Daily Echo* at your party?"

"Oh, them! I was talking to them earlier. They were passing and heard the music and decided to come in. I told them it was OK as long as they plied me with champagne." A wave of foreboding washed over me, but after another hour planning Carol's assault on all males born after 1960, it was soon forgotten. But not for long.

I woke up with a decidedly minty taste in my mouth—the only bonus from drinking something that resembled toothpaste all night—and made for Kate's fridge in search of anything liquid and non-alcoholic to rehydrate my thirst-ravaged body. I settled for a gallon of Sunny Delight. It matched my mood. Not.

Kate was already up and in the midst of cooking breakfast. I sat down and put my head on the table. Last night tiles, this morning Formica. This was getting to be a habit.

"How did I get here?" I asked.

"You couldn't remember your address so we took pity on you and brought you here. Carol is on the couch and Carly slept in the bath. This place gets more like a refugee camp every day," she smiled.

"Did Carly get away on time?" Carly had booked to fly to Glasgow to start her ex-boyfriend hunt that morning.

"Bruce is taking her to the airport now. He should be back any minute."

By the third glass of Sunny D, I started to get flashbacks. Oh no.

"Kate, when I regain the power of my legs, can I use the phone? I'd better check how the wounded warrior is."

"Sure," she laughed.

More flashbacks. There was a fight. Then there was drinking. Carol was having a man crisis.

"Kate, did anything else happen last night?"

"You mean apart from your boyfriend having a boxing bout, Paco having a stroke because so many people turned up, and the four of us singing 'Addicted to Love' on top of a table that then collapsed and left everyone around us with splinters?"

"Apart from all that."

"Nothing significant then, that I know of."

But something was still at the back of my mind and no amount of prodding would move it to the front. There was something else. I was sure of it.

Carol surfaced, dehydrated, hungover and still looking like she'd stepped off the front page of a lads' mag. She struggled to pull out a chair and slowly lowered herself into it, her face longer than a wet weekend in Skegness.

"You OK?" Kate asked gently.

"No, I'm in mourning. I've lost Carly and my motor skills in one night. I haven't felt this bad since Benidorm."

Kate and I automatically smiled at the mention of this. Benidorm had been our first girls' holiday: seventeen, virgins (at least we were when we went) and a higher tolerance for alcohol than Oliver Reed. It was two weeks of overindulgence that Kate, Carly, Carol, Sarah and I would spend the rest of our lives trying to recover from.

"Whatever happened to Sarah?" She was the only one of the gang who wasn't still in contact. In fact, we'd lost touch with her years before.

Kate paused, as she turned the bacon. "I have no idea," she said sadly. "I think about her a lot. Last time I spoke to her was about ten years ago and she was at uni studying to be a teacher. I hope she's happy."

I suppressed a smile. Kate just wanted to mother the whole world and for everyone to have a rosy glow. Carol shakily raised her coffee cup—her powers of co-ordination were slowly returning. "To Sarah. And Carly. May we all end up in the same nursing home."

After breakfast Carol and I staggered back to the kids' bedroom. Zoë and Cameron had been bribed with money and a promise of a day at the zoo to let us borrow their bunk beds for the day.

I had decided I didn't want to go home to an empty flat. What was the point? It wasn't as if Basil would be knocking on my door. He was probably still in casualty.

It was late afternoon when I heard the phone ringing. Kate answered. "Home for Drunks and Strays."

There was a pause, then she yelled, "Jess, Carol, pick up the extensions—it's Carly." I groaned as I rolled out of bed and landed on a heap on the floor. Shit, I forgot I was on the top bunk. Carol and I grabbed separate extensions. We uttered obscenities at Carly for waking us, but something wasn't quite right. It wasn't Carly's voice, it was . . . my brow furrowed as I tried to place it. Then, screaming. Lots of it.

"Sarah? Oh, my God, Sarah!!"

It was one those little ironies that God throws at you every now and then to remind you who's in charge. We had only been talking about her that morning and now Carly had met her in the frozen food aisle at a Tesco in Glasgow.

I realised my eyes were filling up. A hangover and all this emotion in one day. It was too much for a girl to take. All I needed now was to see a charity appeal on the telly and I'd be forging a prescription for Prozac.

I heard Kate asking Sarah when she could come visit us.

"Soon, I hope. But right now I'm getting ready to go with Cooper to St. Andrews. I'm going to be Perry Mason's trusty assistant."

There was a simultaneous groan as we all put our head in our hands. Still, I did feel better knowing that Carly wasn't going to track down ex number one by herself. At least Sarah could try to keep her out of jail.

As I hung up, I breathed a contented sigh. I'd had a great night out with the girls (if you ignore the fact that my boyfriend was now a victim of a violent street attack that had probably left him with a victim complex), found one of my best-ever friends after years of lost contact and I now had the prospect of a whole day in bed, a take-away pizza tonight with the girls and just a few glasses of Lambrusco to top up my alcohol level. Maybe this weekend wasn't going to be a washout after all.

* * *

I awoke on Sunday morning with neck cramps from sleeping on Kate's two-seater sofa. Carol and I had tossed for the three-seater the night before and she'd won. I'm sure she cheated. It wasn't fair that she was that drop-dead gorgeous *and* lucky.

I wandered through to the kitchen, deciding that I would make breakfast for Kate and the kids. It was the least I could do after squatting in their house for the weekend. I had just poured a coffee and was formulating a cooking plan when I heard keys in the front door. Bruce must have been out for his morning jog. God, I hated such motivation. He entered looking sheepish.

"Morning, Jess. I think, em, that you'd better sit down."

I looked around me. "I am sitting down." Bless Bruce. For all his strengths, he was crap in a crisis.

"So you are. Well, em, look."

He thrust a newspaper in front of me and my hand flew to my mouth. The *Sunday Echo*. Not only did I now know the full story of Friday night, but so did the rest of the British public. On the front page was a grainy photograph of Basil sprawled on top of the Ford Fiesta with George looming over him, his face contorted with rage.

Bruce placed down another two newspapers. They all carried the same photo, probably sold to them for a small fortune by the boys at the *Echo*.

The words of the headlines screamed out at me:

BAD BOY BASIL AND BROTHER-IN-LAW BRAWL
STREET CRIME RISES, BASIL FALLS
BASIL BITES THE DUST

My head thumped back down on to the table, one question at the forefront of my mind. "Bruce, do you have any crème de menthe? I think it's going to be one of those days."

There was a huge bouquet sitting on my doorstep when I finally plucked up the courage to go home that evening. Now I felt terrible. I hadn't called Basil for fear of losing an ear when he blasted me for causing such trauma to befall him and the poor man had been thoughtful enough to send me flowers. He obviously wasn't taking the small-minded view that had I not dragged him to Paco's, he would still have a straight nose and the use of both his eyes. Sometimes he really surprised me.

I grabbed the flowers and went inside. My answering machine was flickering like a strobe light. "You have seventeen new messages."

Holy shit. I hadn't had that many since a fault in the phone lines had diverted all Asda's calls to my number. I pressed play. The first fifteen calls were from Basil. They rose in an escalation of anger and desperation.

Message number one: "Jess, it's Basil. Call me back, please." Terse. Succinct.

Message number seven: "Jess, bloody answer the phone or call me back straight away. Don't think you can just hide from this bloody mess." Anxious. Pissed off.

Message number fifteen: "Jess, this is fucking ridiculous. This is all your fucking fault. Miranda is fucking furious and there's no fucking telling what this will do to me in the House. Call me now!" Upset. Going for the world record for saying "fuck." About to hire a hitman to have me annihilated.

I slumped on the stairs. Now I was confused. Flowers/hitman/fuck. There was something wrong with this picture.

Message number sixteen: "Miss Latham, this is Bert, the window cleaner. I did your windows today so I'll be round to collect the money tomorrow."

I was no wiser.

Message number seventeen: "Hi, Jess. This is Mike Chapman."

Who? Oh, shite, the *Echo*.

"We met on Friday night, remember? I peed while you insulted me. I hope your head's better. I'd like to talk to you again. My number is on the card I gave you, so please give me a call . . ."

Not in a million years. Did he think I was nuts? Well, I suppose if he did think that I could see his point—I *was* sucking a wall when he last saw me. ". . . Oh, and I hope you liked the flowers."

I put my head in my hands. It suddenly felt like a good day to emigrate. Why bloody not?

CHAPTER 5

Why not
utter the ultimate ultimatum?

September 1999

"Wanted. Single guy, no baggage (unless it's Louis Vuitton), great personality, affluent, accustomed to the finer things in life, to treat ageing but still stunning super model in the manner she was born to. No time wasters or poor people may apply."

Carol slapped me with her Fendi baguette. We were in the back of a cab on our way to Kate's and her petted lip was trailing on the floor. She obviously didn't appreciate my idea of placing a personal ad to try to solve her current manless state.

Carly interjected. "Or how about 'raging stud with trust fund required for quickie sex and quickie marriage to highly shallow beauty, who is prepared to act as trophy wife for a large fee. Non-refundable deposit required for all dates.' "

Another slap. Carol was having a major sense of humour bypass.

"Look, Carly, just because you're overcome with smugness since you've met Mr. 'Right Enough to Marry Because I've Adopted the Policy of Any Port in a Hurricane,' don't tar us all with the same duster. I'm highly selective about my men."

Now Carly's lip was on the floor too. But not for long. She hadn't stopped smiling since we picked her up, when we spotted her lugging three bags of Lambrusco out of the off-licence nearest to Kate's.

Much to our utter shock and astonishment, her mental manhunt had actually worked. Her first encounter in St. Andrews had crashed like a bus with no brakes. When she finally found Nick, the poor bugger to whom she'd lost her virginity, she was horrified to discover that all traces of sexual attraction had vanished. Not a nipple erection in sight. Not to be deterred, she'd flown to Amsterdam, only to find that the second love of her life, Joe Cain, now had the clog on the other foot and was happily shacked up with a male Adonis called Claus.

These experiences would have had a lesser female applying for holy orders, but not Carly. She'd returned to London to find Doug, meaningful relationship number three in her wild youth, and despite the fact that he'd caught her in bed with another guy first time round, he'd forgiven her and they were now picking the flowers for their wedding service.

How romantic. If you liked Mills & Boon.

The cab pulled up at Kate's house. The driver turned for his fare. "Thanks, love. And I couldn't help hearing what you were talking about earlier." He winked at Carol. "I don't have a trust fund but the cab's bought and paid for and I play a mean game of dominoes. So how's about it?"

Sparks came off her heels as she did a sprint up Kate's path, the sound of one chuckling cab driver echoing her steps.

"Landlady, we're home," Carly yelled as we entered. She'd been sleeping on Kate's couch since she returned from Amsterdam. Bruce deserved a medal for his charity work. As we

launched ourselves into the kitchen, I saw Kate hastily throw a
magazine into the bin. I knew what it was. That week's *Hello!*
had a twelve-page spread of Basil and Miranda "happy at home
on their country estate." I had a sudden mental picture of Basil
pleading for his life as I slowly tortured him with a cow prod.

"It's OK, I've seen it," I reassured her. "I slapped Basil round
the head with it earlier."

The bastard hadn't even warned me about it. Since his bout
with George, he'd been trying desperately to redeem his public
image. I'd even noticed that he'd put on a pound or two, as a
result of too many appearances at coffee mornings and
fundraisers. If he wasn't careful the tabloids would latch on to
the fact that, for the sake of positive publicity, Basil would now
accept an invitation to the opening of a cupboard if he thought
the press would be there.

Miranda was obviously still playing the game. I couldn't
help wonder what was in it for her? Was she just trying to save
face with the other FANNIES? Or did she have a master plan
that would result in the destruction of Basil and all who tickled
him? Or maybe she was just reminding us that she was the
puppet-master pulling the strings and that we were at her
mercy. Call me Pinocchio.

Well, whatever her motivation and plan, it was working.
Basil lived every moment in fear of his image being further tar-
nished and I lived every moment in fear of my sanity being lost.
It was like having a sackful of Christmas presents and not being
allowed to open them. When would she just let us get on with
our lives? My target of being the next Mrs. Asquith by the end
of the year was looking as likely as Carol getting a metaphor
right. Every now and then I would consider cutting my losses
and my ties to Basil, but then he would reassure me that it

would all be worth it when we were happily ensconced in our honeymoon bungalow in Barbados. I looked on it as doing my bit for Queen and country. Carly read my thoughts again. She was getting spookily psychic. If the National Lottery show knew about her, they'd sign her up for the next year.

"Jess, I can't help thinking that you're going to have to do something to nudge this situation along," she said as she wrestled with the screw-top on the Lambrusco.

"I agree," nodded Carol. "You can lead a horse to water, but you can't make it canter. You're going to have to take control of the situation."

They were right. It was time that Pinocchio stood on his own two wooden feet and brought an end to this puppet-show farce. But how?

The answer came to me as I watched *Fatal Attraction* for the tenth time a couple of weeks later. I would boil his bunny. OK, I'm kidding. Knowing Basil, his bunny would have two arms, two legs and be called Felicity. I still wasn't a hundred percent convinced that he'd relinquished all his other "dalliances."

Nope, bribery, blackmail and violence to animals hadn't worked for Glenn Close, so I decided to go for that old-fashioned last resort, the ultimatum.

In hindsight I could have chosen a better moment. First thing on a Monday morning, when Basil had just returned from playing happy families in Oxford, I had PMT and we had a major press conference an hour later to discuss the pollution levels of the Thames, wasn't the most auspicious opportunity to get assertive. But the lady wasn't for turning back.

"Basil, we need to talk." He had that automatic reaction of all men when faced with the prospect of discussing emotions—

his eyes glazed over and he frantically searched his brain for an excuse to leave the room.

But I was unstoppable. The brain was engaged and the gob was on a roll. I took a deep breath. "Basil, I think we've waited long enough for Miranda to grasp this situation. We've been seeing each other now for three years and I think it's time to either make this public or call it a day. I'm not prepared to wait any longer. So what's it to be?"

Bold. Succinct. Assertive. Bloody stupid.

His glazed-over eyes closed and there was a long pause. Say yes, say yes, I willed him.

Eventually, he spoke. "Jess, I know it's frustrating, but please be patient. After all, I've got the children to consider."

"Basil, they're thirty-two and thirty-four. I think they'll cope."

He sighed. "And there's my position to think about."

"Which position is that, Basil? You're the Shadow Minister for the Environment, Basil, not the reigning monarch. The British public couldn't give a damn who you were married to."

He didn't reply, so I forged on. "I'm sorry, Basil, but I want an answer by the end of the week. That gives you plenty of time to speak to Miranda."

With that I grabbed two bars of Dairy Milk and strutted out the door. I was an assertive woman of the nineties with PMT: a combination more deadly than a Scud missile.

A Scud missile that crashed and burned.

The following Friday afternoon, Basil asked me to come into his office. By the uncomfortable way he was sitting and shuffling the papers on his desk, I knew that either he was about to deliver bad news or he had a severe case of piles.

Unfortunately it was the former and I was in no mood to be

receptive. The previous night I had been called on a mission of mercy to Kate's house to find a devastated Carly in the foetal position in the corner of the kitchen, her head being held up only by a two-gallon drum of Ben & Jerry's. Turns out that Doug wasn't the man of her dreams after all. She'd discovered this when a surprise visit to his flat had revealed Doug seminaked with an air hostess called Saskia. That would have been disaster enough, but it further transpired that Saskia was his fiancée and he'd only been stringing Carly along to avenge the fact that she'd two-timed him when they were nineteen. Honestly, some men were bastards.

And women were all above reproach of course, I thought, as I sat in front of my married boyfriend after giving him an ultimatum that would put his (adult) children into broken-home statistics. Double standards? Try telling that to a woman with a hangover (I'd consoled Carly with three buckets of Lambrusco) and PMT.

"Jess, I've spoken to Miranda and we've decided that we should wait just a little longer before taking action. So I'm sorry, my darling, I'm going to have to ask you to be a little more patient."

We've decided!!! *Be patient???* Good God, he made it sound like he and Miranda were my parents and I'd asked for permission to go to a rave. Did he honestly think that I'd sit around and wait for him and Mrs. Whiplash to decide the rest of my life? Obviously yes.

I gave him my best "How could you, you horrible, snivelling bastard" look before sweeping out of the office for the second time that week.

I called Carol. "Paco's in an hour, it's an emergency."

"Oh shite, not another disaster. I've just called B&Q and

asked them not to sell a hosepipe to any females answering Carly's description."

But in the spirit of a true girlfriend called to help in a crisis, she was at the bar before me. "What would you like?"

"Anything except crème de menthe."

Four Tequila Sunrises later and I'd told her the whole story.

Six Tequila Sunrises later we'd decided that capital punishment should be reinstated for all crimes against women. Including stalling your mistress.

Eight Tequila Sunrises later it was Carol's turn and she was bemoaning the lack of sex in her life since she decided to dump the OSCARS. I couldn't quite understand it—most of her OSCARS had been too old to have sex without the aid of medication anyway.

Ten Tequila Sunrises later we'd decided life would be far better if we were gay. Imagine a life where blow-jobs didn't exist. Bliss.

We were just about to ask the barman for directions to the nearest gay club when I felt that familiar longing for a cold tile on a hot head. A wrong turn later, I was back in the gents.

"We'll have to stop meeting like this." Oh God, not again.

"Do you stalk drunk women in bars, hoping to catch them in compromising positions?"

But, again, that's what was in my head.

"Piss off, Mike, I'm not in the mood. Your species deserves to die," came out.

"Do I detect something is amiss with the honourable MP?"

"You mean Mercenary Prick?"

Mike Chapman just laughed. I don't know if it was his mockery, PMT, or the forty-seven cocktails, but rage overcame me. Suddenly, a plan became clearer than perspex.

"Mike, you shtill want a shtory about Basil Ashquith? I'll give you gosship that'll make you editor."

Is your head in your hands yet? Now you know how it happens. Kiss and tell stories do not always come from publicity-loving females shacked up at the newspaper's expense in a flash London hotel. No, they sometimes come from a wasted woman, sounding like Sean Connery and holding up a toilet wall in a rundown bistro. That thought will give your Sunday mornings a whole new perspective.

I recounted the whole Basil saga in a slurred voice, in graphic detail, with as much bitterness as I could spit out. Mike couldn't believe his luck. He got the scoop of his life and an empty bladder simultaneously. Talk about an efficient use of time.

And me? Well, I got a hangover, an apoplectic boyfriend and ritual humiliation. Plus a lifelong hatred of tequila.

As I lay in my bed the following Sunday morning, my stomach was turning. And not because I'd eaten a kebab from Donner You Just Love It? the night before. Ever since Friday night, it had been the same. I couldn't believe I'd been so stupid. Or drunk.

I'd spent the whole of the previous day on the phone trying to get through to Mike, but the *Echo* group obviously only had one phone line and a demented receptionist, because after four hours of listening to the engaged tone, I finally got through to a woman who was convinced I was a topless model and repeatedly put me through to the picture desk. In the end I settled for believing that Mike was a decent person and surely he wouldn't take advantage of the fact that I was tired, emotional and had a gob the size of Newcastle?

A commotion outside finally roused me from the safety of my duvet. The noise of cars and voices had been building up from a dull roar to an ungodly racket for the last hour. If Mrs. Picket next door was getting another extension built, then I was phoning the council. Her house already looked like Southfork.

I pulled back the curtains and screamed as I was blinded. Bugger, that sun was strong. But when my eyes focused, I realised that it wasn't the hottest day on record—the light was being emitted from forty flashes attached to forty cameras being clutched by eighty arms belonging to tabloid photographers. Well, seventy-nine—one was munching on a bacon butty as he snapped.

My heart stopped. I was under siege. Oh fuck, beam me up, Scotty.

I snatched the curtains closed. Breathe, breathe, breathe, I told myself as I prayed to God to send me an oxygen mask and a new life. There was only one thing for it—run! I threw on the first clothes that came to hand (what was suitable attire for a fugitive?) and grabbed my sun specs. I'd need them to run the gauntlet of flashes. Now I knew how contestants on *Gladiators* felt.

Change of plan. The front door was a bad idea. I surveyed the options. It was either the back window or the cat flap. Back window. I could imagine the indignity of getting stuck in the cat flap and having that image plastered across tomorrow's tabloids. "Rumbled Researcher Takes Tiddles' Way Out."

It didn't bear thinking about. No doubt the old dear at the *Daily Echo* would shake her head and mutter, "It's amazing what these topless models will do for publicity . . ." I climbed out of the back window and landed with a thump on Mrs. Picket's patio. I crawled like a commando through the back fence and for once in my life there was an empty taxi coming towards me at exactly the right time. Maybe there was a God, after all.

I threw myself in front of him, giving him no choice but to stop, but when I stuck my head in the window I realised that there was already an elderly lady sporting an extremely dubious hat in the back seat. Bugger, I was an atheist again.

"Sorry, love, I'm off duty. Just taking my mum to Tesco for a bit of shopping."

This was no time for shopping. "Fifty quid if you'll take me to Richmond first."

Mrs. Dodgy Headwear snapped the notes out of my hand. "Right, Geoffrey, we're off to Richmond and put your foot down. I think this young lady is in a hurry." She turned to me. "Ooooh, it's just like *NYPD Blue.*"

After twenty minutes, a flying stop at a newsagent's and a five-pound donation to Help the Aged (I'm sure the old dear used it to go to the bingo that night), I disembarked outside Kate's house. "There's another fifty if you'll wait five minutes, then take us to Heathrow."

"Stay where you are, Geoffrey," the old dear warned. She'd be telling this story at basket weaving class for a month.

I battered on the door like the SAS on a terrorist bust.

Bruce answered the door, Kate and Carly hiding behind him. Carly told me later that she was sure it was the heavies from Mastercard calling to collect her debts.

"Jess!" he exclaimed.

"Sorry, Bruce, this is an emergency," I yelled as I climbed over him. "When's your next trip, Carly?"

"There isn't one. I've given up on the whole idea. I'm joining a convent."

"No you haven't, you're not and you're going. Where was the next one supposed to be?"

Her brow furrowed as she thought for a moment. Only Carly would have to really concentrate to remember the order of her ex-fiancés. Does Liz Taylor have the same problem with husbands?

"Em, Tom in Dublin, but I'm not . . ."

"Yes you are!" I bellowed. I was really getting into this commando thing. I was born to be a sergeant major. Hup, two, three, four.

"Now, get your bags packed, quick."

Kate spoke up. "What's going on, Jess? Tell us what's happened."

I rummaged in my bag and pulled out a newspaper. I held it up. The headline screamed,

BAD BOY BASIL AND THE RANDY RESEARCHER.

"Kind of says it all, doesn't it? The press have got my flat surrounded. I'm leaving the country before they find me. Cooper, why are you still bloody standing there? Get a bloody move on, I'm not keeping the taxi waiting all day."

CHAPTER 6

Why not do the Snoopy shuffle?

November 1999

Some women use boxing, some go for aromatherapy and some resort to the old faithful combination of St. John's wort, evening primrose oil and Dairy Milk to combat the stresses of everyday life. I deployed my working-class roots to vent my aggression—a game of darts with a photo of Mike Chapman pinned to the dartboard. The tosser now had more piercings than a tapestry.

I also held the world record for unanswered phone calls from a tabloid journalist: 106 at the last count. I decided to conveniently overlook the fact that I had actually given him the story and blamed the whole episode on his lack of morals. Denial is a wonderful thing.

I learned that from Basil. The sordid exposé did nothing to bring our relationship to a conclusion that would have us leaping up the aisle, the "Wedding March" blaring from a church organ and my gran sitting in the front pew wearing her Sunday best. In fact, if anything, it had the opposite effect. The party publicity machine had creaked into overdrive and Basil and

Miranda were everywhere, declaring their undying love and claiming that the affair was just the product of sleazy journalism. I had to give Miranda some grudging respect for being as resilient as bullet-proof glass, a view reinforced when I took a call from her the week after my return from Dublin.

It was my fourth day back at the office. Basil had been giving me the cold shoulder, despite my indignant denials that I had anything to do with the story. The only reason I still had a job to go to was that those in authority knew that to fire me would be second only to releasing a photo of us copulating as an admission of guilt. No, far better to retain me in the position and act like nothing had happened—even if I was the laughing stock of London. The worst thing was realising what my life had come to. I'd always despised those tarts who made money out of spilling the beans on their private affairs. I was *so* above that. Well, wake up call, Jess, now I was one of them. How *had* I come to this? How *had* I sunk this low?

When the phone rang at lunchtime, I answered it wearily. Lifting the receiver had become an emotional minefield. So far I'd had fourteen offers of big bucks from tabloids to give my version of the story while wearing a basque, suspenders and a feather boa, twenty-seven abusive calls from Tory faithfuls, saying I was the biggest tart since Cynthia Payne, eleven calls from the girls to give moral support and an irate doctor's receptionist claiming that I'd missed my appointment for a smear test. Did she not read the papers? I think in view of the circumstances, I could be shown some leniency. But no, I was now blackballed from my local surgery.

With a heavy heart I picked up the receiver.

"Miss Latham, this is Miranda Asquith."

Shite, another crank call. "Yes, I'm sure you are, and I'm

Camilla Parker Bowles, now piss off and get therapy, you nut."

I slammed the phone down. How the hell did these loonies get my number?

It immediately rang again. "Yes?" I barked.

"Miss Latham, this really is Miranda."

That was it! I'd had enough of these mental cases with nothing better to do with their time than harass me. I'd show them.

"Prove it," I demanded. That would put her on the spot.

There was a long pause. Then, "Miss Latham, I don't have the time or the tolerance for your games, but since you insist on playing them, let me just say that the last time we met was in my husband's apartment."

The voice. The accent. The wife.

"And you rather rudely interrupted my husband and me . . ."

It was a wonder I could still hear her over the noise of me thumping my head repeatedly on my desk.

"And we had a nice cup of tea and a Cherry Bakewell. Have I refreshed your memory?"

My eyes were clenched shut in embarrassment. But then, why should I be embarrassed? She was the one with her nipples hanging out. I took a deep breath and repeated the mantra, "In control, in control, in control."

"Vividly, Miranda. What can I do for you?"

She was deadly calm. "It seems, my dear, that you've created quite a stir."

"The story was nothing to do with me," I cut in. The House of Commons lie detectors were screaming like car alarms in a pile-up.

"Well, that's as may be. But the fact remains that you've broken the terms of our agreement."

So shoot me. But I didn't say that out loud. I was too busy losing the will to live.

"And I therefore expect you to go some way to make amends."

Here it comes, I thought. She wants my resignation and my internal organs. But it was worse than that.

In fact, it couldn't have been any worse, I pondered the next morning as I entered a hot, sweaty studio to be interviewed by the most popular daytime television show hosts in the country. I sat on *Richard and Judy*'s sofa, next to an utterly composed Miranda and a lightly perspiring Basil, backing up their theory that the press were out of control and calling for the ritual flogging of all tabloid journalists.

As I squirmed in my seat, I caught Judy's eye. She knew I was lying, I was sure of it.

For weeks I was more reclusive than Greta Garbo. I stopped answering the phone at work. What was the point? Even my mother was using it to launch all-out assaults on my ears. I left home only to go to the office and even when I was there I spent most of the day with the door locked so I didn't have to listen to people sniggering as they passed. I couldn't even talk to Basil. The official story was that he was concentrating on issues in his Oxford constituency, but the truth was that he'd booked himself into the Priory suffering from acute stress and a homicidal wife. A homicidal wife who, if rumours were to be believed, had last been seen swinging her stuff in Stringfellow's with a French rugby player on some mad "Tory wives entertain the visiting sportsmen" jolly. FANNIES having a knees-up—it didn't bear thinking about.

Meanwhile, the profits in my local pizza delivery shop

doubled as a trip to Tesco became another study in ritual humiliation—full of old ladies who tutted at me in the dairy section. I couldn't even vary the menu, because if I had fish and chips I ran the risk that they'd be wrapped in a newspaper with my photo plastered across it. It was desperate. Initially, the girls had been more supportive than control top tights, but even they gave up after every call went unreturned. I couldn't face anyone. I was wallowing in a pit of self-pity that four jeeps and a crane couldn't have dragged me out of. It was my first major trauma in life and I just wasn't up to the challenge. In fact, my life was over. My boyfriend, my privacy, my credibility and my ambitions were long gone and I couldn't see any way to retrieve them. If I had had the money I'd have been in the plastic surgeon's queue begging for a new face, new identity and new life.

On a freezing Wednesday night in November, the *EastEnders* theme roused me from my Hawaiian twelve-inch thin and crispy. I switched off the telly—I was suicidal enough without being confronted with Pat Butcher having another breakdown. I pulled my dressing gown tightly around me, put on my Snoopy slippers (I inherited them from Carly when she left the country) and was halfway up the stairs to seek refuge once again under the duvet, when the doorbell rang. Bugger. If it was the Mormons on a recruitment drive I might just join up. At least I'd get to meet the Osmonds.

I decided to ignore it, but by the time I reached the top of the stairs the persistent ringing had escalated into a cacophony of bangs and thuds. Mother of God, the Mormons were getting aggressive these days.

I relented and after putting on the door chain and my most Catholic expression I opened the door just wide enough to tell them that I was Sister Patricia from the Little Nuns of Bernadette, doing care in the community work.

Kate rammed her foot into the gap. "Open up, Latham! We're freezing our arses off out here. I'm a hormonal, pregnant woman—don't mess with me."

I smiled despite myself.

"Bloody let us in," Carol shouted, "my feet are turning blue."

I looked down. Only Carol would wear three-inch, strappy Manolo Blahniks in November. I removed the chain and opened the door. In charged a massive Kate, holding her stomach and making a beeline for the loo, an irate Carol muttering expletives and a female whom I'd never seen before, grinning like a Halloween pumpkin.

"Look, girls, I appreciate the thought, but I'm really not in the mood for company."

"Oh, shut up, Jess," Carol replied. Sympathy had never been her strong point. "Look," she went on, motioning to the other female, "we've even brought a trauma counsellor."

"I don't need a fucking trauma counsellor," I yelled, turning to face the stranger. "I'm sorry to have wasted your time . . ."

Why was she still grinning at me like a demented clown?

". . . but I'm perfectly fine and the last thing I need . . ."

God, she looked familar. Where had I seen her before?

". . . is interfering friends who don't know how to mind . . ."

She was still smiling. I knew her. I was sure I knew her. ". . . their own bloody . . . Oh, holy cow, Sarah!!!"

I flung my arms around her and to my eternal embarrassment burst into floods of tears.

I clung on to her like a liferaft in a storm. It had been so long that I didn't even recognise the girl who'd been my best friend since the days of navy-blue knickers and plimsolls. Kate returned from the loo with a toilet roll and a face cloth. They marched me in to the living room and laid me down on the sofa.

"We can't talk to you like this," Kate said as she put the cold cloth over my face, "You look like a turnip in distress."

It was true. Too many tears and not enough facials had left my eyes looking like they needed puncturing. The soothing iciness of the cloth immediately began to seep into my pores.

Carol disappeared and returned ten minutes later with four glasses. "Jess, that kitchen is a tip. You could lose small children in there. What's happened to you?"

"Depression," I answered in a muffled voice.

"Yes, well, consider yourself officially over it. You'll end up sick as a budgie living in this squalor," she added. "I'll send my cleaner round tomorrow. Call it an early Christmas present." She was all heart, our Carol.

Sarah poured the wine. She looked so happy that it was impossible not to feel my spirits rising. I leaned up on one elbow.

"So tell me," I asked, "what've you been up to for the last twelve years?"

She smiled. "Do you want the pamphlet version or the full *War and Peace?*"

"*War and Peace.* If it's really bad, it'll only make me feel like my life's not such a fuck-up after all," I answered.

Sarah took a deep breath and started to talk. Halfway through, I began to wish I'd watched *EastEnders*—it was light entertainment compared to Sarah's story. Turns out she'd been married to a brute who was an obsessive compulsive. He'd stopped Sarah from working, from socialising, from having any communication with anyone other than him or their two children. That explained her disappearance from our lives all those years ago: she'd been too afraid to talk to us. Instead, she'd endured years of hell until she finally found the courage to leave him a year earlier, taking her children, Hannah and Ryan, with her. And I thought I had problems.

"I'm so sorry, Sarah. If we'd known, we'd have done something years ago." I was furious with myself. Why had I not persisted and got to the bottom of her withdrawal when it happened?

"Carly said the same thing when I met her again, but honestly, there was nothing you could have done. But things are great now. Fantastic, in fact. I've even met someone else. That's why I decided to come down to see you all for a few days."

We gave her a round of applause. Then I noticed she still look worried.

"But there's just one slight problem."

I was so close to the edge of my seat at this point that I was in danger of landing face down on my un-hoovered carpet.

"Go on," I prompted.

"Well, you know I went to St. Andrews with Carly to track down Nick Russo, her first boyfriend."

"Yes . . ."

"Well, when Carly realised that he no longer set her knickers alight, she went off to Amsterdam to look for fiancé number two, and I stayed behind in St. Andrews for a couple of days."

"And?"

"I kind of got to know Nick and I continued to see him and now I think I'm in love with him and we've all just found each other again and now you're all going to hate me and Carly's going to kill me for going out with her ex." She blurted all this out without stopping for breath. Now she was on the verge of tears and turning pink through lack of oxygen.

I looked at Kate in astonishment. She looked at Carol. Carol was still looking in disgust at the crumbs on my carpet. She was hopeless at focusing on more than one thing at once.

Eventually, Kate spoke. "Are you happy now?" she asked Sarah.

"Enormously."

"Then Carly won't be pissed off. I promise. In fact, she'll be delighted for you," Kate reassured her.

She still wasn't convinced. "Even though I'm dating a guy she was in love with?"

Carol laughed. "Sarah, Carly has been in love with half the straight and at least one of the gay men in this hemisphere. Kate's right, she'll be really happy for you."

I looked at the others. "We all are," I added.

She visibly sagged in relief. I love a happy ending. Where was the face cloth—I was filling up with emotion again.

"So where's Carly now? Is she in jail yet?" I asked, suddenly realising that I'd been in hiding for so long that I'd lost track of the manhunt mission.

Kate turned to Carol. "Do you want to tell her or will I?" Oh no. I sensed another drama.

Carol took over. "I'll just give you the arrow points, shall I?" she asked.

"You mean the bullet points," I corrected.

"Whatever. OK, Carly is still on the hunt. I met her in New York last month. So far, she's met five of her ex-men and, so far, none of them have marched her down the aisle. She's on her way to Hong Kong to find the sixth now."

"What else happened, Carol?" I asked suspiciously. My extrasensory perception was telling me that there was more to this story. She and Kate collapsed in giggles. Sarah was looking as puzzled as me; they obviously hadn't had time to bring her up to date.

"Well, there has been a minor development—nothing to fax home about," she teased.

I gave her my serial killer look. She folded immediately.

"OK, OK, so we got to New York and Cal was there on a photoshoot . . ."

"You mean Cal, Carly's brother? Sex god, male supermodel and the most gorgeous specimen of manhood that God ever put on this earth?" I had to check, this was all getting too much for a woman who'd been out of contact with the human race for the last two months.

"The very same," she concurred, her pearlies glinting. "And to cut a long movie short, Cal and I sort of got together."

"Whaaaaaaaat? As in hung out together or naked and sweaty together?"

"And we're getting hitched on Christmas Eve!"

My carpet didn't need a Hoover now as I had collapsed on it and was gasping so heavily for breath that I inhaled two months' worth of pizza crumbs. This was a disaster! What the hell was it with the Cooper family? Was it a defect in their genes that forced them to get engaged within ten minutes of meeting someone of the opposite sex?

But in the way that only a true woman can, I changed my mind in an instant. I suppose Carol and Cal *had* known each other since we were kids. And he *was* under forty. And gorgeous. And the sweetest man. In fact, he was like a brother to all of us. Wait a minute, that meant it was incest! This couldn't be right.

Then the expression on Carol's face dispelled any doubts. She was the happiest I had ever seen her without champagne in one hand and an American Express card in the other. My brain was racing. And it *did* make sense—they were even in the same job. Why hadn't we thought of it before? They would be perfect together. Mind made up. It was the most fantastic news I'd heard since ten minutes ago when Sarah told us about Nick.

Even the thought of Basil couldn't depress me now. And never, I vowed, would I go out of circulation again—there was the potential to miss too much excitement.

I was still hugging Carol when the phone rang.

"Just leave it," I shouted to the others, "I'm still in hiding."

"But it might be Carly, we told her we were coming here tonight."

"Well, you answer it, Kate. If it's not Carly, then just tell them you're my cleaner," I begged.

"In which case you're crap at your job," Carol snorted.

Kate came back two minutes later, looking stunned.

"It was Basil. He obviously thought I was you and he didn't give me a chance to explain that I wasn't. I'm sorry, Jess, but he says he's on his way over and he'll be here in twenty minutes."

Bloody typical. Just when things were going so well.

"OK, girls, let's make a move and leave Romeo and Juliet to punch this out on their own," Kate said as she rounded the other two up.

"No way!" Carol objected. "Sorry, Jess, but you officially have the willpower of a cabbage when it comes to that man."

"Don't be ridiculous, Carol," I assured them. "Anyway, if he's out of the Priory now then I'd have to face him at work tomorrow and I think I'd probably rather have the first encounter here rather than in front of sixty civil servants trying to gauge my reaction. I can handle him, I promise."

Wrong. Carol Sweeney-soon-to-be-Cooper: one. Jess Latham-deserves-to-be-shot: nil. As soon as they were out of the door, I scrambled to my bedroom. Rule number one of encounters with the enemy: never expose weakness to the other side. I realised that the fact that I resembled a bag lady with a hygiene problem would put me at a distinct disadvantage.

I whipped off everything that was made of terry towelling, in other words every item I was wearing, and opened my Dirty Weekend Emergency Tote Bag. It contained everything I needed: red Agent Provocateur bra and G-string (so small it could slice cheese), Obsession body lotion and perfume, Revlon Dragon Red quick-drying nail varnish and everything that was needed for a Clinique "flawless face in five minutes" session. It took a bit longer. I don't think Clinique knew about my eye bags. I threw a fine rib black polo-neck sweater and flared black hipster trousers over the lot, pulled my hair into a high ponytail (disguised the fact that it hadn't been washed for about the same length of time that the carpet had been bereft of the Hoover), then gave myself a quick scan in the mirror. Passable. Chic even. As long as I kept the lights low and the perfume didn't wear off too soon.

As I ran around the living room clutching a black bin bag and throwing in everything that wasn't nailed down, I did mentally rebuke myself for being so stupid as to even care what he thought.

I tried to second-guess him. Was he was coming to bribe me to resign from my position and disappear quietly? Or perhaps there was another prime time television show that he wanted me to humiliate myself on. Had he found proof that I gave the story to the tabloids and he was on his way to murder me and dispose of my body under Mrs. Picket's new patio? Oh, the pressure! So many options and all of them leading to my emotional, physical or financial demise.

Be positive, be positive, I chided myself. Look on the bright side; he had to be coming here for a reason and since there was nothing left that he could take from me, I could only gain from this meeting. That thought cheered me up from clinically depressed to just the wrong side of pissed off. By the time the doorbell rang, I'd talked myself into a frame of mind that was detached, aloof and bordering on arrogant. I would *not* let this man walk all over me.

Wrong. Just call me Astroturf.

I stood behind the door for a full minute before answering it. I didn't want him to think I was anxious or desperate. When I finally swung it open in the most nonchalant manner I could muster, an alien sight confronted me. It *was* Basil, but he was, well, ruffled. The last time I'd seen him look this dishevelled, disconsolate and depressed was when he was sprawled across the bonnet of a Ford Fiesta after receiving a violent right hook.

Before I could even move to the side to let him pass into my newly air-freshened pad, he threw his arms around me and clutched my head to his shoulder. I looked behind him for Louis Theroux and a camera crew—he had to be doing this for dramatic effect of some kind. Either that or the Priory had drugged him and given him a full personality transplant.

He held on to me for what seemed like an age. I couldn't help casting my mind back to a similar situation a few months before when he'd stood in my living room and promised to leave Miranda after the local elections. Ding ding. Bullshitometer was ringing again.

I prised him from me and held him at arm's length. "You look dreadful," I commented. "Don't they have a spa and sunbeds at the Priory?"

He gave me a rueful smile. "We need to talk," he replied. For about the tenth time that night I was taken aback. I didn't think men's brains were capable of forming those four words into a sentence, never mind vocalising them.

"I've been a complete prat," he continued. I nodded my head.

"I know you didn't sell the story of our relationship to the tabloids. I know that you'd never even contemplate such a thing."

I donned my best martyred expression. And prepared for a bolt of lightning to strike me down.

"You see, Jess, I've learned a lot about myself over the last few weeks and I've come to two conclusions that I'm absolutely sure of."

The Tories would never win the next election and waxing is better than shaving? I stayed silent.

"The first is that I am absolutely committed to my career and to politics."

I nodded my head. No newsflash there. I could have told him that and saved him the therapy bills.

"And the second thing is that I want . . . no Jess, I *need* you by my side. I've spoken to Miranda again and demanded a divorce. We were meant to be together, Jess, and this time we're going to be," he finished triumphantly.

Wow! This was unexpected. I definitely hadn't anticipated this one and I had no idea how to react. Did I want to be with him? I had no idea. I'd spent the last few weeks hating him so much that I couldn't remember if I even *liked* him, never mind loved him. Confused, confused. I bloody hated all this emotional stuff. By the expression of anticipation on his face, I could see that he was waiting for an answer. Bugger.

I quickly switched to my far more efficient business head and briefly weighed up my options.

Option number one: tell him to stick his red box where he'd

need three packets of laxatives to retrieve it. But then I'd be back to square one: single, career in tatters, and all the drama and humiliation would have been for nothing.

Or option number two: grudgingly give him another chance to prove to me that we had a future life together that didn't include sneaking around like members of the Territorial Army on a dawn patrol.

What does it say about my powers of rational thought that I plumped for option two quicker than you could say, "Bog off, you lying, cheating bastard?" I blame it on the happy vibes that the girls left in the house. Carol was in love. Kate was in love and pregnant. Sarah was in love. And within fifteen minutes I was in bondage.

I couldn't help wishing that it had been the Mormons at the door—at least I'd have great teeth.

CHAPTER 7

Why not
cool everything down . . . ?

December 1999–
three days to Carol and Cal's wedding

The week before the wedding was hideously frantic. It seemed that every time I picked up a phone or had a conversation with another human being it ended in the potential for disaster. I decided to make a logical list.

Problems to be Solved

1. Basil won't come to the wedding because he doesn't want to risk the repeat of a tabloid fiasco.

   Possible solutions: bribery—a weekend of sexual pleasure in a hotel for the perverted. Nope, too expensive.

   Blackmail—if he doesn't come, I'll spill the Heinz baked ones again. Nope, still denying that I did that the last time.

   Death threats—I'll plead hormones and unreasonable behaviour. As long as I get a jury of Labour support-

ers, they'll never convict me. Mmmmm. Best option
I think.

2. Carly is supposed to be matron of honour but she's vanished from the face of the earth. In fact, she doesn't even
   know about the wedding.

   Possible solutions: call Interpol. Nope, too risky. They'll
   probably arrest her for credit card extortion and
   fraud.

   Do a television appeal in Hong Kong—nope, we've had
   enough media intrusion for one life, thank you.

   Conduct a séance and ask the spirits to intervene—
   nope, who knows what literal skeletons would come
   out of the closet if we did that.

3. Kate is in the final stages of pregnancy and terrified that
   she'll drop before the big day and miss it, or on the big
   day and spoil it.

   Possible solutions: take large bucket, towels and a tea
   urn filled with boiled water. Nope, Carol would use
   all of above to wash her hair.

   Give Kate major shock and hope it induces birth today
   so that she is recovered in time to be bridesmaid.
   Nope, so far she's survived more shocks than a
   wrongly wired toaster and babe is still inside.

   Tie elastic bands around her ankles and keep her horizontal at all times. Possible, but we'd need to hire a
   big bus to get her to Scotland for the ceremony.

   I'm losing the will to live.

The telephone rang, saving me from attempting self-mutilation
with a biro. It was Kate.

   "Panic over," she yelled.

"Which one?"

"Carly! She just rang from Hong Kong—she's been in Thailand all month, that's why we couldn't reach her. She'll be home for the wedding."

Relief.

One problem solved in two minutes. Two, if you count the fact that Kate was excitable again and the baby still hadn't shown signs of appearing. It was obviously going to be in there for the duration. Now for Basil. I rang his apartment.

"Look, Basil, this really means a lot to me. I'm going to ring Miranda and beg for compassionate leave on the grounds that your mistress will make your life a living hell if you don't accompany me to this wedding."

There was a nervous pause, a stutter, a cough, then a resigned tone, "Don't call Miranda. I'll make it to the wedding. Just let me sort it out."

All problems solved. I was getting a better success rate than the Citizens' Advice Bureau. The very organisaton that I'd need some time later.

The hotel that the soon-to-be Coopers had chosen for the nuptials was on the banks of Loch Lomond, and the views were breathtaking. Amazingly for Scotland in December, the morning of the wedding was a mild day with blue skies overhead. The wellies and thermal vests stayed firmly packed in our suitcases. It was probably just as well; our beautiful, sapphire-blue, sheath bridesmaid dresses would have looked a bit odd if they were accessorised with knitted undergarments and rubber boots.

Carol had issued us with a strict schedule: breakfast at nine a.m., hairdressers at ten a.m., make-up at eleven a.m., nervous breakdowns at noon. Unfortunately, she couldn't stick to it and was tearing her hair out in the dining room over her croissants and three jugs of extra-caffeinated coffee by eight forty-five.

"Where the fuck is Cooper?" she yelled the minute I popped my head round the door.

"Cooper the groom, or Cooper the matron of honour?"

"Cooper the fucking dead if she doesn't get here soon," she replied in a murderous tone.

"She'll be here," I answered with more conviction than I felt. I knew that Carly would do everything in her power not to let the supposed-to-be-happy couple down, but in Carly's life sometimes the gods just conspired against her. It was divine revenge for too much time spent bunking off Mass when she was a teenager.

Carol did the mature thing and burst into tears. "I'm sorry, Jess. You know I don't mean it. I'm like Yogi with a migraine this morning. I just really want everyone to be here. It wouldn't be the same without any of you."

Kate and Sarah arrived. "What's going on?" Kate asked when she registered that Carol was having a full-scale wail into her napkin.

I was in mid-explanation when I realised that in the midst of the drama, Sarah was wearing her pumpkin face again.

"Sarah, why do you look like you've just won the Lottery and decided to blow it all on hedonistic pleasures?"

For a fleeting moment she looked embarrassed. "Because I have, metaphorically speaking."

"What does that mean?" Carol asked, lifting her head from the napkin.

"I'll tell you tomorrow," Sarah replied. "Today is *your* day."

But Carol wouldn't be deterred. "Sarah, I love you, but I'll have to kill you if you don't tell me what's going on. I hate surprises and I'm working up to major tantrum here. Clear a space so that I can throw myself on the floor and thump my fists."

"OK. Well, em, last night Nick kind of . . ."

"SPIT IT OUT," Carol yelled. We were going to have to sedate her soon.

"HE ASKED ME TO MARRY HIM," Sarah screamed, her eyes and mouth wide open with glee.

Even the waiters were moved to tears. But that was probably just because they'd been holding hot plates of breakfasts for the last ten minutes, too scared to bring them to our table in case Carol assaulted them with four square sausages and eight rashers of streaky bacon.

As we converged on Sarah, I had a realisation. I was the last one. Of all my friends, who were the most important people on my planet, three had found their soulmates. Carly probably had too and that's why she'd gone absent without leave. So out of the five of us, only I, Jess Latham, shagger of the political one and minor tabloid celebrity, had made as much progress in the marriage stakes as a commitment-phobic. But it wasn't the comparison to the girls that saddened me. It was the reminder that I wanted to share my life with someone. I wanted to have children. I wanted to be part of Mr. and Mrs. Average, taking the family to McDonald's on a Saturday and consoling the kids when they got the wrong Happy Toy. I wanted to have it all—the family, the career, the size eight figure (well, maybe some dreams were just too far-fetched) and so far, nothing in my life plan was going right. I shrugged off the melancholy before the others noticed. I'd worry about minor things like my whole life being a complete fuck-up tomorrow: today was a day for wedding bells and happy thoughts. Now where the hell was Cooper? Surely she wouldn't miss this? No way on earth.

By two thirty though, all the doubts were back with a vengeance. The wedding was at three and we were all ready except for Kate, who'd had to remove her dress for the tenth time in the last hour to pee.

Carol was the most stunning bride I'd ever seen. Her perfect bod was draped in a strapless ivory silk sheath and her hair flowed in loose curls from a glistening pearl and diamond tiara (a past gift from a long-forgotten OSCAR). She was the princess that she'd always aspired to be. The only detraction from this picture of beauty and innocence was that she was chain-smoking Marlboro Lights and swigging Moët from the bottle. Well, even princesses have bad habits.

Suddenly, the door flew open and I felt my face crumble. Behind the door was an unfortunate choice of places to stand. Through the fog of a minor concussion I saw Carly lunge in, wearing dark glasses that didn't conceal the fact that she looked like an escapee from a secure mental ward. But at least she was here.

As we strolled down the aisle to the strains of "Love Me Tender" (Cal's middle name was Elvis), I scanned the crowd. It was an eclectic mix of the extended Cooper family (why was Carly's gran wearing a frisbee as a hat?), the marital couple's fashionista friends complete with "must have" poodles, an assortment of Carly's ex-boyfriends and Basil, looking about as comfortable as a snowman in a heatwave. He jumped three inches every time a camera flashed, obviously convinced that there were *paparazzi* behind every plant pot. It didn't help that he was seated next to Joe Cain, Carly's now-gay ex, who was dressed from cravat to toe in Versace pink satin. This meant he was having to do his most politically correct "I'm not homophobic in any way" act, while trying to demonstrate with body language that he wasn't Joe's partner. I could tell from the amusement on Joe's face that he knew exactly what was going on in Basil's head and was relishing it. I had to admit though, Basil did look handsome. My heart swelled like a tongue with a peanut allergy, as I contemplated the fact that this gorgeous man would one day walk up the aisle with me. Although it would be with the aid of a Zimmer if we didn't get a move on.

There were more tears than an episode of *The Waltons* when Carol and Cal said their vows. To a rousing cheer, the newlyweds danced back up the aisle and after coaxing Carly out of a toilet where she was hiding from her mother we posed for what seemed like hours for photographs. My jaws were frozen into a grin that bordered on that of a homicidal maniac and I was contemplating what sentence I would get for assaulting a photographer with his Olympus, when he finally said we were done. How did Carol and Cal do it? I'd rather have my teeth pulled out with pliers than stand in front of a camera all day.

I grabbed Basil's hand as we returned to the main ballroom and couldn't stop myself from whispering that famous line that all men know to avoid at all costs. "What are you thinking, darling?"

To his credit, he turned to me and kissed me, showing no signs of wanting to call the National Union of Bastards to concoct a suitable reply. "Just that one day we'll be saying those very words to each other."

"What, one more smile for the camera?"

He smiled indulgently. "I love you, Jessica Rabbit."

Don't throw up. I know what you're thinking, but in the moment it was really sweet. Honest. I forced him into a head-lock and snogged his face off. He might be a big-shot politician, but to me he was just the love of my life and I couldn't wait to marry him. One deluded bridesmaid of the year award coming up.

My hormones surged and I looked around surreptitiously to check if anyone would notice if we retired upstairs for a quickie. Coast clear. Carly was in deep conversation with her mother. Carol and Cal were mingling. Sarah was whispering something into Nick's ear and he was rubbing her back as she spoke. Oh, happy day. A wave of contentment washed over me. It didn't get any better.

I scanned the room again. Where was Kate? I spotted Bruce. "Where's the mother of your children disappeared to?" I asked.

"Toilet, ten minutes ago. Can you check on her for me, Jess? I know she's probably just gabbing, but can you just have a quick peek."

I put my libido on hold and turned in the direction of the loos. As I did so, one Carly Cooper, tears streaming down her face, bridesmaid dress hitched up to reveal a pair of past their best Nikes, streaked past me. Conversations with her mother often had that effect on her. I knew all that harmony was too good to last. What should I do first? Check on the pregnant one or follow the distraught one?

I rushed to the toilet. No one there. I was just about to turn and flee after Carly, when I heard what sounded like the voice of a dirty phone-caller coming from one of the cubicles.

"Kate, is that you?"

More deep breaths. Then a moan. Oh my God. Either Kate was in labour or a couple of the guests were having sex in the loo. I tried the door. Locked. I ran back to the main hall. Basil grabbed me as I passed him.

"Shall we go upstairs, my darling?"

His sense of timing had always sucked. I quickly grabbed Carly's gran and thrust her towards Basil. "Keep him talking for ten minutes," I begged her, "and I'll take you to bingo every night for a week." She was attached to Basil's leg within ten seconds. I dragged Bruce to the toilets, where he gallantly broke down the cubicle door. Soon I had my arms around Kate and was supporting her out to the seat at the mirror area. Thank God for posh loos. If this was in Paco's I'd have had to prop her up against a wheelie bin.

She was still breathing like a marathon runner. I left her with Bruce as I dived to the reception to call an ambulance. Carol saw the look of panic on my face and rushed over. "Kate's giving birth in the loos. We need an ambulance," I panted. Physical exertion in two tons of taffeta is not to be recommended.

"Ambulance now!" she yelled to a stunned receptionist. Then she turned back to me. "Oh my God, it never rains but it soaks. Tell her the ambulance is on its way and we'll be with her in two minutes."

Sarah appeared at our sides. "But you can't go anywhere, it's your wedding day."

"Sod the wedding. Cal will understand—he's a Cooper, he thrives on drama. Tell him I'll be back for the dancing. And find Carly," she shouted as she ran to the loos.

Fifteen minutes later, Kate, Bruce, Carol and I were in the back of the ambulance as it started down the drive. Suddenly there was a loud thumping on the side of the vehicle. It screeched to a halt, the back doors opened and Sarah and Carly jumped in.

"I'm sorry, you can't all come," muttered a confused paramedic as he surveyed the scene. I bet never before had he rushed a pregnant woman to the emergency ward, accompanied by her husband, a bride and three bridesmaids.

"They're, *gasp, gasp,* coming," whispered Kate. The paramedic shrugged his shoulders. He knew better than to argue.

"Bee baw, bee baw, bee baw," the ambulance screamed as it hurtled through the countryside, a white train trailing from its back door. Kate looked panic-stricken and in pain. I took her hand.

"Don't worry, sweetie, we'll get there on time."

"I'm not worried about that," she gasped between contractions.

"Then what's wrong?"

"Carly's sitting on my foot."

Tallulah Carly Sarah Jess Carol Smith came into the world kicking and screaming eight hours later. Unusual name, but believe me, Tally got off lightly. It took us two hours of coaxing to persuade Kate not to call her Santa Mistletoe Smith, because she was born minutes before midnight. If Tally doesn't rebel against her parents when she's a teenager, it'll be a miracle.

Carol and Cal finally got to do the first waltz the next morning over breakfast, much to the amusement of the staff. We all celebrated Christmas morning before they flew out to Milan that night for a few days' honeymoon (oh, Utopia—a husband who would shop *with* you as opposed to standing outside boutiques, reading the paper and checking his watch every five seconds), leaving the rest of the bridal party to make their own way back to London. We waited until Kate was discharged on Boxing Day and then piled into a minibus for the trip. It was like a football team tour bus—full of beer and people hanging out the back windows for a ciggie, so as not to pollute the air of our latest addition. Luckily, Basil flew back to London first thing on Christmas morning. It was just as well really—we couldn't have the Shadow Minister for the Environment chugging down the M6 in a petrol-gulping, smoke-belching minibus, where the on-board refreshments consisted of two cases of Budweiser and three boxes of cheese and onion crisps.

I was quite glad really. Much as I loved Basil, some parts of my life were as alien to him as the latest fashions and street credibility. I just couldn't picture him swigging beer from the bottle, singing a rousing chorus of "Angel Eyes." He probably thought Wet Wet Wet were a splinter group from the National Meteorology Society. Carly had started that song as she sat on the buckling knees of Mark Barwick. Mark was her first love (the only boyfriend she hadn't actually discussed marriage with and who was therefore not on her original manhunt list), who had found her on the banks of Loch Lomond after her hundred-metre dash to escape her mother. His role as Cal's lawyer had secured him an invitation to the wedding and amazingly, he was still single, still solvent (I had a feeling Carly would soon change that), and still in love with Carly, even though he hadn't seen her since she was nineteen. He'd just had time to profess his undying devotion before being rudely interrupted by Kate's labour pains. So she'd done it. Thousands of pounds and more air miles than a BA pilot after she'd started her hunt for Mr. Right, she was sitting on his lap, slightly inebriated, feeding him cheese and onion crisps from her Wonderbra.

Carly was still glowing like a red light on a brothel a few days later, as we descended on Kate's house for her grand Millennium bash. We'd offered to hold it elsewhere, due to the fact that she shouldn't be hosting a party before her sutures had healed, but she was adamant—she wanted everyone she loved under her roof to see in the new century. Carol and Cal had returned from Milan, several pounds lighter due to over-exercising their conjugal rights, and thousands of monetary pounds lighter due to exercising their credit cards in Gucci, Armani and every local bar.

Sarah and Nick were still joined at the hip. His Christmas present to Sarah was a week in London, staying at the Dorchester and as much shopping as she could manage. Basil had bought me a book called *Twentieth Century Political Heroes.* Was I bitter? Think three-day-old lemon. I had to admit, if there was a prize for romance, he'd be so far at the back of the queue he'd need a sleeping bag and a Thermos. Still, no one was perfect. I could live without romance, when our time was filled with fascinating conversation and achievements. I should have plumped for someone slushy and joined a debating society. Carly stumbled across me (literally—I was lying on the floor) hiding in the kitchen, slugging a bottle of Hooch. I couldn't drink that in front of Basil as he'd recently called for all alcopops to be outlawed.

"So Miss Latham, this is a Samaritans update call. I do remember that a year ago today, you were sitting in this very kitchen, concocting a cunning and devious plan to march his lordship up the aisle. What's the progress?"

I paused to let a conga line dance past me before answering. "About as successful as the Middle East Peace Agreement."

"Bloody talk in English, Latham. All I know about the Middle East is that it costs £899 for a week's all-inclusive break in Dubai. And by the way, Basil wants another glass of port."

For a minute I was tempted. Would he be able to tell the difference if I gave him Cherry Hooch in a posh glass?

"Sorry, Coop. What I meant to say is that my grand scheme is no further forward. Miranda still refuses to call in the lawyers and dissolve the marriage. She says she'll do it when she's ready. By the looks of things, I'll be going to my wedding using my bus pass. At least we'll get a cheap honeymoon with Saga tours."

I was trying to be jocular. But it wasn't working. Desperation was seeping through me quicker than the Hooch.

Carly was silent for a moment but I could hear her brain whirring. Either that or someone had left a blender on.

"Bollocks!" She finally spoke. "Bollocks, bollocks, bollocks."

"Is this a new song?" I couldn't quite understand her point.

"No, babe. It's my opinion on the whole situation. You've got to stop letting someone else control your life. When we were kids, who always took charge of every game we played?"

"Em, me."

"Who gave us lectures on lung cancer when we first tried smoking?"

"That would be me too." I didn't want to point out that it had been futile—she still smoked like an Australian bush fire.

"And who arranged every night out, holiday and visit to the family planning clinic?"

I didn't even answer. I could see where this was heading.

Suddenly, she lifted a French loaf from the table and started swinging her arms around like she was fending off a swarm of killer bees.

"Carly, what are you doing?" I asked.

"I'm being graphic, you daft cow. I'm conducting an orchestra."

Now I was completely lost. There wasn't a trombone in sight. She'd obviously let her new romance impair her faculties.

"Em, Carly, we're in a kitchen . . ." What was the number for the mental health advice line?

She stopped and put her hands on her hips. "God, you're slow, Latham. I'm just trying to tell you what to do. Remember Fergie? After the royals chewed her up and spat her out, she said she had to be in charge, to conduct her own orchestra, metaphorically speaking. So grab that baton and take charge, girl. Stop playing the bloody tambourine and letting everyone walk all over you."

Obtuse. But she was so right. I'd failed miserably by agreeing to Basil and Miranda's plans, so maybe it was time to put my foot down. Once I got off the kitchen floor, that is. I struggled up, grabbed her hand and dragged her to the hall. I lifted the receiver and dialled a number. Thank God I had a good memory for figures.

"Good evening, can I speak with Miranda Asquith, please."

"Who shall I say is calling?" a male voice replied in affected plummy tones. It was probably the butler. And he probably came from Clapham.

I gave him my name and waited for what seemed like ten minutes. All the while, Carly was conducting Beethoven's Fifth in front of me as a means of encouragement. It wasn't working.

My knees were shaking and she was creating a draught. And what was the racket on the other end of the line? It sounded like French rugby songs . . .

Miranda finally came on the line with an acerbic, "Yes?"

I ploughed right in. I nervously explained that I understood her viewpoint (always start a negotiation with understanding and compassion), empathised with her situation, but I really felt that this situation had dragged on long enough. It was time to bring things to a conclusion, to release Basil and grant him the divorce that we were waiting for so that we could move on with our lives. Please?

Another pause before she finally spoke. "Miss Latham, when did you last speak to my husband?"

"He's with me tonight. Why?"

"Well, perhaps you had better direct your questions to him. You see, I told Basil to start divorce proceedings on the night he discharged himself from the Priory and came to my house begging for a reconciliation. I told him again in October, and then in November. And I restated my wish to end this marriage on Christmas Day, when he arrived uninvited at my home and once again expressed his wish to reconcile. A futile plea, I might add. So you see, Miss Latham, you're actually talking to the wrong person. Good evening." With that she hung up.

I stood, open-mouthed, trying to absorb what I'd just been told. Carly stopped in mid-swing. "Well?" she asked.

Rage consumed me. Once again I grabbed her hand and this time pulled her into the lounge. The timing was perfect. Kate had just entered from the kitchen (slowly, as the sutures limited her movements), carrying two buckets of champagne. I took one from her and went to Basil.

"Ah, darling, champagne for midnight. Just the job," he bellowed.

Just the jobby, I thought. I took the bottle of Bolly from the bucket and placed it on the floor. The whole room had stopped, and the girls were looking at me questioningly, as if sensing a drama about to unfold. The deranged and desperate look on Carly's face had obviously given it away. Drama? This could win an Emmy.

"Darling, when will we be free to marry?" I asked in the sweetest tone I could muster.

Basil furtively glanced around the room. The girls were pretending they weren't listening to every word as if their lives depended on it. Carly's head was in her hands.

He nervously pondered his feet. "Well, er, darling, you know how it is . . . The minute I'm free, we can start making plans."

He glanced around again, looking like a teenage boy who'd just been caught with his first porn mag. "Perhaps we could discuss this later, darling, *in private.*" He tugged at his tie as his face turned a soft shade of pink.

"Are you hot, darling?" I enquired. There was nothing like bare-faced lies to an audience to raise a bastard's temperature.

"Just a little, my sweet. I, em, think I'll pop outside for a breath of air."

You couldn't have stopped me if you'd tied me down with restraints and injected a horse tranquilliser into my butt. Slowly, methodically and savouring every second, I lifted one silver ice bucket over one two-faced lying politician's head and tipped out the contents. Twenty sets of teeth bit twenty bottom lips, while forty eyes opened wide with shock.

"Temperature problem solved, *darling,*" I spat. "Oh, and Miranda asked me to wish you a happy New Year."

I turned and marched out of the room. If I'd stayed any longer I'd have assaulted him with the bucket.

There was a deathly silence in my wake. Then out of the corner of my eye I saw Carly, never one to cope with uncomfortable moments, raise her French loaf.

"Right, em, who's for a song? You sing it, I'll conduct it . . ."

Book Two

Year 2000 DMC (During Mike Chapman)

CHAPTER 8

Why not start again . . . ?

13 February 2000

I was looking forward to Carly's party about as much as a turkey looks forward to Christmas. Who invented Valentine's Day? Whoever it was, they should be shot for crimes against all single women. It's just so nauseating. All those hearts and flowers. Not to mention the slushy cards and poems. Valentine's Day should be strictly limited to kids under the age of sixteen who are desperate for their first snog.

I pulled out three possible outfits. Black dress, stockings and shoes. Positives: will disguise pre-menstrual bloat. Negatives: will look like my dog has died. Red dress, with killer black stilettos. Positives: very sexy, will stand out in a crowd. Negatives: red perhaps a tad too hooker-like for a single girl. Also don't want to stand out too much as then it'll be obvious that I'm the only woman at the party with no man. Navy trouser suit with boots. Positives: smart, chic, understated. Negatives: may look slightly butch for cocktail party, leaving strangers to assume lesbian tendencies. At least that would explain why I was obviously manless. The navy blue suit was looking like the best option.

Or maybe I could just plead illness, insanity or flooding of kitchen by erratic washing machine, as valid reasons not to go to the soirée. The truth was I'd rather have a colonic irrigation than nibble canapés while everyone around me was gazing lovingly into their beloved's eyes. But I couldn't give in to my reclusive moods or I'd start the anti-social ball rolling, which could potentially end with me locked in the house with forty-six cats, the curtains drawn and a lifetime subscription to the *Reader's Digest.*

The oven timer buzzed hysterically. Or maybe it was the smoke alarm. Either way, it signalled that my heart-shaped shortbreads, which would later be adorned with strawberries and cream, were ready. Ironic really. For a woman who struggled to operate the microwave, I'd been instructed by Kate to provide "sweet nibbley things." I hadn't attempted baking since fifth year at school when I'd set the Home Economics classroom on fire making a Victoria sponge. I was sorely tempted to buy ready-made cakes in Sainsbury's and pass them off as my own creation, but I knew I'd get rumbled quicker than a kleptomaniac at a security guards convention. Oh, bollocks. If they were a disaster, I could just start again. It wasn't as if I was pushed for time. The only constraints on my schedule were fitting things into daytime television's commercial breaks.

I had been officially jobless ever since I had assaulted my employer with a deadly ice bucket and given him hypothermia at New Year. It wasn't exactly a career-enhancing move. On the first day of work of the new century, I had been handed my P45 and escorted from the building. I couldn't blame him really. If I'd stayed, he would have had to employ tasters to ensure I didn't lace his lunchtime baguettes with strychnine. The only positive result of the whole fiasco was that I was given six months' salary in lieu of notice. Good point—I now had enough dosh not to have to work for at least a year. Bad point— only if I avoided Bond Street, Regent Street and Sloane Street, all my favourite places. In return for this blatant bribe, I'd had to sign a confidentiality contract that would prohibit me from divulging the Dishonourable MP's secrets to the world.

I was also prohibited from seeking any other form of employment within the Conservative Party for the rest of my natural life and no employment within any other party for at least six months. At first, it had been a bit of a shock to the sys- tem—Mrs. Career Obsessed High Flyer with nothing more to do in the day than get washed and dressed in the morning, then washed and undressed at night. It was hardly a challenging exis- tence. I'd even bordered on slipping back into the woe-is-me state of self-pity that I'd inflicted on myself after the tabloid scandal.

Carol had reinforced this viewpoint one night over dinner in Paco's, in her usual consoling manner. I'd just finished bemoan- ing the terms of my sacking when she had her first blurt.

"Well, personally, I think it's a good thing," she declared. I stared at her, aghast. Did she really hate me? Or was her regular overdose of Botox finally affecting her brain? She pressed on. "Sorry, Jess, but it's true. I think you've had a lucky escape. If you'd married Basil you'd have been miserable within months and you'd have been stuck with him forever, because married politicians win more votes than single ones. As we now all know, that's why he was so anxious to hang on to you when he was being rejected by Miranda. You were plan B. You deserve more than that, Jess."

I nodded my head. Although I'd rather have sat there naked with horns on my head than admit publicly that Carol was right and I was wrong about anything, I had to concede that I'd never been in love with the Mercenary Prick.

"OK, Carol, but you've got the last bit wrong. I never want to be anyone's plan A. I've had it with all that emotion crap. I'm returning to an official robotic state."

Blurt number two. With an accompanying frustrated hand slap on the table. "Don't you get it? Jess, if nothing else, this whole débâcle must have shown you that woman cannot survive on career alone. You only got involved with the MP because he fitted in with your working hours. Now your career is gone and what's left? Nothing! You don't need a new job, Jess, you need a *life.*"

I looked at the others for support. They were suddenly fascinated by their assortment of Mexican main courses.

"Is this what you all think?" I asked tentatively. Now I knew what being the target of a mutiny felt like.

Kate was the first to answer. "We just want you to be happy, Jess. Maybe it is time to think about having things in your life other than work. Give it a try," she urged in a concerned and encouraging tone.

Once I stopped sulking, I did just that. I applied the same fierce concentration and determination that I'd always shown in work into relaxing, chilling out and taking time to reassess my priorities. And what had happened? I was now more addicted to daytime television than a housebound pensioner. There was a whole world out there that I hadn't even realised existed. The grief at the death of my career lasted throughout most of January, but that whole time/healer theory is so true. How could I worry about the trifling issue of the loss of the love of my life, when Oprah was counselling attempted suicide survivors? And I might be jobless, but my payoff was sitting happily in my bank account, so how could I complain when appeals to help the homeless were flashing across the screen?

By the middle of the second month the chilling out thing was beginning to kick in in a big way. I had accepted the fact that I'd led a blinkered existence for far too long. I'd even resolved that in future the most important things to me would be balance and quality of life. I was determined to stay optimistic and positive. This wasn't life-threatening. I was smart, accomplished and resilient. I'd get a new job, a new life and a therapist to rid me of my telly addiction. I was moving on, over, and up. And turning into Delia Smith. Before she learned to cook.

I rescued the shortbreads. Slightly burnt on the top, but after a quick skoosh of cream in a can, they were decidedly passable. Another triumph.

My alarm clock rang. Time for *Live Talk*. I'd just settled on the sofa with a cup of tea and a Chelsea bun (not baked by me and therefore edible) when the phone rang. I considered leaving it. On the fourteenth ring, I gave up and answered it—it was breaking my concentration.

"Can I speak to Jess Latham, please?" a male voice asked.

"Sorry, Miss Layfam no heer. Me is Maria, cleaning lady. She come back later. Tatty bye."

I hung up. Back to the TV. The phone rang again. What was Spanish for "Piss off, I'm watching the telly?"

"Yeeeeees, amigo?"

"Jess, your Spanish accent is crap. You sound like Julio Iglesias on speed." I struggled to place the voice. Why did I suddenly have the taste of grout in my mouth? Oh hell, Mike Chapman. I thought he'd given up stalking me long ago, when he realised that I no longer wished to provide him with career-boosting scoops.

"What's up, Mike? Running out of lives to ruin?" Now, I have to point out at this time that I didn't really blame him for my downfall. But it was fun making him suffer and it made life a lot more bearable to apportion blame elsewhere.

"Look, before we start—"

"I think we've already finished," I spat and was in the process of thrusting down the receiver when his frantic pleas made me hesitate. I raised the phone to my ear again. "Ten seconds then the line goes dead," I warned him.

"OK, I'm really sorry, I understand that you hate me, I'm not looking for another story, I don't want anything from you and this call is not being recorded."

Five seconds left.

"Except, well, I kind of miss hearing your answering machine twenty times a day, miss you being abusive to me and miss the sight of the back of your head as you do a hundred-metre sprint every time I'm in your vicinity."

I must have been wearing a mask because I couldn't quite see where this was heading.

"So I was wondering if you were free tomorrow night and would let me take you out."

The audacity of the bastard! The bare-faced cheek! Did he think he could just call me up and I'd melt quicker than vinyl on a hotplate just because he was drop-dead gorgeous, built like a power-lifter and wickedly amusing. Well, he could fuck off.

"My place, seven o'clock, dress smart and bring wine." I blurted as I slammed the phone down. That told him! Now where was my red dress?

I didn't have second thoughts, I had four hundred and forty-six thoughts, but I was still standing in my kitchen at six fifty the next evening dressed like a jalapeño pepper. I must be mental, I decided.

When the doorbell rang, my hair stood on end. The cat flap was suddenly an attractive escape route again. I undid the lock and opened the door just wide enough to see Mike standing there, in a glorious tuxedo, nervously shifting from foot to foot, clutching a massive bouquet of roses. On Valentine's Day, they must have cost as much as a small cottage in Dorset. I stared at him, my motor skills broken down, on the hard shoulder and waiting for the AA.

"Jess, I'm here to take you out, not mug you, so it's safe to open the door a bit wider."

"I've only agreed to this because it's Valentine's Night and I'm desperate," I warned him.

He smiled, showing two rows of not quite perfect, but therefore perfect teeth. And his eyes crinkled up at the sides when he did that. Get ye behind me, Satan—this man is the Devil's spawn, I reminded myself.

"Well I only asked you because I'm desperate too," he chuckled. "Now where are we going?"

Maybe it wouldn't be so bad after all, I pondered. After all, he was male, easy on the eye, he had a pulse and he was here. It was more than some females got on 14 February.

I snatched the flowers, grabbed my wrap and strutted down the path, leaving one slightly disconcerted man to follow me.

I directed him to Carly and Mark's house. They'd rented the house next door to Kate and Bruce, a master stroke in efficient socialising, and Mark was commuting at weekends from his law practice in Glasgow. As we drove, I was more guarded than the Pope. I kept all my replies to one-word answers, except for the occasional "no comment" when a yes or no wouldn't suffice.

As he brought the car to a halt outside a house festooned with pink balloons, red hearts and multi-coloured streamers (Carly always did go overboard with decorations—at Christmas her house resembled Lapland), Mike reached over and touched my arm. My instant reaction was to recoil like I'd been shocked by a live jump lead.

He raised his voice, so that he could be heard over the strains of Aretha Franklin's "Chain of Fools" emitting from the house. Apt.

"Look, Jess. I'm not in this for anything but your company. Believe it or not, I've liked you since the first time I saw you holding up a toilet wall at Paco's. I know a lot has gone wrong since then, and I understand your reservations, but give me a chance. And if I do one thing you don't like—"

"Then I'll have to kill you," I completed the sentence. Somehow I don't think that's what he was going to say, but he grinned anyway.

"Deal," he answered. Despite myself, a smile was beginning to cross my lips and if I didn't know better I'd swear I was giving him my very best flirty look. Ovaries out of control again. Well, why not? They'd been in a coma for weeks.

Carly did her best to contain her shocked expression when she opened the door to us and succeeded in appearing slightly deranged and borderline manic. As she stood to the side to let us in, she grabbed my arm and whispered an order to meet her in the kitchen in five minutes with a full explanation as to why I was accompanied by the number one male on our Most Wanted list.

There was the sudden sound of a smashing glass and I spun

round to see Kate, hand still in a holding position for the champagne glass which was now shattered across the floor, staring at Mike with undisguised astonishment.

"New mother, her co-ordination's not what it used to be," I whispered to Mike. I had to admit, for a man who was obviously as welcome as a sexually transmitted disease in a convent, he was bearing up remarkably well.

On the sofa, Sarah and Nick were too busy staring into each other's contact lenses to register our arrival, but Carol moved like a bullet from an AK47 and was in front of us in an instant. She was just about to grab Mike's lapels and hustle him back out of the door when I stopped her. I calmly explained that he wasn't stalking me and I'd actually invited him. For once, she was speechless. For about two seconds. Then she let go of Mike's jacket and turned back to me. "Well, whatever floats your dingy. Em, can I speak to you in the kitchen?"

Cal gallantly intervened (how did Carol get anything done? Cal was so perfect that I'd lock him in a room and just stare at him all day) and took Mike over to meet Bruce, while I was propelled out of the room and pinned against the Aga by three (Sarah still hadn't budged) highly strung girlfriends.

"Are you mad?" Carly screeched, "that man is the Anti-Christ!" She always was one for over-exaggeration.

"Look you lot, you were the ones who banged on ad infinitum about how I needed a life, other interests, and romance," I stated defensively.

Carol tried and failed to keep her voice under control. "Yes, but not with the modern-day equivalent of Jack the fucking Ripper."

My back was up further than a paraglider's. "Deal with it, Carol," I ordered. "It's Valentine's Night, I'm here with Mike, I can handle him and I know exactly what I'm doing." Pause. "And anyway, it was either that or I was hiring a male hooker for the night and my severance pay doesn't run to that."

There was simultaneous groaning, not of the orgasmic kind. And then a snort. Then a giggle. Then a full-blown laugh. And before I could plead temporary insanity, the four of us were clutching our sides and doubled in hysteria.

"Oh, fuck it, Latham. I suppose there's no point crying over spilt cappuccino," Carol spluttered.

"Any port in a tidal wave," I replied.

That did it. Kate and Carly rushed out, still chuckling, sudden urges to pee overtaking them. Carol and I grabbed two bottles of champagne and headed, red-eyed, back into the lounge. I caught Mike looking at me as I entered and he winked. I smiled back as I made my way to his side. I hated to admit it, but we actually looked quite good together.

It was after an hour of spin the bottle (our parties are always so cultured), that I realised I was having a great time. And it was nothing to do with the fact that Carly had belted out "Hey Big Spender" in her Shirley Bassey voice. Or that Bruce had done a diabolical "Green, Green Grass Of Home." Or the fact that everyone had cheered after my tuneless attempt at "Puppy Love." It had everything to do with Mike, who had fitted into our group like an old friend. Remarkable, considering we were hatching plans to render him destitute last week.

The males had all accepted him without question; no big surprise there. As long as you could discuss football, golf and Anna Kournikova for three hours then you were practically family. Even the girls had warmed to him, though. He struck exactly the right chord, charming but not smarmy, funny but not overbearing, gorgeous but not Brad Pitt, to be endearing and likeable. The ten pitchers of margaritas helped too. Saddam Hussein would have seemed like our new very best friend after those.

Hunger pangs diverted my attention to the kitchen. In my nervous state, I'd neglected to eat for the last twenty-four hours and now I felt ravenous. The first things I spied were twenty individual cream trifles, all with smiley faces consisting of two grapes for eyes, orange segments for mouths and chocolate vermicelli for freckles. They had Carly Cooper written all over them. Against my better judgement (Carly had cooking skills that could fell even those with the strongest constitution), I tucked into one. Delicious. Then another. I was on the third when I heard a scream behind me. Rumbled!

"Spit it out, Jess!" A horrified Carly was thumping my back. My God, she was being a bit possessive about the trifles.

I swallowed a grape whole. At least I thought it was a grape. Through my splutters and chokes I managed to beg for mercy.

"What are you, the Weight Watchers hit squad?" I asked, my face the colour of the strawberry jelly.

A big, fat tear slid down her cheek as she contemplated the mass trifle genocide. "You don't understand," she wailed, "You just ate Mark's trifle."

I was still missing an episode. As far as I could see there were seventeen more to keep Mark happy. How much custard and jelly could one man consume?

She slid down the wall and put her head in her hands. I spat out a grape pip then joined her. "Carly, I'm sorry. Honestly. I didn't realise they were all for Mark." I couldn't believe I was apologising for eating a trifle. But although mystified, I sensed there was some significance to this. She looked up.

"Was there something hard in that last one?" she whispered.

"A grape," I replied, more confused than a man in the feminine hygiene aisle at Tesco.

"It wasn't a grape," she wailed. "It was an engagement ring." Clarity blinded me. "I was going to ask Mark to marry me, so I put a ring in the trifle and left it at the front so that I'd know which one it was."

"And it was . . . ?" Oh no. Sometimes life was just too cruel.

"The one you've just eaten." Oh, pants. I could see a long night with a box of laxatives looming. I just hoped it wasn't stuck somewhere or I'd be setting off alarms in airports for the rest of my life.

Kate came in to the kitchen. "Not legless already, you two?"

I haltingly explained the dilemma. Kate was aghast.

"Did you feel it when you swallowed it?"

I nodded my head. At least I think I felt it. At the time I'd thought it was a grape.

"Only, maybe, you didn't," she replied sheepishly. "I'm sorry Carly, but why didn't you tell us? Then I wouldn't have moved the trifles earlier when I was cleaning the worktops."

Carly's face lit up.

"And my grape had pips!" I yelled.

"And that would be exciting why?" asked Carol as she staggered in clutching two empty pitchers. This was like a bad episode of *Fawlty Towers,* I mused as we stared at the remaining trifles, hoping that the romantic one would give us a sign, maybe turn pink or something, to identify itself. There was nothing else for it. I grabbed the nearest one and headed for the living room. I thrust it into Mark's hands. Please make him take it. There was a multiple sigh of relief when he did.

"I'll have one too," Bruce offered and was thwacked by a

nervous Kate, studying Mark intently as he ate. Our shoulders sagged in disappointment when he reached the bottom without striking gold. Back to the drawing board. Carol appeared with another and thrust it into Mark's hands. He'd need a tooth sweeter than icing sugar to demolish the lot. He carried on chatting as he ate, oblivious to the tense undercurrents that were now shooting around the room like an escaped budgie.

Once again he reached the bottom of the tub with no surprises. Fifteen left to go. I let out a long groan and Mike turned to me in surprise.

"Wind," I explained with an apologetic shrug.

Carly retrieved another trifle, but Mark put his hands up. "No thanks sweetie, I've had enough."

"EAT IT," we chorused. The others stopped to stare. Had we lost our senses? Were we trying to turn Mark into Desperate Dan?

"It's just that . . ." Carly was lost for words.

"Carly has a bet with us that you can eat five of her trifles," I interjected. Not bad for a spur of the moment excuse, I congratulated myself. "She's bet us a whole month's salary."

Mark seemed confused. I admit that betting on trifles was a bit lame. Even for us.

"But she doesn't earn a salary—she's unemployed." That had slipped my mind.

"Exactly!" shouted Carly, "that's why we've got to win the bet. Now, tuck in, darling."

Mark shook his head. This was bizarre, even in Cooper-land. But he raised another spoonful to his mouth. Then another. Then . . . he stopped and chewed. Then chewed again. Please don't let it be a grape. Eventually, he reached into his mouth and pulled out a gold band. He stared at it incredulously.

"YES!" we yelled. Carly rushed to him, tripped over the "spin the bottle" bottle and landed at his feet. She clutched his ankles.

"Mark Barwick, I know I'm a complete disaster, but I love you and will you please, please marry me?"

There was a long pause as he looked again at the ring, then at the crowd, then back down at Carly. Either the smoke was irritating his eyes or he was getting emotional. He reached down, took her hands and pulled her up to face him. He ran his fingers through her hair (that was over in a second—Carly's hair was the length of a sheepskin rug).

"In a heartbeat," he whispered.

Even the dog screamed. The standing ovation lasted longer than my crap attempt at singing.

Mark released his stranglehold on his fiancée. "Did we win the bet?" he laughed. "Only, I think we'll need the money for dental treatment. The ring has dislodged a filling."

The rest of the evening was a veritable love-fest. Carly was glued to Mark's side and it took three of us to remove her when he wanted to go to the loo. It was ironic really. For a woman who'd said yes to four proposals in her lifetime, only for all of them to end in disaster, you'd think she'd have a phobic aversion to engagements. Yet she looked like she'd won the Lottery, discovered gold and the secret of eternal youth all in the same instant. She was euphoric. And it was contagious. Four trips to the corner shop for champagne later, we were still toasting the future bride and groom.

As Marvin Gaye knocked Aretha from the CD player, Mike took my hands and led me to the garden. It sounds romantic, but it was minus four degrees and my fingers were threatening to drop off with frostbite. He thought I was smiling at him, but I was just desperately trying to stop my teeth from chattering.

He put his arm around me. That's allowed, I thought, but purely for the sake of my body temperature, of course.

He smiled. "I like your friends."

"I know. They're good people. Insane, but good people."

"Listen, Jess, I know we didn't exactly get off to the best start . . ."

"Bigger understatement than Joan Collins in black."

He ignored me. "But I was wondering if I could see you again. Without the company of your armed guards." He motioned to Carol, who was loitering at the back door, clutching a ladle and watching us out of the corner of her eye for signs of trouble. What was she going to do? Spoon him to death?

I contemplated his offer. I suppose I'd never really given him a chance. As far as I was concerned he'd ruined my relationship with Basil by revealing our affair and making us targets for the press, public and Miranda. But if I were honest, it wasn't Mike who'd destroyed it, it was the Mercenary Prick himself. Even if we'd conducted the whole affair in private, he'd never have left his wife. Ouch! The truth stings. In fact, had it not been for Mike I'd probably still be sneaking around Mayfair in the middle of the night. I suppose I should thank him really. Well, if I was a nicer person I would.

He mistook my silence for reticence. "Come on, Jess. I know you've had a crap time lately. Let me make it up to you."

Mmmm. Keep going.

"And remember, we had a deal. One wrong move and you can call in the boys with the baseball bats. Or the girls with the ladles in your case." Carol was still loitering with intent.

Try as I did, I couldn't think of a single reason not to go out with him. What was the worst that could happen? I was a new woman, seeking balance and emotional fulfilment in my life and here was the first candidate. Anyway, life had been severely lacking any love and affection lately. Sod it, why not?

I nodded my head. "Don't mess me around, Mike," I warned.

He leaned over and kissed me. "Never," he promised.

Did you hear that noise? That was the garden bullshit alarm screaming. Unfortunately, I didn't hear it either. Marvin must have drowned it out. Bitter? Call me Angostura.

"I'd better be going. Would it be all right to leave my car here and collect it in the morning? I think I've had one or ten glasses over the limit. I'll take you home in a cab."

"It's OK, I'm staying next door at Kate's."

I was glad. It saved any uncomfortable "will we or won't we have sex" kind of moments. Not that I thought for a minute that he would ravish me on my doorstep. I was more worried that due to several years' drought of decent sexual activity I'd drag him kicking and screaming to my boudoir, from where the poor man would emerge three days later, requiring oxygen and a pacemaker.

He kissed me again. A number four on the snog scale. A peck on the lips is a number one, graduating to full scale tongue combat at ten. There is a number eleven, but it involves other parts of the anatomy.

No, this was perfect. A slow, tender, not quite knee-trembling, kiss. With hands on face. He got an extra point for that.

When his cab arrived, I walked him to the door, passing a blissful Carly and Mark in the hall, slow dancing to "Heard It

Through the Grapevine." Carly had her head on Mark's shoulder and behind her back he was holding up his engagement finger to admire his ring. It made my heart flip. Much to the astonishment of the waiting cab driver, Mike got assaulted with a full-blown number eight on the doorstep. Open mouths with hands in hair and subdued panting sounds.

"I'll call you tomorrow," he whispered, when he'd managed to reclaim his teeth. I waved goodbye and turned back into the house.

Cal was waiting for me. "Is he gone?" he asked urgently.

"Yes."

"Then will you please tell my wife to drop the kitchen utensils and the bodyguard act. I haven't had a bloody word from her all night."

I hugged myself as I smiled. Valentine's Day was a wonderful invention.

CHAPTER 9

Why not
"Row, Row, Row the Boat?"

May 2000

Our lives were fast turning into the sequel to *Four Weddings and a Funeral*: Three Weddings (Carol, Sarah and Carly), a Birth (Kate) and an Unemployed Spinster (me). I felt like I was spending most of my life dressed in taffeta, with a short-sighted seamstress pricking my cellulite with a pin.

Sarah and Nick had decided on a traditional Scottish bash at the Old Course Hotel in St. Andrews, where they'd first met and where Nick owned a restaurant. Carly's wedding would be two months later in New York. Well, it *was* Carly—only New York was crazy enough.

Sarah had taken care of all her own wedding plans, because Nick was immersed in the preparations for the opening of his first restaurant in London. We were delighted—now Sarah would be living in London too. And to make life even better, we were invited to weekly tastings of potential menu dishes prepared by a chef whom I'd have married for his cooking alone, despite the fact that he was 56, eighteen stone and had the temperament of a serial killer.

We decided to go to the hotel a couple of days early for an extended hen night. We dropped Kate and Sarah's kids at their respective grans' houses in Glasgow en route. Two happy grannies, two liberated mums.

The five of us piled into our small hired car and made our way to the Fife coast. Carly turned to Sarah.

"God, it seems like another lifetime ago that you and I were tearing up here in search of my Mr. Right," she grinned.

"And instead I found mine," Sarah squealed.

The rest of us made vomiting actions.

Sarah's face suddenly took on a serious expression. "Carly, does it ever bother you that I'm with Nick and he was your boyfriend before me?"

"Are you kidding?" Cooper replied. "Sarah, I couldn't be happier than I am with Mark. Nick and I were never right together. And anyway . . ." a wicked grin crossed her face, "he was crap in bed."

"He. Bloody. Is. Not," Sarah yelled.

"Children, that's enough. If you can't play together nicely, then you're going to bed early," Kate giggled.

It was great to see Kate having a bit of unrestrained fun. Lately, she'd been looking exhausted—I supposed that's what three kids and a high-flying job in one of London's "so in, it's nearly out" salons did to you. When did she ever sleep?

"You seem remarkably light-hearted today, Mrs. Smith," Carol observed. She must have read my mind.

"Well, I am! I was just thinking how happy I was. I've got a fantastic husband, three gorgeous children who are not within shouting distance and I'm on my first girls' break since Benidorm." She grinned. "Oh, and I got fired yesterday."

I slammed on the brakes. Not good news for the minibus

behind me, whose driver fortunately displayed stunt-driving techniques to avoid us.

"What happened?" I gasped. This unemployment thing was contagious.

"Tamara was getting right on my tits, banging on about her trust fund, so I threatened her with a roller brush."

Even though I had no idea who Tamara was—it seemed that all the clients in Kate's salon were called Tamara, Tara or Portia—my gob was smacked. Kate had the most even temperament of all of us. I'd never even known her to raise her voice past discussion level. If it were any of the rest of us, I'd have believed it. Carol had a temper that would intimidate Liam Gallagher in a rage, Carly was irreverent to everyone, Sarah had a tough side borne of years living with a serial abuser and I had to admit being prone to the odd tetchy moment. But not Kate.

"I think it was PMS," she added. "I'm relieved really. Bruce is doing so well that he's even being considered for an Architectural Design of the Year award, so we don't need the money as much now. Anyway, I was getting tired of being superwoman. Whoever said we could have it all must have three maids, a cook and a nanny. So now I'll be there for the kids every day and not breaking my neck trying to be Mrs. Super-efficient all the time. Everything happens for a reason."

There goes Doris Day again. "Que Sera Sera." I was singing it before I realised it. The others joined in.

We only stopped when the hotel came into sight. It was an awesome spectacle. A glorious white vision set against the backdrop of a lavish golf course and a beautiful coastline. The sea air flooded into our lungs as we quickly extinguished our Marlboros. We made our way through the foyer to the reception. The Old Course is one of those hotels that immediately makes you want to stand with perfect posture and speak in a posh voice. As the receptionist checked us in, I scanned the area. Such grandeur! The walls were cream and with rich oak wood panelling and exquisite artworks. The chandeliers were so huge that if they fell they'd definitely make a large dent in the earth's crust. What was I doing here? I didn't even have a proper job, for God's sake.

As we were shown to our adjoining suites, there were five sharp intakes of breath. I resolved right there and then that they would have to forcibly evict me with a crane from this place—it was just stunning. Each suite had its own kitchen, dining area, office and lounge with floor to ceiling windows leading to the balcony. And the bedrooms! The beds were so big that all five of us could have slept in one with our arms outstretched and we *still* wouldn't have made contact with each other. The décor had a distinctive Japanese theme, with cream carpets so thick that I lost sight of my toes. I stepped on to the balcony. Not only was I unemployed, I decided, I was also dead. This is what heaven looked like. In front of me was a glorious golf course. In fact, I was sure I could see St. Peter and St. Thomas teeing off at the ninth hole. Beyond the golf course was a massive expanse of golden sands, with crystal blue waters ebbing over it.

When the porter left, I turned to Sarah. "I knew Nick was wealthy, but you didn't tell me that he had more money than Bahrain!" I exclaimed. "This must have cost more than a small yacht."

The others were still gazing around in wonderment. "I don't know what to do first," Carly added, "attack the minibar, check out the movies or steal the shampoos and soaps." I could understand her dilemma—the toiletries *were* Bulgari.

"None of the above," Sarah replied. "I've booked us a day of pampering in the spa downstairs."

"It has a spa, too?" Kate gasped. "Well, bugger me, I'm never leaving here. It would take me a whole five minutes to get used to this lifestyle. Carly, do me a favour, call Bruce right now and tell him I've left him."

The rest of us giggled. We were all thinking exactly the same thing. The last holiday we'd had together was to an ant-infested, cupboard-sized flat in Benidorm. Somehow or another, we hadn't half managed to claw our way up in this world.

We were all lounging in the Jacuzzi when the girls demanded an update on my romantic status. I pondered my answer. How to say it without sounding pathetically slushy?

Mike had taken things slowly at first. In comparison to a missile launch. The day after the Valentine party, I got home to discover even more roses on my doorstep with a note that said "Got them cheap—nobody buys flowers on the fifteenth." Cute.

That night he'd appeared with a Chinese take-away and copies of *Sleepless in Seattle*, *Top Gun*, *An Officer and a Gentleman* and *Pretty Woman*. I was beginning to think he was born a female, when he said that he'd been promised by the owner of the video shop that at least one of them would be my favourite. She was obviously a wistful soul. I didn't want to disillusion him and confess that *A Few Good Men* or *Lock, Stock and Two Smoking Barrels* were top of my "night in with a vid" chart. You can't knock a guy when he's trying his best. And anyway, what were the options? *EastEnders*, the scintillating drama of *Coronation Street*, and a Marks & Sparks micro-meal for one.

We talked until dawn. We systematically worked our way through our families, our childhoods, our careers and our previous relationship disasters (he already had a head start on me there, since mine had been all over the newspapers for the last year, but I decided not to hold a grudge).

As the sun came up, I realised that I hadn't enjoyed the company of anyone with a penis this much in years. Basil who? The Mercenary Prick was fast becoming a dim and distant memory.

It took me three weeks to work up to the bare bum wrestling stuff though. Mike had taken me to a press awards ceremony and when we returned to my flat, we kissed at the door. Now here is the all-time greatest dilemma for the modern woman. When in the mood for a spot of anatomical discovery, how do you invite a man under your duvet without sounding like a slapper? Or worse, how do you reassure him that just because you've been intimate with his hairy bits, it doesn't mean that you expect him to appear the next morning with two wedding rings, a marriage license and a minister? When will guys realise that sometimes we're just plain horny and it doesn't mean we're looking for a commitment any greater than a cup of tea and a bacon butty the next morning?

Anyway, somehow I obviously got the right message across, and as he nibbled my nipples I felt a huge sense of relief that for the first time in years I was having a sexual experience without the aid of law-enforcement equipment. Bliss.

I realised that I'd met my match in Mike. He was as focused, determined and quick to make decisions as me. We went from zero to full-blown relationship in about six seconds. It struck me as ridiculous that I was a woman in my thirties and yet this was my first real boyfriend. Our relationship was my new career replacement and I was shocked to discover just how amusing a real-life romance could be. A month later I couldn't imagine life without his three phone calls a day, forty-six text messages and long nights of lurve. I even started buying his newspaper and glowing with pride when I read his by-line under the latest kiss-and-tell exposé of a famous figure. It amazed me that such a caring, sensitive guy could be responsible for such vitriolic journalistic assassinations. It was in the public's interest, was his stock defence whenever I questioned him about it. I could see his point. I suppose it was useful to know if the person you voted to fight in your corner and represent you in government was a sex-mad bankrupt with a past conviction for shoplifting. Mike was doing a public service, I reasoned.

No, this was perfect. I kicked myself for wasting so much time with a tosser like the MP, when there was this amazing guy right under my nose. I should have molested him that first night in Paco's and saved myself all the heartache.

What's more, to my eternal shock, Mike seemed to feel the same way. The night before my trip to St. Andrews, we'd ventured out to celebrate the fact that I'd secured some freelance work, researching for a former MP who was writing his memoirs. The extra dosh would top up the bank account and besides, my new employer amused me. Cecil Woodrow was a gruff octogenarian, with a monocle, a midriff that resembled a bean bag and a wooden leg, so I think Mike felt secure that I wasn't going to be whisked off my feet by his House of Commons anecdotes. Much as they made me laugh. If the voting public knew what went on behind the political scenes, they'd demand rebates on their council tax.

Over coffee, Mike reached out and took my hand. I couldn't stop myself from flinching. It wasn't that I was opposed to public displays of affection, I was just so wary of them after years of checking for lurking paparazzi.

Mike smiled. "Jess, I'm allowed to hold your hand without the potential for a law suit."

"I know," I replied. "Force of habit."

He stared at me. "How do you feel about us now, Jess?"

Here it comes, I thought. Just when I'd finally learned to relax when he scribbled in his notebook, no longer terrified that anything I said would be taken down and used in the following day's tabloids against me, he was going to give me the "I think things are moving too fast" line. Well, I'd be damned if I let him do it first.

"I think maybe we're rushing things a bit, Mike. I mean, we've only been seeing each other for three months and already we spend every free moment together." There. Men of the world, pay attention—women can do that line too.

I expected him to nod in agreement and take off as quickly as his beautifully formed thighs would allow, so I was completely surprised when his face contorted into a crestfallen expression.

"I see," he stuttered. "I've obviously got this all wrong then. I thought we were pretty good together. More than good, in fact. I thought you felt the same."

Oh, bollocks. I back-pedalled furiously. "Shit, I'm sorry, Mike. I do feel the same. I was just being defensive. Another force of habit." Time to 'fess all, I decided. "In fact, I think I'm happier now than I've ever been. Not bad, considering my life has gone downhill faster than an avalanche."

He laughed. Eyes crinkled. Hormones surged. My libido should have been on double-time, considering the amount of extra work it was doing. But it wasn't just the sex that was fantastic. Mike made me laugh, he kept me interested, he knew when to be tender and when to be glib. If my mum had knitted me a man, she couldn't have done a better job than the one sitting before me.

He called for the bill and then helped me on with my coat. Changed days. Basil would have charged it to an account then sprinted out of the back door, leaving me to wait ten minutes before crawling commando style into a car with smoked-out windows.

"Thanks for dinner, Mike."

"My pleasure. Oh and by the way, I love you. Now where do you want to go next?"

My brain struggled to decipher his last sentence. Something about gloves. No, I didn't bring any with me. Or did he say he loved his meal? No, I'm sure his steak was on the wrong side of chewy.

I turned slowly. "Pardon?"

"Where do you want to go next?"

"No, before that, what did you say?"

He laughed. "I love you, you daft bint. I've been wanting to tell you since the party at Carly's."

The other diners had now stopped mid-chew and were listening intently, the women with expressions of wistfulness and the men with their heads in their hands, as they witnessed another of their species succumbing to the evils of the female race.

"As in 'good to be around, enjoy my company, think I'm adorable like a German Shepherd puppy kind of love?' "

He took my hand and kissed it. Jess Latham, one melted puddle on floor.

"As in don't want to spend a minute away from you, never met anyone like you and I'm totally in love with you."

Every man in the restaurant groaned—they'd have to go some to match up to this. Much to my eternal embarrassment, I snogged him right there and then. The waiters were reaching

for fire extinguishers by the time I released him from my suction grip. I was thirty-three years old and for the first time in
my life a gorgeous man had told me he was in love with me
without threats, bribery, blackmail or a hard-on. I was ecstatic.
Who needed job prospects when they had a man like this?

"Anytime today would be good, Jess," Carol moaned. I realised
they were still waiting for the update. I kept it brief, which was
just as well, because Carol was turning a definite shade of cerise.
She stood up to get out of the tub and plummeted back down
again. We all jumped to catch her, causing a tidal wave to soak a
rather large lady who was passing. We frantically fanned Carol
with her towels. If this was the result of another mental diet for
a photoshoot, then I was going to drag her kicking and screaming to the nearest McDonald's.

"Sorry, been feeling a bit off-white lately," she groaned, as
we supported her to a standing position and helped her climb
out. As we did, I suddenly realised that there was something different about her appearance. I did a top to toe. New hairdo?
Thinner thighs? I dismissed that one immediately—Carol's
thighs were the width of my forearms. Pierced belly button? I
couldn't put my finger on it. Then a gasp escaped me.

"Jess, why do your eyes look like side-plates?" Carol muttered.

"You've had a boob-job!" I knew there was something different. Carol had always had breasts like peanut M&M's, to go
with the rest of her wafer-thin body. Now there were distinct
satsumas stretching her bikini top.

Carly obviously agreed. "So you have! You sneaky cow! You
might have told us and I could have come and had my wrinkles
done at the same time."

Carol grabbed the towel and pulled it round her torso. "Don't be bloody ridiculous. My body is a church—there's no way I'd let a madman with a scalpel near it." The rest of us were puzzled. It was out of character. Unusually for a model, Carol had the most secure body image of anyone I knew. And she was such a hypochondriac that she went everywhere with a medical dictionary. Last time she had flu, she obviously opened it at the "Ts," because she swore she had typhoid or TB. There was just no way she'd willingly subject herself to surgery of any kind. "They're just a bit swollen, that's all. Time of the month, probably."

Kate was pensive. "Carol, when was the last time of the month?"

Carol racked her brain. "Can't remember. I can't think straight these days. I think I've either got Premature Menopause, Pleurisy or Post Traumatic Stress Disorder." She was at the "Ps" this time.

"How about," Kate suggested with concern, ". . . em, *pregnancy?*"

There was an abrupt pause, then we all jolted to catch Carol as she threatened to faint again. There was a barely audible "Oh, fuck."

Kate dived up and reached for her towel. "I'm going to find the nearest chemist. My room. Twenty minutes. Bring a crash cart for the patient."

Carol was still frozen to the spot. We prised her up gently and, like a child, got her dressed and steered her back to Kate's room. She still hadn't uttered a sound when Kate arrived back with the test kit.

Carol regained the power of speech and went into overdrive. "I can't be pregnant, I'm on the Pill," she said adamantly.

It was a lame argument. We all knew that Carol only remembered to take the Pill on alternate days, and then only if someone reminded her. Organisation had never been her strong point. In fact, probably the only reason this hadn't happened before now was that the over-fifties had a lower sperm count.

Sarah, ever pragmatic, ushered her into the bathroom to do the test. Carly dived head first into the minibar and surfaced with a half-bottle of champagne and a Toblerone. If she was going to be an auntie, she was determined to celebrate in style.

They emerged from the bathroom with the white stick. We started counting backwards from sixty as we watched the colour change in the first window and the test line appear. Thirty-two. Thirty-one. The colour change slowly crept across the second window. Twenty. Nineteen. Our knuckles were turning white as we gripped various parts of Carol's anatomy. I had a foot.

Sixteen. Fifteen. Oh, holy crap. There was no mistaking the vivid blue line that was forming in the second window. Ten. Nine. It couldn't be more definite. Or more blue. Or more terrifying, if the expression on Carol's face was anything to go by.

We stared at it for what seemed like hours, before Carol spoke. I could have given her a full reflexology session in the time it had taken her to absorb the news.

"It must be a mistake," she whispered numbly, shaking her head. "I can't be pregnant. I'm a model. I don't do big."

Kate rummaged in the bag and pulled out another three tests. She'd known Carol would need convincing. Soon, we had four white sticks with four blue lines in the pregnancy window, a discarded Toblerone wrapper, an empty bottle of champagne and a pissed Carly, singing "I'm going to be an auntie, I'm going to be an auntie, darum dum dum, darum, dum, dum."

Oh, and an ex-supermodel, whose entire vocabulary now stretched to "Oh, fuck."

The next morning I treated myself to the top to toe beauty package. I tried to get Carly to join me, but apparently she'd had a bad experience years before when a beautician waxed, plucked and pummelled her body into pulp and she refused to repeat it. Anyway, she was nursing a raging hangover.

I joined her later in the pool.

"How's our mum-to-be this morning?" I enquired.

"Last seen throwing up in her room. Quite an achievement—she managed to throw up and swear at the same time. She's now my female icon."

Kate and Sarah arrived, in deep conversation.

"What's up?" Carly asked.

"We can't get Carol out of her bedroom, housekeeping are threatening to break the door down, the wedding's tomorrow and Sarah's nerves are tighter than Pamela Anderson's jeans."

I turned to Sarah. "Why, babe? Are you having second thoughts?"

"Of course not. But I'm worried that Nick is. I mean, what do I have to offer him? I'm a divorced thirty-three-year-old, with two kids, I'm still at uni and I've got more debt than a dot.com company. I keep having the same nightmare, where I walk up the aisle and discover that Nick has tunnelled his way out of the church with my mother's hat," she groaned. "And Carly, why are you writing this down?"

Carly was leaning over the poolside writing ferociously in a notebook. She stopped in mid-scribble and stammered like a fourteen-year-old who'd been caught with four condoms and an edition of *The Joy of Sex*. She muttered something about her

Matron of Honour's speech. Sarah pointed out that not only was she not Matron of Honour, but that none of us girls were making speeches.

We waited for Carly's reply. And waited. That's the thing about Carly—her life was so full of unbelievable episodes that she didn't need to lie to make herself interesting and was therefore hopeless at it.

"OK, I surrender. I'm making notes for my book. I've decided to write a novel about relationships and I was just . . ." she tailed off and stared at the floor.

We were stunned. I was about to break into a full-scale incredulous laugh, while interrogating her for further details, when my attention was drawn to a couple snogging at the other end of the pool. I could only see the back of the guy: ripped deltoids, huge lats, crewcut, but it was the female who was familiar. I struggled to focus. Where had I seen that hair before? Why hadn't I brought my specs? And why didn't I posses a pair of prescription goggles? The female broke off from Godzilla's grip and started to swim towards our end of the pool. I didn't know what was going faster—her body as she ripped through the water doing a front crawl, or my heartbeat.

She stopped about a metre away from me, stood up and wiped the water from her face. She was about to turn and streak back to the other side when she registered my presence.

"Well, well, well, it's amazing who they let into these places these days." Carly made a dive for her throat, but Kate clutched her ankle just in time, forcing her to sink and resurface coughing and spluttering. Not her most intimidating moment, but I appreciated the effort.

I summoned my best Vinnie Jones expression. "Yes it is. I'd have thought your friend there . . ." I motioned to the hunk of meat that was observing us from the other end of the pool, "would have struggled with the registration card." Miaow.

"You too, my dear. I saw a tick box for 'Mrs.' and 'Miss,' but I didn't see one for 'mistress' or 'harlot' (who even *used* that word in the year 2000?). "You must have been terribly confused." With that, she turned and glided back to the Incredible Hulk. The others were still staring, open-mouthed.

Of all the swimming pools in all the fuck-off flash hotels, I had to dive into this one . . . If I'd paid attention at check-in I'd have noticed the sign that said "The Old Course Hotel welcomes the French Rugby Squad." I'd have realised that they were here preparing for their imminent match against Scotland at Murrayfield. I might even have wondered if their girlfriends would be allowed to visit.

"Christ, she's a cross between Sharon Davies and Anne Robinson," Sarah exclaimed.

"What did you ever do to her, Jess?"

"Sarah, meet Miranda Asquith. Basil's wife."

Groans. Eight eyeballs were raised to heaven. My two closed in disbelief.

Carly lunged for the side of the pool and started scribbling in her notebook again. At this rate, it would be a best-seller.

We finally tempted Carol out of her room with a promise of food and shopping. We lied about the last bit—St. Andrews isn't renowned for its late night shopping malls. Two gift shops, a petrol station and a twenty-four-hour laundry were all that were open. Still, the food compensated admirably. We dined at Nick's restaurant, where we were treated like royalty due to the fact that Sarah was about to become the wife of the owner. Our food arrived almost before we'd even ordered it.

Over starters, we discussed Carly's potential novel. The plot was to revolve around her relationships with her girl-friends and her search for all her ex-boyfriends, culminating with her finding Mark. It was a great idea; I couldn't believe no one had thought of it before. She was so determined not to return to a life of working in mind-numbing sales, that Mark had agreed to support her while she strove to conquer the lit-erary world. He was looking more like a candidate for saint-hood with every passing day. She'd come to St. Andrews armed with a huge notebook, four Bics and a copy of the *Writer's and Artist's Yearbook.* Her optimism was so contagious that by the time our plates were cleared we had dispelled our doubts and were already planning what to wear at her first book launch.

"I'll be in a tent. Oh, Christ, I'm going to turn into Demis Roussos," Carol wailed. Call me perceptive, but somehow I didn't think she was taking the news of her prospective moth-erly condition too well. And she couldn't even drown her sor-rows in alcohol. Instead, she skipped her main course and went straight to dessert: two portions of sticky toffee pudding.

We distracted her by diverting our attention to Sarah. After all, it was her big day tomorrow. Strictly speaking, we should have dressed her in a bin bag, with a potty on her head, and paraded her around the town, but we decided on a night of food, cocktails and Marlboros instead. Her last one as a single woman. The drinks waitress had been stupefied when we gave her our cocktail order—a lethal mixture of vodka, gin, tequila and pineapple juice. Our own invention, The Legal Inter-course, is a must for every girl who's about to embark on the marital path. Oh, and a fresh orange juice for the good-looking one who kept contemplating her navel with a terrified expression, as she imagined the imminent time when she'd be able to lick her belly without bending.

"Still nervous?" I asked Sarah. She bit her lip as she nodded.

Carly tried to comfort her. "Look, Sarah, Nick loves you. Of course he'll be there tomorrow."

"He loved you too and you didn't end up waltzing up the aisle." This was heading into dangerous territory, but luckily Carly was in tact and diplomacy mode.

"Sarah, we didn't even get past holiday-romance status. Our suntan lotion lasted longer than our relationship. Nick told me you were everything he'd ever wanted and he couldn't wait to marry you, so get that cocktail down you and start being nice to me, otherwise I might just make that speech tomorrow after all."

That did the trick. The drinks waitress sprinted back to the bar for refills.

They poured us out of the restaurant at closing time. We were heading for the hotel when Sarah diverted our course. "Beach. Need. Fresh. Air," she ordered. Manoeuvring a U-boat in a paddling pool would have been easier than co-ordinating a change of direction for four inebriated women. Carol stayed on the original course. She claimed she needed to return to the hotel to think about how she was going to break the news to Cal, but in truth we knew she was planning to set a new world record in comfort eating. Thank God room service operated twenty-four hours.

We staggered along the shore until we came to a dinghy resting upside down in the sand. In our intoxicated states, it took seven attempts to turn it over and another four for us all to climb in. Carly grabbed an oar. "Row, row, row, the boat gently down the stream . . ."

It got worse. We went from "Sailing," to "The Skye Boat Song," to "I'm Getting Married in the Morning." Well, there are a limited number of songs about boats. The last I remember was the middle verse of that old chestnut "I Will Survive." Gloria Gaynor would have drowned herself if she had heard us. In my liquefied state, I realised that I had two options: sick or sleep. I chose sleep. But unfortunately, so did the others. We really shouldn't have been allowed out without a responsible adult and an armed guard.

An almighty roar roused me from my slumbers. My brain struggled to comprehend my situation. Why was my nose pressed against wood? And what was the blinding light? Had I fallen asleep on the sunbed again? I tried to turn around, but I was paralysed from the waist down. Then I realised I had an oar up the leg of my jeans. This couldn't be a good thing. I squinted in the vague direction of the deafening noise. Nick was towering above us, Bruce, Mike and Mark just behind him, their expressions varying between horrified, concerned, relieved and amused.

Nick reached down and swept Sarah up into his arms. Somehow, I knew that the rest of us would be made to walk.

"What time is it?" Kate asked, rubbing sand from her eyes and simultaneously trying to pat down the haystack that had replaced her hair.

"Nine o'clock," Nick replied tersely. "You lot have three hours to make yourselves presentable." He turned and whisked Sarah off.

I groaned. It would be impossible—not without the aid of a Clarins factory and the Makeover Squad.

Mike held out a hand and I latched on to it.

"How did you find us?" I whispered. Anything louder than that would have shattered my eyeballs.

"Carol. We found her at the breakfast buffet and she said you might still be here. At least one of you had the sense to go home. In saying that, she looked a bit grey. What *were* you all drinking?"

"Petrol, if my head's anything to go by," Carly replied. "Carry me, Mark, I don't think I can stand."

"In your dreams, Cooper," he laughed. "I'm off to the pool. The French rugby squad are in there and I want to sabotage the Jacuzzi. Coming, guys?" The three of them strode across the sand, shaking their heads and chuckling as they went. I glanced at the others. Kate looked like she had been sandblasted and Carly resembled a contestant on *Survivor*. Oh bugger. This was going to be a long day.

There were tears in my eyes when Nick and Sarah said their vows. Of course, it could have been due to the fact that my head was threatening to explode. Or that there were still three buckets of sand under my lashes. Or that Carol and I had inadvertently got our bridesmaid's dresses mixed up and I was wearing her size eight and therefore hadn't managed to breathe for the last hour. Minutes before the ceremony, Carol's depression had momentarily lifted, when she realised that her dress had plenty of room in it. "Maybe I won't get so fat after all," she exclaimed. "This dress fitted me perfectly two weeks ago." I couldn't disillusion her and tell her that she was wearing my size twelve.

No, I was pretty sure it was just the loveliness of the occasion that was moving me to tears. It had taken every member of the beauty team staff to restore us to human-being status, and

Sarah was now resplendent in her gold Victorian gown. It was an awesome sight. She and Nick were oozing happiness and excitement. I was still oozing tequila.

Out of the corner of my eye, I spied Mike. Instead of watching the bride and groom exchanging rings, he was staring straight at me. I surreptitiously winked at him. I still wasn't sure if my previous night's escapades would have him screeching back to a single life, with only a brief stop to buy me paracetamol and a season ticket for Alcoholics Anonymous.

He smiled and winked back. I started to feel better—at least I'd now confirmed that he had a sense of humour.

It was a huge relief when the photographs were over and we could all sit down to dinner. Due to the over-zealous number of bridesmaids, we were seated at our own table with our partners, leaving the top table for family only. The other guests stared in bewilderment as three bridesmaids threw their heads on to the tabletop and the fourth launched straight into the breadrolls. Exit all wedding etiquette.

I can assure you that it was our love of Sarah and certainly not Carly's mad "hair of the dog" theory that compelled us to drink champagne all through dinner. By the time the profiteroles arrived, the Bollinger had acted as an anaesthetic and pain was a thing of the past.

Carol had restricted herself to one glass, which she nursed through her four courses and the next table's bread basket. When the liqueurs arrived, she politely refused. Cal raised a perfectly formed eyebrow.

"You must be feeling terrible, darling," he cooed. "I've never known you to refuse a Grand Marnier. Or to eat this much, for that matter."

The rest of us buried our heads in our profiteroles. She obviously hadn't broken the news to him yet. I tried to second-guess his reaction. Cal was one of the most laid-back guys I had ever encountered, so surely he would take this in his stride. But then, he and Carol *were* very career-focused and loved their jet set lives, unencumbered by responsibilities any greater than paying their credit card bills at the end of the month. I'd have preferred the baby—it would be cheaper.

I was distracted from my thoughts by Nick, who stood up to make his speech. There was an almighty din, as everyone banged on their glasses with their spoons and cheered. The crowd finally settled.

"On behalf of my wife and me . . ." Almighty din number two. Sarah beamed beside him. He went on to thank his parents, the best man (strange, he forgot to mention the brides-maids), the vicar, the hotel staff and the rest of the world. Then he nudged Sarah's children to their feet.

"And I'd like to thank Hannah and Ryan for letting me marry their mummy. I promise I'll be the best daddy I can, which won't be hard because I already love both of you very much."

We were now sobbing and blowing our noses. Nick leaned over and took Sarah's hand. "I love you more than anything or anyone I've ever known, and I can't tell you how ecstatic I am to be spending the rest of my life with you."

The walls shook to the sound of tumultuous cheers and every guest was on their feet. The ovation lasted longer than the speeches.

The band burst into action and Mr. and Mrs. Russo swept to the floor, to the sounds of Otis Redding's, "These Arms of Mine." We hastily repaired each other's mascara, before joining them for the second dance. Mike put his arms around me. I was so drained by champagne, emotion and excitement, that I wanted to put my feet on top of his and let him carry me round the room.

"Are you OK, Miss Latham? I haven't seen tears like this since the opening night of *Titanic.*"

"Don't read anything into it, Mike. I'm tired, emotional and overjoyed at seeing my best friend so happy," I chided.

"And here's me thinking that you were ecstatically imagining us up there," he retorted.

The arrogance. I *was not* imagining us. Well, maybe just my dress. And his tux. And the rings. And how gorgeous the girls would look in silver, off-the-shoulder, bias cut . . . I snapped back to the present, the direction of this conversation now permeating my brain.

"Mike, does that mean that *you* were imagining that scenario?"

He leaned over and kissed me. "Maybe, darling. Maybe one day."

That was good enough for me. I didn't have to stand on his feet, because I was now levitating ten inches above the floor.

We spent the rest of the night alternating between dancing, snogging and chatting to the others. When Sarah and Nick made their exit, we almost drowned them in confetti. As soon as they were gone, the band played the last dance then downed instruments and headed for the bar. Carly was distraught. She wasn't ready to stop partying yet and drunkenly started rounding up volunteers for an *a cappella* karaoke session. Mark's head was in his hands. Cal shouted "Go, Sis," and stood on a chair to announce that the party was continuing. There are definitely defective genes in that family.

Carol was still nursing the same glass of champagne, the expression on her face suggesting that her dog had died, she'd discovered a pimple and lost her credit cards all in one day. As I walked past her in a determined effort to find the loos while I could still focus, I gave her a hug. She gazed up mournfully. I said a silent prayer that the baby couldn't yet sense its mother's moods, otherwise it would be requesting Prozac before the night was out.

We sang until the hotel staff were on their knees begging for mercy and threatening to call the police. For someone who'd been born south of the border, Mike took to the traditional Celtic after-wedding sing-song like a duck to a cartoon. He even appeared sorry when we finally made a move to vacate the ballroom.

Carly was still in full song, with her head on the table. But only when everyone else had ceased their performances, did we register what she was chanting.

"I'm going to be an auntie, I'm going to be an auntie, darum, dum, dum, darum, dum, dum . . ."

Carol gasped in horror and Cal spun round (at least I think he did—it could have been the room that was spinning and Cal was rooted to the spot), confusion knitting his brow.

"Carly, what are you singing? What are you talking about?" Cal demanded.

Carly stopped immediately. She lifted her head to see a sea of horrified faces, all staring at her with threatening expressions. Carol stared intently at the floor, her life flashing before her.

After a few seconds, Carly regained the power of speech.

"Em, I'm going to wear my panties, I'm going to wear my panties, darum, dum . . ." She broke off lamely. I had to hand it to her, it was a valiant cover-up attempt. Not exactly Watergate, but a good attempt none the less.

Cal was now even more confused. And so was Mark.

"I thought you were a G-string girl?" he asked, the whole situation whooshing over his head like a Harrier jump jet on a training exercise.

Cal faced Carol. "Babe, what's she on about?"

"I don't know, but I think I'll have to kill her anyway." Carly stared at the table, saying a silent prayer to the gods to grant her three wishes: a smaller gob, a hole that she could crawl into and a rewind button.

But Cal wasn't to be appeased. A lightbulb went on over his head as he mentally recounted Carol's behaviour that night: the glum mood, the impersonation of Dawn French in a chocolate factory, the lack of alcohol.

"Carol?" he asked searchingly.

Carol's whole body slumped as she exhaled a sigh that made the room temperature drop by twenty degrees. "OK, Cal, I'm kind of, sort of, definitely, well . . . have you ever wanted to be a daddy?"

CHAPTER 10

Why not
have a Virgin experience?

July 2000

I decided that weddings were like orgasms—you don't get one for ages then they all come at once. I tried to analyse the reason that three of my four closest friends ended up marrying within seven months of each other. Was it the same principle that applied to nuns' menstrual cycles? I'd read somewhere that when females lived together for a prolonged period of time, their bodies automatically fell into sync with their companions and they developed the same menstrual patterns.

En route to New York for Carly and Mark's tying of the knot, I flipped back the seat on the Boeing 747 (we always flew Virgin—we liked the irony of it), to the disgruntlement and discomfort of a very large lady sitting behind me. Well, it's never too late to diet.

Almost the whole section of the plane was taken up with guests going to the forthcoming nuptials. Except the large lady—I have no idea how she managed to sneak in. In fact, I couldn't imagine her sneaking anywhere.

In total there were thirty of us heading across the Atlantic.
Carly's parents were sitting in front of me. Or rather, her dad
was lying across her mum's lap having taken his usual medication, a bottle of Jack Daniel's, to combat his fear of flying.
Her gran (whom I swear was using collagen—she didn't look
a day over fifty) was sitting across from them, intently chatting up an air steward called Edwin. I didn't want to disillusion her, but Edwin's hips definitely swung in the other
direction. I was about to intervene when she switched her
attentions to the vicar sitting on the other side of her. It's a
sad day when there's more chance of scoring with an ageing
vicar than a gorgeous, thirtysomething guy with his own
teeth and hair.

Carly's brothers were there, of course. The youngest,
Michael, and his girlfriend, Karen (who was also Kate's
younger sister—it's an incestuous world we live in), were bat-
tling heatedly over a computer game. Cal was sitting content-
edly rubbing Carol's stomach, much to her annoyance. I
hoped her maternal instincts would kick in soon. At this point
she gave the impression that she'd rather *eat* her firstborn than
nurture it. Thankfully, Cal had the opposite reaction. He had
been ecstatic from the moment that he'd heard the news and
every time he returned from a modelling shoot he was armed
with new things for the baby: Gucci jeans, Nike trainers,
Prada papoose. The cost of one of this child's outfits was more
than my monthly shopping bill. But I knew he'd be a great
dad.

Carly was sitting across from me, typing furiously with two
fingers on her laptop (a combined early wedding present from
us girls—she kept losing the notebooks). To everyone's eternal
shock, not least her own, she'd sent a synopsis and the first four

chapters of her book to every publisher in existence and had received three requests for the finished manuscript. She was ecstatic! The chances of an unknown novelist being published were about as low as her gran's chances of shagging Edwin, so she was overjoyed at the interest.

I suppose it also removed any pre-wedding nerves. She didn't have time for last-minute jitters when she was concentrating intently on forging her way to her first bestseller.

But then, I was jittery enough for the two of us. I tried to convince myself that it was only because the bridesmaids were going to be wearing unbearably tight sheaths at the ceremony and frankly, my hips were threatening a revolt. But the truth was that I was far more terrified that my boyfriend was planning a revolt of his own. My stomach turned. We'd been together now for five glorious months and he'd made me happier than I ever thought possible. He was interesting, he was tender, he was great to be with and he obviously adored me. Or so I had thought.

I had first noticed a change in his behaviour a few weeks before. Mike spent so much time at my flat that inevitably it seemed ludicrous to retain his flatshare with a fellow journalist. When he moved in with me I wanted to hang bunting from the front window. Oh, happy day! For about five minutes.

He occasionally worked from home, so he'd converted my spare room to a makeshift office. One afternoon I made him a cup of coffee and took it to him, but instead of a polite "Thanks," he'd flushed bright red and hung up on the person he was talking to. Strange. Even stranger was that he'd asked me to knock in future, in case he was on an important call. I didn't understand it. It's not as if I was causing a disturbance—I was only taking him a coffee and a sticky bun.

Old familiar doubts began to overtake me. Surely I wasn't unlucky enough to meet two complete bastards in my lifetime? I pushed the doubts to one side. Mike loved me, I was sure of it. But then I'd thought the same about the MP. He was just under pressure at work, I decided. No need to overreact.

Until, that is, the following week when he installed a minishredder in the office and started to destroy his incoming mail. What did he think I was going to do? Sell his stories to a rival tabloid? My name changed to Jess Insecurity Latham as I became more vigilant than a sniffer dog at Heathrow. Where *was* he on that Saturday afternoon that he swore he was watching Arsenal, not realising that the game had been called off at the last minute due to a waterlogged pitch? When I confronted him, he refused to budge from his hastily concocted story that he'd spent the day in the pub with his mates. So how come there wasn't the slightest whiff of lager? This had more signs of impending doom than Armageddon. I only wished I had the nerve to spit my dummy, demand explanations, then dump his stuff in my wheelie bin, but I had the resolve of a draught excluder. And a fierce determination to make this relationship work. This time, I would *not* fail.

But still, a Nobel Prize in self-delusion was looking likely. I realised he'd changed the password on his e-mail program, taken to locking the keypad on his mobile phone, and had a shopping spree in Harvey Nicks when he said he was at work (I'd pieced together the receipt after it had been through the shredder—how sad am I?). But *still* I did nothing about it. Everyone is entitled to their privacy, I reasoned. Don't get me wrong, I hadn't slipped into victim mentality. I wasn't a candidate for the next Ricki Lake show, "Hi, I'm Jess and I have the self-esteem of a cabbage." No, I was just experiencing a realisation that the fairytale didn't exist—no relationship was perfect, and on balance I still felt that the fantastic outweighed the bad. OK, so Mike was a little on the secretive side. But he was still so loving. And funny. And gorgeous. And spontaneous. And exciting. And amazingly, fantastically, wonderful in bed. I could honestly visualise us down the bingo hall together when we were eighty.

He was truly everything I had ever wanted in a man and more. Surely he couldn't be all those things if he was dipping his stick elsewhere? Please God, don't let him be shagging the cleaning lady. Or Tony Blair's cleaning lady—he *was* always trying find new sources for scandal. Maybe he was a government spy. Chapman, Mike Chapman. Budweiser, shaken not stirred.

I'd blurted out all my doubts to the girls the night before. It was officially Carly's hen night, but Mark forbade her from any activities other than a girls' night at Paco's. He was terrified that we would miss the plane the next morning and he'd end up bride-less in the Big Apple. After seven Legal Intercourse toasts to Carly and Mark, another four to celebrate Carly's progress towards securing a publishing deal and three to Sarah who'd graduated teacher training college the week before, I poured out my fears.

I never thought I'd say this about the girls, but they were about as supportive as Sunday knickers—you know, the ones with the burst elastic that you throw on under your joggies when you're having a chill-out day.

My drama queen crown glowed as I spouted the endless list of niggling events that had cast a stormcloud over my sunny world. The phone calls, the shredder . . . The girls listened intently. For the first five minutes. Then Carly stifled a yawn. A bloody yawn! I'd dug that girl out of so many bad situations I was a qualified miner, and here she was yawning in the middle of my trauma. Well, excuse me.

The tears were welling up (well, OK, it was just the smoke irritating my eyes, but it *could* have been tears) when Kate stopped listening and diverted her attention to catching the eye of the waiter to order more drinks. Even Doris Day was proving to be a traitor. The cow.

I knew there was no point seeking sympathy from Carol. Since I'd started my story, she'd had the same glazed-over look that guys get when they're watching soap operas. Indeed, all she'd done all evening was sip orange juice and slip into mourning for her lost waistline. Amputating a toe would have been less traumatic to Carol than losing her figure. We'd already spent thirty minutes consoling her that just because she had a bump the size of a tennis ball on her abdomen, it didn't mean she was obese. When I finished my diatribe, she just looked at me and muttered something about it just being a storm in a mug.

In one of my more immature moods, I stomped back to Kate's in a full-scale huff. It had originally seemed like a good idea to stay overnight there together, to ensure that we made it to the airport on time and in one piece. The guys were all ensconced next door at Carly's, helping Mark celebrate too. At least we'd spot any strippers sneaking up their path and chase them for their life. If ever I needed a Dial A Friend service . . . Maybe I wouldn't chase the strippers, I could just pay them to listen to my worries and provide a sympathetic ear.

I only snapped out of my petted lip state next morning,

when Carly produced the outfits that she wanted us to wear for the journey. White, white and more white. It was all part of the wedding theme.

My kit was a pair of white leather jeans, a matching basque and boots. Not exactly practical travelling gear, but at least I'd stand out in a crowd and they wouldn't lose me at the terminal. I looked like a Tampax applicator. Albeit a rather hip, cool, and trendy one. The things I did for my friends. My ex-friends, that is. I hadn't quite recovered from my strop.

Carly's outfit comprised of a white leather mini and a vest top that I would have sworn were two of her gran's handkerchiefs tied together. Kate was a bit more respectable in a white cashmere polo-neck and denim knee-length skirt, and Carol was wearing a floaty lace dress. Very Laura Ashley.

When two impatient taxi drivers simultaneously sat on their horns to announce their arrival, we gathered together for one last look in the hall mirror. There would never be a better advert for Daz.

We lunged out of the door, dragging more luggage than Madonna, as the guys alighted from Carly's. I screamed in delight. Five gorgeous men, all wearing beautifully cut tuxedos, marched towards us. We collapsed in fits of giggles. Mike leaned over and kissed me.

"You're gorgeous," he whispered.

"Not bad for a feminine hygiene product," I agreed. He was puzzled. "And you're gorgeous too, Mr. Chapman." I felt an overwhelming urge to explore his tonsils, but was pushed out of the way by Carly.

"Come on, you lot. I want to get bloody married this week, before my unsuspecting groom has time to come to his senses."

Mark flashed his pearlies. He adored every bit of this mad bird.

Somehow I had the feeling that this whole wedding experience would be one to tell the grandkids about. When they visited us at the bingo hall.

We were buckling our seat belts and taking sneaky sips of our duty-free vino, when I noticed that Mike was looking decidedly red in the face. I nudged him, spilling the contents of the bottle of Chianti that was halfway to his mouth.

"Are you feeling OK? Your face is a bit flushed."

"Just the after-effects of last night," he stammered. "Too many Fantas and sweets."

I smiled. He was so perfect. And he was mine. At least, as far as I knew he was. I pushed my worries as far as possible to the back of my mind. "Why don't you take off the dinner jacket and tie, then?" I urged. Anything to stop the development of his facial colour from pink to a shade of magenta. But he made no move to divest himself of the excess clothing. Fine. If he wanted to arrive in New York resembling a sun-dried tomato, that was his problem. Just as long as he didn't sweat over my new leather trousers. I was getting quite attached to them (and them to me—I had no idea how I'd get them off in the loo). I stuck my nose back into *The Thatcher Years*. I always liked a book that you could use to light fires with when you'd read it.

The cabin crew were about to close the doors when I caught a glimpse of four bodies with blankets over their heads being escorted on and ushered to the front of the plane. Fantastic! Celebrities on our flight! Calm down, I chided myself, it was probably some boy band. You know, the ones who hadn't even developed body hair yet. Then my imagination kicked in. Maybe it was four dangerous prisoners being extradited to the US. Oh shite, I hoped not. I'd seen *Con Air.*

Bing Bong. "Good morning, ladies and gentlemen, this is the captain speaking. Welcome to this Virgin Atlantic flight to New York . . ." I tuned out. Just for once I'd love the pilot to come on and say, "Morning, everyone. Sorry the plane was five minutes late in taking off, but I got pissed last night and then shagged this big blonde . . ."

Mike's elbow, directed sharply at my ribs, brought me back to the present.

". . . and on behalf of the crew, I'd like to congratulate Mr. Barwick and Miss Cooper who are travelling to New York to get married."

We did a drum-roll on our lap tables. I was a bit too enthusiastic and mine snapped on one side.

Ten minutes after the captain's announcement, there was a sudden rise in the volume of the cabin. Great! Hopefully it was either more duty-free or the lunches—either way I needed sustenance. It was neither. I slapped Mike's thighs, simultaneously exclaiming, "Well, bugger me, look who it is, babe."

But Mike was already staring, and grinning.

Coming towards us, in full flight uniform, was Richard Branson. Personal service or what! One of my entrepreneurial heroes! I had to admit, he cut a dashing figure. But then, I'd seen *An Officer and a Gentleman.* You could put Pavarotti in a pilot's uniform and I'd fancy him.

Suddenly, he was standing right in front of me. Everyone else in the cabin craned their necks to look.

"Miss Latham?" Oh, shite, he was talking to me. Now there's a weird thing. When I was Miss Professional, I'd spent time in the company of some of the leaders of the political world without a weak knee, a stomach tremor or the urge to ask for a single autograph. Now one of the most successful entrepreneurs on the planet was standing in front of me and I'd lost the power of speech.

Eventually, I summoned up enough brain power to nod my head.

"I'll take over from here, Richard," Mike intervened. Whoa, boy! Did he *know* Richard Branson?

"Jess, I know you hate surprises, but I asked Richard to come here today. You see, I'd like him to be my best man." I wasn't taking any of this in. I was still trying to think of something witty and interesting to say to Richard Branson.

"Jess, pay attention," Mike chided.

"Sorry. Em, what?"

"Jess Latham, will you marry me?"

My head exploded. "Whaaaaat? When?" I mumbled in a tone that only dogs would have been perceptive enough to understand.

Oh, fuck. Fuck. Fuck. Realisation dawned in a stream of expletives. The phone calls. The secrecy. The girls' indifference. The tuxedos. The Daz advert. This was a bigger set-up than *The Sting*. And Richard bloody Branson was still grinning at me. I scanned the cabin. Even the fat lady had a tear in her eye. But that might just have been because her girdle was killing her.

I suddenly realised that I was still nodding my head.

"Is that a yes?" Mike asked, now resembling an extremely anxious sun-dried tomato.

"Oh fuck, yes," I whispered. It was a wonder the oxygen masks didn't drop with the dramatic decrease in cabin pressure,

as everyone broke into a chorus of cheers and a standing ovation.

The vicar sitting next to Carly's gran climbed over her and
extended his hand to Mike.

"Morning, Mike, I believe this is where I come in." He *knew*
a vicar? A real one?

"Hi Ted, thanks again for doing this."

My God, Mike was a tabloid journalist—I thought the only
vicars he knew were the ones that visited lap-dancing clubs.
Suddenly, I was reluctant to shake Ted's hand—I didn't know
where it had been.

I moved as if in a trance. The girls sprang into action. Kate
dived to the cabin crew section and returned with four small
posies of white carnations and a massive one of lilies. He'd even
remembered my favourite flowers. He was a god. No wonder he
knew Ted the vicar.

Carol ran to the business-class section and returned with my
parents and Mike's. I gasped at my mum. "It was you? With the
blankets over your heads? I thought it was *Westlife!*"

Sarah ushered everyone around the space in the seating next
to the fire exit, where the ceremony would be performed. At
least if I changed my mind I could make a quick escape. With
the aid of a parachute. And Carly? She started a rousing chorus
of "Here Comes The Bride," then dived to my aid as I tried to
fight off her gran, who was trying to pin a doily to my head.

So that's how it happened. The most unexpected event in
my whole life was saying "I definitely bloody well do" to Mike
Chapman, in a Virgin 747 halfway across the Atlantic. There
were no stress-inducing preparations, no church organ, no
flash hotel and no drunken Uncle Bert trying to pick a fight
with his ninety-two-year-old brother, Uncle Ned, as happened

at the last family occasion a couple of years before. Instead, there was everyone I loved most in the world, a groom I would have died for and Richard Branson. It didn't get much better than that. Who needed a 747? I could have flown the rest of the journey to New York fuelled by delirium and duty-free Lambrusco.

CHAPTER 11

Why not
double the celebration?

October 2000

We'd all been summoned to Carly's house for an emergency summit. At least she'd said it was an emergency. To be honest, I had my doubts. This could just be the eleventh successful manoeuvre she'd deployed over the last three months, to get us all to her house to watch her wedding video *again*. I already knew every word of the dialogue verbatim. Don't misunderstand me, it was great to see it the first time. And the second. Maybe even the third. But I firmly believe it should be illegal to force your friends to sit through your video any more than two weeks after the ceremony. It should be punishable by six months' community service, posing as mourners at the funerals of people with no friends. That would put you off ceremonies for life.

I suppose, though, I did understand her obsession. It seems ridiculous that you spend a large part of your life dreaming of the day that you'll saunter up the aisle (mine with floor lights to guide guests to the emergency exits), and then it's over within a matter of hours. I'd be all for week-long ceremonies. If a political party added that to their manifesto, they'd get my vote.

And Carly's wedding *was* spectacular. She and Mark had married at New York's City Hall. Carly wore the tackiest, most fantastically stunning dress I'd ever seen: a Stars and Stripes flag that had been made into a strapless corset above a floor-length body-hugging skirt with a six-foot train. Mark was gorgeous in a black tux with a Stars and Stripes waistcoat and the brides-maids looked great (if a bit lumpy in Carol's and my case) in our sheaths: Kate and Sarah in red and Carol and I in blue.

They'd had to prise my hand from Mike's with WD40 to make me take my position next to the bride. I hadn't been able to let him go since we were pronounced man and wife by the lap-dancing vicar.

I still couldn't believe the effort he'd put into making my wedding day the most exciting one of my life. Since the day I'd met him, I'd loved the fact that he was an adrenalin junkie. I suppose it was what made him so good at his job—he thrived on the bizarre and unexpected. He thought nothing of coming home at night, telling me he had a couple of days off and flying me to Paris for a picnic. He loved to go to a party or a première every night of the week. He thoroughly enjoyed meeting new people and finding out about their lives. And he had an outra-geous anecdote about the majority of people in the public eye—most of them deeply embarrassing. He was the ultimate dinner-party guest.

And husband, I thought smugly, as I watched Carly taking the same vows I'd taken only a few days before her. This was a momentous day in history. After more false starts than a ner-vous sprinter, Carly Cooper finally became a Mrs.

We celebrated afterwards at the Four Seasons (we'd need to

remortgage our homes to pay the credit card bills) on Bollinger, hot dogs, popcorn and Ben & Jerry's ice cream. Ted the vicar shocked us by revealing that he was also a Tom Jones impersonator. We switched off the specially requested jukebox and he had us dancing until dawn to the strains of "What's New, Pussycat?" "Delilah," "It's Not Unusual" and the rest of T.J.'s greatest hits. He was phenomenal. The only worrying moment came when Carly's gran threw her knickers at him. We had to put her to bed after that.

The celebrations continued for three days. The days (or rather, the afternoons—we didn't have the stamina to rise before one p.m.) were spent alternating between shopping and sampling cocktails in bars that were straight out of an episode of *Sex and the City.*

After dark, we went out to play. We took a moonlight, black-tie cruise around Manhattan on the night after the nuptials. The following evening we invaded Nirvana, the "so upmarket it's got a doorman and private lift" Indian restaurant, overlooking all of Central Park. It was a great concept, but I have to say the location is slightly wasted when you eat at nine p.m. and it's so pitch black outside that you need night goggles to see the trees. Still, we had the time of our lives and the hangovers to prove it. Even Carol had a blast by her recent standards, managing a smile as she ate her pakora.

But best of all was just being able to spend every minute with my husband. My stomach danced every time I looked at him and I beamed like a blowtorch every time he kissed me. Sod work, sod ambition, sod reputations and aspirations. This, I thought, as I sat on a cushion in Nirvana's thirty-ninth floor restaurant, was the closest to heaven I'd ever be.

*   *   *

Sarah opened the door to us when Mike and I arrived at Carly's. She was radiant. Marriage and her new job teaching in a Richmond primary school had transformed her from a woman who always seemed to have the weight of the world on her shoulders, back to the glowing beauty she'd been as teenager. Nick was a lucky man.

"What's it about this time?" I smiled as I asked her. "I've brought us all mags in case she's going to make us watch the video again."

Sarah laughed. "Don't worry, I've already dismantled the plug on the telly when she wasn't looking."

I was puzzled. Carly hadn't sounded in any way perturbed on the phone, so I knew it wasn't bad news. I had a sudden thought. Maybe she was pregnant! She'd made no secret about the fact that her wedding present to Mark was to throw a family size box of condoms, two diaphragms and three packets of contraceptive pills down the loo.

That was it—she was pregnant! I was going to be an adoptive auntie again. I was distracted from my theory by a dishevelled Cal (I know, I find it hard to say "dishevelled" and "Cal" in the same sentence), heading down the stairs towards us. I stared at him in undisguised shock. Here was Mr. Armani, Mr. Porsche and Mr. Omega, resembling a bleary-eyed gambler who'd just lost everything on red. Beer-swilling, football-watching, couch potato males all over the country must have been doing a victory dance.

"Don't ask, Jess," he warned me.

"I have to, Cal. You look like death. What's happened?" I was fearful. Whatever it was, it must be serious to land Cal in this state. Please don't make bad news be the reason for tonight's gathering. We'd all had such a good run of luck lately that I couldn't bear anything to go wrong.

"Carol kicked me out."

"*Whaaat?*" I blurted. "But why?" I couldn't comprehend this. Carol might be stubborn, fiery, and more explosive than a tin can in a microwave, but she adored Cal and he worshipped the ground she walked on. I couldn't imagine anything that could come between them.

"She had a berzy last night because she couldn't fit into the dress she was going to wear to dinner. Apparently, it was a size fourteen and apparently that's not good."

My bottom lip automatically assumed a petted position. I'd been straying into a fourteen lately and I thought I looked OK. Maybe it was time to check my mirrors. "Anyway, the next thing I know, she launched her hairdryer at me, and started screaming the she was a fat cow and it was all my fault. Something about Rambo sperm. Then she screamed that if she ever saw me again she'd have to kill me and pushed me out the door."

The poor soul was more forlorn than a deck chair attendant on Brighton beach in December.

"So I stayed here last night. Carly says I can stay as long as I need to."

My shoulders sagged with relief and I fought to suppress a giggle. "Don't worry, Cal," I consoled him through my mirth. I turned to my husband (I still loved the sound of that—*my husband*). "It's all down to one thing, Mike, isn't it?" I automatically knew that Mike would be on the same wavelength as me on this one.

He nodded his head and put his arm around Cal's shoulders. "Hormones, mate. Bloody hormones," he sighed. "They'll be the death of all of us. C'mon, I'll get you a Bud."

Cal visibly brightened. An explanation for his wife's unrea-

sonable behaviour and the promise of a beer . . . it was amazing
how little it took to keep men happy.

I followed the guys into the living room. The whole gang
(except Carol—she was still on a field trip with her pregnancy
hormones) was already ensconced there, all with faces stricken
with fear that we were about to be chained down and made to
re-watch the union of Mr. and Mrs. Barwick. Mortuaries had a
better atmosphere.

Carly came in from the kitchen with a tray of glasses, followed by Mark, lugging two ice buckets full of champagne. I
was right! They were definitely pregnant.

"OK, everyone," Carly announced, "I just thought I'd get
everyone together because it's been a while since we watched
our wedding video."

There was a combined loud groan from everyone in the
room and Sarah hastily shoved the plug she'd removed from the
telly down the back of the sofa. Carly might be going to torture
us, but we weren't going down without a fight. Just as well I
hadn't started knitting bootees.

Everyone was suddenly compelled to stare at their feet.

Although my head was bowed, I sneaked a glance at Carly—
she was grinning from ear to ear. Mmmm. Somehow I didn't
think she was telling us everything. Maybe I hadn't been wrong
after all.

"OK," she blurted, "I'm only kidding." I was right! Baby
under construction! "The reason I wanted you all to be here
is . . ." She paused, brimming with excitement and desperation
to share her news. My face was turning pink because I'd stopped
breathing in anticipation of the bombshell.

"Today I spent the day at an agent's office in London
because I GOT A PUBLISHING DEAL FOR MY FIRST

TWO NOVELS!!" she screamed, so loudly that cats all over the street outside were diving for cover and taking paracetamol.

Mark popped the champers as the rest of us shrieked in delight.

Carly had tears the size of grapes rolling down her cheeks, as we descended on her. When we finally disentangled ourselves, everyone spoke at once, all demanding to know the details.

My flabber was gasted once more. Carly Cooper would still be shocking the pants off me when we were wrinklies. She was a one-woman amusement arcade.

It transpired that her manuscript had landed on the desk of a female editor of one of the UK's most reputable publishers. The editor, Camilla (something told me she wasn't from north of the Watford Gap), had absolutely loved it and despite the publishing house's policy of not signing first-time authors, had persuaded the management to contract Carly immediately. They'd pointed her in the direction of an accomplished agent and after some negotiations, had purchased the first novel and commissioned a second. She'd done it! She was Danielle bloody Steel.

I was beside myself with excitement. And not just because Carly had promised us that if she ever got a book deal she was taking us all to the Caribbean for a week. She was obviously on the same wavelength as me yet again.

"The only problem is, girls, Antigua will have to wait. The amount of money they've given me won't cover the cost of my tights for the next year. But who cares? I'm an author!"

The doorbell rang. Carly staggered to answer it, returning with a doleful-looking Carol. Cal didn't know whether to be delighted or don a bulletproof vest. Carol spotted his frantic glance around the room to check the nearest exit.

"Don't think about moving, Cooper, I need to talk to you."

She made straight for him. He scanned the room again, this time for somewhere to hide, but he was too late. When she reached him, however, she threw her arms around him and burst into tears.

"I'm really sorry," she sobbed. "I know I'm a maniac," *sniff, sniff,* "and Attila the Hun would be easier to live with," *sniff, sniff,* "but I'm so sorry. Please come," *sniff,* "home."

Cal squeezed her tight and lifted her into the air at the same time, her bump forcing her arse to knock over what was left of the tray of glasses. We didn't even notice. We were too busy drying our eyes and doing a drum-roll with our feet.

"And anyway," she sobbed, drying her eyes on the sleeve of the largest jumper I'd ever seen, "I'll need you there to carry the other baby."

You could have heard a teddy bear drop. Another baby?

Cal stared at her in disbelief for a few seconds, then muttered, "Twins?"

Carol slowly nodded her head. Which was unfortunate, because Cal whisked her off her feet again, leaving her with whiplash. "Twins! Holy crap, we're going to have twins!" he screamed. Another drum-roll. More champagne. Enough tears to refill the ice bucket, and those were just Cal's.

Carly went into the kitchen and returned with a man-size box of Kleenex. "You know what this means?" she giggled through her tears. "We'll have an even bigger audience to watch our wedding video every week." Several cushions flew in her direction, as she headed out to the off-licence for more champagne. It was going to be a long night.

They poured Mike and me into a taxi at three a.m. I was still in party mode, much to the annoyance of the taxi driver, who I'm sure could have lived without a woman singing a drunken version of "Love Is All Around" in his cab in the middle of the night.

It was impossible not to be caught up in all the happiness and excitement. Mike obviously thought so too.

"The room is spinning, we're round the bend . . ." I warbled.

"Stop singing, Mrs. Chapman, I want to say something."

"To get my love, you'll have to spend. Ooooooh oooooooh."

He clamped his hand over my mouth. The taxi driver cheered. Rude git.

"Jess, I'm serious. I want to say something."

I gave him my undivided attention. "Whassamater, my sweetie?" I slurred. He wrapped his hand around mine.

"I was thinking about the whole baby thing." Understandable. It was impossible not to. "What about having a wee addition of our own?"

I hoped he didn't mean that he wanted to buy a hamster. I stared at his face. Nope, he definitely meant baby—he was too serious for a hamster.

"You want a baby? With me?" I had to check. I had a track record for misunderstanding things after a few glasses of bubbly.

He nodded his head. A baby? Ours? It was the best idea I'd heard all lifetime. I wailed in delight as I launched myself at him like a torpedo and smothered him in kisses. I was going to be a mum! Life just got better and better.

It was all too much for the driver. I didn't realise that there was a law against being happy in the back of a hackney. Or that we'd reached our house. He slammed on his brakes like a getaway driver at a police roadblock and I landed face down on the floor. Now Carol and I would have matching neck braces. "That'll be ten quid," he spat.

Mike threw the money at him, lifted me up and carried me up the stairs to our flat (he must have been working out lately—either that or the champagne had been spiked with steroids).

"Inside and naked quickly, Mrs. Chapman," he panted as he heaved me over the doorstep. "We've got a baby to make."

CHAPTER 12

Why not sack Doris Day?

December 2000

It was my turn to host Christmas lunch. Just my luck. The one year that I was feeling about as festive as an unemployed Santa, I was up to my queasy stomach in chipolatas. And who was the sick bastard who discovered that putting sage and onion up a turkey's arse made it taste better? They should have been jailed without parole.

I contemplated the criteria for martyrdom. I definitely qualified. I was sick, exhausted, totally feeling sorry for myself and cooking lunch for ten adults and five children on my own. Mike was being about as helpful as an aerobics instructor in a home for the elderly.

At least, I thought as I rubbed my protruding stomach, this time next year I'd be celebrating Christmas with my own little present. I smiled despite my gloom. It had been four weeks since I discovered that I was pregnant and I still had a Ready Brek glow every time I thought about it. My own little baby. *Our* little baby. Although it hadn't appeared to have the same effect on my husband as it had on me. Maybe Mike was in shock, I contemplated. That was the only explanation I could muster for his strange behaviour lately.

His initial reaction, as we sat huddled over the loo waiting for the test result, had been one of total elation. Until he did a jig in the shower, slipped and broke his leg in two places. But even in the ambulance on the way to the hospital, he clutched my hand and told me over and over again how delighted he was, how much he loved me and how we were going to be the happiest family since the Waltons.

The following week, as he hobbled around on his crutches, he was still lavishing my ovaries with compliments on their efficiency. We calculated that we must have conceived on the very night that we decided to start trying. I must have been more fertile than a genetically modified field.

We made a pact not to share the news until after the three-month landmark, which by my reckoning was around today. Thank the Lord. I couldn't keep this a secret from the girls for much longer. If only I'd told them last week then I'm sure one of them would have insisted on taking over Christmas lunch duty.

But no, St. Jess, the Martyr, kept her mouth closed and ventured off to Sainbury's for enough food to sink a small ferry and now I was spending Christmas morning staring up the bottom of the fattest turkey I'd ever seen in my life.

It was no use calling Mike for moral support. After his initial elation, he seemed to have gradually withdrawn into a world of his own. I was beginning to think I'd imagined that it was his idea to breed. True, with his broken leg he was about as mobile as a lamp-post and that was guaranteed to depress anyone. And yes, he was struggling to bring in the most sensational scoops, because he was working daily from the scandal-free environment of our front room. And fair enough, since morning sickness that lasted all day and a leg of plaster of Paris ruled out most of the positions in the Kama Sutra, our sex life had dwindled to that of a eunuch. But surely his joy at the knowledge of impending fatherhood should have outweighed even these not so minor hiccups? So why was he shrouded in a wave of gloom that had me considering spiking his tea with antidepressants?

I had tried everything I could think of to cheer him up. In between vomit-induced sprints to the loo, I had served all his favourite meals, told all my best bad jokes, bought all his favourite videos and cuddled him at every opportunity. But he shrugged me off every time. And as for the cosy conversations about our future child's name, nursery, potential as the next Prime Minister . . . he was less interested than a bull in a Tupperware shop. There was more chance of me reaching the space shuttle that was currently orbiting the earth than reaching my husband in the next room.

As if to reinforce my worries, his Christmas present to me that morning had been two jars of anti-stretch-mark cream, two maternity bras and a jumper that was big enough for us to camp in. Something told me romance was either dead or at least terminally ill. I finished the preparations, bunged the turkey in the oven and snuggled down on the sofa for a nap. Mike hobbled by, en route to the kitchen for a coffee refill.

"Hey, husband. Come and rub my bump! It needs some stroking," I cajoled him. That would make me feel better. We could cuddle up on the couch for a few hours before the mass descent of friends.

"Later, babe," he waved his hand dismissively, "I'm busy just now." Par for the course.

"On Christmas Day? Oh, come on, Mike. The world of journalism can survive without you on Christmas Day."

My shoulders sagged at his reaction. If this had been a few months ago, he'd have pounced on me without me having to beg, and spent the rest of the day ravishing my bits. What was going on with him?

He realised that he was cornered and wearily lowered himself on to the sofa, his plastered leg dangling over the side. I ran my fingers through his hair.

"I love you, Mike," I whispered.

"I love you too, babe," he replied. How come I wasn't convinced?

The doorbell woke me with a start. Oh shite, I'd slept all afternoon. I gently pushed Mike to wake him.

With hair resembling a burst sofa and mascara streaked down my cheeks, I opened the door to Carly, Mark, Kate, Bruce and the kids (Zoë, Cameron and Tallulah, looking gorgeous in red tinsel headdresses). It was like a procession of elves as they marched down the hall, all dressed in their Christmas outfits. Carly was a masterpiece as usual, in her full Santa suit, complete with pillow shoved up her front for effect.

She nudged me as she passed. "Having an afternoon siesta?" she asked with a wink. She obviously thought Mike and I had been having a festive frolic.

"Unfortunately, it was just that. A sleep and no more," I replied. Sex? It was the number after five and before seven.

Luckily, I'd prepared everything that morning. I allocated Carly to Christmas present distribution, Kate to check the food and the guys were put on bar duty, while I headed to my boudoir to repair my face. I'd just crossed the bedroom door when I felt that familiar bubbling feeling in my stomach. I lurched for the bathroom, just in time to see Mike sitting on the loo, snapping closed the mouthpiece on his mobile phone. Who had he been talking to?

"Em, just calling my mum to wish her a happy Christmas," he stuttered. Strange. I didn't know that he was in the habit of chatting to his mum while his trousers were down. I shoved him out of the door and dived for the loo. It was the first time that I consciously thought that God must be a man—no woman would put another through this unless she was a psycho bitch.

I fixed my face, brushed my teeth, tied back my hair and changed into my Rudolph the Red Nosed Reindeer jumper and red jeans (with elasticated waistband—chic or what?). It was my token effort to generate Christmas cheer. By the time I returned downstairs, Cal and Carol, Sarah and Nick and their two children, Hannah and Ryan, were swapping pressies with the others, all those under five feet tall squealing with delight at their assortment of roller-blades, skateboards and Barbies. Tallulah just played with the boxes. Unconsciously, a smile crossed my face, as I realised that every Christmas from now on would involve cookies left out for Santa, milk for the reindeers and a gorgeous wee bundle opening his or her presents at six o'clock in the morning. I spotted Mike and tried to gauge if this scene was having the same effect on him, but he was in deep conversation with Bruce and Cal in the corner. Oh well, at least he was speaking. That was this year's Christmas miracle.

Kate ushered the older kids out the back door to play with their new toys. The girls congregated in the kitchen, Carly and Carol comparing their stomachs to see who won the award for Biggest Over-Hanging Belly.

"Don't even think about giving birth today, fatty," I warned Carol. "The flat's not big enough and I've got no clean towels."

"Don't worry. It's all booked for the twenty-seventh. I'm having a caesarean under doctor's orders, followed by five days' rest and recuperation. I'll be out in time for the January sales!" I had a vision of Carol tearing round Harrods on the first of January with one twin attached to each breast.

"I'm going to be an auntie, I'm going to be an auntie, darum, dum, dum . . ." Carly had been in at the egg-nog already. I had an overwhelming urge to share my news with them, but stopped myself just in time. We'd planned that Mike would announce it later and I didn't want to steal his thunder.

Over dinner, the conversation revolved around choosing names for the impending twins. The top five favourites were Peters and Lee, Donny and Marie, Huey and Duey, Porsche and Mercedes (Carly spoiled that one by pointing out that they could get nicknamed Punto and Corsa—it immediately ruled out all car brands), and Kylie and Jason. Carol wasn't impressed. Kate slammed her hand on the table. "I've got it!" We all turned to her in rapt expectation. "You want the names to mean something to you. Something close to your heart, that you love dearly. Names that say something about who you are and what you believe in." We were all nodding frantically in agreement.

"Then you only have one option, Carol. American and Express."

We all collapsed in hysterics. Even Carol was looking a bit moist in the eye area, though I think they were tears of outrage.

Cal agreed. "American and Express it is! At least then, Carol will have no problem bonding with them and taking them out every Saturday."

A turkey leg attached to Carol's hand smacked him across

the face. "Be careful, Cal Cooper, you're on a shaky screw," she warned.

When the meal was finished I went into the kitchen to retrieve the Christmas pudding (sticky toffee—I know it's not very traditional but it's our favourite) and mince pies. Carly was already there, fishing several bottles of Budweiser out of the fridge.

"You on bar duty now?" I asked her rear view.

The back of her head nodded. Then came a huge sniff. I rushed over to her and turned her around. Two big fat tears were rolling down her face.

"Carly, what's wrong? Tell me," I urged. This was unprecedented. Her whole life normally sailed by on a wave of enthusiasm and optimism.

She dried her eyes with the fur on the sleeve of her Santa jacket.

"I'm sorry, Jess. I'm just being bloody pathetic. It's all this talk of bumps and babies, it just gets me down sometimes. Mark and I have been trying solidly since the day we got married and I'm *still* not pregnant. The poor guy is bloody terrified to come home, because the minute he walks through the door I molest him."

I gave her a long, tight hug. "It'll happen, sweetie. You just have to be patient."

"I know," she nodded her head in agreement. "But it's just so difficult sometimes when everyone else seems to fall pregnant at the drop of a condom. If I hear about one more person getting pregnant without so much as a hormone chart, I'll fucking scream."

I gave her another hug, my mind whirring. Today was not the day to announce our news. I'd just hide my condition with baggy jumpers for a while, until I thought that Carly could cope with it. I ushered her back into the dining room, desperate to warn Mike and derail the planned announcement. Oh no. Somehow I knew that the ball was rolling and David Seaman couldn't have stopped it. Mike was on his foot, plaster and crutches, hitting his glass with a spoon, the others staring at him in bewilderment.

No, no, no, I tried to silently motion to him. Don't do this now.

"OK, everyone, Jess and I have a major announcement to make." All eyes widened in anticipation.

"Yes," I hastily interjected, "We're, em, we're buying a puppy. But it's no big deal. Now who wants some sticky toffee pudding?"

Around the table, everyone stared straight at me in confusion. It was the biggest anti-climax since the demise of my sex life. But it was tradition that every announcement should be acknowledged and celebrated in some way.

"Should we clap?" Carol asked lamely.

Mike's brow furrowed in incomprehension. Then with a wave of the hand (which unbalanced one crutch and almost left him flat out on the floor), he dismissed my interruption.

Stop, Mike. Please stop. But it was too late. He gave me another confused glance, mistaking my reticence for bashfulness, before proceeding.

"Jess is joking. She's just doing her usual 'hates to be the centre of attention' thing. The thing is, Jess and I are . . . I mean we're going to be . . . em, we're pregnant," he finished triumphantly. Why is that? Why do men get all proud of themselves for spawning offspring, when we do all the crap stuff? I didn't have time to dwell on it. Amid cheers of congratulations, copious hugs and a riot of back-slapping, I was too busy trying to clear up the four bottles of Budweiser that had just slipped out of my best friend's hands and crashed to the floor.

After a few seconds, Carly visibly pulled herself up, then leaned over and hugged me.

"I'm sorry, Carly, I'm so sorry," I whispered.

"No, it's me who's sorry. And not just about the fact that I've just ruined your carpet. I'm pleased for you, Jess. I promise." She gave me a tight squeeze. Then suddenly, she was back in Cooper mode. "Right, you lot, I think it's time for a song. Who knows the words to 'Baby Love?' "

I paced nervously up and down the waiting room of the maternity unit in the Chelsea and Westminster. It had been an hour now since Carol had been taken into the delivery suite for the operation to bring her family into the world.

We had all gathered in her private room that morning to give moral support. It was like a star's dressing room on opening night. Carol was propped up in bed, her manicurist putting the final touches to her nails, while her hairdresser primped her mane and her make-up girls added the final touches to her lip gloss. So much for childbirth preparation being a time of private turmoil. Carol would have been just as well giving birth in the middle of Elizabeth Arden.

In the corner, the *OK!* magazine team was setting up for their agreed exclusive "first shots of the Cooper babies." Well, it wasn't often that two of the country's most famous models became parents to twins. And Carol reasoned that the dosh would make up for the income she lost due to the fact that she'd been the size of a wardrobe for the last three months.

Carly returned from the canteen with coffees for Kate and

Sarah and a herbal tea for me. I still felt terrible about Christmas Day. I couldn't believe I'd kicked her when she was down, even inadvertently.

She handed me the tea. "Listen Jess, I just wanted to say that I truly am happy for you. Sorry I was a nightmare the other day. Just ignore the ramblings of a hormonal woman."

I took her hand and squeezed it. "I'm sorry too, Cooper. My timing has never been brilliant."

She bounced back quicker than a bungee rope. She never had been one for prolonging emotional moments.

"OK, we're over that now. So tell me, for a woman who has a gorgeous husband, financial security, her own home and a baby on the way, why do you seem on the wrong side of ecstasy these days?"

I was surprised. I hadn't realised that I was emitting miserable vibes. I explained the "Mike" situation. The three of them groaned.

"For God's sake, Jess, he's just adjusting to the new situation. Bruce went into a coma for a month when I first fell pregnant," Kate rebuked me.

"But what about the sneaky phone calls and unexplained disappearing acts?" Mike had started hobbling out every day for a couple of hours and was less forthcoming than a teenager when I asked him where he'd been. "Out," was the standard reply.

Sarah piped up. "Jess, he's on crutches. He's probably just getting a bit of exercise. What have you been thinking? That he's swinging his plaster cast around a nubile twenty-something?"

I nodded my head. I hated to admit it to myself, but given my past experiences with the deceit of married men, that was exactly what I was thinking.

"Jess, can I point out that the last time you thought Mike was having a rampant affair, he was actually planning your wedding?" Sarah continued. "Has it crossed your mind that maybe you're being a wee touch paranoid?"

She was right. I was turning into a totally neurotic, paranoid, control freak who thought if a man was unaccounted for at any time he was as trustworthy as an adder. I really needed to relax and focus on happy thoughts. Mike was my husband, we were going to have a gorgeous baby and he loved me madly. See, I was starting already. My karma was turning a fluffy shade of pink at that very moment.

Suddenly an alarm sounded and we all jumped. What was going on? Was there a problem in the delivery room? My heart was beating louder than a boy racer's Ford Fiesta. I got up to demand to know the condition of the patient, but Kate stopped me with one arm, as the other one rummaged in her handbag.

"Calm down, Jess—it's not an alarm, it's just my mobile phone alert that I've received a text message."

I took several deep breaths. "Give me the bloody thing so I can drown it in the water fountain. It nearly gave me a heart attack."

Carly was laughing. "Bet it's Bob the Builder, bet it's Bob the Builder," she stage-whispered in a sing-song voice.

I turned to Kate. Her face was turning puce. Who the hell was Bob the Builder? Carly filled us in while Kate blushed furiously.

Bob the Builder, alias Keith Miller, was the rather handsome, thirtysomething owner of a construction company, who'd bought the other half of Kate's semi in Richmond. Apparently, he spent a large part of the day stripped to a T-shirt and jeans in spite of the fact that it was December, overseeing the renovations of his new property. He and Kate had struck up a friendship when she took him out a cup of tea and a vanilla slice on his first day on the job. Since then, she'd been adding her woman's touch to his ideas for the interior design. Now he was texting her to ask if the curtains she suggested were muslin or voile. Mmmm. We didn't need Poirot to deduce that there was more to this than met the eye. Since when could a member of the male species even spell "voile"?

"Tell you what, girls. Come round to our house tomorrow during the day and you can check him out—it's like the Diet Coke advert from nine till five," Carly offered.

Kate was squirming in her chair.

"Something you want to share with us, Mrs. Smith?" I asked her.

She shook her head fiercely. "Look, he's just a friend."

Oh dear. That's what Charles said about Camilla Parker Bowles, right up until the moment he admitted that he'd been rummaging in her stable box for years. We all eyed her with scepticism.

"OK, OK." Kate would have been a crap spy during the war. The minute she was caught behind enemy lines she'd have folded like a travel cot for fear of offending anyone by lying to them. "Maybe he's a kind of flirtation," she relented, then swiftly, "But definitely no more than that. I love Bruce and I'd never be unfaithful to him." Bugger, the "u" word again. I'd just stood on all my fears about Mike and now they were rising back up and biting me on the bum. If Doris Day could stray . . .

She held up one hand and put another on her chest. "I swear I've done nothing wrong."

"Kate. We're not in the Brownies any more, you can put your hand down. Just tell me that you haven't even *thought* of checking out his properties," I grilled her.

There was a long pause. Oh no, Doris what's happened to you? If Carol was here she'd have muttered, "There's no smoke without a cooker."

"Well, I admit I've had the odd un-pure thought." Had Kate regressed to childhood? First the Brownies, now she was nine again and stuck in Father Kelly's confessional box.

"It's OK for you lot, all in the first flushes of married life, but Bruce and I have been together for nearly fifteen years. Let's just say that sometimes I miss that romantic excitement stuff and it's nice to have a daydream once in a while. So Keith's my daydream," she finished weakly. Then almost as an after-thought, "But I'd never act on it."

What was that old line about protesting too much? But there was no time to cross-examine. Sooner than I could say, "Call me Perry Mason," the doors to the delivery room swung open and Cal charged out, sprinted over to us, dived across two rows of chairs and grabbed us all into a bear hug. "It's two girls!" he announced breathlessly. "I've got two new beautiful girls!"

CHAPTER 13

Why not call in big Barry?

March 2001

I woke up with that familiar *Titanic* sinking feeling in my stomach. I stretched my hand behind me across the bed, at the same time willing my fears to be unfounded. But they weren't. Where my loving husband should have been lying, poised and ready to rub my back at any moment, there was an aching big void. He hadn't come home last night. Again.

I tried to inhale deeply to slow my racing heart. If the reports about a connection between stress in pregnancy and hyperactive children were true, then I was on target to give birth to the Duracell bunny.

I clenched my eyes tight shut to stop the tears. I'd cried so much lately that the skin under my eyes resembled Venetian blinds. I reached for the phone and dialled Mike's mobile number, pressing 141 before I dialled, so that he wouldn't realise it was me who was calling him. I mentally gauged his situation, depending on the time it took him to answer. Two rings: he *had* come home last night and he had now slipped out for a morning jog. Four rings: he'd worked through the night and was at this very minute sitting at his desk putting the final touches to his latest story. Six rings: he'd worked all night and was in the deli next to his office getting an espresso to keep him awake. Eight rings: he was having a power breakfast with some female journalist and flirting mercilessly. Ten rings: He was lying in someone else's bed . . . I didn't even want to think about it. He answered it after twelve rings.

"Hello." He sounded sleepy.

"Hi, babe, it's me," I replied, forcing cheerfulness into my tone. I could have won an Oscar, either for my acting skills or my determination not to accept that my relationship was going downhill faster than an Olympic ski-jumper.

"Oh, em, hi. I was just going to call you." And my name is Michael Caine.

"Where are you?" Still cheery. Still positive. Still certifiable.

"I'm in, em, Manchester. Don't you remember that I told you I'd be away for a couple of nights covering a story up here? Honestly, Jess, those hormones are affecting your memory."

He was lying. I was sure of it. Just because I was six months pregnant and had developed slight lapses of memory, didn't mean I'd forget something like this. Where I'd put my handbag when I came in last night, maybe, but not that my other half was leaving town. And anyway, how could he have told me when the full extent of our communications lately were two-minute, frivolous, false conversations, that mostly revolved around the status of his dry-cleaning?

"When will you be home, Mike? I think we need to talk." There was no use carrying on this pretence any longer. It was time for a grown-up conversation. I just need to find a grown up to advise me on what to say.

There was a pause, then, "Tomorrow, Jess. I'll be home tomorrow."

I replaced the phone, every muscle in my body aching with heaviness. I rubbed my huge stomach. There were three of us in this now. I had to fix my marriage, I just *had* to. I thought back to the first time that I felt sure that Mike was no longer just mine. It was on 14 February, exactly one year after our first date and our first Valentine's Day as man and wife. I'd spent all day preparing a romantic homecoming for him; I cooked his favourite meal, his favourite wine was on the table, Barry White was on the CD player. Even Mike's non-existent libido couldn't defy Barry, I reasoned, as I pulled down the hemline on the black Lycra dress that was threatening to cut off all circulation to my feet. I'd have to keep my legs above my head for the next three days to recover from this. I'd placed his gift next to his champagne glass. It was the Gucci watch that he'd had his eye on for months. Bugger the cost, I'd decided. In the space of one year, Mike had transported my life from chaos to the happiest I'd ever been. I'd even bought bloody rose petals for the pre-dinner bath we'd have together.

By six o'clock, I was beginning to wonder where he was. Mike never stuck to office hours, his job prohibited that, but surely he'd make an effort to come home early tonight. By seven o'clock, the dinner was ready and the rose petals were wilting. At eight o'clock I turned off the cooker. Tonight's food now looked like road-kill. By nine o'clock I wanted to hunt down Barry White and assault him with a Gucci watch.

At eleven thirty I heard his key in the door, and he wandered in, whistling. He stopped with a jolt when he saw the table, the wine and the tear-stained wife. At least he had the decency to look humbled.

"Oh, Jess, I'm sorry. I didn't know I was to be home early tonight. You should have said."

I stared at him mournfully.

"I didn't think I'd have to," I replied. He seemed embarrassed, as he pulled off his tie and headed for the shower. No kiss. No card. He was a Valentine-free zone. How long would a judge give a pregnant woman for murder?

When I heard the water hitting the bath, I went to the bedroom. He'd be in there for ages. Ever since his double-back somersault with pike that resulted in multiple fractures, he showered in slow motion, lest he repeat the experience.

I spotted his mobile phone on the bed. I wanted to ignore it but I just couldn't. I quickly grabbed it and scrolled to the message section. There was one message in the inbox. I pressed "read."

"Thanks for the flowers—they're beautiful. See you soon, S xxxxx."

My legs gave way beneath me and I plummeted down on to the bed, my mind racing for a feasible excuse. He couldn't use his mother as an alibi this time—her name was Marge. I had been right all along. Mike was playing away from home and still using me to get his strips dry-cleaned. Rage consumed me. Manslaughter was looking more likely by the minute—I'd just have to pray for a female judge—but I was too shocked even to lift the nearest blunt object.

I was still sitting there when he came out of the shower. He looked at my face, then down at the phone, then back again. His expression was that of a six-year-old, caught red-handed with his hand in a packet of Wagon Wheels.

I stared at him. "Who's 'S,' Mike?" I asked. Cool as a Mars Bar ice-cream. But it was a façade. Inside my blood gushed like lava.

He hit the roof quicker than a champagne cork exploding

from a bottle. How dare I check up on him? How dare I go through his phone memory? When was my next appointment at the doctor's, because I had to get this sudden paranoia checked. What was I accusing him of—being out shagging when his wife was sitting at home pregnant? (Yes . . .) Did I honestly think he was the type of guy who could do that? He ranted on and on. What had happened to me since I became pregnant? I'd turned into someone that he didn't recognise and certainly didn't want to spend time with. In short, I was a neurotic, moaning annoyance and who could blame him for working long hours, just to get some relief from the nagging.

He huffed and puffed and vented his fury until he was breathless. Through it all, I sat in complete silence, completely numb.

I waited until he ran out of insults and condemnations, then I summoned up every ounce of energy I had left.

"You haven't answered my question, Mike. Who's 'S'?"

He threw his towel down on the floor in exasperation. "S" he screamed, was a model who had given him a tip-off on a story he was working on. She'd supplied invaluable details of an MP (not another one!) who secretly visited London's upmarket boutiques and cosmetics houses, gathering the equipment he needed to live a double life as a drag queen called Blossom. He'd simply sent her the flowers as a thank-you for the information. The fact that it was Valentine's Day was a mere coincidence.

"You know, you really need to get your head checked, Jess. This mad behaviour is destroying our relationship!" With that, he pulled on the rest of his clothes and made for the door.

"Where are you going?" I shouted after him.

"Out!" he replied, immediately followed by the slamming of the front door.

Exit one man acting like a stroppy teenager. He'd have a skateboard under his arm and be wearing a baseball cap backwards by the time he came back. If he ever did.

I lay back on the bed, my head threatening to explode, my stomach on spin cycle number nine. What had I done? Was he right? Had I turned into the wife from hell? Was I like an alcoholic, who totally denied their problem while sipping on a bottle of paint thinner? Had I really become a paranoid neurotic who was forcing her husband to the brink of homelessness? I *had* been more tightly strung than a banjo since I became pregnant, but only because I was so damn tired and sick all the time. And yes, my *joie de vivre* had deserted me lately. Realisation dawned. Oh, my God, I was a one-woman home wrecker and this time it was my home I was destroying. Mike was right. I'd turned into a volatile, pregnant terrorist! He wasn't having an affair, he was just trying to dodge the bullets.

For the first time in my life, I sobbed into my pillow for hours. How was I going to sort this out? It wasn't just my life I was affecting—I had to think about my baby. I had no right to deprive it of a father before it was even born. I had to mend our relationship, I resolved. I had to prove to Mike that I was still the female he'd married only eight months before. Maybe then we could claw our way back to some semblance of happiness.

It was eight a.m. when I heard the door slamming downstairs. He'd come back! I quickly dried my eyes and heaved myself off the bed. I caught sight of my appearance in the mirrored wardrobes: Lycra dress now sagged like Nora Batty's stockings, face looked like it had been sunburned and someone had swapped my hair for a cheerleader's pom-pom. I could understand Mike's revulsion—the cross-dressing MP would have been more attractive than me.

He slowly climbed the stairs and leaned against the bedroom door. I didn't even give him the chance to speak. I wobbled across the room and into his arms.

"I'm so sorry, Mike," I sobbed. "You're right, I've been a nightmare. Just tell me that we can fix this. Please, Mike, say it's going to be OK." Even as I spoke, I was stunned at how weak I sounded—I was 5 foot 10 inches of pure hormones, all of them unbalanced. For a horrible moment I thought he was going to push me away, pack his bags and burst into a chorus of, "It must have been love, but it's over now."

But he didn't. Every bit of me shuddered in relief, as he wrapped his arms around me and ran his fingers through my hair. The tangles almost amputated his thumb.

"Ssshhh, Jess," he soothed. "I'm sorry too. I love you, babe and we'll work it out. It's all going to be fine, I promise."

He led me over to the bed and we climbed under the duvet, still wrapped in each other's arms. We stayed like that for hours: kissing, whispering and vowing to each other that we were going to make it through this. It was late afternoon when eventually hunger forced us to the kitchen. I was in the fridge, retrieving last night's champagne, when I heard Mike opening the oven door and then retching.

"Jess, what the hell is this mess in the cooker? It looks like something crawled in here and died."

"Last night's dinner. It was a Valentine's Day surprise."

He broke into a smile. "It has to be said, Jess. I certainly didn't marry you for your culinary abilities."

"Nope, but I can rustle up a mean Chinese. Pass me the phone and I'll call it in." I giggled and it was infectious. It was a great feeling. We were going to be fine. I just knew it.

* * *

Manchester? I racked my brain all morning. Alex Ferguson, David Beckham and an airport, that was all that was coming into my brain. There was definitely no recollection of Mike making plans to go there. I flopped on the sofa with a pile of reference books and biographies. May as well take my mind off the chaos with the last of the work that was required for the eccentric MP, who had now almost finished his memoirs. The progress slow due to Cecil's failing memory, propensity to fall asleep at least once an hour, and his dalliance with the local bingo caller called Vera. Still, at least what should have been a couple of months' work had now provided an income for the best part of a year. Mike could never accuse me of being a drain on his finances. His sanity, maybe, but not his bank account.

By lunchtime, my head was throbbing and my back was aching due to my unborn child's decision to practise the samba. It was either going to be a soccer player or a contestant on *Gladiators,* if the current level of activity was anything to go by. I gave my belly a wee rub.

"Hello in there, this is Mummy." I'd read in all the pregnancy books that talking to your bump helped it to recognise your voice after it was born. If this poor little soul had been eavesdropping on all my arguments with its father lately, it would be putting itself up for adoption and calling Childline the moment it popped out.

"Listen, I'm really sorry for all the shouting that's gone on. I do love your daddy, more than anything. Except you, that is. I'm going to love you more than you could ever believe. We'll always be OK, you and I. I'm going to make you so happy. We'll go to the park, and sing songs, and read stories every day. And I'll never let anyone make you sad. I promise. I love you, baby . . ."

Oh no, tears welling up again. I wiped my eyes furiously. For a woman who had never cried before the age of thirty-two, I was now the personification of Niagara. Nothing, I vowed, would ever make my child unhappy. I would make everything right with Mike and we'd raise this baby together in a house full of laughter. And nothing, *nothing* would get in the way of that.

I put the books down and manoeuvred my body into a position that would help me get from sitting to standing. With difficulty. I finally propped myself on the edge of the sofa and was levering myself up and taking a step at the same time, when my foot slipped on page 302 of *The History of The British Parliament*. I crashed on to the floor like a 747 with no landing gear. The earth shook. And so did my entire body. I frantically checked my bump for signs of trauma and my limbs for signs of breakages, the whole time trembling from head to toe in panic. I tried to raise myself up, but the ache everywhere was excruciating. My legs were in agony, but much worse than that, to my devastation pain ripped through my abdomen. Please God, if I never ask you for anything else, make my baby be OK. I held my breath. Dance little one, dance. But there was no movement. Oh, fuck, what had I done?

Fear racked my body and hysteria took hold. I'd hurt my baby. I gasped for breath. Please don't let this be happening.

I reached for the phone and dialled 999. Through deafening sobs, I explained what had happened. They assured me that an ambulance would be there quickly.

"Now," I implored, "Now. Please get it here now, my baby's not moving." I fought to control my breathing, everything that I'd remembered in antenatal classes now a blur to me. It's too soon, my mind screamed, as my stomach tightened. I'm only six months. It's too soon.

I reached for the phone again and somehow, on the tenth attempt, managed to call Mike's number. He answered straight away. I didn't even give him a chance to speak, just shrieked and wailed down the phone.

". . . fell . . . hurt . . . and the baby's not moving, Mike, it's not moving."

I could hear the panic in his voice. "I'll be there, babe, just hang on."

How long would it take him to get back from Manchester? I needed him here now, not in three hours' time. I could hear a banging at the front door. The room began to blur around me. Suddenly, it was like I wasn't there, like everything was happening to someone else. My baby, please help my baby, I begged, as I lost consciousness and blackness consumed me.

There was a blinding light shining in my face, as I forced my eyes to open. I tried desperately to remember where I was, but my brain wouldn't focus.

"She's awake!" a female voice yelled. "Jess, Jess, can you hear me. Somebody get the bloody doctor! Jess, CAN YOU HEAR ME!"

I nodded hesitantly. God, my head hurt. But I recognised that voice.

"Carly, the next street can hear you," I whispered. I peeled back my eyelids to see Carly, Kate, Sarah and Carol, their faces streaked with tears, terror and relief.

"Where am I?" I stuttered. "Is my baby all right?"

"Your baby is just fine, Mrs. Chapman," boomed a strong, authoritarian voice, belonging to a middle-aged woman in a white coat who was entering the room. "And so are you. Apart from a few bumps and bruises, you're still in one piece. But we do want to keep you in overnight for observation."

My head fell back on to the pillow. That was it. I was going to become a born-again Christian, or a Buddhist, or a Jehovah's Witness, or a servant to whatever God had saved my baby. But preferably not one of the religions that banned alcohol—I had a bottle of champagne all prepared for after the birth.

The doctor explained that they'd had a foetal monitor around me since my admission four hours before and the baby's heartbeat was completely normal. I felt a jolt and gasped with relief. The bump was doing the samba again.

"But the pain . . . ?" I asked.

"You've pulled a muscle at the side of your abdomen. It might be a bit tender for a few days, but it's nothing to worry about. You've also sprained both ankles and bumped your coccyx, but nothing is broken. You're going to be just fine, dear," she assured me.

Before I realised it, I was laughing heartily. Even though it hurt. But I didn't care. My baby was healthy and I was more or less in one piece. Nothing else mattered.

"I'm afraid that's not strictly true. The bit about nothing being broken." Carly spoke up. Had she been watching *ER* again? Was she overruling the doc's diagnosis? "Your door, Jess. We broke down your door. Sorry sweetie," she finished lamely.

I laughed even louder. And so did the others. Carly explained that she'd popped round with a box of chocolate eclairs to visit me and had been banging furiously on the door when the ambulance arrived. When they said that it was my house they'd been called to, Carly had panicked.

"So you told them to demolish my door . . ." I finished her narrative.

"Are you kidding?" she contradicted. "They were wee guys—they couldn't have knocked down a row of skittles. I kicked it in myself. Just call me Muscles!" she finished proudly.

There was a commotion at the door and Mike raced in. He flew over to the bed. "Jess, are you OK? The baby . . . ?" He enveloped me and was frantically kissing my face. How had I ever doubted him? Mike Chapman loved me and he loved our baby. He was a good man.

"We're fine, Mike. We're both going to be fine."

"I'm so sorry it took me so long to get here," he panted. "The traffic was a fucking nightmare. Oh, Jess, I can't believe I wasn't with you. I'm not leaving your side again, I swear."

The girls made a discreet exit, leaving Mike and me clutching on to each other, awash with relief. Mike pulled up a chair and positioned himself beside me, his head resting gently on my bump, listening to its heartbeat via the monitor. It was the sweetest sound I'd ever heard. I had my baby and I had Mike. I sighed in contentment. You're coming to a happy place, I told the baby. And life's going to be great.

It took five days, endless cajoling and the promise of a round-the-clock guard by the girls, to persuade Mike that it was safe for him to leave the house. The doctors had pronounced me fit and well and apart from aching ankles when I walked, I felt almost back to normal. The girls had organised a fat-lady-sitting rota, a copy of which was pinned to my fridge. Carly and Kate alternated most days, with Carol fitting in at least one day a week around work and the twins (who were eventually named Charlotte and Antonia, or Charlie and Toni, as they soon became). She'd been modelling again for the last three weeks and was hugely disgruntled because she was only being offered work for the "larger lady" catalogues. And that was at a size twelve! Was it any wonder the female population of the country was having a perpetual body image crisis? Carol included. "The way the bookers go on, you'd think I had an arse the size of Devon," she'd moaned. "Don't they know who I used to be?"

"A shallow, skinny bird with tits the size of golf balls?" Carly replied, only to be smacked by a flying Ryvita.

Sarah filled the gaps between the end of the school day and Mike returning from work. She was my daily enthusiasm boost. She was so happy with her new life in London, her gorgeous kids, Nick and his flourishing new restaurant, that it was impossible not to get caught up in her joy.

By the time Mike came home every night, I was in a state of euphoria. We'd cuddle up on the sofa, eat pizza, watch movies or just read. I'd even persuaded Carly to give me a copy of the manuscript for her forthcoming novel, but I'd had to stop reading it after fifty pages, because it made me laugh so much that I was in danger of re-pulling a muscle. Who'd have believed that she'd be so talented? Dippy, unpredictable, hilariously accident-prone, yes. But a comedy writer? She'd certainly kept that well hidden.

I raised it with her the next day, as she lay across an armchair devouring two packets of cheese and onion crisps and that week's *OK!* magazine. She laughed as she explained that writing the book was easy. After all, between her personal escapades and those of our group, she had enough material for an epic trilogy. I supposed that she was right—there was definitely never a dull moment.

I carefully formulated my next sentence in my head. I wanted to acknowledge the fact that she was here with me most days despite her own problems. We'd never discussed her

pregnancy-free status since she ruined my carpet with four bottles of Budweiser on Christmas Day.

"Carly, I just want to say I'm really grateful for the mummy-
sitting service. I know it can't be easy for you."

She smiled and shrugged her shoulders. "No problem,
Jess—your company's not *that* bad."

I laughed. "That's not what I meant and you know it, you
cheeky cow. Are you and Mark still trying for a baby?"

"Let's just say we're having more sex than an overworked
porn star. Honestly, Jess, I never thought I'd say this but I'd be
happy if I never saw another penis again as long as I live. Mark's
even had to cancel his gym membership because he's always too
knackered to go."

"Have you been to the doc's?" I asked.

She nodded her head mournfully. "They've said it can take
up to eighteen months to fall pregnant naturally, so we have to
wait until then before exploring any fertility options. Another
six months of frantic sex . . . I'll be walking like a cowboy by
that time. And it's just so unfair!"

She was right. "I know, babe. You'll make a great mum and
it is unfair that it's taking so long."

"No, I don't mean that," she wailed. "It's bloody unfair that
I've spent half the money I've earned in my lifetime at the Boots
contraceptive counter! If I'd known that my reproductive
organs were on bloody strike, I'd have saved the money and
bought a Jag."

We were interrupted by the sound of a key turning in the
door. I was perplexed. I'd given all the girls keys to my house,
because raising the dead would have been easier than getting me
off the sofa to answer the door, but no one else was due today.

Carly and I stared at the door in anticipation as Kate

stormed in, breezily announcing that she'd just wanted to pop over to check on us. Carly and I glanced at each other suspiciously. Kate hadn't made eye contact with either of us—something was afoot.

"What's going on, Kate?" I asked, as she busied herself clearing away plates and then pulled the Hoover out of the hall cupboard. Oh no, it must be something terrible. Kate always resorted to manic housework in times of tribulation.

"Kate, have you already cleaned your own house from top to bottom today?" Carly asked, obviously trotting along the same train of thought as me.

"Yes, and then I nipped next door and did yours too, Carly." Carly was now caught between being grateful for the maid service and panic at what could be wrong with Kate. This was the most frantic Mrs. Mop session in years—had someone died?

"Kate, SIT DOWN," I barked. After a few seconds, she reluctantly perched on the arm of Carly's chair. "Now tell us what's going on," I ordered. She made a gesture to dismiss the interrogation, but then slumped, realising it was pointless— Kate could be facing a firing squad and she *still* wouldn't be able to tell a lie to save her skin. Her eyes filled with tears.

"I kind of, well, sort of, I, em, oh fuck, I *nearly* kissed Keith Miller."

"Builder Bob?" Carly yelled. Kate nodded her head then hung it in shame. I was in shock. It was like finding out that Florence Nightingale had a secret life as a serial killer.

We forced the details out of her. She'd been up a ladder first thing this morning, hanging the voile curtains in Keith's kitchen. When the job was done, Keith had leaned over to give her a peck on the cheek as a thank-you, and an irrepressible urge had overtaken her. She barely managed to stop herself from assaulting his tonsils at point blank range. She was so shocked when she realised what she was thinking that she'd taken off like Sally Gunnell, leaving Keith Miller open-mouthed in astonishment. She'd spent the rest of the day obsessively cleaning. Poor Kate. She wasn't equipped for dealing with situations like this happening in her life—in our lives, yes, but not in hers.

It took Carly and me a while to recover from speechlessness. Carly spoke first.

"Let me get this straight. You're traumatised about the fact that you contemplated snogging a member of the male species other than your husband, even though you didn't actually lay lips on him?"

Kate nodded tearfully.

Carly shook her head and laughed. "Bloody hell, Kate, if that was the criterion for trauma then I'd have to employ a full-time therapist. I can't sleep at night unless I've had at least one erotic thought about a bloke other than Mark. It's *normal*, hon."

Kate sobbed again. "Not for me. I've never thought about anyone other than Bruce," she wailed. Pure as filtered water.

"So what now, Kate? Are you in love with him? Is this marriage-threatening?" I prompted.

She shook her head. "Of course not! I love Bruce. I just think I've been fantasising about Keith because he made me feel attractive again. If I'm honest I don't even think I fancy him, really. It was just nice to have that excited feeling again. Oh shite, what have I done?"

Carly threw down her crisps and wrapped her arms round Kate. "Nothing, sweetie. It was just a moment of diminished responsibility. It's not as if you went near any of his body parts, so just forget about it."

"It's OK for you—you've got no morals, but I can't live with myself. I'm a trollop!" Carly's face contorted into an indignant scowl, but she bit her tongue.

"Carly's right, Kate. Just forget about it. And if Keith comes near you again for curtain advice, just give him the number of the nearest blinds salesman. It'll blow over, babe."

But she wouldn't be placated. "I'm. A. Slag. Need. To. Clean," she sniffed as she heaved herself up and headed up the stairs. Something told me I'd be able to eat my pizza off the bedroom floor by the time the day was out. I pushed myself up to go after her, but Carly stopped me. "Let her be, Jess. Wait until she's calmed down, then we'll reason with her. There's no talking to her when she's in cleaning mode."

I reluctantly sat back down. The clock struck two and instantly Carly sprang into action. There was only one thing for it, only one thing that would take our minds off our devastated friend upstairs. She grabbed the remote and flicked on the television, just in time to see a demi-god of our times fill the screen. We reached for some bagels and snuggled down into our seats. It was the antidote to all the problems of the world. Montel Williams said, "Welcome to the show . . ."

Like a great holiday, the time flew by and all too soon the credits were rolling. As the last glimpse of Montel was about to leave our screen, I wanted to snog the telly. You didn't get many men like that to the pound. I was just contemplating what I would do to him if he walked in the door right now when Kate reappeared. I should have told her what I was thinking about Montel; that would have reassured her.

She was clutching the pile of Mike's clothes that had been lying on the bed, ready for him to take to the dry-cleaner's. I scanned her face. She almost looked human again. It was amazing what two bottles of bleach and a duster could do.

"I'll just nip down to Mr. Wong's with these," she announced. "I need some fresh air."

"Check the pockets first, Kate. Mike's never forgiven me for the time I left a biro in his best Armani shirt and it came back looking like something they'd wear in Hawaii."

She rummaged through the clothes and pulled a pile of papers out of the inside pocket of his favourite jacket. "Just some receipts." She handed them to me.

To this day, I don't know why I felt compelled to look at them. Normally I'd just have stuffed them into his desk. Two bottles of wine from Oddbins. A can of shaving gel and a pack of razors from Boots. Lunch for two at The Ivy. I sighed. It had been a long time since Mike and I had gone anywhere that trendy. But I could understand it. He took colleagues and work contacts there and to the other "in" London restaurants so regularly for meetings, that he preferred to eat at home with me. I was about to consign the lot to the bin when some figures on the last receipt caught my eye. I gasped as my hand flew to my mouth.

"What's wrong, Jess?" Kate exclaimed, registering my shock. But for the second time that day, I was speechless. I could only shake my head and hold out the receipt.

Carly took it and they huddled over it, reciting the contents out loud. "Lunch for two at The Ivy. Very flash." They were struggling to comprehend my reaction. Was I unreasonably opposed to Mike eating mid-afternoon? "Total bill, £126.00. Fuck, that's a night out for two with a new outfit thrown in," Carly observed. But still they were confused.

"Look at the date," I uttered wearily, my knees automatically trying unsuccessfully to draw up to the foetal position.

"Fifteenth of March," Carly read. "What's the problem with that?"

There was a pause. Then, "Oh, no." Kate understood. "The fifteenth of March. That's the day that you fell. That's the date that he said he was in Manchester. I remember because it was the day after Bruce's birthday." She winced when she said "Bruce"—her conscience was still locked in a wrestling bout.

I raised my eyes to them, my vision blurred with shock and tears. "It took him four hours to get to the hospital," I whispered, "and he was only twenty miles away . . ."

CHAPTER 14

Why not check the small print?

May 2001

Kate and Carly stayed with me until we heard Mike's key in the door, at which point they slid out, neither of them able to say "hello" in case "bastard" slipped out on the end of it. Both had protested when I'd asked them to leave. But I knew that this was something I had to do on my own. It was going to be one of those life-defining moments that I'd play over in my mind again and again and I didn't want the memory of me literally hiding behind my mates in cowardice.

We'd spent all afternoon dissecting the new information, searching for any plausible explanation. The horror of the reality was just too excruciating to bear. Carly had even called The Ivy, posing as the accountant of a soap actress, to check that their till was working correctly and couldn't possibly have printed the wrong date. They were mortally offended that she'd even suggested such a thing. At The Ivy *everything* worked efficiently, she was assured.

You would have thought that I'd have been climbing the walls like a bionic aspidistra, but bizarrely, the opposite was true. Maybe I'd slipped into a state of shock. It was almost as if, now that I knew the truth, the fatality of the situation was clear and a protective instinct had kicked in. For both the baby and me. At least I now knew that it wasn't my imagination—I wasn't neurotic, paranoid or hormonal. I just had abysmal taste in men. My only fury was with myself, that I hadn't listened to my instincts when they were screaming so loudly that they could have drowned out a rave. In the back of my mind, I'd known all along. I just hadn't had the guts to admit it to myself. In my desperation to build the family unit I'd come to dream of, I'd dismissed every dangerous instinct and dark suspicion.

I laid out the evidence on the coffee table in front of me as Mike entered the room, armed with an extra-large Meat Feast and two bottles of Diet Coke. He'd be having them "to go."

"Pack your bags, Mike, it's time for you to leave," was my opening line. Deadly calm, resolute and dignified, with a "don't fuck with me if you know what's good for you" overtone.

He eyed me in confusion. I could tell he was thinking that I'd taken leave of my senses. Nothing new there then.

He uttered a nervous laugh. "Having another hormonal day, babe?" he added weakly. But his body language betrayed his fear. He knew the game was up.

I was going to stay silent, but in a perverse way I was enjoying watching him squirm. "Mike, I have the receipt for The Ivy. On the fifteenth of March. The day I fell. Unless you've suddenly developed the powers of Dr. Who, you couldn't have been in Manchester while I was lying in hospital waiting for you. Now I'm not going to repeat myself again. Pack your bags and go."

It was strangely empowering. Here I was, ending my marriage to the love of my life, and I had an overpowering feeling of invincibility. Now I know why men constantly bleat that they don't understand women. Trigonometry was easier to comprehend.

His reaction took me by surprise. There was no rage, no anger, no accusing me of being a candidate for an institution. For the first time since we'd met, Mike Chapman cried.

He couldn't leave, he wailed, because he loved me. He'd been a fool. A complete tosser. He *had* been having an affair, but she meant nothing to him. He started to go down the road of "you've been so distant since you became pregnant that I sought affection elsewhere . . . ," and for the first time since I gave him his marching orders, I was compelled to speak.

"Don't even go there, Mike," I warned him, in a tone that made it clear that it would be a fatal mistake.

It wasn't my fault, he conceded, it was all his. Oh Christ, he was on a roll. Like a mass murderer facing the electric chair, he felt an overwhelming urge to confess all. He should have realised that there would be no last-minute reprieve and the Meat Feast was going to be the dying man's last meal. Instead, he bleated on about how he needed a constant fix of excitement, that adrenalin junkie thing that had been part of him since childhood, and since I could barely speak for throwing up for the first four months of pregnancy, he'd become restless. The model he was working with at the time was throwing herself at him (his words) and eventually he'd given in (poor soul—my heart was bleeding for him. Not). And he *had* sent her flowers on Valentine's Day. He *was* with her when I was lying in hospital. But that was the episode that had forced him to his senses. The fact that he'd had to wait for hours before coming to me had been devastating for him and made him realise what a fool he'd been. He regretted it bitterly and he'd known since then that the baby and I were everything he would ever want; He loved us more than life. I *had* to believe him.

I contemplated his defence. One of the things I'd always adored about Mike was his spontaneity, his thirst for adventure. It was those very aspects of his personality that were responsible for some of the best times of my life: the speed that our relationship developed, the impromptu wedding, the decision to have a child. And it was true that since that day in March, his behaviour *had* transformed. Since I was released from hospital, he'd been attentive, loving, funny . . . the old Mike Chapman had indeed returned. I sighed. Shame the stable door was already padlocked and made of reinforced steel.

Would I please, please give him another chance? Just let him prove to me that he loved me and would never, ever so much as glance at another woman. He'd spend the rest of his life making this up to me, he vowed. He'd make me happier than I'd ever been. He'd be the perfect husband, if only I'd give him the opportunity. Could I really end everything because of one stupid mistake, one episode of madness?

Absolutely. You see, the affair would have been terminal enough, but what was even more vicious was the fact that he'd battered me with insults and questioned my sanity when he was cornered. He'd deflected all the heat like tinfoil by accusing me of being insane, forcing me to struggle with the persistent fear that I was losing my grip on reality. I would never forgive him for that. He begged, pleaded, remonstrated and beseeched for over an hour. Then he broke down again and fell into a mournful silence.

"I'm going out now, Mike. By the time I get home, I want every trace of you removed from this house. There's just no going back."

I stumbled out of the door, grabbing my handbag on the way. I wandered in a daze to the end of the road and flagged a passing taxi.

"Where to, love?"

I realised that I had no idea where I wanted to go. I was already in hell. What was the next stop down from there? I falteringly gave him Kate's address. As in all times of pain, joy or suffering, the mother ship was calling me in.

By the time I arrived, I was trembling from head to toe. When she opened the door, I collapsed into her arms and for the first time that day, cried until I could barely breathe. I let her take me inside, rub my hair while I sobbed and comfort me until I fell asleep, exhausted, in the middle of the night. It was over. My last thought before my eyes finally closed, was that it was all over.

Carly insisted on returning with me to the flat the next day, in case Mike was foolishly still there. My stomach was rising as we entered my street, in my throat as we went up the path and in my mouth as we got to the front door. As soon as I opened it, I knew he was gone. There was a gaping space where his jackets hung in the hallway. His books, CDs and pictures were missing from the living room. I slowly climbed the stairs. There were ring marks on the bathroom shelves where his toiletries had been. I conducted this whole macabre tour in an unemotional, robotic trance. I entered the bedroom and pulled open his wardrobes. There was nothing but a row of empty hangers. It was too much. I crumpled and only Carly's quick reflexes stopped me from sliding to the floor. She guided me over to the bed and laid me down. For the first time I noticed that there was a letter lying on my pillow.

"Open it for me, Carly. I can't bear to do it myself."

"Are you sure? Maybe you should leave it until later."

I shook my head. The aching pain of devastation was eating my insides. I wanted to throw up, to beat down a wall, to scream at the top of my lungs. I clutched my massive stomach. I had to be stronger than this. This wasn't just about me and Mike. This baby didn't need hysteria, it needed a calm place to grow.

I took a deep breath. "Just read it to me," I asked her.

She sighed as she opened the envelope. "Fine, but I still think you should burn it."

" 'Dear Jess,' " she read. " 'How can I even begin to tell you the things I need to say. I am so, so sorry for the pain that I've caused you. You have to believe that it wasn't intentional. I love you, baby. I can't believe I was so stupid, so bloody callous and so wrong. This is truly the biggest mistake I have ever, or will ever make . . .' "

"Ain't that the truth. The prick should be fucking shot." Carly's face was purple.

"Just keep reading, Carly."

" 'Jess, you've got to give me another chance. From the first moment I set eyes on you, I knew that we were meant to be together. I knew that I wanted to spend the rest of my life with you. Please, baby, don't throw away everything we've built together because of one mistake . . .' "

"That's it, this is going in the bin." Carly scrunched up the note.

"Stop! Please, Carly, just read the rest of it. Please." With a dramatic sigh she unscrunched the paper.

" 'Most of all, Jess, think of the baby. Together we could give it the best home, the best childhood. Please don't deprive me of that and even more importantly, deprive the baby of a father. I will love it more than I can say in words. Please reconsider, Jess. Please help me work this out. All I want is for us to be together. You, me and the baby. Always . . .' "

I closed my eyes to try to calm the storm that was battering the inside of my head. It felt like my life was flashing before me—and not the good bits. Was this payback? Was this a bizarre punishment for getting involved with a married man? Was this how Miranda felt when she discovered the truth about me and Basil? Was I Hitler in a past life and this was some kind of cosmic revenge? I squeezed my eyes shut to stop the tears. Stay calm, stay calm. My poor baby. Was Mike right? Did I really want to deprive it of a full-time father? Was I being a self-ish cow by putting my pride before its need to have Daddy there in the morning when it woke? The storm was now working its way up to a full-scale hurricane. "Carly, what if I'm making a huge mistake? What if there's a chance that we could work things out?"

"Don't give me 'what if's,' Jess—they're a total waste of time. You don't need him, Jess, not after what he's done. Now I'm going to make tea, so climb under the duvet and I'll bring it up to you—I've just appointed myself as your personal maid and minder."

She pulled the cover over me and gave me a kiss before leaving the room.

"Thanks, Cooper. For everything," I murmured.

Gallows humour kicked in. "Don't thank me now, babe, you haven't tasted my tea yet. It'll give you indigestion for days."

The next few weeks passed in a blur of confusion and pain. Had I not been pregnant, I'd have been wailing at the moon, but I fought to maintain a modicum of composure, for the baby's sake and for mine.

The telephone rang relentlessly and every time I dialled 1471, it was Mike's number that was announced. I'd switched off the answering machine after he'd left seven messages on the first day, begging me to talk to him.

He even came to the house several times, until he realised that he could knock on the double-locked-from-the-inside door for a month and I would still ignore him. He sent me flowers. Returned. He sent me e-mails. Deleted. He sent me letters. Burned.

I had good days and bad. On a good day, I could manage a whole five minutes without thinking about him. On a bad one, I struggled to even get out of bed in the morning. Eventually, though, his persistence started to wear me down. By the end of the first month, I could actually say his name without retching and started to contemplate the fact that I'd have to meet with him at some point to discuss the logistics of the separation, the baby, the future. I was determined not to see him, though, until I was sure that I could manage a whole conversation with dignity, without attempting to harm him or throwing myself at him in submission.

You see, that was the worst part. In some ways, I'd actually started to miss him. After the first week, when I just wanted to die a quick death, the pain had very gradually started to subside and now it was at amputation level. I still felt devastatingly and desperately hurt. But I was beginning to realise that although I *could* live without him, I wasn't sure that I *didn't* want him back.

For fleeting intervals, between rage, hurt and anger, memories of the best parts of our time together would sneak in and

ambush me. I'd lift the telephone to call a divorce lawyer and
suddenly get a vision of the two of us at the top of the Empire
State building, wrapped in each other's arms, me smiling in the
certainty that I wanted to spend the rest of my life with this guy.
Or I'd be lying in bed at night wondering who he was sleeping
with now, when I'd imagine his familiar touch as he started to
make love to me. And it broke my heart. No matter how furious I was, I couldn't overlook what we built together. It was just
a pity that he had.

"What are you thinking, Jess?" Sarah asked gently, snapping
me from my memories. She was on guard duty that day.

"Don't hate me if I tell you the truth, Sarah."

She eyed me curiously. "Go on."

"Sometimes, I can't help myself, I just miss him. I know it's
crazy and I should despise him, but every now and then I just
want to talk to him. He's my husband—I can't go on avoiding
him for ever. Shite, the others would have me jailed if they
heard me now."

Sarah shook her head. "Jess, it doesn't matter what anyone
thinks. It's up to you, and no matter what you decide we'll support you. Well, except maybe Carly and Carol—we'll still have
to chain them down next time they see him. But you've got to
do what's right for you. And for the baby," she finished, giving
my belly a rub.

She was right. It was time I stopped hiding and did something positive, even if it was just calling a good lawyer. The
phone rang. I knew it would be him. For the first time in weeks,
I lifted the receiver. It was like speaking to a stranger. After the
initial shock that he was talking to me and not a machine, he
showered me with apologies and adulations, then begged me to
meet with him.

"Just half an hour, Jess, please. You at least owe me the chance to speak to you."

"I owe you nothing, Mike. You cashed in your chips when you decided that I wasn't enough for you."

There was a pause. Let him suffer.

"But I'll meet you tonight. My place, seven thirty, and you'll be gone by eight, just in case you have other social arrangements to fit in," I added sarcastically.

If I was going to make an appearance on *Stars in Their Eyes*, impersonating early Madonna in a conical bra, I wouldn't have been more nervous. Another new emotion. I'd always prided myself on my ability to be calm and methodical in any situation.

At seven twenty-five, the doorbell rang. He obviously figured that I'd changed the locks, so he didn't even try his key. I'd let him think that was the case—it made me feel more in control. My fingers were shaking so much that it took three attempts to negotiate the Yale. When I finally managed to prise open the door, I was stunned at his appearance. His face was ashen, his eyes had three sets of Louis Vuitton under them and his hair looked like it had been in a fight with a lawnmower. It gave me perverse pleasure to see that he was obviously coping as badly as me with this whole situation. Or maybe he just appeared a bit rough because he'd been out on the town all last night with Model Minnie.

I stood back and let him pass. He headed into the lounge and I reluctantly followed him. Now that he was here, I wasn't sure what the next move should be.

He started with small talk. "How are you?"

"Shite." No point in pretence. Then, some long-forgotten strength rose up from wherever it had been hiding, and took control. I'm in charge of this, Mr. Chapman, I vowed. "Where are you staying?" I asked dryly. "Moved in with the model?"

He shook his head in resignation. "I told you that it was over with Saffron." At least now I knew her name. "I'm staying at the Central." It was a small hotel near his office that he occasionally used for entertaining. Of the non-sexual sort. At least I'd thought it was, but now I wasn't so sure. He was probably having daily orgies there.

He changed tactics and aimed for neutral territory. "How's the baby?"

"The baby's fine, Mike. Still doing the samba all day long."

That did it. He threw his arms around me. "I'm so sorry, Jess . . ."

It went on for minutes, but it seemed like hours. Eventually, I shook him off. I had wondered all day how I would feel when he touched me. Would I melt into a wobbly jelly and capitulate to his caresses? Or would my knee automatically make violent contact with his genitals? The answer was neither. I felt detached. I was cold and ambivalent. I just wasn't ready to make any moves to forgive him.

"Let me come home, Jess. Please. I swear you'll never regret it." I stayed silent, my heart and my brain locked in a furious battle to the death. I'd be lying if I didn't admit that a huge part of me wanted to say yes, to tell him to come home, that we'd put this whole fiasco behind us and start again. Logic prevailed though. It was too soon. The wound was still too raw, too devastatingly painful. I couldn't guarantee that I wouldn't suffocate him as he slept.

I shook my head. His face contorted in grief. I almost felt sympathy. Maybe he'd been right about the "insane" stuff.

"Never?" he gasped.

"I don't know what I want for the future, Mike," I answered honestly, "And I don't know when I will."

The girls arrived at eight fifteen sharp. It wouldn't have surprised me if they'd come armed with kitchen utensils, ready for battle. There was a definite clanging noise when Carly walked in. I recounted the whole story to them, ending with the honest declaration that I had a glimmer of hope for us. I'd been thinking everything over since he left. Maybe I did owe it to the three of us to try again. Maybe it wasn't a lost cause after all.

"I can't believe you would even *consider* having him back, Jess," Carly exclaimed, but Kate kicked her ankles, making her add, "but of course, it's up to you and we'll support you whatever you do." We all smiled at her effort to camouflage her true feelings. They were more obvious than Thatcher's views on Europe.

"I know her," Carol said calmly.

Who? Margaret Thatcher? Had I said that out loud?

"Saffron. His fluff. It's a pretty unusual name. If it's who I think it is, I've worked with her a few times."

"Tell me she's a complete cow, who only does 'before' pictures for adult acne solutions," I begged.

"Sorry, Jess, but she's not. In fact, she's really nice. I used to have the odd drink with her, before I was condemned by motherhood to the social life of an outcast. I don't understand this, though. I didn't think she was the type to go after a married guy. What a slapper."

I ignored the last bit. My past indiscretions were belting me in the face like a broken brolly. I hadn't thought I was the "type" either.

"Call her. Call her now," Carly barked.

"And say what? You stole my best friend's man and we think you're a tart, na na na na boo boo?" I asked, bewildered. But the others outvoted me. It would be useful for background information, they decided. Just to check Mike's version of events.

Carol called Cal to get the number from her Rolodex. Only Carol would still have that eighties' status symbol—mine was now used to hold cooking recipes that I vowed to attempt if I ever worked out how to use the oven properly. My nerves were jumping as she dialled. Saffron answered after a few rings.

Carol explained that she was just calling to catch up, since they hadn't spoken for a while. Pause. Yes, it was great to speak to her too. Pause. The twins were doing great. Pause. And yes, married life was fab. Pause. Yes, they must get together for a gossip. I bit my lip at this point. I didn't want my friend meeting with the enemy.

So, Saffie, how was the love life? Pause. A journalist? Pause. Mike Chapman? No, I don't think I know him. Pause. How long have you been seeing him? Pause. Really? On/off. Most of last year and then for six months this year? Should I be buying a floppy hat and flowers anytime soon? Pause. Well, fantastic! Listen, I must go just now, but I'll call you later in the week and arrange that drink. Talk to you soon, sweetie.

Carol slowly replaced the phone. I put my head in my hands. Last year! So he *was* seeing someone else when he was planning our wedding. I'd been right all along. It gave me no comfort. And then for the last six months! I was only eight months pregnant. He'd started seeing her before the pee on the pregnancy test was dry! And he was *still* seeing her. The lying, cheating, fuckwit. I wanted to tear him apart. It was all becoming so clear. He was like one of those guys who lead double lives and only get caught when they die and three wives turn up at the funeral. How could he do this? And how could I not have realised it?

After an hour of hysterics, threats and vows of vengeance, Sarah went into the kitchen and returned with three bottles of wine. "Where's your corkscrew, Jess?"

"It's OK, I've got one here," Carly replied, pulling a large metal corkscrew from her trouser pocket. I didn't ask. For the first time in my pregnancy, I nursed a large glass of wine, while the others demolished the rest of the bottles. A vineyard wouldn't have been enough to numb this pain.

I woke the next morning with a crushing pain in my chest. For a fleeting moment, I thought I was having a heart attack, then I realised that it was Sarah's legs lying across my torso. I thought back to the night before. It had been after three by the time we'd poured the others into a taxi, after a night of deep debate, discussion and Lambrusco. The first couple of hours had focused on Mike, then we moved on to Kate's Builder Bob dilemma. Doris Day was beside herself with disgust at her impure thoughts and temptations.

Carol was just as disgusted, but with her body, not her brain. "If beauty is skin deep, I must be fucking gorgeous," she wailed, pinching two millimetres of flab at the side of her waist. If she'd mentioned liposuction one more time, we would have attacked her with a bicycle pump and done the job ourselves.

At midnight, Sarah had called Nick, given him a rundown on the latest developments and checked that he could drop the kids at school the following morning, before announcing that she was going to stay the night. Nick told her to give me a hug from him. He was a sweetheart.

In fact, all the guys had been fantastic since Mike had been caught with his willy in the cookie jar. Cal had appeared weekly with gifts for the baby—he'd almost single-handedly kitted out the nursery. Nick arranged for food to be sent from his restaurant most nights. Bruce and Mark had been over every weekend, building wardrobes, putting up shelves and decorating the nursery. I was so grateful. Most of all, though, I appreciated the fact that they didn't resent the endless hours of babysitting duty they'd been encumbered with, as their wives kept me company. They were all such good people. How come I'd ended up with the Devil's spawn, when there were men like those on the planet? It would take me years to repay their kindness.

I woke up Sarah, telling her it was time for work and promising that I was safe to be left alone until Carly came that evening. Kate was going to miss her shift because she had Zoë's sports day to attend. In a way, I was glad. I needed a few hours on my own.

I made breakfast and headed for the sofa. Even the smallest exertion exhausted me these days. I had to lie down for half an hour after every visit to the loo. I lounged there for hours trying to digest the latest developments. To my surprise, I didn't even feel pain any more. Instead, I just felt an overwhelming void. Numbness had overtaken every part of me. It was like a death in the family. Mike Chapman, R.I.P.

I analysed the situation from every angle. It was over, of that there was no question. I instinctively reached for my stomach, passing soothing vibes through to the baby. We'd manage, I promised my bump. I just needed to sort out a few things, including having its father assassinated.

I picked up the phone and dialled the number of a female divorce lawyer, who was renowed for her aggression and delivery of results. I wanted this marriage ended and ended quickly.

What would Mike say to this? I knew the answer. He'd deny everything. Lying was obviously an intrinsic part of his make-up. If he could come here and plead for me to return to him, while at the same time continuing his affair with Saffron (now named the Yellow One), then he was more two-faced than a double agent. I pondered this for hours. It was late afternoon when the realisation came to me. I wanted to see him squirm. I needed to catch him in the act. Well, not in *that* act, that was too stomach-turning to comprehend, but I needed *him* to know that *I* knew everything. I needed him to see with his own eyes that there would never, ever be any going back from this point and that the only contact he could ever make with me again would be to arrange to see his child. My blood ran cold. The very thought of that gave me shivers. I never wanted him to so much as set eyes on this innocent babe, but I'd cross that bridge when I came to it. First, I needed closure. And a cunning and devious plan. I called Carol on her mobile and asked the favour. Would she call Saffron and find out what nights she was free this week? She called me back within ten minutes. Saffie wasn't available tonight because she was seeing her boyfriend, and then she was going away tomorrow for a two-week shoot in Tobago. Why did I want to know this? Just curious, I assured her. Just wanted to check that they were still together.

So it had to be tonight. I called Hertz and requested that they drop off a hire car—something small, dark and unobtrusive. The agent probably thought I was a drug dealer and I'm sure she was on to the police to check for prior convictions while she told me she was authorising my credit card.

The car arrived at five o'clock. I dressed for the part: long, black overcoat, shades and a scarf around my hair. I looked like a cross between Puff Daddy and a Kosovan refugee. I grabbed my mobile phone and bag and wedged myself into the driver's seat. Perhaps I should have gone for a bigger model.

The gods were on my side (for the first time in recent memory), as I pulled into a parking space right outside the Central Hotel. I just hoped Mike would bring Saffron here and not head for her place, but I remembered Carol telling me that most models shared flats because they travelled so much. Surely they'd want their privacy?

The six o'clock news came on the radio. Shite! Six o'clock. Carly was due round at seven. In my intense concentration on my plan of action today, I'd forgotten all about her. I rang her number.

"Hello," she groaned.

"Carly, it's me. What's up? You sound like crap."

"I've got the hangover from hell. I think that wine at your house last night must have been off. I haven't been able to lift my head from the pillow all day. I think I've died. Anyway, where are you? I can hear noise in the background."

"It doesn't matter. Listen, give tonight a miss and I'll buzz you tomorrow. 'Bye, babe." I tried to cut it short. But even in her death-like state, she wasn't to be humoured.

"STOP! DON'T YOU DARE HANG UP! Where are you?" she bellowed.

There was no use lying. She'd never believe anything I said anyway—after all, how many places can an eight-month-pregnant female go to on her own at six o'clock at night?

"I'm sitting outside the Central Hotel. I want to catch him, Carly. I want him to see me catching him."

There was a loud groan. "Oh, fuck, Jess, you're a mad cow. But I'll be there in twenty minutes." The phone went dead.

I turned the radio back up. "Endless Love" blared from the

speakers. I resisted the urge to smash it to pieces with my bare
hands and snapped it off. I hummed Whitney Houston's
"That's Not Right" instead.

A while later, there was a thud at the window. I opened the
door and let in Carly, carrying two Styrofoam cups of coffee, a
box of paracetamol and a Kodak camera. Good thinking: we'd
need photographic evidence.

As she climbed in, she looked like she needed a blood trans-
fusion. She handed me a cup. "If we're going to be Cagney and
bloody Lacey, then I thought we'd need sustenance. It's decaf,
oh fat one." I laughed. This was one of the most dramatic,
tension-filled moments of my life and I was laughing in the
front of a Micra with a hungover woman. Well, why not? My
life got more bizarre by the day.

Carly popped two of the headache cures, then removed a
Stetson and a pair of dark glasses from her bag and slipped them
on. If we didn't get arrested it would be a miracle.

It didn't happen like it does in the movies. In fact nothing
happened for hours. At nine o'clock we were still sitting there,
the street outside almost deserted, with not so much as the sight
of a bastard husband. We'd worked our way through every Bea-
tles song, every Elvis number, every modern-day classic and
now we were on to Steps' greatest hits. With actions.

Carly was deteriorating faster than an iceberg in a heatwave.

"Listen, Jess, why don't we call it a night. He's obviously not
coming back here."

"No way. I'm not moving until I've seen him. I just can't."

"What's the plan if he ever does show up? Are you going to
assault him with your brolly? Only, I've never seen Cagney or
Lacey do that."

"I don't have a plan. We're making this up as we go along."

"OK," she sighed. "I'll stay here with you all night if we have to, but I really need some food. I'm sweating pure Lambrusco here and I'm going to keel over at any minute." She spotted a McDonald's on the other side of the road and made a swift exit, returning with two Big Mac meals with extra fries. She offered me one, but I refused it—my stomach was too stressed to welcome any visitors.

She quickly unwrapped her burger. "God, I need this."

Her mouth was open and the bun was halfway there, when I grabbed her arm. "It's him, Carly, it's him." Mike's black BMW had pulled in one car in front of us. And there was someone in the passenger seat.

"Fuck!" she exclaimed. "The bastard didn't even give me time to eat my burger."

We slid down further into our seats. I didn't want the target to see us now and blow our cover—I wanted to catch him with the goods. We waited for him to exit the vehicle. And waited. And waited. "What the fuck is he doing?" I murmured to no one in particular. "Bugger it, I'm going in."

Carly grabbed my arm. "No way, Jess. You stay there. You can't do a commando crawl in your condition, you'll get stuck."

"Carly, I need to see him. And I need him to see me."

"Oh, shite. Well, I'm coming with you."

We ducked down and edged our way out of either side of the car. With my knees bent as far as they would go, so that only my head was visible above the car window level, I slowly worked my way past the Mondeo in front. I hoped it was empty, otherwise the occupants would think they were being ambushed. Luckily, it was. I crept further forward until I was level with the back of Mike's car. I peeked up. What on earth were they doing? It looked like they were snogging in the front seat. Please! Could they not at least wait until they were inside? Had they no dignity? I already knew the answer to that one.

I edged further forward. Now I was touching the driver's door and Carly was at the passenger side. I peeked my head above the parapet. I couldn't believe it! They weren't snogging—Mike had his head buried in the Yellow One's chest area and she had her eyes squeezed shut in enjoyment. Where were the bloody police when you needed them? It had to be illegal to do this in a public place.

Through the two panes of glass, I made eye contact with Carly. I motioned her to wait. If this was going to be a simultaneous attack, I needed time to get myself to a standing position.

Saffron was still oblivious to my presence as I heaved myself upright, my thighs screaming in agony. Carly did the same. Our eyes met over the roof of the car. Now! I signalled.

I rapped on the glass and Saffron's eyes and mouth simultaneously opened in shock. There was a sudden flash as Carly caught the view from her side of the car on film—a clear image of the face of Mike Chapman buried in the bosom of a brunette. David Bailey, eat your heart out.

Mike was momentarily startled, then he spun round in his seat, his mouth wide as he shouted expletives. I was glad the window was closed. Then, I couldn't resist it. I pressed my lips against the window and blew him a kiss, then waved as I waddled at speed back to the Micra.

I later found out that Mike had lunged at the door, attempting to come after me, but Carly spotted his actions. She rapped on the passenger window to cause a diversion. It worked but it wasn't enough, she needed another stalling tactic. So she did what only Carly would do—lifted her T-shirt and flashed them. Two leopardskin-clad breasts were pressed against the window of his BMW. It didn't last for long, but it was enough time for me to get the car started and draw alongside them. Carly jerked down her top and jumped in, and we screeched off into the night like Bonnie and Clyde.

And we laughed until tears flowed down our cheeks and our jaws ached. I'd just caught my husband exploring the cleavage of another woman and in that moment it seemed like the funniest thing I'd ever seen. Well, why not?

Book Three

Year 2001 AD (After Dickhead)

CHAPTER 15

Why not use a sperm bank?

June 2001

The sun streamed in the window of my room at the Chelsea and Westminster, as I eased my head from the pillow. I tried to move my arm, but it was dead from shoulder down. I smiled as I saw why. Cradled on my elbow was the most perfect little boy God had ever created. A son. My son. My eyes filled again, but for the first time in months it was from sheer joy. Nothing else mattered now. I had my boy.

Aaww! And sore nipples. I winced as my cotton nightdress brushed over my chest. Why had no one warned me that breast-feeding was like having your nipples sucked through a lathe? I pondered again that God was definitely male. If He was female, She'd have installed two taps.

The baby stirred and stretched his hands above his head, before returning to a deep snooze. He was obviously as exhausted as me. That journey down the birth canal must have been the equivalent of a full marathon.

I gently stroked his face and his lips pursed as he slept. My stomach did a somersault. I just couldn't believe how perfect he was. And beautiful. I'd always thought that most new babies resembled a cross between ET and a bulldog. I'd never quite understood all the declarations of gorgeousness that surrounded them. But now I did. My wee bulldog was the most stunning sight I'd ever witnessed.

A wave of sadness washed over me. Mike was missing this. He'd missed the birth of his first child (at least, as far as I knew it was his first—he'd told me so many lies that it wouldn't surprise me if he'd fathered a football team). Now, he was missing every moment of his son's first day. Oh hell, more tears.

I heard footsteps approaching and the door to the room opened. I instinctively put my arms around the babe. A fascist nurse had been popping in throughout the night, trying to persuade me to put him in the cot at the end of the bed, but I had refused every time. Now that I had my son in my arms, I never wanted to let him go. It would be tough when he was going to school and I sewed the arm of my jumper to his backpack.

A massive bouquet of lilies popped round the door and I held my breath. Mike? Oh shite, would I hug him or kill him? My eyes were wide with fear when Carly's head appeared behind the flowers.

"Morning, Mum," she cooed, before planting a huge kiss on the babe.

"How did you get in?" I asked her, shocked but delighted that she was here. "I thought it was partners only outside official visiting hours."

"It is. But I thought you'd like company, so I told them we were a lesbian couple and that we'd had the baby via artificial insemination at a sperm bank. Hope you don't mind."

I laughed. I could hear the chatter of gossip from the nurses' station at the other end of the ward. This would keep them going until lunchtime.

Suddenly, a young nurse appeared with a vase. She was so busy trying to conceal her curiosity about the same-sex parents that she tried to replant my breast pump. Carly made it worse by holding my hand and saying, "Oh darling, I don't know if he looks more like you or the photograph of the sperm donor." Exit one purple-faced junior nurse. I swatted her hand. "That's no way for my son's other mummy to behave," I giggled.

She pulled up a chair, then lifted the baby and snuggled down with it, her face etched with joy, amazement and sadness all at the same time. Friends. It struck me how lucky I was. Carly was in a perpetual turmoil about her inability to get pregnant, yet her only concern was for me. I had the best friends. They'd climb mountains for me. Literally. I just hoped I never got stuck halfway up Everest, or there'd be an order at Jimmy Choo's within minutes for snow boots. Mike might not be here, but this baby would be surrounded by love always. Oh, more tears coming. Is this the way it would be from now on? Was I going to be the emotional equivalent of Bianca on *EastEnders*, snotting my way through every day?

"What are you going to call him?"

"I don't know," I sniffed. "Mike wanted to call him Michael."

Carly bit her lip, obviously not wanting to decry my son's father in his presence.

"Joshua," I announced. "I'm going to call him Joshua." I smiled. Carly smiled. And Joshua let out a contented sigh. He liked his new name.

*   *   *

I left hospital after three days amid a flurry of kisses and good wishes. The nurses had been fantastic. Even the fascist had warmed to me when she finally realised that the fight to separate my arms from my boy was one that she wasn't going to win. They didn't even bat an eyelid when Carly showed up to collect me in a man's suit and Doc Martens. She was taking the butch thing a bit far.

If I was truthful, I was terrified about going home. It was one thing dealing with the baby when there was a trained nurse only a few steps away, but quite another when I'd be at home alone. What if something went wrong? What if Josh was upset and I didn't know what was wrong with him? I was racked with panic as we drove back to my house. I squeezed Josh tightly. We'll be fine, I promised silently, for the millionth time.

The first thing I spotted as we turned into my street was a banner hanging from my window proclaiming "Welcome home, Joshua." Did I also mention that those great friends were incredibly tacky? But it made me scream with laughter. Standing guard at the front door were Kate, Carol and Sarah. They ushered us inside and I looked around in amazement. They'd transformed the place. In one corner was a beautiful swinging crib, decked in white silk and trimmed with blue lace. In another was a baby box filled with everything Josh would need for bathing and changing. And the whole room was filled with presents and balloons. But the biggest surprise was standing by the window, tears flowing down her face. My mum. The girls had flown her down from Scotland and she announced that she was staying for a couple of weeks to help. I fell into her arms. Although we'd never been especially close, I felt for the second time in three days like I'd won the Lottery. And Mrs. Doubtfire was here to help me spend it.

"The girls told me everything that's happened with that bastard," she whispered in her soft Scottish burr. I was shocked. I'd never heard her swear in her life. "Why didn't you tell us, Jess?"

"Oh, Mum, I'm sorry. I didn't know what to say. Everything is such a mess."

"Nonsense," she said softly, taking her grandson from my arms. "Everything is going to be fine, my darling. Just you wait and see." And I knew she was right. At least for now.

Josh was passed around so that all his new aunties could fuss over him. He was less than impressed and slept throughout the whole experience, waking only when he was hungry. With trepidation I whipped up my shirt, unhooked my nursing bra and latched him on. The pain shot right down to my toes, which were now curling and levitating off the floor. "Sorry Mum," I apologised for the expletives that automatically accompanied the pain, "but I swear this baby's first words are going to be, 'Oh for fuck's sake.' The poor wee thing hears that at every mealtime." My mum gave me a light thud on the back of the head. I wasn't too big to be scolded, she warned me.

I don't know what I'd have done without her. For the rest of the day, she made tea, took care of Josh, chatted to the girls and sent me for sleeps—all that with a duster in one hand and a broom in the other.

It was five o'clock when the phone rang and she answered it with a curt, "Latham residence." She'd obviously decided to completely ignore the fact that I was now married and my surname was Chapman. I stared at her for signs of distaste. Was it Mike? Had he called to say he was coming to see the baby? I knew that he was aware of the birth, because Kate had let slip that Bruce had bumped into him at a golf tournament the day before and told him about the arrival of his son. How should I react? On the one hand, I hated every ounce of him and never wanted to see his face again as long as I lived. But on the other . . . he *was* my baby's father.

"It's a Miss Dunhill." My lawyer.

I took the phone. "Hello."

Miss Dunhill didn't waste a second on pleasantries. I didn't mind. Her time was more expensive than Michael Jackson's.

She'd contacted Mike's lawyers to discuss the new developments, she explained. Mike had petitioned for an official separation order. Yes, he knew about the baby. No, he didn't want to pursue visitation rights at this point. Mr. Chapman was now involved in a new relationship. My world went black again. He *knew* that he had a son and he *didn't* want to see him? I couldn't believe it. Not only had he tossed me to one side, but now he was doing the same to his baby. Had he no heart? Was he *that* unfeeling? How on earth could I ever have been with this man and not realised that he was the biggest prick on the planet? He was a monster. I wanted to hug Josh tightly and protect him from this. He was only three days old and already he'd been rejected. Well, fuck Mike Chapman. This was war.

Miss D. was still reciting her update in a completely unemotional voice. Was she a robot? Mike had refused to agree to an interim payment for the baby. He was claiming that I'd been stalking him and therefore was refusing to co-operate any further. He might even wish for tests to confirm paternity. He'd see me in court. End of story.

At that point I dropped the phone. He was questioning that the baby was his? Oh, please, God, not that. Even Mike couldn't stoop that low. Please let me wake up from this nightmare.

The girls were all staring at me with concerned faces. What

was going on? I told them. Their hands flew to their mouths in horror and disbelief. Carol was the first to speak.

"That's it!" she spat in a furious tone. "We haven't got involved before now because we didn't know what you would want us to do, Jess, but it's gone too far. Mike Chapman has gone too far." All around the room, the others were nodding in agreement, their faces thunderous with rage. Mike Chapman would pay for this. And not just financially.

I still struggle to recall any event that took place during the two weeks that followed my heart being ripped out and torn to shreds. The pain of it all was just too searing to live with. So I didn't. It seemed like my whole body and brain shut down and I veered in a trance-like state from feeding Josh, to sleep, to feeding again. It devastates me that for the rest of my life I'll have little or no recollection of the first fortnight of my child's life. Add that to Mike Chapman's list of crimes and misdemeanours.

My mum was a godsend. Much as her gentle nagging to eat and shower irritated me, without her I'd have starved and smelled like a skip. It was a monumental effort even to get dressed in the morning. Mum must have been shocked at the change in her daughter, but she never said it out loud. When I'd left home all those years before, I was a strong, indestructible character, determined to conquer the world and leave my mark in history. And now look at me. I'd married a bastard, had no visible means of employment and resembled a bag lady. She must have been proud.

The nights were the worst. The pain of breast-feeding had now dulled to the level of walking on glass and I lay in bed every night unable to sleep, pouring my heart out to the baby

slumbering beside me. He'd either be a fully qualified psychia-
trist, or in desperate need of therapy by the time he could talk,
if I didn't stop burdening him with my problems. He was
already bearing a distinct resemblance to Woody Allen.

Josh was eighteen days old when I finally snapped out of it.
As we lay there one morning, his face damp with my tears that
were splashing down, his head turned to me and he smiled. I
know it was probably just wind, but in my diminished state, I
chose to believe that it was a genuine smile. Inside me something snapped. This couldn't go on any longer. Somewhere in
my crazed head, I realised that he needed his mum. He'd
already lost his daddy—the last thing he needed was a mother
who was incapable of functioning. I jumped out of bed and I
took my first voluntary bath. I even broke out and blowdried
my hair. It was time to stop wallowing. I'd had enough of self-
pity. They were erecting bunting on the street outside when I
also applied lipstick and mascara. When I descended the stairs,
my mum registered my appearance with surprise.

"You look nice today, love," she said with a smile.

"Thanks, Mum." She shrugged her shoulders in an "it's
nothing" gesture.

"No, Mum, I mean it. Thanks. For everything. I couldn't
have survived the last two weeks without you."

She gave me a hug. "Of course you could have, dear. You've always been strong, Jess, remember that. You can cope with anything life throws at you. You'd have managed fine without me—
you'd just have smelled really bad," she finished, as she picked up
a cup and bustled into the kitchen, her face pink with embarrassment. That was Mum. Walking down the street with her knickers
tucked into her skirt was less shaming than an outward show of
affection. Her generation didn't do the touchy feely thing.

I called Kate and detected the shock in her voice when she realised it was me. The girls had been constant visitors over the previous two weeks, even though my conversational ability had rivalled Barbie's.

I asked her to round up everyone who was free and invited myself for lunch. It was time Josh met all his adopted cousins.

The afternoon was mayhem. I'd forgotten that it was now school holidays. When Josh and I arrived, Kate's oldest two were swinging from the curtains and Tallulah was using the kitchen wall as target practice for a plate of spaghetti hoops. Carly came in right behind me, muttering obscenities about the editor who'd asked her to rewrite several sections of her novel. Carly was outraged—the parts she was referring to were completely autobiographical, yet the editor claimed they were too far-fetched. She'd obviously never lived in Cooperland.

Sarah appeared with Hannah and Ryan. After hugs all round, all children who could walk were dispatched to the garden, the wine was opened and lunch was served. For the first time in recent memory, I felt human again. I hadn't realised how much I'd missed everyday life. It was great to hear Carly launching into a diatribe of moans about the pressures of being an "artist." Even better to hear that Kate had finally got over her crush on Builder Bob. She'd confessed to Bruce that she felt the pilot light had gone out in their relationship and to her surprise he'd agreed. They'd decided to put more effort into their romance and he'd responded by being super-attentive and demanding mad, passionate sex at every opportunity. Now she was grinning like a pumpkin and walking with a limp. But she was happy.

Sarah was full of news about the imminent opening of Nick's restaurant. Bugger, it had completely slipped my mind.

It was next week and I had nothing to wear. I could feel a raid of Carol's fat wardrobe coming on—her old designer pregnancy clothes would still fit me perfectly. Carly informed me that Carol was on the Mothercare modelling shoot that day, so I'd have to call her later. This was such a breakthrough: lunch with the girls *and* making plans for a night out all in the one day. I was a new woman. A new mum, I reminded myself as Josh demanded his two o'clock feed.

We avoided the subject of Mike all day. I'd rather have talked about cervical smears than my husband. In fact, I'd rather have *had* a cervical smear. I was having fun for the first time in ages and I had no wish to depress myself.

It was six o'clock when I arrived home. I called to Mum.

"Up here, Jess," she answered.

I climbed the stairs, desperate to give her another hug. I had so much to thank her for. As I entered her room I stopped dead in my tracks. She was packing.

"What are you doing, Mum?" Dumb question, but I was having another reality denial.

She turned to me and I realised she was wearing the same expression on her face that she'd had on the day I left home and set off for London. It was time for her to go, she explained. I was fine now. She needed to get back to Dad. But she was only a phone call away and could be back in two hours if I felt I needed her again. I was distraught. I wanted to clutch on to her ankles and beg her not to leave. But I knew she was right. I had to get on with life and learn how to be Josh's mum on my own. Even the worst trapeze artist had to lose the safety net eventually.

To her mortification, I gave her another hug. Two in one day. She'd need a month of counselling to get over this.

"Thanks, Mum. I love you." Oh God, the "L" word—that was illegal in the West of Scotland—make that six months.

"You'll be fine, Jess. I'm really proud of you," she replied stutteringly, to my complete astonishment. This was the closest to full-scale emotion I'd ever known her to be. This was my mum's equivalent to a breakdown. Call the RAC. Call Oprah. She pulled herself up and wiped her eyes. Back in control. Breakdown averted.

As I watched her taxi leave for the airport, I squeezed Josh. It's just you and me now, babe. We're home alone. What would you like for dinner—one nipple or two?

CHAPTER 16

Why not
form an alliance with the enemy?

July 2001

On the evening before the launch of the new restaurant, my house looked like it had been bombed. Don't get me wrong—it was spotlessly clean, as I was now never without my baby wipes in one hand and my Dettox spray in the other. It was just that you couldn't see the pristine surfaces for the piles of clothes that covered them. How had my mother managed to keep the place so tidy and take care of us at the same time? It seemed like I had no sooner finished tidying up, than it was time to start all over again. Washing hung from every radiator, ironing was piled everywhere. In my pre-motherhood life, this disorganised environment would have brought me out in a rash.

Somehow, though, I sailed through it unperturbed. Josh was growing every day, he was happy and contented and I was still sane. Therefore, life was bliss. I refused to let anything trivial, such as the fact that I couldn't see my floor for clutter, get me down in any way. I consulted my eleventh list of the day for my next action. I was convinced that several thousand brain cells had slipped out with the placenta. How else could I explain that I kept finding my bras in the freezer, my shoes in the bath, I hadn't seen my handbag in days and I now needed to write everything down in lists otherwise I'd never remember what to do next? Did God automatically swap the power of logic for motherhood? I must write that on the list so I'll remember to ask him.

The doorbell rang. That would be Carol with my choice of fat clothes for tomorrow night. I checked Josh was still sleeping and dived to the door.

"Come in, watch your feet—you'll lose your shoes in the mess. How're you d——"

I stopped. Stunned. In front of me, were ten coat-hangers trailing various adaptations of the not-so-little black dress. Behind those, was Carol. Behind Carol was a massive bouquet of flowers. And behind the flowers was . . . Saffron. I recognised her from the stakeout and photos that Carol had dug out after we'd discovered that she was the fluff. I froze. Should I welcome her in or attack her with the coat-hangers?

Carol read my mind. "Hold on to your hat there, Tonto, we come in peace."

I didn't know what to do. This wasn't on any of my bloody lists. "Welcome husband's fluff into home in a charming and gracious manner." I silently stood to the side to let them enter. They fought their way through the debris.

"Time to send my cleaning lady round again, methinks," Carol observed. No shit, Sherlock. I was mortified. If I'd known the Yellow One was visiting, I'd have enlisted the services of Molly Maid and Helena Rubinstein. She was probably standing there thinking that no wonder Mike had gone elsewhere. I was more defensive than the Manchester United back line. The enemy was standing in my front room and my ammunition was lost under a pile of knickers on the couch. Oh, bollocks.

I surveyed Saffron from the perfectly conditioned follicles on her head (even that gave me a sore neck—she was the height of Michael Jordan) to her pedicured toes. I could see what Mike was attracted to: she was simply gorgeous. Her brunette hair flowed past her poised shoulders, her size eight bod was resplendent in a black vest and bootlegs with a gold chain around her non-existent hips. Her brown eyes were the size of chestnuts and you could file your nails on her cheekbones. There was no contest really. She was Cindy bloody Crawford and I was Roseanne Barr. Game, set and match to the supermodel.

Saffron hesitantly cleared her throat and pushed the flowers at me. "Em, hi, Jess. I know this is a bit weird, but Carol has told me everything and I thought we should talk."

My back was so far up I looked like a turtle and you could have cut the atmosphere with a chainsaw. "Why? It's a bit late to compare notes, don't you think?"

She shifted from Manolo Blahnik to Manolo Blahnik. I bet she didn't even have a sliver of hard skin on her feet. Cow.

Right on cue, Josh let out a yell and we all turned in the direction of the crib. Thank God, the cavalry was here. At least this would provide a distraction till I composed myself, although in my present state that would take about a fortnight. I gently lifted him and snuggled him into my chest. I just hoped he wasn't hungry. There was no way the saggy ones were coming out in front of Saffron.

"Can I hold him?" she asked hesitantly. Oh sure. And while you're at it, here's a stake to ram through my chest. Why didn't she just go away? What had Carol been *thinking* about in bringing her here without warning? I was torn between acting like a civilised adult or reverting to pettiness and telling her to piss off. The mature genes won. After all, she may have run off with my husband, but there was no way she would abscond with my son too. And anyway, I'd bolted the front door—her escape routes were blocked. I glanced at Carol for moral support but she was still surveying the untidiness in distaste. She never could concentrate on more than one thing at a time.

I reluctantly handed Josh over to Saffron and she instantly cooed at him. Don't be taken in by her, Josh, I telepathically told him, she's the Anti-Christ. But he wasn't listening. He nestled cosily into her arms. Traitor.

"He looks so much like Mike," she exclaimed in wonderment. I nodded my head. Much as I hated to admit it, she was right. There was no mistaking who Josh took after in the looks department. I just hoped he had someone else's morals.

She stroked Josh's face, murmuring soothing noises, then lifted her head again. There was a distinct shine in the eyeball vicinity. What the hell did she have to cry about? Had she broken a nail?

"I'm so sorry, Jess. I know you must hate me. I would. Hate me, I mean. But I had no idea. I honestly knew nothing about this. I think he lied to me too."

Nooooo! Don't do this! my head screamed. Don't make me feel sorry for you. Don't make me like you. I was much happier when I hated your guts.

But sympathy was rising. She looked so bereft. And genuine. But then, I'd thought Mike was honest and had integrity, so what does that say about my character-judging skills?

Carol finally spoke up. "Come on, Jess, at least listen to what she has to say. There're two sides to every poem."

She was right, I realised. It must have taken a lot of courage for Saffron to darken my door. I had nothing to lose by talking to her. And who knows? I might discover she had some fatal flaw in her character that would make her not quite so perfect after all.

The thought cheered me. "I'll go put the kettle on. Have a seat if you can clear a space."

I returned carrying a tray with three mugs of coffee and a plate of Wagon Wheels. I was being petty again. I knew that in line with her profession she couldn't eat chocolate, but I wanted to waft them under her nose and watch the temptation make her squirm. No such joy.

"My favourites!" she exclaimed, as she dived in head first, and was picking chocolate off her chin before I'd even put the plate down. I hated her again. But I knew when I was beaten.

"Right, Saffron, if you want to compare notes, let's go for it. I want facts and figures and complete honesty. And I reserve the right to kill you if I don't like anything you say." It gave me a small sense of achievement to take control.

She smiled. "Yes, miss," she agreed reverently. Carol surreptitiously departed to the kitchen. She'd always hated the sight of blood.

"OK," I continued. "For the purposes of this discussion, Mike Chapman, my distinguished husband, will hereafter be referred to as 'the prick.' Any objections?"

Saffron agreed with a smile. She was even more gorgeous when she did that. "None."

"Right then. When did you start seeing the prick?"

"December 1999." That was a shock for starters. She'd been seeing Mike longer than I had. She went on to tell me how they'd met. It was at his newspaper's Christmas party. He spotted her at the bar and bought her a glass of champagne. Flash bastard. The most I ever got was a bottle of Lambrusco and a pizza.

Mike had showered her with flowers the next morning. No wonder the man didn't own his own house—he must spend his whole salary on floral arrangements. That evening, he'd turned up at her house with a meal and four videos: *Pretty Woman*, *Sleepless in Seattle* . . .

"*Top Gun* and *An Officer and a Gentleman*," I finished the sentence for her.

"How do you know that?" She was amazed.

"Call me psychic. Carry on," I urged.

They were an item from that night. It had never been an all-consuming relationship as she travelled so much, but whenever she was in town they'd hook up. That explained all those late working nights he claimed to have to endure. And how he had time to practise the very same seduction techniques on me. Zero out of ten for originality, Mr. Chapman. They'd continued to see each other over the following year, apart from a break in the summer when she was temporarily reunited with her Formula One racing driver ex-fiancé.

My heart sank. "Was that around July?" I asked her, not really wanting to know the answer.

She nodded her head. "How did you know?"

"That's when we got married. July 2000. On the way to New York." She bit her lip.

"I knew about New York. He told me he was going there on a boys' holiday, with a few old schoolfriends."

It was all becoming clearer than jet-washed crystal. Saffron had blown Mike off in favour of her ex, and his ego had crash-landed. His warped mind had then decided to repair the damage by leading unsuspecting me up the aeroplane aisle and having me declare undying love for him. Bastard! I was reporting him to Richard Branson. He'd never fly the Virgin skies again.

Saffie's (we were on nickname terms by now) dalliance with her ex had blown over after a couple of months and she and the prick resumed their fling.

"Did you never wonder why he didn't take you back to his house, Saffie?"

She shook her head. "He told me that he lived with his widowed sister and her kids. He said that he liked to be close to them to make sure that they were OK, and that the lack of privacy didn't bother him because the *Echo* paid for him to stay in hotels whenever he wanted to be in the city."

This was getting worse by the sentence. "Saffie, Mike, sorry, the prick, is an only child."

She gasped in amazement and horror. As Carol would say, the pound had dropped. Both of our relationships with the big P had been based on a concoction of lies and deceit. Saffron's face was still frozen in shock. Mine was just wrinkled in resignation. It was all so ludicrous. Outrageous. How could two adult, intelligent females have been so duped?

We moved on to the rest of the year 2000 and a second batch of Wagon Wheels. Mike had returned from our honeymoon and they'd kissed and made up after her reunion with her ex had hit the crash barriers. Between her modelling trips, they'd continued their affair until October, when a conversation about children had caused a huge bust-up. Apparently they'd attended the christening of a friend of Saffie's new baby, when Mike had asked her if she ever visualised having a family. He was astounded when she declared that she'd never wanted kids. Exit one model, enter one fertile stunt double. That was the very month that Mike had decided he wanted us to start a family. My stomach was churning like a tumble drier. Had I really just been his second resort for everything in his life? Was I like the old sweatshirt that you wore around the house because you didn't want to wear out your good ones? This was sick. And yet I still wanted to hear more.

"Tell me about last Christmas," I probed. Carol had come in with refills for the coffee, but when she heard the question she put her head in her Marigolds and returned to the kitchen.

Saffron thought for a moment, then had a flash of realisation. "I remember. I met him briefly on Christmas Eve. He was a bit grumpy because he'd broken his leg at a cross-country speedway race . . ."

"He fell in the shower."

"And he couldn't come to a party I was having on Christmas Day because he was working at a homeless shelter . . ."

"He was here with me, announcing that I was pregnant." It was too much. In spite of my determination not to make myself look even more unattractive in front of Miss Gorgeous, my bottom lip began to tremble.

She flew over and put her arms around me. "Oh, Jess, I'm so sorry. I can't believe I did this to you."

I waved away her apology. "It wasn't you, Saffron. It was him. Keep going." Like a horror film that I couldn't switch off even after the fourteenth slaughter of an innocent victim, I needed to hear the whole story.

During the whole of my pregnancy, they'd been together. When I was suspicious that he was seeing someone else and he'd blamed paranoia and hormones, he'd been in a full-blown romance with Saffie.

"Valentine's Night?"

"He sent me flowers. Then we went to Quaglino's for dinner. But he had to leave fairly early, because he had a big story to work on the following day." I would never listen to Barry White again. He was officially sacked.

"Was there a cross-dressing MP?" I had to know if there was even a shred of truth in his alibi.

Saffron giggled and nodded her head. "That did happen, but that was a few weeks before. I told Mike some gossip about Jeremy Brown and his liking for frillies."

Was there no end to this? Jeremy was the MP for my constituency—I'd even bloody voted for him in the last election.

I racked my brain for further episodes. "Lunch at The Ivy on the fifteenth of March?"

She thought for a minute. "Can't remember, hold on." She rummaged in her Gucci handbag and pulled out her diary, flicking furiously through the pages. She shook her head. "Nope, not guilty. I was in New York that weekend, so that wasn't me. But I do remember him calling me on that morning. He told me it was his sister's birthday and he was taking her out for the day. She's a single parent, so she doesn't get out much."

We stared at each other in mutual realisation. It wasn't me. It wasn't her. There was no sister. Bloody hell, he had someone else too. Where did he get the energy? He must be on Viagra.

Suddenly, I had an uncontrollable urge. My shoulders started to shake and the corners of my mouth crept up. This whole scene had just graduated from the ridiculous to the unbelievably bizarre and like the night of the stakeout I had a compelling need to laugh. I fought to control myself, but it was no use. Saffron came over to me again, anticipating a breakdown and ready to mop up more tears. Her face was a picture of confusion when the first snort escaped me.

"Jess?" But I was gone. The hysteria was uncontrollable. And contagious. Within seconds, we were both shrieking with giggles. Carol dived in, clutching a broom (there was a once in a lifetime Kodak moment), but stopped short when she saw that we were laughing.

"Oh, thank Christ. I heard the screams and I thought you were killing each other—I was coming to split you up. What's the joke?"

"There's. Someone. Else," I managed to stutter through the mirth. Saffron was still bent double next to me.

"You're kidding!" Carol exclaimed, clutching a Marigold to her forehead. "The man's a maniac!"

Saffie eventually regained the power of speech. "It does explain some things, though. When I came back from New York, he broke things off. He said he couldn't live with the thought that I'd never want children. But it only lasted a week or so and then he called me again and said he'd changed his mind."

"Nope, that was me. That was when he was being Mr. Super Husband." I explained about the fall, Mike's four-hour, twenty-mile dash to the hospital and how I'd found the receipt for the lunch the following week and duly evicted him. That was when he'd returned to Saffron. I wondered what happened to his mystery lunch date. Hopefully she gave him crabs and he never saw her again.

"The bastard!" she gasped. Then, "And here was me thinking it was my good looks and charm that brought him back," she added with a chuckle. I was *so* beginning to like her. She was taking all this with the attitude that it demanded. She refused to allow Mike's behaviour to reduce her self-esteem to the size of an atom. I decided to take a leaf out of her book. I would not let him beat me.

"So what's happened since?" I asked.

She and Mike were still together. There *was* a minor blip last month, when a very fat refugee and a mad flasher in a leopard-skin bra accosted them, but Mike explained that we were two crazies who'd been stalking him ever since he wrote a story claiming we should be deported back to our country of origin. She'd believed every word. She'd carried on seeing him right up until that afternoon when she'd bumped into Carol at a studio and Carol had confronted her.

"Well, I can tell you where I want to stick this broom," Carol said forcefully.

"No, that's not enough," I contradicted. Mike Chapman had single-handedly trashed two and a half of the three and a half people in this room. He wasn't going to get away with this. This time he'd bitten off more than an adder could swallow. "We need a plan," I declared.

"What do you want me to do?" Saffron asked. I paused. I had absolutely no idea. I needed to write a list and see if anything came to me in a flash of inspiration. But I did know that we needed to keep the target in our sights.

A telephone started to ring. Saffron dived back into her bag and read the number on the screen. "Oh, fuck, it's him. It's the prick. What do I do?" she asked desperately.

"Act like nothing's happened," I answered quickly.

She pressed the receive button. "Hi baby," she cooed, while making vomit gestures with her fingers. Who said models couldn't act? She gave a faultless performance as she promised to meet him the next night, then signed off with, "And I adore you too, baby." "Yuk!!" she screeched as she hung up then threw her phone behind the sofa in disgust. "Why do you want me to keep seeing him? Are you mad?"

"Look, Saffron, what's the point of concocting a plan of attack if we don't know where he is to execute it? Or execute him. It won't be for long, I promise. It'll only be for a couple of weeks at most. We'll come up with something soon. Think of it as drama practice."

"I'm not having sex with him," she vowed. "It would turn my stomach. Oh, God, I'm going to have to claim the longest-lasting menstrual period in history."

Carol and I smiled, the noise of our active brains drowning out Saffie's moans. We had the target. We had the conspirators. Now we just needed a plan.

I went through four of Carol's dresses the next night, before I even managed to get out of the door. Joshua was sick on two of them, peed on another and an unfortunate accident with my breast pump took care of the fourth. Leaving home now required more strategic planning than a military coup.

On top of that, I was racked with guilt at leaving Joshua for the first time. I tried to reason with myself. I *was* leaving him at Kate's, where Bruce's mother (no stranger to little people—she'd had seven children of her own) was looking after Kate's three too. I was also leaving enough expressed milk to nourish three calves for a week, a suitcase of clothes, nappies and a first-aid kit. I'd leave the phone number of the restaurant, I had my mobile phone with me and a pager as back-up in case there was no signal in that area. I did everything short of installing a microchip in my shoe that was connected to a satellite radar and a panic button. Maybe I should invest in one of those for next time.

I arrived at Kate's in a flurry of activity twenty minutes later. The whole gang was there, but something was amiss—they were still in their jeans and T-shirts, slugging Lambrusco and eating chicken sandwiches.

"Oh, bugger, I've got the wrong night. I don't believe it. When's the launch? Is it tomorrow?"

Kate laughed. "Don't panic, you've got the right night. I just remember what it's like trying to get ready with a new baby, so I told you to be here an hour earlier than necessary. Now, give the baby to Betty and get yourself a glass."

"But I'm all ready," I objected.

Carly spoke up. "Jess, did you iron that dress?"

"Em, no." So the scarlet strappy number was a bit crushed, but I'd had a baby to organise.

"Have you done your hair?" she continued.

Good point. It was tied up with the elastic band that was normally used to keep my cornflake packet sealed.

"And have you even threatened your face with the sight of cosmetics?"

"Carly, I don't have time for make-up. I don't even know where my make-up bag was last seen."

She held up her hands. "Our point exactly. Now get your kit off, get this robe on and pour yourself a drink. We're going to make you over until you bear some kind of resemblance to the sex goddess that we used to know and love."

What use was there in objecting? It was so long since I'd been pampered that I thought foundation was what went under bricks when a house was being built.

Betty prised Josh from my arms. "I'll take care of this little one, won't I, sweetheart?" she murmured to him. "Oh look, he's smiling at me."

"It's just wind," I snapped. The others laughed and after my indignant moment, I joined in. I supposed I could do with loosening up a notch or two. I simultaneously reached for the Lambrusco and unzipped my dress. I was a mother—I could multi-task. I caught Carol's eye. "Have you filled the others in on what happened last night?"

She shook her head. "I thought I'd let it come straight from the donkey's mouth."

I took a large slug of vino. "Right then, girls, you work and I'll talk. You'll never believe the latest episode."

I recounted the story of Saffron's visit as Kate attacked me with a hot brush, Carol worked on my face, Carly ironed my dress and Sarah gave me a manicure and pedicure. It was bad timing. I ended up with three hotbrush burns to the neck, a trail of nail varnish that reached to my ankle and an "only visible in daylight" singe on my frock, caused by outrage and astonishment at various points in the story. By the end of the hour, I was unrecognisable as the harassed mother who'd entered and the others were in a state of shock.

"Incredible. Bloody incredible. This will make a fantastic plot for the next book—I couldn't have *dreamt* it up," Carly spluttered.

"So we need a plan, girls. Any suggestions?"

"A hitman sounds like a good bet to me," Carly declared.

"Too messy. Not to mention illegal. I don't want Josh to be visiting me in prison for the rest of his childhood." The others muttered in agreement.

"Why not get Saffie to lead him on then dump him like a stone? Let him see how it feels to be devastated." That was Sarah's suggestion.

"Because, knowing Mike, he's probably got someone else on stand-by already. I honestly don't think he has a heart to be broken." More sounds of concurrence.

"I've got it!" Carly yelled triumphantly. "Why not set him up with a false story for his front page, so that he then gets sued, loses his job and lives the rest of his life in destitution." She grinned like she'd just won the biggest teddy bear at the fair.

"I'd thought about that one, but I definitely *don't* want him to lose his job. You see, I also want to hit him where it hurts and with Mr. Materialistic Mike, that's his wallet. I want him to pay child support for Josh and if he's got no career then I'll get no dosh."

"Mmm. You'd be cutting off your nose to spite your ears," Carol agreed.

Kate interjected. "So we can't destroy his love life, his career or his financial status. What's left?"

"My quandary exactly. But there must be *something* we can do—we can't let him get away with this. I know it's incredibly shallow, but I want revenge. Big time. The only question is how?"

There was silence in the room as we each pondered the problem. We'd come up with something, I was sure. We always did.

As we entered the restaurant, I held my head up high. I might not quite be in Carol or Saffron's league, but if I did say so myself, I scrubbed up pretty well. Kate had piled my hair on top of my head, with tendrils framing my expertly made-up face. It was bloody amazing what make-up could do—I'd even redis-covered my cheekbones. I realised that it was the first time in almost a year that I'd actually felt anything even approaching sexy and desirable. I made a mental note to control myself or I might actually start to look at men again.

The restaurant was fabulous. Nick had managed to achieve a

balance between the rugged interior of a Scottish castle (lots of stone, beams and roaring fireplaces) and the elegance of a stately home. It felt so grand. And I was there. Without a baby strapped to my chest. The gathering was an eclectic mix of London's "in-crowd" (although a tad too many half-naked girls for my liking—didn't they ever get cold?), minor aristocrats, politicians, journalists and celebrities. Oh, and Sean Connery, Ewan McGregor and Billy Connolly. Unfortunately, I got caught trying to switch name cards so that I'd be on their table. Only intervention from the owner saved me from being ejected by a large man in a kilt.

For a dreadful moment, I wondered if Basil or Mike would be there, but then I relaxed—there was no way that Nick would have invited either of them. I took a glass of champagne from a passing waiter. Nothing was going to spoil tonight. Nothing.

We took our places at our table when summoned, Carol on my left and Sarah on my right. Nick had warned her that he wouldn't be able to spend any time with her because he'd be too busy with the formalities, but he'd promised to make it up to her with a week in Barbados. Oh, the deprivation! Somehow, she was struggling through.

The meal was sumptuous. The conversation, as always, was hilarious. We grilled Cal, Mark and Bruce for ideas for the "Get Mike" campaign, but they were useless. Burning his boxer shorts and smashing the remote control for the telly just didn't go far enough. Men have no imagination.

We were sipping our coffees and munching on tiny Scottish tablet squares when Carol kicked me under the table. What? Did I have crumbs on my chin? I looked at her quizzically.

"Diet Coke man approaching," she whispered out of the corner of her mouth.

I followed her eyeline. Wow! This wasn't the Diet Coke guy, it was an early forties Brad bloody Pitt! He was well over six foot tall, with shoulders the width of the Humber Bridge. His blond hair flopped forward in that "just ran his fingers through it after a shower" way, his green eyes were surrounded by lines that said he laughed a lot and his smile had a definite 100-watt glow. And he was heading for our table. Kate suddenly became engrossed in her espresso as Brad shook hands with Bruce and Mark and then said a collective, friendly "Hi everyone" to the rest of us. While he crouched down to chat to Bruce, I leaned back over to Carol.

"That's Builder Bob? What's he doing here?" I asked.

"Nick's builders let him down a couple of weeks ago—flu epidemic or some other lame excuse—so since Bruce was the architect for this place, he asked his friendly neighbourhood builder to step in. Keith's boys finished the place off in record time to meet the opening night deadline. Nick is eternally grateful and Keith's now all the guys' new best friend. They'll be discussing Anna Kournikova any minute now."

I glanced at Kate. She was chatting to Carly and trying her best to pretend that nothing was amiss, despite the fact that she'd downed her espresso in one gulp and was now shaking like an electric whisk.

I could understand the attraction. "Christ, no wonder Kate's anatomy developed a mind of its own when he was around," I muttered to myself. Only I didn't. Carol heard me.

"Good grief, Jess, did I just hear you say something positive about a member of the male species?"

I turned to her in alarm. "No you bloody didn't. I hate all men. Even the ones that come in nice packaging," I whispered bitterly. I had to admit he was certainly an attractive package, but then, so was Tom Cruise and he left Nicole Kidman devastated. They were all bastards.

Keith stretched back up and scanned the table as he said goodbye. To my horror, his eyes stopped at me. "Sorry," he said as he reached over, his hand outstretched, "I know everyone else, but I don't think we've met."

My face turned the colour of my dress. "Jess. Jess Latham," I haltingly replied as I shook his hand. I was astonished with myself—since when had I reverted to my maiden name? Had my hormones just kidnapped my brain? Bloody behave yourself, I silently warned them, we're in enemy territory.

"Keith Miller. Pleased to meet you," he replied with a smile. He turned his attention back to the group. "Well, I hope you all enjoy yourselves. And don't forget to enthuse wildly about how great the restaurant looks—my ego will love it." Everyone laughed except me. He might think he was being funny, charming and self-effacing, but I knew differently. He had a penis, therefore he was an anti-female terrorist in a tux. All men (present company seated at the table, my dad and Joshua excepted) were to be avoided and possibly shot on sight. They should be held in detention camps and only let out in the presence of their mothers. Not that my viewpoint was bitter, twisted, or extreme in any way whatsoever. I mentally shook myself back to my happy, I'm having a great night out, frame of mind. No man would spoil anything for me ever again.

After dinner, Nick gave a short speech to thank everyone for coming and was rewarded with a standing ovation. The restaurant would be an overwhelming success—it was a certainty. The band took their places and the ceilidh began. We were first on the floor. All those years of school dance lessons weren't to be wasted as we whooped, wheeched and flung

around the floor. After twenty minutes, I was weak at the knees
and requiring oxygen. I excused myself and headed for the
ladies. I didn't need to pee; I just wanted somewhere cool to sit
for five minutes.

It was a bad choice. The toilets were more crowded than Top
Shop on a Saturday. As I joined the queue, I decided that the
bladder must be prone to psychosomatic tendencies because I
suddenly needed to get to the loo urgently. The line moved
slower than a funeral procession. What were they doing in those
cubicles? Having a sleep?

I tried counting to a hundred backwards. Nope, didn't take
my mind off my urge. After a few more minutes, I was having
difficulty moving, because my legs were crossed in four places.
One of Carol's dresses had already been peed on and I'd never
explain the same fate befalling another.

Finally I reached the front of the queue. Almost there, bladder, almost there. I stared at the four doors, willing them to
open. When the first one did, I dived at it, almost knocking
over the unsuspecting female trying to make a dignified exit.

"Ooops, sorry," I blurted, as I pushed her out of the way,
scrambled inside and assumed the position. Phew. Just in time.
Wait a minute. My brain frantically tried to register an event
that it had overlooked in its haste to the porcelain bowl. The
female I'd just assaulted . . . I stood up and fixed my clothing.
There was something about her. I reached for the door. Something familiar. I unbolted the lock and opened . . .

"Good evening, Miss Latham."

She was standing facing me, dressed in a stunning red sheath
(Bulgari, I was sure), looking even more glamorous than I
remembered and wearing the look that cobras assumed right
before they killed you.

"Good evening, Miranda."

Go on, bite me. Put me out of my misery. I held my head high and strutted past her to the wash-hand basins. She followed me. The reptile had me in its sights and was moving in for the kill.

"I was hoping I'd bump into you here tonight. I'd like to speak with you, my dear." Oh no, same tone of voice my mother used when she discovered my first packet of contraceptive pills.

"What is it, Miranda? Surely we're past the recriminations and insults stage."

"Quite, dear. But I've a small proposition that I'd like your help with. I really think that in view of the fact that you destroyed my marriage, the least you could do is listen to me."

There was a sudden gust of wind, as every head in the room sensed a drama and swished in our direction. I could tell which females read daily newspapers—they were the ones who had lightbulbs flashing above their heads as they recognised the protagonists in the last major political scandal. Wife and mistress in the same room. Both dressed in red. If it came to violence, how would they tell us apart? They'd be selling tickets at the door within minutes. I sighed. Bloody fantastic. I get one night out in a year and I'm a topic of titillation once again.

"OK, Miranda, but not here." Twenty faces fell as I took her by the arm and ushered her into the corridor. I spotted a door with a "Staff Only" sign. Perfect. I pulled her into the closet and fumbled for the light. Eventually I found it and flicked it on. We both burst out laughing at the same time. We were about to have a conversation surrounded by six mops, four Hoovers and enough loo rolls to keep a puppy running for weeks.

"Welcome to my office. Pull up a case and have a seat."

Miranda laughed again. "You are quite amusing, dear. I can see what Basil was attracted to."

Was that a dig? Was she saying that he obviously wasn't attracted to my looks or my brains, just my ability to throw out the odd one-liner? Or was I being paranoid?

"Well, Miranda, you have my attention. What can I do for you?"

She took a deep breath, her posture one of someone who would rather be in a hostage situation than sitting here with me. Shallow as I am, I took small comfort from that. Basil, she explained, was proving to be highly inconvenient to her. Despite all that had happened and the fact that she was happily ensconced with the French rugby team's right hooker, he was refusing to grant her a divorce. It seemed that he was clutching like a man hanging from a cliff to their marital status, in order not to lose credibility, connections and, most importantly, her bank balance.

"So what does that have to do with me?" I asked, confused as ever. If only I hadn't had that last glass of champers.

"Well, to be honest, dear, much as it sticks in my throat, I'm asking for your help. You see, the only thing that will force Basil to the divorce courts would be the threat of another scandal, and since you have previous history in that department, I thought you'd be the perfect person to create the scandal."

I couldn't believe my ears. Was she serious? Did she really think I'd reduce myself to tabloid fodder once again, just to let her get into a legal scrum with Henri the Hooker? "What exactly would you want me to do, Miranda?"

She thought for a moment. "I hadn't exactly worked out the details yet, but maybe a new photograph of you with my husband leaked to the tabloids would be, let's just say, *opportune*."

Now I knew she was mad. What on earth would possess me to see Basil again? Why would I help her? It's not as if I destroyed her marrige. Well, OK, I did. But that was ancient history. I'd rather have my toenails pulled out one by one than see the MP, much less be photographed with him.

But then I had a vision. Not the religious variety, but one of conscience. A picture of Saffron came into my head. I had to admire the way she had handled our situation. There was no hysteria, no dramatics, just a true sense of what was right and wrong and a desire to see justice served on an extra-large platter. She was one of the girls. Was that how I had acted to Miranda? Hardly. It was no use trying to justify my affair with Basil by saying that he told me his marriage was over, because that was the oldest cliché in the book and I should have seen right through him. No, I was a disgrace. And here was my opportunity to make amends. Fuck it, why not? I *would* help her.

"I agree. Miranda, you've got a deal. I'm not having a picture of me plastered all over the dailies, but I'll think of something. One way or another we'll force him into submission." I shook her hand. Yet again, I needed a plan. I had a feeling that I was going to suffer the mother of all headaches the next day and it wouldn't just be because of the hangover I planned to have.

Miranda and I exchanged numbers and agreed to meet at the same place—the restaurant, that is, not the store cupboard—two weeks later (it would take me that long to get over the guilt of leaving Josh for another night), to discuss tactics. I promised that by that time I'd have a plan of action organised. Unlikely—there was more chance of me marrying Basil—but I was carried away with enthusiasm. There was nothing else for it: I needed a conference.

I strutted back to the table, the adrenalin charging through me like a tornado. Oh, the excitement. The intrigue. This was better than a night in with every Bruce Willis movie. At least here the ending was unpredictable.

"Where have you been? We were about to round up a posse and come searching for you," Carly drawled drunkenly.

"In a cupboard with Miranda. It's a long story. But I'm calling an emergency summit. Here, two weeks from tonight, no excuses for absenteeism."

Carly laughed, her face a picture of puzzlement. "Not even a note from my mother saying I've got a runny tummy?" she giggled, using the same excuse that had got us out of games all through high school.

"Nope, not even that."

"Ooooh, fantastic." She rubbed her palms together. Well, she tried to, but her co-ordination was off and she only succeeded in flagging down two passing waiters.

"Yes, madam?" they asked simultaneously. She was startled, but quickly rallied and downed what was left of her wine.

"Another bottle, please, chaps. In fact, make it two. We're celebrating." They nodded and departed.

"What are we celebrating, Cooper? I mean, apart from the opening night of Nick's new place?"

"You. We're celebrating the fact that for the first time in months you look like you're glad to be here. You're scheming. You're plotting. You're our old Jess again. Welcome back, sweetie."

I was so touched. Right up to the point when she leaned over to give me a cuddle and missed. She landed arse first on the floor. Luckily, everyone else was enjoying themselves too much to notice.

But she was right, I thought as I caught Miranda's eye across the room and winked at her. I was back. And it felt fantastic. Until ten seconds later . . .

"Excuse me, Jess. I was wondering, would you like to dance?"

Who knew that builders could do the Highland fling?

CHAPTER 17

Why not call in reinforcements?

August 2001

It was like the Last Supper, only with fewer people and more breasts, I thought as we all sat around the table a fortnight later. I had the feeling of impending doom. I had thought of nothing but revenge for the last fourteen days and had come up with precisely, well, nothing. Nada. Zero. If I was a nation, the war would be lost and I'd be strolling across no-man's-land pretending my white bra was a surrender flag.

I scanned the faces for inspiration, but the others were equally downcast. Carly, Kate, Sarah (looking sun-kissed after her week in Barbados) and Carol had been subjected to interminable nightly phone calls to discuss my bizarre ideas, but each plan had more holes than a colander. It was so difficult. Given the circumstances, how could we sort out not just one, but two errant men?

I felt sorriest for Saffron. Her face was etched with the stress of continuing her relationship with Mike, when really all she wanted to do was eat him for breakfast. With a croissant on the side. She'd confessed on the way there that she'd run out of excuses to avoid sex. There was the time of the month that dragged on for a week. Then the imaginary case of thrush, followed by two days of cystitis. Eventually, in desperation, she had blurted out that she had become celibate due to the suspicion that she might have contracted a sexually transmitted disease and claimed she wanted to wait for test results before resuming carnal activity. She had, of course, pleaded fidelity and accused him of giving it to her. It spoke volumes that instead of outright denial, he rushed to the nearest clinic the next morning. He'd been given the all-clear and she'd had to say that she'd been given the same verdict.

"I don't think I can keep this up for much longer, Jess, he's driving me nuts. I can't bear him even to touch me." She shuddered involuntarily.

"Just think of yourself as being undercover. You're our equivalent of the SAS."

"You mean Stupid Arse Saffie?" At least she hadn't lost her sense of humour.

I sat directly across from Miranda. She seemed mildly uncomfortable, surrounded as she was by a group of women she'd never met before (other than briefly in a hotel swimming pool in St. Andrews), but who already knew the intimacies of her life.

After ordering our drinks, I made the introductions. Her eyebrow shot through her hairline when I told her Saffie was my husband's girlfriend. The irony wasn't lost on me either. Do unto others . . .

The waiter returned with our wine and requested our dinner order. Didn't he realise that this was no time for trivialities such as nourishment? We went for seven of the daily specials. If there's a God it won't be haggis, I prayed.

I decided to chair the meeting. "Let's get this underway. Ladies, we have a two-pronged dilemma. Problem number one. Pathetic as it is, I won't sleep at night until suitable retribution has been attained for the fact that my husband has annihilated my life as I knew it and is now treating my son and me with complete disdain. The constraints are as follows: we can't damage his employment status or his wallet. Problem number two. Miranda wishes to attain a divorce from Basil and we need to encourage him to agree. No constraints on that one, other than I don't want it to involve my face on the front pages."

Everyone was listening with ferocious concentration, which was broken by the waiter returning. The service was swift. Seven plates of haggis were placed before us. It wasn't a good omen.

"Any ideas?" I said as I pushed my plate away.

The haggis made more noise than the diners. Six blank faces stared back at me. After an interminable silence, Carly spoke up. Fantastic. I knew she wouldn't let me down. Wrong.

"How about we plant a rumour that Mike and Basil are having a tempestuous affair? We could have that round London in no time."

"And that would achieve what?" I enquired, not comprehending her train of thought.

She hesitated. "Well, nothing. But it would be fun to do."

Miranda looked less than impressed. She'd have had more success if she just hired a hitman and had Basil bumped off.

"What about using the internet?" Sarah spoke up.

Finally we were getting somewhere. "To do what?"

"Well, we could put on a diary of Mike's history, sort of a Bridget Jones, but real life and then e-mail it to everyone we know. We could do the same for Basil. The embarrassment of having their personal lives firing through cyberspace might be enough to make them realise the error of their ways."

Six of us pondered the thought. Carol was pondering her reflection in the mirror behind me. Goodbye weight problem, hello again vanity.

I shook my head. "Good suggestion, Sarah, but it could backfire. Chances are Mike would become a male icon as some kind of super-stud and Basil would want to refute the claims so much that he'd never let Miranda go."

Another plan bit the haggis. This was getting desperate.

"We need some kind of scandal. Something that would embarrass them both into agreeing to whatever we demanded. What would hit the headlines in a big way?" Kate wondered out loud.

"They were both born women and had a penchant for pink frillies," Carly giggled.

I almost swatted her with my napkin. This was no time for joking. I stopped, hand in mid-air. Wait a minute. I had a seedling of inspiration.

"Saffie, why has Mike never used the story about Jeremy Brown being a cross-dresser?"

"Because he couldn't get photographic proof. Jeremy is more cautious than royalty when it comes to airing his fetishes in public."

"Carly, is Joe in this country at the moment?" I was referring to Joe Cain, Carly's ex-boyfriend, who had discovered after their separation that he preferred the gay lifestyle and had gone on to open a European chain of gay clubs called JC's Heaven.

He and Carly were still the best of friends. Was it any wonder she had enough material for a novel? She could write a trilogy based on her past alone.

The seedling was growing. It was now bordering on a sapling. But could I make it into a triffid?

"No, I spoke to him in Amsterdam yesterday, but he'll be back tomorrow."

"Fantastic," I enthused. Six mystified females teetered on the edge of their seats.

I slapped my napkin on the table. "I think I've got it! It'll take some work, but I've got it!" I shouted.

Carly was so excited that she missed her mouth with her fork and splattered Kate with haggis. Kate was so engrossed, she didn't even notice.

I sat back in my chair. "All right, listen up, ladies, this is what we need to do."

At eleven o'clock the following morning, after seven attempts that were aborted by cold feet and the slamming down of the receiver, I called Basil's private number. No answer. In a way, I was relieved. Maybe I didn't have the courage for this whole scheme after all. The night before, I'd been fuelled with adrenalin (now I knew why Mike was so addicted to excitement—the rush was incredible), but now I was a founder member of Cowards Anonymous. Maybe I should just forget how to even spell "revenge" and go back to my haven of blissful motherhood, domestic chaos and daytime telly.

I was halfway to replacing the receiver when he answered. Bugger.

"Asquith speaking." That voice: more confident than Prince Naseem and more smug than Jeffrey Archer. Before he landed in the slammer. Resolve flooded through me again. I'd forgotten how much I disliked him.

"Good afternoon, Mr. Asquith. This is your former mistress speaking," I purred in my most seductive tone. I hoped it sounded OK. I was well out of practice—how seductive do you have to be to buy Pampers in Tesco?

There was a long pause, then "Jess?" How many other past mistresses did he have? Cancel that question. I probably didn't want to hear the answer.

I confirmed my identity, then launched into my well-rehearsed spiel. I needed his help, I proclaimed. You see, I hadn't been sleeping well lately, because I just couldn't get him out of my mind. I missed him so much (I could hear his ego inflating and chest puffing out as I rambled). I missed his voice, his touch. I had to know, were he and Miranda still together? Was there a chance that we could see each other again? Just one more time, baby. I couldn't stop thinking of the things we'd done together, the times we'd shared. I just needed to be with him again. In *every* way. I was turning greener than cabbage: It was so difficult to act horny when I was retching at the same time. How did the girls who manned the phones on the sex lines do it?

He paused again and I held my breath, willing him to have a positive reaction. If I couldn't get Basil on board, then our plan was scuppered before it even got off the ground. I couldn't let Miranda down. I just couldn't.

When he finally spoke, the sense of relief almost overshadowed the nausea. Almost. No, he and Miranda were no longer together, *but* unfortunately she was still refusing to divorce him. She couldn't let go of the past, poor mare (I made a mental note to tell Miranda that one—I was sure she'd be amused). She was still clinging on to the hope that they'd one day reunite. He *had* thought of me often. He did miss me and yes, he would indeed like to see me again. We must, of course, be discreet. After all, the tabloids were being more vigilant than ever. So when and where should we meet?

I suggested that lunch would be best initially, that way we could catch up on old times and plan a proper evening of entertainment. Had he heard of Nick's new restaurant? Yes, great—they have private rooms there so we could be alone. Friday, twelve o'clock was perfect. I was counting the minutes already. Yes, I was so glad I called too. Goodbye, my darling.

I hung up the phone, relief flooding through me. I could never be a spy—I just wasn't cut out for subterfuge. But I did feel a small sense of victory as I lifted the phone to call Saffron. She answered immediately.

"The MP is in the bag," I told her. "It's your turn now."

My next call was to Carly. I repeated what I'd told Saffron.

"Jammy Dodger, over and out," she answered.

"Don't you mean Rodger Dodger?"

"Whatever, this is no time to get picky, Latham. I'll call Joe right now and set everything up."

"Are you sure he'll agree?" Joe was another weak link in the plan. He had no reason to help us, other than the fact that Carly was one of his favourite people on the planet.

"Are you kidding? He'll love this. Trust me." She hung up and got to work. Operation Bastard was underway.

On the Friday morning, I opened my wardrobe with trepidation and pulled out my favourite Prada suit from my past life. Basil would expect me to be as polished and presentable as ever. If he could see me now, dressed in jeans and a T-shirt that had more food stains than an oven glove, with no make-up and unbrushed hair, he'd walk past me, muttering in disgust about the homeless taking over the London streets. I squeezed myself into the outfit. It would be fine as long as I didn't breathe.

Kate arrived on the stroke of eleven to take care of Josh. She asked me how I was feeling.

"Like I'm about to offer myself up as sacrifice at a cannibalistic ritual," I replied. Actually, that would be a pleasant day out compared to this. I would rather meet Saddam Hussein than Basil Asquith. However, through the veneer of nervousness, determination and power were fighting to emerge. I just hoped they won.

It was a comfort that Nick met me at the door of the restaurant. Sarah had filled him in on our plan and his part in it. He couldn't contain his amusement.

"Everything is all set up. You lot are mental, do you know that?" he observed. "I just hope I never cross any of you—there's no telling what you would do to me."

I pinched his cheek. "You'd never do that, you're one of the good guys. Now promise me that you'll have a member of staff lurking outside the door at all times in case I get rumbled." He nodded.

I took my place at the table in the private room. It was big enough to seat ten, but I removed the extra chairs so that Basil had to sit at the opposite end from me—that way, unless he was wearing stilts, he'd be too far away to play footsie. Relief.

At twelve o'clock, Basil strode into the room, his footsteps echoing the deafening beat of my heart. He looked as distinguished as ever in his navy Savile Row suit and red, handmade silk tie. As he approached me he flashed his killer smile, then enveloped me in a bear hug.

"It's so good to see you again, Jess. I can't tell you how much I've missed you."

I groaned inside. Oh no, he was in the mood for sex already. He only ever said loving things to me when he was planning on having a fumble. This wasn't going to be easy. Right on cue, the waiter came in to take our order, forcing Basil to postpone any notion of molestation. One big tip for one efficient waiter coming up.

We ordered drinks and main courses only. My throat was so tight, I'd be hard pressed to swallow a pea. I did what I always did when under pressure: I took control. I batted my eyelids so fiercely that I got friction burns on my forehead.

"So Basil," I purred, "why don't we start by reminding ourselves just how good the old days were. How long is it now since we first began our little tête-à-tête?"

God, I was good. I hadn't spent years in the company of politicians for nothing, I thought, as I deftly steered him through all the details of our affair. Under the pretext that it excited me to remember every detail of our relationship, we reminisced about everything from our first night together to the intimacies of our favourite sex games. Or should I say *his* favourite games—mine was nothing more sexual than Twister.

By the time coffee was served, I was mortified and he was flushed with anticipation. Time to raise the subject of Miranda.

"Basil, you know that I want you all to myself this time around. When will your divorce be finalised?"

If the restaurant had a bullshitometer, it would have been

wailing. It was merely a technicality, he promised. Miranda wanted him back, but he knew that he wasn't in love with her—it was a marriage in name only. But that was no reason to delay us seeing each other. When would I be free for an evening?

"How about next Saturday evening, sweetie?" I purred. Everything was set up. It had to be that night; otherwise the whole operation would be thrown into chaos. I prayed that he didn't have a prior arrangement. The pause as he checked his palm pilot was excruciating.

"Next Saturday evening is perfect," he smiled, his eyes twinkling at the prospect.

Yes! Slam dunk! Now I just had to wrap up the lunch so that I could go collapse somewhere and breathe into a brown paper bag. I suggested that we leave separately and he concurred. He rose from his chair and walked towards me. Oh no. Beam me up, quick, Scotty, enemy approaching.

He wrapped his arms around me and nuzzled into my neck. "Until next week, poppet," he whispered. Then to my horror, I realised that his hand was working its way down my back. Then round to my front. He turned his head and kissed me on the lips. Crap! Now I know how Sigourney Weaver felt in *Alien*. I too was trapped by a monster with bad breath. His hand crept inside my shirt and cupped my Wonderbra. Help! If telepathy exists, someone help me now!

Basil jumped as the door swung open and turned to see Nick striding towards us. Nick shook his hand, pretending not to notice that one of my breasts was open to the public. "Mr. Asquith, it's a privilege to meet you. I do hope you enjoyed your lunch."

Basil flushed and nodded. "It was splendid. Splendid. Now

if you'll excuse me, I have a meeting with the PM." The bull-shitometer was ringing again. I'd seen the Prime Minister on the news the night before; he was on some jolly in Europe, not sitting waiting with bated breath for an audience with Basil Asquith.

He made a hasty exit. I fell on to my chair in an undignified heap and slammed my forehead repeatedly on the table.

"Tell me again why I'm doing this," I asked Nick between thuds.

"Don't ask me, I'm a male. It would take me three weeks with an encyclopaedia before I could work out why you lot do anything."

I lifted my bruised head and grinned. "Thanks for rescuing me. Have you got the goods?"

Nick handed me a cassette tape. "Every word, you mad bint. Every word." Strike one.

Saffron arrived at Kate's laden down with two bulging plastic bags and panting for breath. Kate ushered her in.

"My God, I'm unfit. As soon as this is over, I'm quitting the ciggies, otherwise I'll have to do a whip-round to buy an iron lung."

She emptied the bags on to the kitchen table. Kate picked up what looked like the fur of one of Miranda's Irish Setters.

"Great wig," she exclaimed as she held it up to Saffie's head. "The colour match is perfect." She pulled the wig on to a dummy head, supplied Saffie with coffee and an ashtray, and then lifted her scissors. Her hairdressing skills kicked in—Vidal Sassoon couldn't have been more meticulous.

"Don't move. This shouldn't take too long," she ordered as she started cutting the wig.

"Don't worry," Saffie replied. "I spend my whole life frozen to the spot while people fuss around me. Occupational hazard."

Half an hour later, Kate stood back and surveyed her masterpiece. It was perfect. She'd just given Saffie permission to relax when the back door barged open.

Carly bounded in and immediately started talking to the fake head wearing the wig. "Saffie, you look gorgeous today. Your skin is glowing, sweetie, honey, darling. No of course all models aren't dummies."

Saffie fired a packet of Marlboro Lights at the back of her head. "Fucking hilarious, Carly," she spat in mock annoyance. "At least we look presentable. What is it they say about writers? All barking and total social misfits. Why else would they lock themselves away alone in a room all day and make up invisible friends?"

Kate refereed. She stuck two fingers in her mouth and whistled. "Ding, ding, end of round one. Now back to your corners, both of you."

Carly and Saffie giggled. Kate removed the wig and gently placed it in a large hatbox before handing it to Carly, followed by a plastic bag containing a dress, jewellery and photographs.

"Now, don't lose these, don't wear them and don't damage them. Take them straight to their destination and don't talk to strangers on the way."

"Yes, Mum," Carly agreed with a grin. "I'll be back tonight with a full report. Wish me luck."

She bounded back out of the door, slamming it in her wake. Ten minutes later, she was in a taxi heading for central London and Kate was on the phone to me.

"Mission successful—the package is being delivered as we speak."

"Message received," I confirmed.

Strike two.

Miranda called her brother George Milford, Carol's ex-OSCAR, aka Rambo, and chairman of the publishing company that owned the *Sunday News*. She was put straight through to him.

"George, darling, it's Miranda. Yes, dear, I remembered Mummy's birthday. Now the reason for my call—are you free for lunch over the weekend? I have a rather interesting proposition for you, which I'm sure will amuse you. Yes, Sunday would be lovely. How about my house at one o'clock? I look forward to it, darling."

She hung up and dialled another number. I answered on the second ring and she relayed the previous conversation. She wasn't entering into the spirit of this at all—she spoke completely normally. Not even an "over and out" before she hung up. It didn't matter though, I thought with relish, she'd fulfilled her first part of the plan.

Strike three.

Saffron rubbed Mike's thigh under the table at Langan's. Think of all this as being drama practice for my next career change, she told herself. I am Meryl Streep. I am Meryl Streep.

"You're what? You leave in two hours?" he yelled, so loudly that the guy at the next table swallowed a mussel whole. "For Christ's sake, Saffie, I need you here. We haven't spent a night together for bloody weeks. How long will you be gone?"

"Only a few days, baby." This wasn't going well. It was crucial that she kept him at her beck and call otherwise everything could fall through. There was nothing else for it. Her hand crept up towards his two-timing, indiscreet, any hole in a storm, penis. "I'll be back next Saturday. And I want you to keep that night free, because I've got an extra-special surprise for you," she whispered enticingly, giving his crotch a rub.

That did it. He was, after all, a man who'd been deprived of sexual activity lately.

He flushed, excused himself and headed at speed for the gents, still holding his napkin in front of him. Saffie suppressed a smile.

Thank God her booker had managed to secure this few days' work in Paris. In saying that, she'd have taken a bikini job in Lapland just to escape from the possibility of having to sleep with Mike.

Mike strode back towards the table. He seemed calmer, sleepy even, as he reached for her hand. "So what's this surprise then?" he asked playfully.

Saffie twirled her hair with her free hand. "I think I might be able to help you with the scoop of a lifetime," she teased.

Mike was immediately attentive. He leaned towards her. "Tell me more."

"Well, remember Blossom, our favourite cross-dressing MP?"

Mike's face lit up as he nodded furiously. "Jeremy Brown. What about him?"

"Well, I was chatting to an old friend today and he happened to mention that he occasionally socialises with Mr. Brown."

"So?" Mike frowned in puzzlement.

"My old friend is a six-foot two-inch guy, with blond hair to his waist, who wears only Versace dresses and goes by the name of Mandy."

Mike gasped in excitement, for possibly the second time that night.

"He's planning to meet Jeremy next Saturday night. I've asked him to tell me where and when. So maybe you'll get those photos after all," she whispered conspiratorially.

Mike leaned over and kissed her, triumph written all over his face. "If that happens, I'll love you forever, my gorgeous one," he cooed.

Saffie shuddered. The very thought . . .

She made a swift exit to the ladies where, once in the cubicle, she opened her mobile.

I snatched my phone from the cradle instantly. I was sure Josh was beginning to think he'd been born into a British Telecom exchange.

"We're on for next Saturday night," she reported.

Strike four. One more home run and the first game was ours.

Joe looked like death. He'd been all over Europe in the last month, checking on the performance of his chain of nightclubs, and now he'd returned to London for some rest. Carly was about to put an end to that idea.

He was reclining on a chair in his office, with his feet on the desk and his eyes closed, when she barged in. She climbed on to his lap, causing his knees to crack, and hugged him.

"So how's my favourite ex-fiancé then?" she asked as she squeezed.

"I bet you say that to all the guys," he countered. "I'm tired, exhausted, glad to see you and crippled," he said with a grimace as he removed her and tried to bend his legs. Carly now perched on the edge of the desk.

"Before we start, Cooper, this 'plan' you alluded to on the phone, is it underhand, immoral or illegal?" he enquired wearily.

"Probably all of the above. No, make that *definitely* all of the above."

He rolled his eyes. "Why am I not surprised? Tell me what you need me to do."

Twenty minutes later he looked like a new man. His eyes were shining (from tears of mirth), his eyebrows had reached his hairline and he was chuckling like the audience at a Billy Connolly show. He'd even stopped Carly mid-story to summon his partner Claus, determined that Claus shouldn't miss out on the action. Now they were huddled like Bill, Ben and Weed, with photographs spread all over the desk in front of them, going over the logistics of the operation.

He lifted the phone and dialled an extension somewhere else in the building. His promotions manager answered.

"Storm, what have we got planned for next Saturday night—any events scheduled? No? Great. I want you to set this up. Next Saturday is going to be Carmen Miranda night. Advertise it on radio, the press and in the club over the weekend. I want the whole place decorated like the Caribbean and a strict dress code—everyone must be in theme. OK, fantastic, thanks."

He leaned back in his chair.

"Sorry about creating work for you, Joe. I wouldn't ask, but this is really important to us."

"Nonsense," he replied. "I wouldn't miss this for the bloody world. Now give me that kit over and I'll check it for size."

*   *   *

It was midnight when I answered the door to a grinning Miss
Cooper. That was a good sign.

"Well?" I asked nervously.

"He's practising his walk already. It's a go."

Strike five. Operation Bastard has lift-off.

CHAPTER 18

Why not
execute Operation Bastard?

August 2001

I arrived thirty minutes early at Kate's, just in time to cross paths with Keith Miller who was heading out the front door as I headed in. Oh no. Don't tell me this was going to be a dramatic night for all the wrong reasons. Had Kate finally succumbed to Builder Bob's biceps? Instead of *Que Sera Sera*, was Doris Day now singing "Where's my bra, my bra?" after a hasty fumble with the workie? This couldn't be a good thing.

"Hi, Jess, isn't it?" He flashed me a smile that suggested his parents must have been dentists; his teeth were perfect as a row of skittles. "It's good to see you again," he continued with an almost embarrassed shrug. My man alert was flashing, "Don't give me that modest demeanour crap." I knew the truth—he was a predator like the rest of them. Just because number twenty-seven on *Loaded* magazine's "How to Get Them into the Sack on the First Date" list instructs: "Act modest, shy and non-pushy—chicks love a bit of sensitivity," didn't mean this chick was going to roll over with her legs in the air. Anyway, even if I wanted to I couldn't. I was wearing my new investment—a rough imitation of a fabulous Julian McDonald dress. The blue shoestring straps struggled to hold the unbelievably tight sparkly bodice, from which the skirt fell to my calves in a bias cut wave. It was so tight that I'd cracked three ribs putting it on and sitting down would be a serious threat to the seams, but I didn't care. This was my big night and I wanted to look stunning.

I barely acknowledged Keith as I strutted past in my most aloof manner. Never, never would I fall for that charm stuff again. Although, I did have to grudgingly admit that if ever I did, I'd forgive myself a lot quicker if he was as attractive as Keith Miller.

I barged into the kitchen, where Kate was having coffee with Carol. I approved. There would be no wine tonight—we all needed clear heads to execute the operation.

"Kate, what the hell was Keith doing here—I thought you were over that?" I asked in mild outrage.

"I am *so* over that. He was putting up shelves in Tally's room." I must have looked cynical. "I swear," she added. "Not one impure thought in weeks."

"I can vouch for her," Carol added. "The shelves look fab. He should do that for a living."

I gave her an exasperated glare. "He *does* do that for a living." I turned back to Kate. "So isn't it uncomfortable being around him now? Isn't he afraid you're going to jump his bones at any moment?"

"Jess, he never *knew* about my lust-fest crisis. He's actually a really shy, unassuming guy; the kind of bloke that you'd have to lie down naked in front of before he realised that you liked him. Thankfully, my period of diminished responsibility didn't stretch to that."

And I'd just given him my best premenstrual Princess Anne act. Oh well. I made a dismissive gesture. I didn't have time for this just now—I had a schedule to adhere to. "OK, here's one baby, one overnight bag, one first-aid kit and the telephone number of my pager. It's one of those vibrating ones, so you can call it anytime without causing disruption."

Kate eyed me up and down. "I don't even want to know where you've hidden the pager."

Carly, Sarah and Saffie arrived while Carol was working on my face again. Soon I was unrecognisable as an exhausted mother of one.

"What time are you meeting Mike?" I asked Saffie.

"Eight o'clock. We're having dinner at The Ivy first. I thought that was kind of apt, since it was eating there that brought about the start of his downfall," she grinned.

I liked her style. I gave her a hug. "Thanks, Saffie, for every-thing."

She looked embarrassed. "It's my pleasure. Or it will be when this is over and everything has gone according to plan."

I didn't even want to contemplate that it might not. This was it. It was a one-time chance to get even and if it failed, I'd be wailing and beating my chest for the rest of my life. I adopted my most confident tone of voice, although in that dress, it was a little more high-pitched than usual. "Let's syn-chronise watches."

Carol checked her Cartier, Sarah her Longines, Saffie her Gucci (present from Mike—he probably swapped the one I bought him for it), and Carly her Teletubbies. Po was at the seven and Lala was at the three. Tinky Winky was racing round, counting the seconds and Dipsy's belly displayed the date. Seven fifteen. Time to get a move on.

"Right then. Everyone knows where they've to be. Carly and Sarah, you're in the security control room at the club. Saffie, get Mike there at ten o'clock, no later. I'll arrive with Basil at ten thirty. Carol, you're by the bar on the ground floor. If there are any problems, call Kate and she'll page me. And remember, just be careful."

I kissed Josh goodbye, mentally apologising to him for what I was about to do to his non-existent father. It firmed my resolve. If tonight was a success, then at least I'd squeeze some kind of support out of him for Josh. He gurgled back at me. He was on my side. As I made for the front door, I gave Saffie another hug. "Good luck, not that you'll need it." I was trying to instil confidence that I didn't feel.

She sensed it and squeezed me back. "Don't worry, Jess, it'll be a walk in the park."

The others shouted their goodbyes. The last words I heard as I climbed in to the waiting cab were Carol's. "Break an arm," she yelled. I laughed. Potential fractures were the least of my worries.

Basil was waiting for me in the private dining room of Home House, the exclusive London club. He must really be expecting a full night of naked gymnastics, I thought—normally he was too stingy to buy dinner. I conjured up an image of Carol in my head and did my best supermodel strut to the table. Heads were swinging to see who I was and I was tempted to announce, "A skint, single mother, con artist, wearing a fake dress."

As soon as I sat down, I went into action. It was imperative that he was hornier than a category A prisoner and more pliant than Play-Doh, to get him to follow the plan. Under the table, I slid off a shoe and worked my toes up his thigh. Thank God I had bactericidal wipes in my bag for later—I'd need to encase my feet in them for days after this.

Basil's eyebrows rose and he gave me his smuggest grin. I wanted so badly to wipe that off his face. Patience, Jess, patience. I asked him to bring me up to date with everything that had happened in his career since we last met. This served two purposes: it kept him droning on for hours and reduced the requirement for me to interact with him, and his ego was boosted with every sentence as he embellished the accomplishments of his favourite subject, himself.

I was bored witless. A day at a garden centre was more interesting than listening to Basil. It was a relief when the waiter presented the menus. I immediately scanned the right-hand side of the page. I was too distracted to do anything but play with my food, so I might as well launch the first strike. I ordered the most expensive items on the menu. I didn't even *like* caviar, but I didn't give a bugger. Luckily, he was too engrossed in his narrative to notice. I just hoped there was a doctor in the house when the bill came.

Through every course he continued to prattle. I zoned out midway through my starter. For all I knew, he could be telling me that he'd eradicated crime, eliminated greenhouse gases (he could have sucked them in single-handedly) and achieved full employment for the nation. In fact, he probably *was* claiming all that. I was having a different conversation in my head. What on earth had attracted me to him in the first place? Was I on drugs? Or temporarily insane? Or just downright desperate? He was *such* a despicable character. Smug, condescending, patronising, two-faced, dishonest, cheating. Not enough derisive adjectives existed in the English language to describe him. I made a mental note to send all future prospective boyfriends to my parents and friends for vetting. I obviously shouldn't be trusted with relationships deeper than the one I had with my postman. Hello, good morning, yes, lovely day, and see you tomorrow, would be my self-imposed limit from now on.

During the main course, I mentally concentrated on the schedule for the rest of the evening. Carly and Sarah would be at the club. Joe would be getting ready and Carol would be checking the escape routes (in theory, that is—the club had a huge mirrored wall so it was doubtful that she would get past that). Claus, Joe's partner, should be on his way to The Ivy. And Saffie? Saffie should be with Mike by now. I was sure she'd be on top of the situation. Or rather, trying to avoid being on top . . .

"Oh, baby, I have missed you so much," Mike whispered, as Saffie pulled into one of the few parking spaces within walking distance of The Ivy. It was unheard of for her to take her car into central London, but it was crucial to the plan. Luckily, Mike was too busy having a testosterone surge to question it. "Let's just skip dinner and go back to my place," he drawled, as his hand wound its way up Saffie's skirt. It didn't have far to go. I'd seen wider belts.

She pushed his hand away. "Now, now, darling. Just you keep *little* Mike under control for a bit longer. Anyway, I told you—Mandy should be here tonight and he promised to tell us where Jeremy Brown would be later." The prospect of his front-page splash brought him back to reality.

The Ivy was crowded as usual. Elle was comparing highlights with Claudia. Geri's pooch was peeing in a pot plant. And Madonna and Guy were smooching at their table. Didn't they ever dress up? Either Oxfam had kitted them out or they'd got dressed in the dark.

Saffie later said that dinner seemed to last longer than Lent. She was suffering from the same condition as me, which was total disbelief that she had ever been attracted to the cretin in front of her. She asked what he had been up to while she was away. Oh, the usual, he said, as he embarked on running up yet another mammoth expense account bar bill. He'd taken his (invisible) niece and nephew to Thorpe Park, worked two nights at the homeless shelter and did a ten-kilometre sponsored run in aid of a local mental health hospice. I think he got that bit confused. I think he did a ten-kilometre run trying to *escape* from his bed at the mental health hospice.

The monotony was broken midway through dinner, when a new arrival stunned the room into silence.

Mike's chin dropped in horror when he realised that the apparition was approaching their table. In four-inch heels, which took his (or her) height to six foot six, with Anna Kournikova hair trailing to his waist, wearing a silver, chain-mail microdress and elbow-length satin gloves, "Mandy" leaned over and air-kissed Saffie.

"Daaahling," he enthused in a mid-European accent, "it's simply *divine* to see you."

Saff suppressed a chortle. "And you too, em, Mandy. You're looking as gorgeous as ever."

"Oh, you." Mandy swatted her shoulder bashfully.

Mike was frantically scanning the room, appalled at being witnessed in the company of a German RuPaul. He downed his drink in one go, rapidly poured another, and then did the same again. Oliver Reed couldn't have matched him.

"Listen, daaahling, about that small favour you asked me last week," Mandy continued.

"Yes?" Saff replied. Mandy leaned closer to her ear. "I've arranged to meet Jeremy Brown tonight at a nightclub in Soho, called JC's Heaven. Do you know it?"

Saff had the wits to ponder this for a second. Mike, who'd been levitating off his chair straining to hear the conversation ever since the MP's name was mentioned, cut in.

"I know it," he blurted.

Mandy turned his attention to Mike. "Mmmm, nice chest," he murmured, stroking Mike's shirt. Mike almost combusted spontaneously. Another drink downed in one gulp.

"Thanks, Mandy, you're a star." She stood up and hugged him, almost garrotting herself in his wig. Mandy teetered off, the sound of his mules resounding through the room.

"How the *fuck* do you know him?" Mike exclaimed.

Saff shrugged her shoulders. "He works as a stylist on some of the jobs I do. Is there a problem?"

Mike sat back in his chair. After a pause, an evil, if slightly inebriated, smile crossed his lying mouth. "Not when he provides information like this," he replied smugly. The man had more faces than a dice. "Next stop Soho," he added with the expression of a hitman who'd just got his target in his sights. "Come in, Jeremy Brown, your time is up."

And so is yours, Mike Chapman. So is yours.

Carly and Sarah were adjusting the views on the twelve monitors in front of them in the JC's Heaven security room. Great. They had every angle in the club covered.

"OK, Carol," Carly spoke into her walkie-talkie, "walk from the door to the bar, then across the room. I just want to check that we've got no blind spots." On monitor one, they could see Carol nodding. Then, as she walked, her image transferred to

monitor two, then three. Perfect. Wherever she went on the ground floor, they had sight of her.

"Carol, that's great. Now let's test the communications." Sarah switched on her handset and spoke. Carol pulled her walkie-talkie out of the inside of her jacket and replied loud and clear. They had sight and they had sound—now all they needed were the players.

Josh demolished every ounce of milk in his last bottle of the day and then burped so loudly that he sounded like the Budweiser frogs. Kate lifted him and gave him a cuddle. He nestled into her chest. "They'll be home soon, little one," she whispered. "Mummy is out causing mayhem, but she loves you very much and she'll be home soon." Josh smiled. He definitely had wind.

The waiter gave me a quizzical look as he removed my untouched fifty-quid plate. At least he noticed. Basil had paid no attention whatsoever. I could have inhaled the plate whole and have string beans dripping from my nostrils, for all the notice he took. But then, he was still on his favourite subject.

"So what do you think, Jess?" What? I'd been less attentive than a trainspotter in a bus station.

"Sorry, Basil. I'm afraid I missed that. I was too busy having a little fantasy, about you and me and what we'll do to amuse ourselves later." Puke! But I was desperate—I couldn't blow it now.

"That's exactly what I was asking you, darling. Shall we retire to the flat now? I think it is time that we were somewhere a little more intimate," he leered. My stomach turned as I surreptitiously checked my watch. Ten o'clock. Lights, camera, action.

"That would be great, my darling. I've thought of nothing else all week. But, Basil, do you mind if we make one teeny stop on the way there?"

His face fell. He obviously wanted to go straight to Mayfair, without passing GO and collecting £200. I purred an explanation.

"It's just that I want to collect something for you. Something that'll make your head spin." He was interested again, because it revolved around him. Basil was definitely one of those guys who talked about himself all night and then said, "Enough of talking about me, let's talk about you . . . what do *you* think are my best features?"

I continued purring. "Do you remember Joe, Carly's friend? You sat next to him at Carol's wedding." He nodded vaguely. He obviously had no idea who I was talking about. "Well, Joe has just been to Amsterdam for a few days and I asked him to bring a few things back for me. I don't want to spoil the surprise, but let's just say that they'll make you a very happy little bunny *all* night long." I held my breath. If he said no now I was doomed.

Eventually, he nodded his head and playfully ran his fingers up and down my arm. *"All* night?" he checked.

"All night, darling. This is definitely going to be one that you'll never forget."

He started to turn pink. If he got up now, he'd be walking with a limp. He summoned the waiter. "Just add this evening's bill to my account, please."

"Certainly, Mr. Asquith."

Shame. I was dying to see his face when he realised that my meal cost more than a week in Majorca. But then, surely I was worth it—after all, the services I'd been providing to this particular MP were priceless.

*   *   *

Saffron and Mike approached the door of JC's Heaven. It was still early in clubland terms, so there was no queue yet. Carly spotted them on the outside camera. She spoke into her walkie-talkie.

"OK, Chad, here we go," she said. Her voice was received in the earpiece of the head bouncer standing at the front door. Carly had known Chad since she was seventeen and first went to work for Joe in a club in the red light district of Amsterdam. He was a gentle giant, but entirely intimidating to those who didn't know him. He was so big that he caused an eclipse every time he moved. "They're approaching from your left. Tall female, long dark hair, shortest skirt in history, with white male, six feet tall, dark hair, slight stagger, wandering willy." They could see Chad fighting to keep a straight face as he stepped forward to greet the approaching couple.

"Sorry folks, strictly themed dress only tonight." Mike and Saffie looked at each other in confusion, then back at Chad.

"What's the theme?" Mike slurred, bewildered.

"Tonight's Carmen Miranda night, sir."

Mike exploded. "WHAT? Look, do you know who I am? I'm from the press," he screamed. "Now stop being bloody stupid and just let us in." He tried to barge past Chad. Big mistake. Chad put his arm out and Mike bounced off it so hard that he almost broke his windpipe. Saffie clasped her hand over her mouth in mock horror. It also served to conceal her grin as Mike landed on his arse on the pavement.

The veins in Mike's neck were throbbing louder than the music coming from inside the club. But not quite as deafening as the screams of laughter coming from the security control room.

"Easy, Chad, easy," Carly whispered through her giggle, "we want to set him up, not kill him."

Chad backed off. Mike pulled himself to a standing position and dusted himself down, his pride more injured than his butt. He obviously decided to change his approach. "Look, mate, it's really important that we get in here tonight," he said in a more amenable tone of voice.

"That's no problem, sir," Chad replied. "But you must be dressed correctly."

Mike visibly struggled to regain his composure. "I'm not dressing like Carmen fucking Miranda. I'll look like a fucking poof," he spat.

Chad, bless him, still kept a straight face. "If that was the case sir, you'd be admitted—this *is* one of London's best *gay* clubs."

Before he lost control of his faculties and his senses, Saffie pulled him to one side. "Look, baby, let's just forget it. You can get Jeremy Brown another night."

There was a horrible moment when he shrugged his shoulders, as if to agree with her. Bollocks! That wasn't the anticipated reaction. But then, true to form, ego and alcohol kicked in and he rallied.

"I can't, Saff. I haven't had a front page in weeks. This could really make things for me. Jeremy Brown is big news."

Saffie sighed, then pretended to think for a moment. "Then I have a suggestion. The modelling shoot I did today was beachwear. And I had to wear a red wig. I've still got all the kit in the back of the car."

You could see his internal struggle. Dressing in female clothes was as alien to Mike as fidelity. But on the other hand, getting this story would mean a huge scoop, huge profile and huge bonus cheque. He could drink champers on that for a year. There was no contest. "OK, babe," he concurred. "I mean, no one has to know about this, right? It can be our secret."

Saffie nodded. He was right. No one had to know about it. Except the entire population of the free world.

The atmosphere in the control room was more electric than the National Grid.

"Fifty quid says we never see them again. There's no way Mike will go for this," Sarah announced.

"Done," Carly replied. "He'll go for it. The prospect of the glory when he gets the exclusive story will force him to do it. There's no way his ego will allow him not to." Behind them, a door opened and "Mandy" teetered in. Carly lunged at him and covered his face in kisses. "Claus, you big darling, you must have been brilliant! They've already appeared and have gone off to change. They took the bait!"

"I should bloody hope so," Claus replied, his face grimacing, as he peeled off his stilettos and threw them at the wall. "This had better be worth it, Cooper. My feet have been permanently damaged in these shoes. And as for waxing my legs this afternoon! If that was a requirement for gay men, I'd go straight."

Carly giggled. "If I'd thought there was any possibility of that, then I'd have saved myself for you, baby," she promised, as she ruffled his hair.

We disembarked from Basil's limo, me with a huge sigh of relief. It had been like wrestling with a hyperactive octopus for the last fifteen minutes. His hands had attempted to slide down inside my dress, but when it became obvious that he'd need a pair of pliers and a vice to force enough room for his hand, he'd changed tactics and launched an attack from the bottom up. As he slid his hand up my thighs, I shuddered. He eyed me quizzically. "Just excited, darling," I promised, "I've thought about your touch for so long." Fool that he is, he believed every word. His hand whooshed up my skirt like a tornado and was just forcing my best Agent Provocateur thong (I liked the irony) to one side when I felt the car stop. Please don't let it be another set of traffic lights, I prayed. Thank God for smoked windows, otherwise pedestrians all over London would have had a full view of one of the Opposition's leading lights drooling as he molested me in his back seat.

"We're outside JC's Heaven now, sir," his driver's voice announced through the speaker.

Phew. Saved by the chauffeur. I twisted and reached for the door handle so quickly that I almost amputated his hand, which was still probing around the knicker regions. But as the door began to open, I froze. Two extremely tall beach babes were strutting past the car. Or rather, one was strutting and the other was concentrating furiously on remaining upright, while he tried to negotiate the paving slabs in four-inch heels. Saffie caught my eye with a horrified expression. Shite! I slammed the door shut, my heart beating like a techno tune. Fuck, fuck, fuck. Had he seen me?

"What's wrong, sweetie?" Basil cooed.

"Not a thing, my love," I replied huskily. "I just realised that I was enjoying what you're doing far too much to stop now." I couldn't believe it. Don't tell me I'd fallen at the last fence. Had Mike seen me? Out of the corner of my eye, I checked the view out of the window to see if Mike showed any signs of recognition, but he was still negotiating the pavement like a baby giraffe trying to walk for the first time. I breathed a huge sigh of relief. He hadn't spotted me. But then my spirits crashed as I realised I'd have to stall the eight-armed one long enough to let Saff and Mike get into the club. There was nothing else for it. I was going to have to let him continue with his exploration exercise. For the first time in my life, I wished that my privates had the capabilities of a Venus flytrap. I'd love to see Basil explain how he'd managed to lose a hand in the back of his limo.

I uttered the obligatory heavy breaths and gasps. Mike and Saff were still fifty yards from the door.

"Oh, baby, that's so good." Twenty yards.

"Oh, yes, darling, right there." Ten yards. My clitoris was wondering what all the fuss was about. Basil would have needed the services of a Sherpa to find it. But I didn't share that with him. They were at the door.

"Oh, yes, baby, yes, baby, YES . . ." Meg Ryan, eat your heart out.

"Unbelievable! Looks like I owe you fifty quid, Carly. Enemy approaching. And he's in full battledress," Sarah exclaimed in shocked tones.

All heads swung to the monitor. The shrieks could have been heard in Clapham. Teetering along the pavement, holding on to Saffie for support as he struggled to balance in his tipsy state and on four-inch mules, was Michael Carmen Miranda. On his head was a curly wig the colour of a satsuma. Saff had obviously applied his make-up with her eyes shut—he wouldn't have been out of place in a circus with his overdone eyeliner, two red circles on his cheeks and lips so bright and prominent, they could have suctioned him to a window for days. Below the neck was no better. He wore a jungle-patterned bathing suit, the breasts obviously padded with the air bags from Saffie's Peugeot, covered from the waist down by a fringed sarong which colour-co-ordinated with his lips. There was a suspicious bulge in the front. Innocent bystanders could have been forgiven for thinking that he was better endowed than Red Rum, but we knew differently—it was the telescopic lense of his Pentax, not so cleverly concealed in his outfit.

Suddenly, Sarah spotted the white limo the size of the QE2 that had parked outside. Not realising that I'd already seen Mike, she had a panic attack. "Oh, bollocks! Houston, we have a problem. I think that could be Basil and Jess. If they get out of the car now, they're going to bump into the others at the door."

Carly grabbed the walkie-talkie. "Chad, mayday, mayday. Get Saffie and Carmen Miranda inside as quickly as possible. The others are right behind them."

Chad stepped out of the doorway and ushered them inside. They stopped at the cash desk to pay. "No need for that sir, just go right on ahead. Tonight, entry is with our compliments." True to form Mike smiled. He was getting free entry and a major scoop in the one night. What a bargain.

They went into the ground-floor section of the club and scanned the dimly lit room. The club was about half full. There were more wigs and false eyelashes here than in Dolly Parton's dressing room.

Right on cue, a distressed-looking Mandy, feet throbbing in time to the music, greeted them. As Mandy was giving Mike a welcoming hug (much to his embarrassment and disgust), Saffie made eye contact with Carol, who was lurking in the corner. Carol gave her a thumbs up sign. Everything was on track and going according to plan. Saffie winked back.

Mandy was still in full flow. "Daaahlings, so glad you came.

And you, you big stud," he exclaimed to Mike with a squeeze, "I could just eat you for breakfast." Mike searched for a sick bag and ordered two double vodkas from a passing waiter. More screams of hilarity in the control room. Putting a microphone on Claus had been an inspired idea. Even if he did refuse to say where he was concealing the battery pack.

Mandy stage-whispered conspiratorially. "Jeremy should be here any time now. He always sits at that table there, so you're probably best just to stay where you are for now." Mike nodded with relief. Walking anywhere else in those shoes would have been a challenge. Mandy ran his hand down the front of Mike's swimsuit. "And tell me, gorgeous, what do I get in return for all this help I'm supplying? If you can't think of anything, I've got one or two suggestions which would have you paid in full in no time," he teased. Mike turned the colour of the apples tucked into Mandy's headpiece and slugged his vodkas.

Carly and Sarah crossed their legs in the control room; tears of laughter streaming down their faces. Carly was trying to decide if she had time for a quick dash to the loo, when another person entered the room. She gasped.

"Joe, you look perfect! Turn round, so I can see the back view." Joe complied. Carly checked the photograph in front of her. "Sen-fucking-sational! You could be identical twins," she exclaimed.

"They're here," Sarah cut in. "Jess and Basil are almost at the door."

"OK, Chad, you're on again. You know what to do." Carly spoke into her microphone. Then, she turned to Joe. "Ready for your starring role, Mr. Cain?"

"Never more," he replied with relish, as he rearranged his fake breasts back into an upright position. "I knew I should have worn a Wonderbra. These things will be at my knees by the time the night is out."

I had my fingers crossed behind my back as we approached the front door of the club. A giant of a man stepped forward to greet us. "Evening, folks, if you'd just like to make your way to the cash desk . . ." Perfect. Chad was wasted as a bouncer, the man should be in Hollywood.

I spoke up. "Actually, I'm just here to see Joe Cain. My name is Jess Latham—I think he's expecting me." Chad made a fuss of checking notes on the clipboard pinned to the wall next to the door. My nerves were strung tighter than the bodice on my dress.

"Ah, here you are," he said, pretending to find my name on the invisible guest list. I'll take you right up to Mr. Cain. Sir, I'm afraid I'll have to ask you to wait in the bar. Mr. Cain is rather strict about security and only the lady's name is listed here."

Basil hesitated. The three-foot poster of Carmen Miranda that was staring at him was obviously making him a bit apprehensive. "Maybe I'll just wait in the car."

"Oh don't be ridiculous, sweetie," I chided. I couldn't let him leave now. We were so close to victory. It would be like Apollo 11 landing on the moon and Neil Armstrong deciding he wasn't in the mood for a stroll. I leaned over and whispered in his ear. "Just wait five teensy minutes in the bar, baby, and if you're good, then I'll show you the private room on the second floor that's designed for encounters of the well, *captive* kind."

He smiled. Or leered. He immediately understood what I was talking about. He wasn't the MP for Sado-Masochist Pervs for nothing.

Chad directed Basil to the correct door. I gave him a wave. "Won't be long, babe. Just amuse yourself until I return."

His face was pink with anticipation as he waved back. There's no greater fool than a man with a hard-on.

I galloped up the stairs and into the control room, passing Joe on the way down. "You OK?" he asked.

"Just about," I replied, "although I don't want another night like this for as long as I live."

"Me neither. My boobs are a disaster." He continued his descent. I had a feeling that, despite his moans, he was having more fun than Joan Rivers in a plastic surgery clinic.

I ran the rest of the way. I didn't want to miss one minute of this. I got a standing ovation as I entered and took a mock bow. Thank you, my public.

"Way to go, Jess, you were brilliant!" Carly exclaimed. "We thought we were finished when you arrived at the same time as Mike and Saffie. How did you manage to stall getting out of the car?"

"Don't ask. But I'll be waiting for Superdrug to open in the morning to buy a wire brush and Dettol."

I checked the monitors. Where was Basil? Ah, got him. He was standing at the bar, sipping what appeared to be a cocktail festooned with umbrellas. I expected him to be impatiently shifting from one foot to another, more uncomfortable than Joe's fake breasts, but surprisingly he was scanning the colourful inhabitants of the room with an intrigued expression. Maybe he was discovering a whole new side to himself. Perish the thought.

I glanced at monitor six. Saffie and Mike were dead centre on the screen. Saff had cleverly manoeuvred Mike around so that his back was to the door and the bar, on the pretext that if Jeremy Brown entered and recognised Fleet Street's most notorious journalist, he'd take off like a torpedo. It was nonsense—Mike's mother wouldn't have recognised her son in that outfit—but again, his inflated sense of importance compelled him to agree.

On monitor eight, we saw Joe enter the room. "OK, Saffie, there's your cue," I whispered to no one in particular. A couple of minutes passed, but Saff didn't move. Then we realised why. Her view of Joe was being blocked by two butch guys in flowery dresses with heaped apples and bananas on their heads. Bugger! I glanced back at Basil. He was still clearly enjoying himself, but was starting to display a restless demeanour, his eyes flitting to the door every few seconds to check for my return. Come on, Saffie. Come on.

I grabbed a walkie-talkie. "Carol, everything's set, but Saffie can't see Joe. You have to get her out of there."

On monitor nine, I could see Carol nodding her head. Then she worked her way around the room until she was in Saffie's eye line. She frantically motioned to her with her head that it was time to leave, much to the concern of all around her, who were immediately consumed with sympathy for the beautiful girl with the violent nervous tic.

A massive wave of relief swept through the control room when Saffie almost indiscernibly winked in return.

"Mike, sweetie, I just have to nip to the ladies. Will you be all right here alone, or shall I fetch Mandy to keep you company?"

Mike shot back his reply with a panic-stricken look. "No, no, I'll be fine," he slurred, patting her on her pert rear end. "Just hurry back, sweetie, you wouldn't want to miss the action."

"You're so right about that. Oh, good grief, Mike, look! Isn't that a politician guy over there?" She motioned to the bar. Mike spun round, twisting his sarong and almost toppling off his heels in the process.

He struggled to focus, his eyeballs swimming in pure vodka. "Christ, it's Basil Asquith. What the fuck is he doing here?"

"Do you know him?" Saff played dumb.

"Em, yes. I did a story on him a few years ago. He was having an affair with someone I used to know. Vaguely. Fuck, what a night. Basil Asquith and Jeremy Brown in one go." His face was rapt with excitement. "Off you go to the loo, sweetie. I'm just going to get a bit closer to Mr. Asquith—I want to see what the old perv is up to now." As Carol pointed out later, that was the pot calling the kettle pink. Mike was the one in four-inch heels with a camera down his crotch.

Saff made a sharp exit as Mike began to slowly work his way around the room like a commando closing in on an enemy troop. From the shadows of her corner, Carol watched his every move. From just inside the doorway, Joe did the same. From the edges of our seats in the control room, we followed Joe watching Carol, watching Mike, watching Basil. I stopped breathing. Carly was whispering, "Come on, baby, come on, baby," to the screens. Sarah's knuckles were turning white around her walkie-talkie. Even Claus, once again seated behind us and rubbing his bunions, had a fine veil of sweat on his forehead. This was torture. I'd rather give birth again than endure this.

Saff burst in. "Have I missed it? Don't tell me I've bloody missed it." Without taking our eyes from the screens, we all shook our heads. She pulled up a chair to perch on.

Mike was closing on Basil. Twenty feet away. Carol nodded to Joe, and he started to cut across the room. She then moved swiftly from her hiding place, so that she was bringing up Mike's rear. Ten feet. Joe was almost there. Carol was still on Mike's tail. Five feet. Joe was in touching distance of Mike now. Two feet. Mike put his hand out to tap Basil's shoulder. Basil sensed the intrusion and turned to face him. He was about to recoil like a bungee rope when a very tall brunette cut in between them. Then everything happened in an instant. Mike heard his name shouted and looked back, just as the brunette landed a full-scale snog on his sink plunger lips. FLASH, FLASH, FLASH. The lights dazed him and his pupils shrunk to the size of blackheads as he groped around, his powers of comprehension lost in the flurry of activity. He drunkenly flailed at his attacker. Behind him, Basil dived for cover then sprinted to the exit in panic. FLASH. FLASH. FLASH. Carol thrust her Olympus down the back of her hipsters and lunged behind the bar. The entrance doors were now swinging in Basil's wake. Chad miraculously appeared and grabbed Mike by the arms. Joe followed Carol behind the bar, his brunette wig getting caught in an optic and being swiftly wrenched from his head. Chad whisked Mike from the room as he repeatedly screamed, "What the fuck is going on? What the fuck was that?"

"Don't worry, mate, I'll get you out of here. Mistaken identity. I knew that brunette was trouble the minute I set eyes on him."

When they reached the door, Mike was still ranting. "Get my girlfriend. Get my fucking girlfriend." I just hoped that my son didn't inherit his father's command of the English language.

"Calm down, mate, calm down, I'll get her for you," Chad promised, his words drowned out by the sound of a limo screeching past, its tyres giving off steam as they spun on the tarmac.

Back at mission control, Saffie panicked at the sound of Mike calling her—the last thing she wanted was to face him now. "Go Claus, go. Get rid of him," she yelled.

Claus bounded down the stairs, through the front door, and over to Mike, who was now pacing up and down (well, as much as he could in those shoes), muttering ferociously to himself. What had just happened? What the hell was going on? Where the fuck was Saffie? They say that shock instantly sobers the mind, but it was having the opposite effect on Mr. Chapman. He was more disorientated than a Brownie without a compass.

"Hi, daaahling, are you waiting for me, you big, gorgeous brute?"

Mike put his head in his hands. This was the icing on the Christmas bloody pudding. "Piss off, you big freak." He pushed Mandy's hand away. Claus had the cheek to look offended. "Piss off all of you," Mike rambled. An unsuspecting cab driver was unlucky enough to be dropping off two Carmens at that very moment. Mike pushed them out of the way and stumbled into the taxi. "And tell my girlfriend that she can piss off too. How long does it take to have a pee, daft cow."

Saffie shrieked with laughter as she watched his cab pull away on the screen.

" 'Bye, Mike," she waved. "See you in the morning, my love." She turned to the rest of us in the control room. "Well, everyone, it looks like Operation Bastard went exactly to plan. Jess, you should take this up for a living. We could form our own company—Retribution Incorporated."

I couldn't answer her. I was numbed. We'd done it. We'd actually done it. All the emotions, the excitement, the nerves, the terror, they all washed over me simultaneously. Everyone turned and watched me nervously. Had this tipped me over the edge? Was this the straw that would finally put the camel in traction? I didn't know whether to laugh, cry or adopt the foetal position and rock back and forwards.

"Jess?" Carly whispered in concern. "Somebody get brandy quick, she's in shock." Then hysteria took over. It started as a weak giggle, then erupted into full scale side-clutching chortles.

"Sod the brandy, Cooper. Make it champagne. Big, bloody great buckets of champagne," I spluttered. By this time I was bent over almost double. "And somebody get me a doctor. I think this dress just cracked my ribs."

There was a loud knock at the door. But it wasn't a member of the medical profession. Mrs. Asquith squeezed her way into the overcrowded room, immediately followed by her brother. I pulled myself up to greet them as Carol dived under a desk, not wanting to come face to face with an OSCAR from the past.

"Well?" she asked apprehensively. I held out my hand to one side. Sarah dropped a roll of film and a cassette tape into it, which I then passed on to Miranda.

"Mission accomplished, Miranda. You've got enough ammunition there to invade Poland."

She smiled, then to my utter astonishment, leaned over and hugged me. "You know, Miss Latham, it's a shame we met in such appalling circumstances. I'm beginning to think that in another life we could actually have been friends."

I hugged her tighter. "Don't scare me, Miranda. I'm only just recovering from shock—don't give me a relapse."

The door opened again. It was a wonder it was still on its hinges with all tonight's traffic. Joe tried to enter, but it would have been like squeezing an elephant into a Mini. "OK, you lot, champagne is served. Form an orderly queue," he shouted from the hallway.

"We have to go, Jess. Our job is just beginning," Miranda said, passing the roll of film to her brother. "Thank you."

I nodded. She didn't have to say any more. I knew exactly how she felt. As they retreated, I switched my gaze to Saffie. I'd never be able to repay her.

"Don't say a word, Latham. I enjoyed every minute of it," she blurted before I could speak.

Carol handed us two glasses of the bubbly stuff. "Right you two; don't go getting emotional again. You've done your bit. It just proves what they say about a woman scorned."

I couldn't resist it. "What do they say, Carol?"

She looked around the room, her face imploring one of the others to bail her out. A parachute wouldn't have broken her fall. "A woman scorned is, em, well, is . . ."

"Yes."

"Is a woman seriously pissed off," she finished triumphantly.

CHAPTER 19

Why not
believe everything
that's printed in the newspapers?

August 2001

The *Sunday News*, Sunday, 26 August 2001.

Headline: IS CHEEKY CHAPMAN OUT?

Tag Line: Exclusive! Britain's biggest source of scandal appears to have a secret of his own!

Editorial: It emerged last night that infamous journalist, Mike Chapman, who has made a career of exposing the private lives of the country's top political figures, is hiding a skeleton or two in his own, now-opened, closet. Chapman, who works for one of Britain's more down-market papers, was spotted last night getting up close and intimate with an unknown drag queen (identified by onlookers only as "Josephine"), in a Soho club and then later in a busy London street. Details of Chapman's personal life have been a closely guarded secret until now, although it was believed that he was married. As these photographs show, the man who has been behind the downfall of many public figures, a leading voice in the campaign to "Clean Up Britain's Morals" and a major critic of the Gay Rights Movement . . .

Photograph 1: Mike Chapman kissing a brunette known only as "Josephine" in a London nightclub.

Tag line: Chapman thoroughly investigates a new scoop

Photograph 2: Mike Chapman with his head buried in the "bosom" of the same brunette, in a black BMW outside a London hotel.

Tag line: Chapman digs even deeper to cover every inch of the story

I laid the newspaper out in front of me. I hadn't even read the story yet. A moment like this needed meticulous preparation. The owner of the newsagent's at the corner of my road had looked at me warily, as I stood outside waiting for him to open at six a.m. I think he was worried that I was about to mug him. When he finally let me in, one foot on the panic button connected to the local police station, I dived to the paper stand. What if it wasn't there? What if Miranda and her publishing director brother had reneged on their side of the deal? Then I spotted it. Wedged between "Rock Star Heads For Seventh Divorce" and "Footballer Secretly Attends AA Meeting With New It-Girl Love," was "Is Cheeky Chapman Out?" I got a warm and bubbly feeling in the pit of my stomach. It took every ounce of discipline not to devour the story on the walk home, but this was like a fine wine or sex with a bloke you'd fancied for ages—it had to be experienced in the right circumstances.

As soon as I got home, I woke up Saffie. Her car was still

parked outside JC's Heaven, due to over-enthusiastic celebrations the night before. When it was time to leave, I offered her a bed for the night. It was the least I could do to repay her conspiracy. I made bacon butties and fresh coffee. As she staggered into the kitchen, despite three gallons of champagne and only three hours' sleep, she still managed to look stunning. I sighed. It would be so easy to hate her. It should be illegal to be that attractive.

"Well?" she asked excitedly.

I handed her a cup and a plate laden with three butties. We took our seats at the table and I dramatically pulled a tea towel off the *Sunday News*. She splurted out a mouthful of her coffee, narrowly missing soaking the images of her ex-boyfriend that took up half the page.

"Fantastic!" she giggled. And she was right. The first photograph was the one that Carly and I had taken on the night of our stakeout, showing Saffie and Mike in a compromising position. The shot showed only the back of Saff's hair and body, but had a clear view of Mike's face as he nestled in her cleavage.

The second photo was taken last night. Mike was engaged in full-scale tonsil tennis with what appeared to be the same person—same dress, same long brunette hair. But that person was most definitely a man and had two-day stubble protruding through his foundation to prove it. The picture it (and the accompanying story) painted was clear. Holier than thou, moralising, get rich from the private lives of others Mike Chapman, was leading a double life. The previous night, not only had he been openly intimate in a nightclub with a man in four-inch heels called Josephine, he had then taken her back to his London hotel, stopping outside for another snog, where she had "allegedly" spent the night. The *News* had been extremely careful to use lots of "allegedlys"—their legal department must have been in uproar over this one. But they had photographic evidence, supplied by an "anonymous" source to back up their theories. And no judge could argue that their interpretation of the photos was in any way unreasonable. Anyway, Mike would probably flee the country when he saw this; he couldn't sue if he was hiding out in Bogota.

I couldn't eat my bacon for laughing. Perverse, I know. This was not the normal reaction of a wife when she was witnessing her husband's infidelity splashed across the front pages. But this was a victory. We'd succeeded in hitting Mike where it would hurt the most: in his ego. Did I feel triumphant? Think Steve Redgrave when he won the fifth gold medal.

My telephone rang and I let it click on to the answering machine. I knew he'd call. I'd asked the girls not to phone me this morning, because I wanted to keep the line free for him.

"Jess, it's Mike. I know you're there. Pick up the phone. Pick up the fucking phone!" he yelled. The sound of his voice made my stomach breakdance. The phone slammed down. Seconds later, it rang again. "Jess, I need to speak to you." He sounded like Vesuvius right before an eruption. "Call me back, Jess. Fucking soon." Murderous tone. I just hoped he'd burst several blood vessels. I bit my lip—had I bitten off more than I could chew with this one? Then reason kicked in. What could he do to me? Desert me? Done that. Abandon our child? Done that. Refuse to provide any support? Done that. Break my heart into fragments smaller than dust-mites? Surprise, surprise, done that too. There was nothing left that Mike Chapman could do to hurt me. We had to see out the rest of the plan. There was nothing else to lose.

"So what do we do now, general?" Saffie asked.

"We wait," I replied. "This is only going to get better."

In the drawing room of a Mayfair townhouse a couple of hours later, a very different scene was playing out. Basil had been astonished when he answered the door (it must have been the butler's day off) to see Miranda standing there. He was wearing a white vest and red baggy boxer shorts. It wasn't pretty.

"Miranda, poochie, how lovely to see you," he stuttered.

"Cut the crap, Basil. I'm here to talk." Basil's astonishment grew. He'd never heard Miranda use language like that before—she'd obviously been mingling with some very unsavoury people of late.

He followed her through to the study like an obedient puppy. "Would you like tea, poochie? Or, em, a spot of breakfast maybe?" He was floundering. He hated to be caught off guard.

Miranda cleared the study desk and threw down a copy of the *Sunday News*. Basil paled.

"Where were you last night, Basil?" Miranda demanded.

Splutter, splutter, splutter. "I was, em, here, sweetie, catching up on some paperwork."

Miranda sighed wearily. "Stop lying, you great twat." She'd learned that word from me too. She indicated the photograph on the front page of Mike and Joe kissing. In the background, barely visible to the naked eye, was the form of a man who bore a frighteningly close resemblance to the MP. Miranda pointed it out.

Basil studied the picture intently, his face now turning from white to purple. "For goodness' sake, poochie, that isn't me. That could be anyone in that photo," he said with as much confidence and bravado as he could muster. He was Bill Clinton. "*I did not have sex with that woman . . .*"

"Correct, it *could* be anyone in *that* photo. But not in this one. Or this one. Or this one." She slapped down a selection of the other photos taken before Basil had done his commando crawl from the club. In the first, he was standing behind Mike, happily sucking his cocktail. In the second, he had obviously registered the first flash and his face was panic-stricken. On the third, you could just see the top half of his face as he hit the deck like he was being bombed. Courage under fire. Not.

There was a long pause. Then he sighed. "So I was in a club last night. And yes, it was a gay club. But that means nothing. These photos don't mean a damn thing."

"Oh, yes, they do, Basil. I want a divorce and I want it immediately."

He was cornered, but foolish man, he decided that attack was the best line of defence. "Never," he spat. Then he emitted a patronising guffaw. "You think that just because I was seen in a nightclub, you can sue me for divorce? Is it now 'unreasonable behaviour' to socialise in London? Now, put these away and stop being silly, Miranda." He pushed the photos to one side. "I took my wedding vows and I intend to keep them. There will be *no* divorce."

Miranda was cooler than a yeti. I don't know how she did it—I'd have been steaming like a locomotive by now.

"What about the other vows? The fidelity ones?" she countered.

"You've got no proof of that. Nothing that would stand up in a court of law," he finished smugly.

Miranda removed a small dictaphone from her clutch bag.

She pressed play. The sound of Basil roaring with laughter filled the room, then, "Oh, yes, Jess, I've thought often of that first night we spent together. Such energy, my darling. I knew from that moment that we were going to have some jolly indecent times . . ." There was no mistaking the leer in his tone or his meaning.

Basil looked ill. His mouth was so wide open that a transit van could have parked in it. "But how?" he stammered.

It was Miranda's turn to be smug. "Do you remember your little lunch with Miss Latham earlier this month? Do you remember the rest of the conversation? Let me remind you." She started to squeeze the play button again.

"No!" Basil stopped her. He knew when he was down. He slumped against the wall. "Miranda, please, after all these years . . . So I made a mistake. Yes, another one. But that doesn't mean we couldn't give it another try, poochie. I adore you, my darling, you know that," he begged.

Miranda cut him short. "All I know, Basil, is that you really are a pathetic excuse for a man." She turned to leave the room. And his life. "You'll be hearing from my lawyers on Monday morning. Co-operate, Basil, or these photos and a transcript of this tape will be on the desk of every editor in the country by the end of the week. Goodbye." She swept out, like a twenty-first century Boadicea. Only her chariot was the mint green Range Rover parked outside. She'd come, she'd fought and she'd conquered. The battle was won. But what about the war?

Saffie's mobile rang at 11:06 a.m. After she peeled me from the ceiling, she answered it. "Hello?" She immediately thrust the phone to arm's length—I could hear the shouting and expletives coming from the earpiece. When they finally halted, she put the phone back to her ear.

"Mike, calm down, just calm down. Where are you?" I could see she was trying desperately not to laugh. She listened intently, making appropriate soothing noises when necessary. Eventually, she spoke. "Look, I'll come over. I'll meet you in the lobby of the hotel in half an hour. Don't worry, baby, I'm sure we can sort this out." She hung up and threw the phone back into her bag.

"He is going absolutely super-bloody-sonic ballistic. He's seen the paper and he's threatening to sue, to bomb their offices and to murder every member of staff. He sounds really distressed, Jess. I feel quite sorry for him."

What? I couldn't believe what I was hearing! After everything he'd done to both of us? I was about to launch into a tirade, listing again every one of his crimes and misdemeanours, when I caught the expression on her face. I threw what was left of my bacon butty at her, as she dissolved into giggles.

"Cow! I thought you were serious! I was about to excommunicate you from our species."

It was strange. I'd only known this female for a couple of months and yet we'd become so close. Maybe we were sisters in a past life. Sod that. Knowing my luck, she was Cinderella and I was . . . I didn't even want to think about it.

We pulled up outside the hotel exactly fifty-five minutes later. I'd called Kate on the way there. Yes, Josh was doing just fine—he'd slept right through the night. Yes, the others had filled her in on last night's events and had already been on the phone fourteen times this morning to find out if she'd heard from me. I brought her up to date. "And Kate, thanks," I finished. "I couldn't have done any of this without you lot." Oh no, emotional woman alert. The men in the nearby cars could sense it and were all giving us a wide berth. Or maybe it was just Saffie's driving that made them do that.

"Jess, just be careful. Mike isn't exactly renowned for his mature, rational behaviour." I told her not to worry and hung up. We could handle this. Although I couldn't help wishing I had riot shields and a SWAT team.

When we reached the hotel, Saffie made her way inside to find a beleaguered Mike slumped in the corner of the lobby. She rushed over to him. "Oh baby, I was so worried after your call. What's going on?" Meryl Streep strikes again.

Mike wearily pushed the paper across the table to her. She pretended to read it and clasped her hand to her mouth. "Oh my God! But that isn't me in the second photo!" she exclaimed. "Who is it? And why were you kissing her? I mean, him?"

Mike shook his head defeatedly—he'd been set up, he explained. Someone that he'd crossed in the past had framed him. Someone with a grudge. Did Saffie remember the females outside the car on the night that the first photos were taken?

"The refugees?" she asked with an expression of incomprehension. "But why would they go to all this trouble to set you up? Surely they'd be in hiding or deported by now."

Well, the truth was, he had a confession to make. In hindsight, he thought that one of the females was someone he used to know. He had only just realised it, because her appearance had changed a lot—she'd put on a considerable amount of weight. Saffie was gobsmacked. Was he finally about to come clean?

"What do you mean, 'used to know?' " she asked.

He adopted a pitiful expression. Well, you see, he was married once. It was a big mistake. He was trapped into it, when a female he barely knew claimed she was pregnant. Of course, he'd had to do the honourable thing and marry her. But then, to his horror, he'd discovered that the baby wasn't his, so he'd left the tart immediately. He was a victim of his own honour. She was mad, this woman, certifiable even. Now, he was divorcing her, so the deranged creature had obviously sold the story to his rivals at another paper and, fuelled by their jealousy of his journalistic skills, they had set him up last night. Saffie had to understand—*he* was the victim in this whole affair.

Saffie took his hand. "Of course, I understand, baby. Everyone makes mistakes in life." Mike sagged with relief. He knew he could count on her. Then she continued, "Tell me, Mike, what does your sister think of all this?"

He was momentarily startled, but recovered quickly. She was devastated, he told her. And goodness knows how much his niece and nephew would get teased at school next week. He was gutted at the very thought of it.

"So what happens next, Mike?"

Well, he had a plan, he gushed maniacally. But he needed Saffie's help. She would help, wouldn't she?

First, he was going to issue a writ against the *Sunday News*. He'd been advised by everyone he'd called already this morning (the ones who could speak through their laughter, that is) that it would be futile—after all, the story was no more subjective than most of those that *he'd* published over the years—but he would do it anyway. It would at least tie them up in inconvenient legalities for a while. But the most important thing, he ranted, was to salvage his credibility. He'd already been on the phone to a friend at *OK!* magazine, and secured an interview for him and Saffie. They would go on record and say that it had all been an innocent prank; photos from a fancy dress party that had been misconstrued. He and Saffie would announce that they were very much in love and had just become engaged. After all, no one would believe that the fiancé of one of the most recognisable billboard girls in the country was anything but as straight as a spirit level.

Saff gasped and fanned her face with her hand. "Mike!" she squealed in delight, "are you saying that you want to . . . *marry me?*"

Another pause. Saff watched his changing expressions. She could read him like a book. Or make that a porn mag. His brow furrowed. He hadn't thought for a minute that Saffron would take his plan so literally. He'd intended it just to be for the purposes of the story. Then his face began to relax. Maybe, he reasoned, it wasn't such a bad idea after all. Saff was gorgeous, she was great company, she was away a lot, which left plenty of time for other recreational indoor sports . . . He grinned from ear to ear, then leaned over and hugged her.

"Yes, I want to marry you, baby. I was going to ask you this weekend anyway. So will you? Marry me?"

Saff burst into tears. Her Oscar nomination was in the bag. She nodded furiously, then reached for her phone. "Oh, Mike, I have to call my mother. She'll be so delighted that her little girl is going to walk up the aisle," she sobbed.

"What, right now?" he exclaimed. This wasn't going according to plan. By now they should be writing the script for their *OK!* exclusive, not announcing their forthcoming nuptials to a housewife in Brighton.

Saff dialled the number. I was so tense that I jumped three inches when my mobile rang in the car outside.

"Mummy, Mummy, it's me, darling. Guess what? I'm getting married," she screeched. That was my cue: the phone call, that is, not the announcement. I didn't have a clue what she was rambling on about. Was she drunk already?

I checked my appearance in the rear-view mirror. Saff had done my make-up and hair (apparently she was under instructions from the girls that I couldn't be trusted with either a make-up bag or a hot brush) and I was wearing my faithful black Prada suit. I was a woman in charge, it said. I took a deep breath and ordered my body to stop shaking like a demented go-go dancer. This was it. This was my moment.

I strutted up the stairs and through the foyer. I immediately spotted them in the corner. I had a side view of Mike, looking decidedly uncomfortable, and a full view of Saffie, who was still crying into her phone. In control. In control.

Suddenly, Saffie, screamed. "Look, Mike, it's my very best friend! I have to tell her my news!"

He turned. I wish I could describe the look on his face, but it just doesn't transcribe to paper. Think of the most outrageous shock you could imagine. Then multiply it. By a billion. His eyes popped so far out of his head that they looked like those fake Groucho Marx glasses. His chin dropped so far I could see what he had for dinner last night. His face turned redder than blood and he looked like he wanted to drink mine. He was a vision of rage. I feared for Saffie's health—if he self-combusted now she'd be scarred for life by the flames.

I quickly walked over to them, as Saff jumped out of her seat.

"What the . . . ??" He'd finally found his voice, but it was only temporary. I didn't give him the chance to finish. I wanted to fire all cylinders while he was still in shock.

"Hi Mike, great photo." I motioned to the newspaper in front of him. "Although I really don't think they got your best side." He was trying to speak. His mouth was moving but nothing was coming out.

I ploughed on. Assertive, Jess, assertive. Bugger Meryl Streep, I needed Clint Eastwood. Are you feeling lucky, punk? "Here's the deal, Mike. Yes, we stitched you up. It was small retribution for what you did to your son and me." Saff nudged me. She was determined not to be left out. "Let alone all the lies you told to Saffie too. But trust me, you got off lightly. We could have done a lot worse. So here's what's going to happen: number one, you're going to send me a cheque for the child support you haven't bothered paying yet." He was now staring at me in astonishment and undisguised hatred. He never was very good at confrontation—he usually preferred the backstabbing method of resolving differences.

"Number two, you're going to let me divorce you on the grounds of adultery. I think I have my prime witness here." Saff smiled. "And number three, you're going to make arrangements to visit your son: under my supervision of course. You may be lower than pond-life, but my son still deserves to have a father. And sadly, you're it," I finished.

There was such a long pause that I'm sure the staff in the hotel went through two shift changes while we waited for him to speak. When he did, it was barely louder than a whisper. I squeezed Saff's hand for support.

"And if I don't?"

"Then you'll always be looking over your shoulder, Mike. You see, this time we were just playing with you. OK, so you've got a bruised ego and today you're a bit of a laughing stock, but you'll get over it. You'll explain the pics away and another scoop will have you back on top. But just think about this. If we were just toying with you this time, what could we do if we really set our minds to it? You've got a lot to lose, Mike: your job, every-thing you've worked for, your salary. If you don't play ball, then we'll have to revise our approach and our target. Don't make me do that, Mike. Trust me, it won't be worth it. I'll expect to hear from you tomorrow."

I'd said everything I wanted to say. Now I had to get out of there before my knees buckled, I burst into tears, or he mur-dered me. As I strutted away I could almost hear the whooshing sounds of the daggers he was staring into my back. I couldn't believe he'd barely said a word. Mr. Big Shot stud, reduced to speechlessness by two women. And not in a good way.

Suddenly, Saff jerked my arm. I felt like a toddler being dragged by its mother out of the ice cream freezer at Tesco. "Hold on, Jess," she said as she turned back to face Mike. No, don't do this, Saff, just keep walking before he kills us.

"Oh, Mike, sweetie, baby, about that marriage thing, I think I'll pass. You see, I'm trying to give up ciggies, chocolate and em, what else, Jess?"

"Bastards."

"Oh that's right, bastards. So I think now's as good a time to start as any. 'Bye, baby."

Mike closed his eyes. I didn't wait to see if the shock had killed him. I'd find out if I got his life insurance cheque in the post.

As soon as we were out of his line of vision, we sprinted back to the car. I let Saffie drive. In my condition, the pedestrians on the pavement wouldn't be safe. She screeched away, turned the corner and slammed on the brakes. Then she turned to face me, her eyebrows raised in expectation.

"Chocolate, ciggies and *bastards?*" I said slowly.

She grinned. "Inspired or what?" she replied. Then it happened. The trembling, the tears, they were back. As I laughed harder than I'd ever laughed in my life.

We'd done it all. One successful mission—we went in, we did the job and we took a hostage. Mike Chapman, prisoner of war.

Now the general was going home to cuddle her boy.

Jammy Dodger, over and out.

Why not
start again, again?

November 2001

The launch of Carly's first novel was a spectacular event—*Nipple Alert* will be on the bestseller list within weeks if the advance publicity that her publisher has generated is anything to go by. It seems like every time I switch on the television or radio, there's Miss Cooper plugging the novel and at the same time denying strenuously that it's based on the story of her life. The Met Office is thoroughly confused about the sudden bolts of lightning that are hitting central London. She's already working on book two and something tells me there'll be an MP, a wronged wife and a fat supermodel in it. Not that she uses us as material of course.

Carol is, thankfully, back into her size six Versace jeans. When she turns sideways, she could slip down a drain grate, but at least she's stopped complaining about her flab. She's switched her neurosis to her wrinkles now, so we've decided to buy her a consultation with a cosmetic surgeon for Christmas. Since we told her, she hasn't stopped singing, "On the third day of

Christmas, my best mates gave to me, two collagen lips, one laser peel and a partridge in a pear tree." It's a worry.

Carol reported that she did a job with Saffie in Milan last week. Saff managed to squeeze it in between the Monte Carlo Grand Prix, where she was in her boyfriend's racing pit, and her imminent wedding in Marbella. I'm sure the invitations will drop through the door any day now. After all, I am her new very best friend.

Sarah is still blissfully happy with Nick and her new life teaching in London. When she's not at school, she spends her time at Nick's restaurant, meeting and greeting the windswept and interesting celebs. She's turned into a bizarre cross between Mary Poppins and Ivana Trump. She's even got her own personal stylist.

Well, it's Kate, but that still counts. Kate decided she needed an interest outside of domestic heaven, so Bruce's mum looks after the kids three days a week and Kate uses the time (and her background in hair and fashion) to ensure that her clients are perfectly groomed. She gets loads of jobs from our circle alone: Carly's TV appearances, Sarah's important events and Carol's modelling jobs. But she's even been booked, thanks to a glowing reference from the soon-to-be ex-wife of Basil Asquith, MP, to do the hair at the next Conservative Party Convention.

Miranda, however, won't be among them. I got a postcard from her yesterday from New Zealand, saying that she's having a very invigorating break over there while she waits for her divorce to be finalised. I'm sure that the fact that the French rugby team are on a six-week tour there is merely a coincidence.

In some ways, it's a shame that she's out of the country, because I'm sure she'd find it amusing that Basil is now a regular at JC's Heaven's Carmen Miranda nights. He's been spotted several times in the company of a rather tall female called Blossom. It's another front page waiting to happen.

And no doubt Mike Chapman's name will be on the byline. Needless to say, Mike bounced back like a rubber ball from his own little scandal by claiming he was working undercover to infiltrate the seedy personal lives of the country's politicians. People still snigger that he looked great in fuchsia. I'm sure that's probably also the colour of his face when he writes my monthly cheque. He takes Josh to the park every Sunday (with me following at a discreet distance). I think to his surprise he's actually starting to enjoy it. Well, it must be refreshing to spend time with someone who has the same emotional age.

And as for me, life seems to be bounding from great to fantastic. There's my new job as a political columnist for the *Sunday News* (courtesy of the lovely George Milford) and my permanent contented-mother glow, which manages to permeate the fact that I'm still crap at doing my own make-up. It must make me attractive in some obscure way. Keith seems to think so anyway. Yes, ever since I decided to give Mrs. Picket next door a run for her money by erecting my very own extension and called in Keith Miller, alias Builder Bob, to give me a quotation, it's been like a permanent Diet Coke ad, only I get the guy after the can has been chucked in the bin. Well, I couldn't continue with my one-woman anti-men campaign forever—a girl has needs! Don't get me wrong, I've made the girls promise to shoot me if I even *think* about getting serious with another man, but Keith assures me that he's happy to wait until I'm ready for something more than a casual relationship. I don't think he realises that that'll be some time in the *next* millennium. He did make a promising start though. On our first date, he turned up with three bars of Dairy Milk, two hot dogs and *Lock, Stock and Two Smoking Barrels.* He even brought a three-foot Tinky Winky for Josh. All that and a stomach that looks like a toast rack. What else could a girl do but explore the situation further? Well, why not?

Up Close and Personal with the Author

THE KEY THEMES RUNNING THROUGH THE BOOK ARE FRIENDSHIP, INFIDELITY AND RETRIBUTION—WHAT INSPIRED YOU TO FOCUS ON THESE TOPICS?

The most important things in my life are my family, my friends and my career—in that order. I have a group of girlfriends who have been like sisters since I was a teenager and although we're all very different in many ways, we've stuck together through years of dramas, tragedies, great times and many nights of endless conversations and empty wine bottles. When my husband and I married, he said he gained a package deal: a wife, two sofas and six other women permanently perched on them! Those relationships are mirrored in the book—I couldn't begin to imagine what life is like without friends to share the good times and bring humour to the bad times.

THAT COVERS FRIENDSHIP—TELL US ABOUT THE INFIDELITY THEME . . .

This book originated as an attempt to turn a dreadful experience into a positive one. The seed was planted when one of my girlfriends discovered that her partner of many years was being unfaithful. Sadly, she was eight months pregnant at the time. The horror of the situation was incomprehensible: she was transformed from being a devoted partner with a beautiful home, a thriving career, a solid relationship and the prospect of a wonderful family life to being devastated and destitute. Shortly afterwards, I sat down to write the sequel to my first book, *What If?* As a struggling new author, I'd been there for my girlfriend emotionally but couldn't help financially, so (with her agreement, of course) I decided to use her experience as one of the plot lines and share the earnings from the book—the proceeds going to her "rebuild her life" fund. We spent many nights laughing until we hurt and crying until we hurt even more, as I wrote and she read the results.

SO IS IT AN ACTUAL DIARY OF THE EVENTS?

Not a verbatim one, but I did reproduce some of the key happenings. The stakeout in the car, for example, happened pretty much as I wrote it in the book. As did the scene wherein the cheating partner took hours to reach Jess in hospital, although it later transpired he was with his girlfriend only minutes away. Despicable!

AND THE RETRIBUTION SCENE?

Sadly, no, that was all a figment of my over-active imagination. Although, as in the novel, my friends and I spent many hours in deep discussion about how Mike Chapman could suffer his comeuppance. However, we couldn't come up with anything that didn't involve pain or illegal activities! I had absolutely no idea how the book would end until I sat down to write the final chapters and thankfully, once I got started, the ideas came and the words flew onto the pages.

SO DO YOU BELIEVE THAT REVENGE IS ALWAYS A BETTER OPTION THAN FORGIVENESS?

I think that every circumstance warrants its own conclusion. In this case, both in the novel and in real life, forgiveness wasn't an option—there was no coming back from the devastation that had been wreaked on the relationship. Personally, I think to betray a woman when she is pregnant with a child is unforgivable.

HOW IS YOUR FRIEND'S LIFE NOW? DID SHE GET HER OWN REVENGE?

Unfortunately not. Yet. She has an adorable child and for that gift alone, wouldn't change anything that's happened. However, we still live in hope that *Why Not?* will become a blockbuster movie and the proceeds will allow us to retire to the Caribbean—now wouldn't that be divine retribution?

WHICH OF THE CHARACTERS IN THE BOOK DO YOU MOST IDENTIFY WITH?

Definitely Carly! Carly is based on me, thirty pounds ago and before I became a (sometimes) responsible mother-of-two. I too had that inbred thirst for mischief, and the ability to delude myself that insane ideas were great ones. It got me into untold trouble and great adventures over the years, as a result of which I now have lots of wrinkles, the odd grey hair and a husband who gets nervous if I'm out of the house for too long!

SO YOU NOW HAVE A HUSBAND AND TWO CHILDREN—HOW DO YOU FIND TIME TO WRITE?

With great difficulty! My boys are two and three, so I'm with them during the day. Then, when they go to bed, I get the lap-top out on my kitchen table and type away furiously until I fall asleep over the keyboard in the early hours of the morning. If anyone ever wants to check the sequence of letters on a key-board, they can just check my forehead, as they are permanently imprinted there.

HOW LONG DOES IT TAKE YOU TO PLAN A NOVEL?

Em, well . . . I'd love to say that I spend weeks setting out a framework and character backgrounds, but much to the horror, I'm sure, of creative writing teachers everywhere, I don't plan a single word before I write it. I have endeavoured to be more methodical but I find that I lose the spontaneity of the words and the unpredictability of the plot lines if I plan it all out beforehand. I think when you are writing prose that is humour based, the best ideas come when you just relax and go with the flow. When I write, I can see the scenes and characters in my head, like a movie, and I just have fun imagining what happens next and putting that down on paper. It's like leading a really fun-filled, exciting, sometimes heart-breaking life without ever leaving the kitchen. There have been many times when my husband has wandered through the kitchen to find me bent over my laptop with tears streaming down my face because I'm writing a particularly sad scene. He's found that the best response is to slip some chocolate in front of me and then make a swift exit. He's a wise man.

WHAT IS YOUR OVER-RIDING EMOTION WHEN YOU FINISH WRITING A BOOK?

Joy! On the first Saturday after I finish a book all the girls come over and cram into my living room, where they're handed a glass of wine and the finished manuscript. They spend the whole day reading it, correcting my typos and telling me which lines work or are too rude and have to be cut. You can see it's a very scientific process!

When I finished *Why Not?*, though, there was an element of sadness, as I'd really grown attached to the characters.

SO WHAT'S NEXT?

Exactly! I decided to write a couple of books with a completely different cast, but one day I intend to write a sequel to *Why Not?* called *What's Next?* Or maybe I'll wait a long time and set the sequel in a home for the elderly, with all five girls in their seventies, comparing false teeth and hatching plans to seduce septuagenarian gentlemen. In that case, it could be called *Almost Done?*

AND FOR YOU, PERSONALLY?

Just more of the same: writing novels, bringing up my boys, trying to make the most of every day. Although I wouldn't say no to a bit of jet-setting! I've spent much of my time in New York over the years and adore the city, and I recently spent the best time of my life living in Los Angeles for a few months. The combination of sun, sea and the hilarious shallowness of the entertainment industry there had me absolutely hooked! I'm now an LA devotee and currently working on my first screenplay. If I could design a perfect life, it would be one that enabled me to split my time between Scotland, New York and LA. That would be fantastic. Throw in a Prada wardrobe and first class flights between the cities and life would be perfect. Well, a girl can dream . . .

Then don't miss these other great books from Downtown Press!